WOLFMAN
CONFIDENTIAL

JUSTIN ROBINSON

Candlemark & Gleam

For information, address
Candlemark & Gleam LLC,
38 Rice St., #2, Cambridge, MA 02140
eloi@candlemarkandgleam.com

Library of Congress Cataloging-in-Publication Data
In Progress

ISBN: 978-1-936460-86-1
eISBN: 978-1-936460-85-4

Cover art and design by Kate Sullivan

Illustrations by Fernando Caire
www.artofernando.com

Editor: Athena Andreadis

www.candlemarkandgleam.com

OF ALL THE MONSTERS...

...they could have dressed me up as, why'd it have to be a clown? Okay, sure, some would have been difficult or impossible. But what about a nice vampire? Or even a ghoul? I'd even have settled for a scarecrow's itchy togs. Impersonating a monster was never safe, but a clown? The things they did to their friends, you'd hate to be an enemy.

Moon and Garou insisted I was going in that night. They really wanted their man back. With a lead this flimsy, I had no idea what I was going to do. Other than spend the evening in blinding terror, of course. That was a given.

PRAISE FOR WOLFMAN CONFIDENTIAL

"As with the prior novels in this series, Nick Moss' assignment [...] is always tied in to [...] schemes and subtexts that further the world-building, deepen Moss's character, and serve as love letters to Los Angeles' culture and geography on a par with those of Tim Powers." —Kate Sherrod, *Skiffy & Fanty*

"Once again, Justin Robinson weaves a complicated tale set in a delightful universe. // As always, his books [...] leave the reader wanting more." —Ashley Perkins, Game Vortexer

"...Robinson brings his deft touch to a story that is at turns delightful and weirdly humorous, yet still manages to offer wry observations on society today." —John F.D. Taff, Bram Stoker Award-nominated author of *The End in All Beginnings*

CITY OF DEVILS SERIES:

City of Devils
Fifty Feet of Trouble
Wolfman Confidential

OTHER CANDLEMARK & GLEAM BOOKS
BY JUSTIN ROBINSON:

Mr Blank
Get Blank

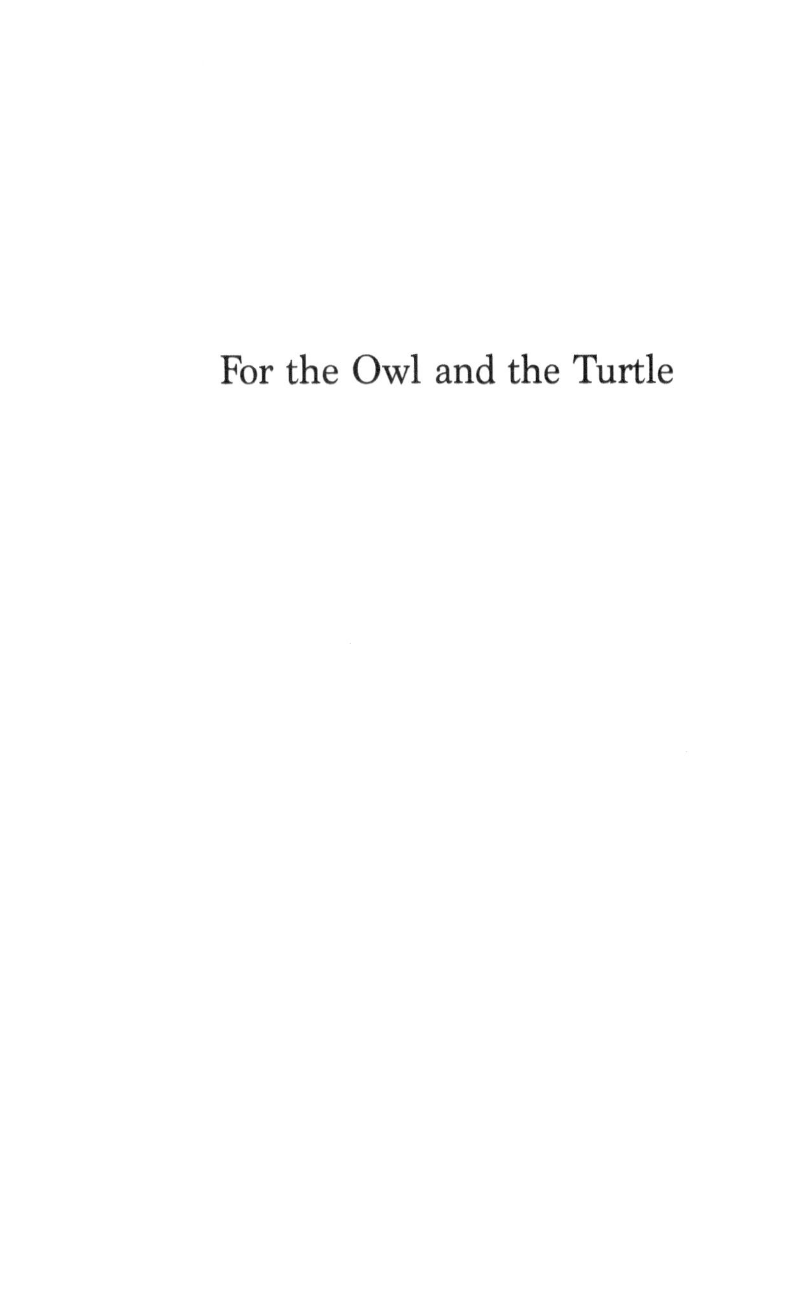

For the Owl and the Turtle

ONE

Thursday, October 27, 1955
Afternoon

T he ogre looked like a Christmas tree, but instead of ornaments, some joker had hung three cops on his boughs. The star at the top was entirely in my imagination, suggested by the love taps the cop near the ogre's zenith was giving him. I don't even think the gargantuan monster noticed he was being played like a bongo drum in a Cuban orchestra. If you planned on arresting an ogre, you needed to bring something a little heavier than a little salty language and ashwood batons. A bazooka, for starters.

The ogre was big, and I mean big for an ogre. Even hunched over like he was, he was scraping the ceiling. That had to be hell on the patrolman clamped around the ogre's thick neck. Every time the hapless wolfman was mashed against the ceiling, he left behind more scraps of uniform and clumps of brown fur stuck in the panels. Viewed from above, it probably looked like a game of Whack-A-Mole, only the mole was a progressively more dazed wolfman, clearly thinking about the length of time he had before he could retire. All three cops—wolfmen, like ninety percent of the force—were wearing the wolf on the outside. Man-shaped, but covered in ropy muscle and thick fur, with underbites crammed full of sharp teeth and hair trigger tempers to boot, they were unholy terrors. To everyone but ogres.

And anybody with wolfsbane or silver bullets.

This ogre looked like he might have been a greaser. He was stuffed into a leather jacket and ripped blue jeans, everything dripping with chains. A half-fallen pompadour perched atop his misshapen head, the first casualty of his running battle with the cops and the ceiling at the 77th Street Station. The three wolfmen he was wearing like decorative scarves weren't the only ones around. No, several more fellas in uniform, along with a couple more plainclothes dicks, were all doing their best to subdue him. Looked like they'd had no better luck: the ogre had ogre-sized cuffs on his wrists, but the chain had been snapped clean in half. They might as well have tried to cuff an earthquake. The LAPD was going to have to upgrade their equipment if there were going to be monsters of his size noodling around.

This was the first thing I saw when Detective Lou Garou opened the front doors of 77th Street Station with my face. I wasn't being arrested—probably the first human who had crossed that particular threshold without a fancy pair of steel bracelets; Garou was just a louse by nature. I wasn't going to make any jokes about how he woke up on the wrong side of the den, either. Not because I worried he wouldn't get it; I was scared he might.

Right through the front doors and the first thing I saw was this giant palooka wrestling with more cops than I was comfortable being around at any one time. Although, I had to admit, it was nice seeing Goliath beating on David for a change. Not that Goliath had much to say to me. That legend needed someone below David before I fit in.

"Keep moving, meatstick," Garou growled in my ear while giving me a shove that sent me stumbling past the melee at the entrance.

"He seems nice," I said.

The thing was, I was armed. Like I said, I wasn't under arrest, so I was carrying the whole shebang. A .32 revolver loaded with silver bullets rode under my left armpit. A vial full of wolfsbane was in one of the pockets on my jacket. I could play havoc with these cops if I got tired of living sometime soon. You didn't pull wolfsbane or silver on cops unless you were damn sure you could get away with it, and I knew for a fact I couldn't. Not here.

I wasn't arrested because, apparently, I was hired. That was what Detective Phil Moon—Garou's partner, and by far the nicer of the pair— told me when he rousted me from my office this morning. He was waddling behind Garou, occasionally whistling snatches from songs hovering maddeningly out of reach.

Here's what surprised me: I was a detective of the private variety, and if there was one thing I thought the LAPD had in plenty, it was dicks. I'm also human, which made me a rarity in the City of Devils. Hell, made me a rarity in the good old U. S. of A., and maybe the whole wide world. I might as well have been the Hope Diamond. This whole thing already stank and I didn't even know what the problem was. At least I still had wolfsbane.

The ogre roared and plowed one of the cops into the floor. The linoleum cracked like a windshield catching a fly ball and the cop came loose from the ogre's arm, counting stars. Never seen a wolfman knocked silly before.

"You might want to move along, Moss." That was Moon. Like I said, he was nicer. Called me by name rather than a racial slur, even.

"Yeah, what's his story?"

"Search me. We just got here."

"What do you want with me, Moon?"

"Not here. These walls have ears."

I didn't like the sound of that, not one bit. The LAPD, if you believed the TV shows, was a model of efficiency and justice. A lot of people, or at least people like me who maybe ran into the seedier side of things, knew that the existence of the Bellum Mob put the lie to that. They'd been in Los Angeles since before the end of the Night War, and they weren't going anywhere. Trust a brainiac to figure out how not to get caught. Her zombie enforcers were everywhere, like roaches with better fashion sense. If Bellum had gotten her hooks, or whatever it was brainiacs had, into the LAPD, we were in dutch up to our necks.

With the ogre's roaring and the cops' cursing receding behind me, we entered the bullpen. The Night War changed a lot of things, but a police station was still a police station. Sure, half the people in it could sprout fur at a moment's notice, and some of those files looked to be floating around on their own, but the rest of it was just jake. Cops at desks doing their paperwork, occasionally glancing in the direction of the melee, clearly wondering if they were paid enough to make that their problem or not.

Garou shoved me past all that into a hallway. Doors opened up on either side. I poked my head into the first one we passed. A corkboard had been covered with a map of the city, along with pictures of monsters, then strings leading to thumbtacks in the map. Every monster in the picture was dead, and it wasn't much of a mystery how they were bumped off. A vampire with a stake still sticking out of him, a mummy half-burned into glass, a martian dead next to a used tissue, a crawling eye shriveled up on a pile of sand. You know the drill.

"What's that?"

"Monster Slayer task force," Moon said, his raspy voice sounding like a dirge.

"What?"

"Some goofy meatstick offing monsters all over the city," Garou growled.

"Monster Slayer?" I wanted to know.

"Nickname the guys gave him. It just stuck," Moon said.

"Catchy. How do you know it's a human?"

"Who else would be croaking monsters?" Despite the phrasing, Garou wasn't asking. "You ask me, it's the Normandie Knights. They got organized."

I was smart enough not to snort at that theory. The Normandie Knights were a bunch of kids. Yeah, a street gang, and yeah, they did blip off monsters on occasion. But if you asked me, most of them didn't know holy water from Bebop Cola. Nobody asked me.

"Not their style," Moon said, and my estimation of him went up a little.

"How many have been killed?"

"We're not sure," Moon sighed. Garou shot him a sharp glare. "Oh, settle down, Lou. Moss here hasn't done anything like this since the war ended."

"I still say that general amnesty was a dumb idea," Garou muttered.

"Not sure on the numbers?" I asked.

"Well, it's different monsters, different styles. The Slayer uses weaknesses, and uses them perfectly. We got a scent at a couple of the crime scenes, and a lot of the rest are, you know, conjecture," Moon explained.

I shook my head. If it was a single human, he was playing roulette with all our lives. Ever since the Treaty of St. Louis was signed back in '53, about half the monsters walking were looking for an excuse to go back to the bad old days of the Night War when every human was on the menu. This could be the perfect excuse to throw the Fair Game Law—the only thing keeping me alive and with my original skin intact—into the trash.

If this wasn't the same person, then it was some kind of snipe hunt by the LAPD. They'd pin it on the first convenient patsy and break their arms patting themselves on the back when they hauled him in front of a grand jury. My guess? It was monsters offing each other and betting the taboo they had against using each other's weaknesses would shield them.

Moon opened another door. "You have other things to worry about than the Slayer." Light glinted off his badge, clipped to the pocket of his ugly suit. Number 452.

I slinked past him and found myself in a small meeting room. A table fit for maybe six people and some plastic chairs all around. A blackboard stood against one wall, cloudy with old, scrubbed-out words.

"Have a seat," Moon said.

I did what he said and faced the two LAPD detectives. Moon was the older of the two. His hair was mostly gray, and he looked like he had been hitting the doughnuts about as hard as that ogre outside was hitting his colleagues. He had a florid complexion, and in hotter weather would already be dripping sweat. His voice sounded like a glass of whiskey with a three pack a day habit. Moon's fashion sense was nonexistent. Today he was wearing an eye-searing pink jacket with green pants that looked like they were designed by an uncaring God.

Garou was younger and meaner. I didn't like to look at him much, since he was always looking for an excuse to give me a cuff. He wasn't slim, but next to Moon he might as well have been a scarecrow. Garou's wolf nature was right near the surface, giving his eyes an odd shine at some angles. He wore a brown suit that looked barely more expensive than mine.

"So what can I do for you fellas?" I tried to project a bravado I didn't feel. Sitting in a police station filled with angry cops was slightly less pleasant than having spiders crawling on my face.

"We need you to find someone," Garou said.

I blinked and turned to Moon for confirmation. He merely turned to Garou. *Wait, was this Garou's idea?* Stranger things had happened, I guessed, but I hadn't heard of them.

"Uh...who?"

Not sure what I expected. Maybe Garou trying to find some human he was sweet on or wanted to turn. Didn't know how to tell him I didn't do that kind of thing. Maybe somebody jumped bail, but I wasn't a bounty hunter either.

Garou slid a file from one side of the table over to me. I looked from Garou to Moon, pretty sure this was going to turn into some kind of practical joke. Both wolfmen were stonefaced. And, I noted gratefully, entirely human-looking.

So I opened the file. A picture was paperclipped to the side. I frowned at it, because it really looked like a flying caterpillar. Then I put it together. Granted, the name on the other side of the file helped clear up the mystery.

"An invisible man?" I demanded. "You want me to find an invisible man?"

Moon sighed.

"Yeah," Garou said, and his tone said he realized how silly it sounded.

"Why me?"

"You found a girl at the bottom of the ocean," Garou said.

I couldn't argue with that. He was referring to a case a couple months back. What he didn't mention was that I didn't find several other people on that same case, or at least not in time for it to matter. I managed to rescue a grand total of one. But yes, I found a girl in a mad scientist's lair at the bottom of the Catalina Channel. Gold star for me.

"Yeah, but you know, she was visible."

"See, Lou?" Moon said, dubious.

The two wolfmen started muttering to each other, and I couldn't help it. I paged through the file. First thing that fell out was a sealed plastic bag holding a white handkerchief. *I surrender,* the file was telling me, spilling its secrets out before me. The hanky looked like something I was carrying on me: you sneezed your last cold into one and presto, the perfect weapon against a martian, should you need one. Didn't think that was what this was, or why it was in a file. Why would you need to protect your files from martians? I had a look at the dossier.

Anonymous Bosch, an invisible man and a vice detective for the LAPD. Monsters could be as circumspect as Victorian ladies when it came to their histories pre-change, and this file had enough redacted to say he was one of those. It started with his war record, and that's Day War: Bosch served in World War II in the Pacific theater. A Marine, he saw action on Peleliu, Guadalcanal, Okinawa, and half a dozen other places I could barely find on a map, let alone spell. His rebirth date was in '51, which meant he was turned in the later parts of the Night War. Monsters like that were among the most dangerous: the Night War toughened them from both ends. As humans they got used to near-starvation and being hunted, and as monsters, they got to face humans who had turned monster killing into an art.

I did my best not to let the memories of those days back in. Me and my friends, especially Mickey and Izzy, we had gotten pretty good at pushing the button on whatever monster hell spat out that week. Still, when one of them died, I always remembered he used to be a man. Or a woman.

Or sometimes even a kid.

"Moss. Moss!" I looked up, blinking myopically. "C'mon," Moon said, waving me to the door.

I stayed put. "What's with the mustache?"

"You know invisible men. They get the screaming meemies if you can see them." It was true. Most invisible men couldn't be within fifteen feet of flour and they hated dust. "Well, Bosch likes people to know where his head is when he's not on duty. Hence the mustache."

"Uh huh." Sad thing, that was what passed for logic with monsters.

"C'mon, Moss. Let's go."

"What'd he do?"

Moon and Garou shared a look. I was on the hook. They both knew it. What I couldn't tell was how they felt about that information. Garou hated me, but he was apparently the one who wanted to bring me into this. Moon didn't like me, but he also didn't regard my continued existence as an insult. Considering he was a cop, that practically made us engaged.

Moon pulled out a chair and sat down, uttering the kind of sigh big guys always do when they park their keisters. "We used Bosch for the kind of work we need invisible men and doppelgangers for."

"Undercover." Didn't take a brainiac to know where they'd be sending their faceless men.

"Yeah. Well, he went under and never came back up for air. We looked for him, but as you pointed out, it ain't exactly easy finding an invisible man."

"Can't you, uh..." I sniffed the air. I wasn't sure how to ask without offending them.

"Doesn't work like that," Moon said, with a glance at Garou. This time the other wolfman was seething. I could swear he had gotten a little hairier since I'd last looked at him. "We can ID people off scent, not track them. The nose isn't that good, and besides, you know how a city smells, Moss? Worse than your cologne."

"It was a gift." I didn't finish the thought. I was too busy thinking about all the humans who had been pinched after the cops tracked them by scent. Yeah, they'd been using that excuse for years. It shouldn't have surprised me it was phonus balonus, but sometimes I wondered how brazen they'd get.

"So how do you know one invisible man from another?"

"Scent. We keep them on file," Moon said, gesturing to the handkerchief. "Normally those are in a locked cabinet along with the rest of their information. Don't want it getting out just how many glass men we have out there."

"Right, okay. Where was he under?"

"You heard of the Gobfather, Moss?" Garou growled. He was leaning against the doorframe and looking at me like I was wearing a rare steak for a tie.

"I don't think so. Should I?"

"Mab doesn't get down to Watts much, Lou," Moon said with a raspy chuckle. Then, to me: "New boss, as in mob. Showed up a little over a year ago trying to muscle in on the Bellum rackets."

Moon slapped another file down. I tucked the plastic pouch back into Bosch's file, set the whole thing aside, and opened this new one.

The picture was of a sidhe. That's pronounced "she," as in the fair sex. I originally figured it was because, when it came to sidhes, the hes and shes pretty much looked alike, but then someone told me it was Irish. The sidhe were gorgeous in an ethereal kind of way. Lean, usually tall, with features that could cut glass. This one was no exception. He was dressed all in white, a fitted suit complete with waistcoat, his blond hair short and slicked back from a high forehead. His eyes were large and slanted upward, staring right at me, as though he could look through a photograph and size up the viewer.

"Goes by the handle Titanio Mab," Moon said by way of explanation, "but most everyone just calls him the Gobfather."

"Why?"

"Mob is mostly goblins. Some banshees and headless horsemen in there, but mostly goblins."

"I heard there were a lot of, um, zombie businessmen getting the wrong end of blunt objects lately."

Garou snorted. "Yeah, someone is rubbing them out left and right."

"We had a double murder in Hollywood the other night," Moon said. "Los Angeles is supposed to be the safest big city in the world. We can't have this kind of thing."

"They'd have to change the plot of *Dragnet*."

"Cute, meatstick," Garou said. "Keep being cute."

"We think this double murder means the Gobfather is on the move," Moon said.

"So all this..." I trailed off.

"Mob war, Moss."

I wasn't quite sure what to think. On one side, people were getting knocked off, and for once they weren't humans. Still, it was the same old story as always. Zombies and goblins were working stiffs, serving the more intelligent, more powerful monster races. They were the ones getting the push, while their royalty lived it up.

"Bosch was looking into Mab?"

"Bosch is the only reason we know what little we do."

Moon turned the page on Mab's file. Another picture, this time of three goblins, greeted me. They were on a street, probably in Hollywood, getting ready to climb into a car. Or, considering the way the door looked like fancy vine-shaped latticework, a carriage.

"These are Mab's top three guys: Flux, Murk, and Sawbones." Moon pointed to each of them as he named them off.

As monster races went, goblins were among the most mutable. These three might never have been mistaken for the same race if we didn't already know about goblins. Just about the only thing they had in common was their height: goblins were all around three to four feet tall. That, and they had a strange thing about speaking in rhyme.

Flux had pointed ears that rose a good foot over a misshapen head, and a nose that called to mind the worst image of witch crones. His skin was slimy and his eyes were black. Murk was stouter, with a piglike snout and an underbite, complete with miniature tusks. Sawbones wore an old kraut helmet and a gas mask, like he was ready to do battle in the trenches. In the photo, he was lighting a cancer stick for Flux, the flame coming from Sawbones's bare fingers.

That was the worst part of goblins. Their damn magic tricks.

"When we lost him, Bosch hadn't managed to pin anything on them, but everything he said made these three sound like real live wires."

"Oh, good."

Moon turned the page.

My heart had skipped beats before. Most recently for a certain former witch who had to leave town after I'd managed to botch an investigation for her. It did this time, too, though the feeling wasn't quite as pure. I didn't know the girl in the picture from Eve. I *did* know she might have been the loveliest woman alive. Her skin was olive, edging darker, and her hair was long and glossy black. Her features were large and well-defined. She looked like a living doll, although some of that was because it was hard to believe someone so lovely could be real.

"Who," my voice faltered, and I tried to cover it with a cough, "who is she?"

"Already forgotten that witch of yours," Garou needled. I wanted to hit him.

"Dulcinea Ramos," Moon said. "Mab's human girlfriend."

"Human?"

"Yeah, the Gobfather has a type. He's gone through several. Real dishes, all of them."

"Gone through? What happens to them?"

"Who knows?" Garou said. "Not our problem."

"Yeah, why would you investigate missing girls?"

Garou's snarl sounded like someone had ripped a car door in half. I sat up straight, my hand reaching into my jacket on its own.

"Settle down, both of you," Moon said. He turned to me. "More motivation for you to want this elf behind bars where he belongs."

"Don't need to tell me twice. Where was Bosch last seen? Uh…no, I mean—"

"I know what you mean, Moss. Bosch was following the Gobfather to a club in Hollywood. The Nocturnist. He was a regular."

"The Nocturnist?"

"Looks ritzy, but it's a tough joint. Last Halloween we had a pair of murders: a martian and a gremlin. No arrests for it, but let me tell you, everyone in that club knows just who is responsible."

Moon paged backwards and poked his finger onto the Gobfather's picture.

"But nothing sticks."

"This place is a mob front?"

"Not exactly. It's a place where the mobsters can go, be themselves. Not get bumped off for wearing pinstripes. Neutral ground, if you will. So anyway, that's the last we heard of Bosch."

"One minute he's going into the hive of all the mobsters in LA and the next he's gone. I don't know, gents. I might have cracked this one already."

"Oh God, Phil, can I just pull his head off?"

"You're the one wanted him, Lou. And yeah, Moss, we know. Bosch might have been bumped off, but we want to know for sure. Bosch goes in and then he's gone. Missed his next meeting, which wasn't unusual, but then missed two more, which is."

I paused. "Does this mean you two are working for the Wolf Pack?"

The looks were back, and this was the first time I'd ever seen a hint of panic on their faces. The Wolf Pack was an elite squad from all over the city, charged with policing the mob. The only public name was Detective Lieutenant Hunter Moore, the man who headed things. He was famous for surviving more assassination attempts than Hitler.

"You keep your mind off that, Moss," Moon told me.

"Oh, I was going to congratulate you fellas. I don't want to tell you your business, but if you're with the Pack, have you thought of just taking Mab to the Falls?"

The Falls were a section of Mulholland overlooking the entire city. The Bellum Mob liked to give their enemies free skiing lessons down them. Rumor had it that the Wolf Pack did the same thing. There were more bones at the bottom of that slope than a slaughterhouse.

"Can't do that to an elf," Moon said with real regret. "Cold iron or nothing for them."

"And Bellum never surfaces," Garou growled.

"The Nocturnist is our only lead, Moss. That's how far down Bosch was."

The cops stared me down, their expressions telling me they were leasing me and strongly considering the option to buy. There was no backing out of this job. No way to tell these two no. Yeah, I was working for the LAPD to find an invisible man, or Moon was going to let Garou pull my head off like a bottlecap.

"Yeah, okay. I'll look into it."

"One catch," Moon said. "The Nocturnist doesn't open until sundown."

My heart skipped more than one beat then. Because after sunset, monsters had a free pass to do whatever they liked to me. All nice and legal, according to the Fair Game law. When the sun went to sleep in the Pacific, I was prey for the entire city.

It was the City of Devils for a reason.

Two

Thursday, October 27, 1955
Heading for sunset

Of all the monsters they could have dressed me up as, why'd it have to be a clown? Okay, sure, some would have been difficult or impossible. But what about a nice vampire? Or even a ghoul? I'd even have settled for a scarecrow's itchy togs. Impersonating a monster was never safe, but a clown? The things they did to their friends, you'd hate to be an enemy.

Moon and Garou insisted I was going in that night. They really wanted their man back. With a lead this flimsy, I had no idea what I was going to do. Other than spend the evening in blinding terror, of course. That was a given.

They brought me into a room below the station with cardboard boxes in shelves from floor to ceiling. There had to be a ghoul creeping around somewhere looking after the musty, spider-ridden oubliette, but he never poked his head out. Moon, muttering and swearing, rooted around in the boxes before pulling one out, ripping it open, and revealing a costume of blue and white.

"Is this the evidence room?" I asked as the horror sunk its claws into me.

"Where did you think we were? Our undercover guys are either invisible or they can look like whatever they like. You think we're in the habit of keeping costumes around?"

Garou barked a quick laugh.

"You're dressing me as a...*murdered clown*?" Somehow it was worse that the clown had been murdered. Don't ask me why.

"Living clowns ain't in the habit of dropping their get-ups at the police station," Moon said.

"What happened?"

"Search me, Moss. Wasn't our case."

"Someone probably dropped a piano on him," Garou said with another chuckle.

"Pianos don't kill clowns!" I told them.

"Yeah, I don't think you should be yapping about how you kill monsters. Liable to get my partner, you know, tense," Moon said.

I looked at Garou. He nodded.

"At least I'm getting paid," I muttered, pulling out the flappy shoes, the baggy outfit, the whole kit and caboodle. There was even a full seltzer bottle, but I was guessing it was full of some kind of acid.

Put together the clown costume, plus some makeup Moon was nice enough to pick up from the local drugstore and a wig I was pretty sure had a bug-eyed monster in mind, and I looked passable. Passable? I didn't even recognize myself.

"Something's missing," Garou said, staring me down.

"Balloons," Moon said.

"Balloons."

It's difficult to describe the fear I was feeling as Moon and Garou drove me into Hollywood in the back of their unmarked jalopy. This situation was exactly what I had been trying to avoid since I found out monsters existed, and even more so after the Treaty of St. Louis gave all our interactions some rules. Garou had been threatening to turn me since he met me, he said because I was a good detective, but I'm pretty sure he did it just to get under my skin. Got worse, too. The cops weren't exactly pals with local humans. Turning was the good end, but just as common was a beating or worse.

And I really didn't want to die dressed like this.

They dropped me off a block from the Nocturnist, and I probably should have been grateful Garou pulled the car to a complete stop.

"Poke around, Moss. See what you can see," Moon told me.

"Did I mention I charge extra for night work?"

"Maybe ten, eleven times now. Go find our man. He's probably not at the bottom of the ocean."

The car merged back into traffic on Sunset. That's a hell of a name for a street in the City of Devils. Just a nice reminder of the last time the humans were safe from being shanghaied into some kind of weird new life no one ever wanted.

I looked down at myself. I looked like a clown, I thought. Hard to tell. I would have loved a good disguise hex, but I only knew one witch powerful enough, and she lost her powers and skipped town. I waddled down the street toward the glittering gothic-style sign proclaiming THE NOCTURNIST. All around me on the street, well-heeled monsters enjoyed the nightlife, laughing, chatting, even window-shopping as they headed for their exclusive clubs and restaurants. If they thought of the humans huddled in their homes in neighborhoods like Watts or Boyle Heights, it was only a flicker of a thought, quickly banished by the glitz of Hollywood.

Certain monsters could see right through disguises, I knew. The change gave them some kind of super-sense, or at least something keener than anything we humans could understand. Made fighting them in the Night War a pain, too.

The Nocturnist was in an art deco edifice shoved between two other buildings, with only a narrow alley along one side. Didn't take a genius to know that alleyway had been used for more than one illicit rendezvous. Probably was a selling point of the property. The front was a pair of double doors, each one tall enough even for that ogre I'd seen at 77th Street, thrown wide to a foyer where security could have a look at the guests.

Okay. Time to see how well this get-up works.

The foyer was dark, the carpet a deep charcoal gray; the walls were painted with shadowy tree trunks, the ceiling a deep velvety blue. Security was an ogre shoved into a tux, and he looked about ready to burst it at the seams. His spiked club leaned against the wall next to him.

He patted me down with a pair of piggy eyes. He was hardly drooling, too. Real classy joint, this. An ogre was a decent beginning test. They weren't known for their perception; more for mashing stuff that annoyed them into tiny, perfectly flat discs. Still, my blood had dropped a couple degrees as I waited for him to give me the bum's rush.

"Welcome to the Nocturnist, sir."

With one mitt he opened the inner door for me. That was the first perfect manicure I'd ever seen on an ogre, too. They say you see something new every day.

I started walking, then remembered that if I wasn't going to get made, I should probably start playing the role.

"Thank you very much, my good man!" Then, thinking of the one clown I'd met recently, I added a "Hyuck, hyuck, hyuck!" I swear, the ogre shuddered the tiniest bit when I hit him with the laugh. I'd go ahead and put that one in the bank.

I stepped into the Nocturnist, and my breath went right out of my lungs.

The club was decorated like the edges of a dark forest. Leafless trees and craggy peaks were painted onto the walls, giving way to a deep sky ruled over by a blood moon. More trees, these ones real, ran along the sides of the walls to enhance the image of the forests. Toward the far side of the club, the natural imagery gave way to a glowering castle, with the stage styled to look like an open drawbridge.

I was more concerned by the cages at the front, where a pack of wolves—real wolves—padded back and forth, sniffing the air. Bones littered the floor of their enclosure, and I wasn't about to check to see if they were human or not. Bats hung from the top bars as well, occasionally fluttering to another upside-down perch.

I moved past them, hopefully not so quickly as to mess up my disguise. The monsters in the crowd were the upper crust. Vampires, mummies, doppelgangers, your occasional jaguar person, crawling eye, or robot. Meat golem waitresses in cigar girl outfits circulated through the tables, bringing drinks and light food.

The big band on the stage was in the middle of a slower number. The band leader, in his white tux, was singing in some kind of accent that sounded vaguely Latin and entirely muddled, but he was hitting his notes. He was a phantom, so missing a note would have sent him screaming out onto Sunset. I noted with horror that most, if not all, of his band appeared to be phantoms. I couldn't stand phantoms.

They weren't looking at me, so I figured it was safe to ignore them for the time being. I cased the crowd. I wasn't going to find an invisible man for obvious reasons, but finding who he was staking out, now *that* was doable.

I waddled past the tables doing my best not to trip over the flappy shoes and looked without looking like I was looking. Sounds strange, but it's about half of the job.

A nattily dressed zombie smoked at a table near the middle of the club, watching the stage with disinterest. His blue suit was tailored to his skeletal frame. The bite wounds on his face were fuzzy with some kind of green mold. He was the only zombie in the joint, unless they were hiding a couple dead men in the orchestra. He had to be a Bellum enforcer; no other zombie would have the juice to darken a door like this one. He might have been a trouble boy, but he didn't look like he was keen to start any. I'd keep an eye on him anyway.

I recognized Nyx Nocturne, the owner of the club, from the description Moon and Garou gave me. At the time, I thought their editorializing was unnecessary, but if anything, they'd undersold her. She had the complexion of a Greek statue, the looks of a movie star, and the attitude of a lion in a room full of lambs. She flashed a brilliant white smile with little to no provocation, but I think some of that was to show off the fangs she had for canines. I wasn't sure if vampires like her could smell my blood under the greasepaint, but I sure wasn't going to check.

My real target was front and center, best seat in the house. Titanio Mab, looking just like the picture the wolves had shown me. His lean body reclined in his chair as he brought a slender cigarette in a holder to his lips. He wore a white suit, tightly fitted and perfectly tailored. He seemed to be watching everything and nothing at the same time, projecting an air of ownership over everyone and everything in the place.

Three goblins sat around the table with him, and I recognized them as Flux, Murk, and Sawbones. They watched the crowd while their boss enjoyed himself. There's a difference between a man who will kill when he has to, and a man who does it because he likes to. Those three were in the latter camp. No way I wanted to get within spitting distance.

The phantom wrapped up his tune to enthusiastic applause.

"Thank you," he said in his muddled accent. "Once again, I am Capriccio Español, and this is my orchestra."

More applause.

"We have a special treat for everyone tonight," Español went on. "A guest singer, graciously loaned to us from our dear friend." Español put his palms together and gave a little bow to the sidhe sitting front and center. Mab nodded back with practiced *noblesse oblige.* "Ladies and gentlemen, please join me in welcoming the Songbird, Miss Dulcinea Ramos."

The room exploded in applause as the lights went down. A spotlight banged onto the top of the stage, well above the orchestra. A shape descended into the circle of light, throwing it back in blinding glitters. I watched, breathless, as I slowly put together what I was seeing. It was an egg formed of a silvery lattice, big enough for a human.

The light shifted, and the surface of the egg no longer shone back. The occupant was suddenly illuminated and haloed. I had seen her picture in the police station, but that hardly did her justice. She was the kind of woman people invented poetry to describe, because otherwise it would have been nothing but incoherent stammering and whistles.

A second wave of applause greeted the revelation, followed by a hush as she began to sing. Her voice belonged to an angel, or a whole choir, the way she was hitting her notes. She had pipes to put a phantom to shame. The song was something in Spanish, so I shouldn't have the foggiest idea of what she was singing about. From the longing she put into her voice, I knew. It was a love song, and not one that ended well. Wasn't that always the way?

Didn't take a big jump from a Spanish love song to Hexene Candlemas. I was still mooning over her like a schoolboy. It was a stupid thing to think of. She was a witch, I was human. She'd had her choice between me and her power, and she picked her power.

No, that's not true. I didn't have the guts to tell her how I felt, didn't let her know there was a choice at all. I just took it on the chin and let her go. Sure, she probably would have picked the power over me—and I had to believe she knew what I'd almost said—but I should have said it. A man says it. But it was too late for that. Hexene was gone, maybe for good. Time I accepted that.

It was tough. You don't meet a girl like Hexene every day. Or ever.

I turned away from the stage to keep poking around, and to stop thinking about the one that got away. I nearly ran into a group of fellas. That wasn't the strange part. The strange part was that I recognized the man in the lead. He was in his forties, shorter than me by a couple inches, and a lot pudgier than I remembered. His dark hair was fleeing from a high forehead. The long, crescent scar under his left eye was unmistakable, and I knew it was from a prizefight that went the wrong way, because he'd told me the story. The eyes, too, the way they twitched around while still looking dead, and the mouth, thick-lipped and pursed in distaste. He was dressed a lot better than I remembered, too, in a gray suit with pants pulled high over his new belly. Yeah, this was my friend Mickey from the Night War. Wasn't sure what to say, what with me dressed as a clown.

Mickey squinted at me. "Holy cats, Nick, is that you? Oh, shit. I'm sorry. Dunno what your new name is. Never thought you'd get changed. And by a clown! Of all the bum raps. Y'know, no offense."

"Mickey, yeah, it's me. I'm not...um..." I lowered my voice and leaned in. His guys behind him flinched, but they didn't get close. Mickey, tough guy that he was, leaned in to listen. "I'm not changed. I'm in disguise."

Mickey's face brightened. "Scared the shit out of me for a minute there, Nick. Don't do that to a fella. I always figured you'd die before you was changed."

"That was the plan."

Mickey broke out laughing. "That was the plan! Yeah, same old Nick. It's good to see you, even if you did join the circus while I wasn't looking. Yeah, yeah, I know, you're incognito. Lemme introduce you to the fellas."

I finally got a look at the group. I had been too shocked from going from my woolgathering about Hexene to seeing a fella I hadn't seen since the Treaty was signed to really take much of anything in. Next to Mickey floated a ghost, who looked like she was a pretty girl before someone had taken a tommy gun to her. The way Mickey stayed close to her said she was his dame.

A handsome Italian man stood next to Mickey, almost like a bodyguard, but he looked more like he'd be more at home in front of a camera than behind a gun. "This is my good friend Johnny Stompanato," Mickey said, then pointed at the other two. "The pale one is Jack Whalen, and the darker one is Rob Sampson. Say hello, boys."

I shook hands with Johnny, but the other two looked like they didn't want to give up their places. Or they didn't want to shake hands with a clown.

"Who's the lady?" I asked, gesturing at the ghost, who favored me with a demure smile.

"Where the fuck are my manners?" Mickey wanted to know. "Nick Moss, meet my lady friend, Florence Fantasma."

"Charmed," I said.

"Likewise," she said. To date, that was the nicest interaction I'd ever had with a ghost.

"Were *you* changed?" I asked him.

Mickey laughed. "What, because of the spook?"

I jumped, glancing guiltily at Florence. She hardly blanched at the slur, but she did blanch. Just slightly.

"Uh, yeah. The, uh, the ghost."

"Oh, it ain't like that. You can housebreak a monster same as a puppy. Just have to know who's boss, and Florence, she knows. What about you? A man don't go in disguise for no reason."

"I'm working a job."

"Yeah, I heard somewhere youse was a dick."

"Not my favorite term."

"Youse can tell me all about it later." Mickey handed me his card. "Gimme a call, Nick. Been way too long."

"Sure thing, Mickey."

Mickey and his group moved away, taking a table near the back of the room. Jack and Rob, the big guys, were alert to the activity. Humans? I could hardly believe it. Four actual humans out at night and not instantly being kidnapped and changed. It hardly seemed possible, but there it was, clear as day.

I knew what Mickey did before the war. Everyone who knew him did. He liked to brag about how he knew Al Capone and Bugsy—he called him Benny—Siegel. I never knew how much was bunk, but there were enough details that it sounded more like exaggeration than outright lying. If Mickey was back to his old tricks...just seeing a human out at night, unafraid, made my chest puff out like a pigeon.

I had an invisible man to find. They were a strange bunch. I'd had a friend back in the war by the name of Harry Braden. Back in '48, when we still thought we had a chance of winning it, Harry vanished from our camp in Debs Park. It was one of the early camps, too, when military men like me got weapons and ammo, and we had guards and perimeters and everything. Hell, we even had a Sherman tank for all the good it did us.

Two nights after Harry goes missing, and I'm on that perimeter staring out into the night with a sickness creeping in my gut wondering what's going to step out of my nightmares and into my gunsights. Well, I hear some rustling, then some cursing. Then I see footprints appearing in the dirt, getting closer but no feet, no legs, no nothing.

"Is that you, Nick?" I recognized that voice, even with the way he was whisper-yelling.

"Harry? What happened?"

"I'm invisible."

"No kidding, Harry."

Well, we thought everything was going to be jake. We now had a monster of sorts on our side. Harry got changed, but it wasn't like he had a thirst for blood, or went bugs every full moon, or had an irresistible urge to take over the world with some kind of cockamamie giant ants. It was still the same old Harry Braden, just a little more transparent than we were used to. Also, naked. That took a little getting used to as well.

Started out great too. Harry could scout for us like nobody's business. He could get the drop on most monsters, too, and old Harry did that with relish. Maybe a little too much relish.

The thing was, Harry couldn't see himself anymore. That's the strange part about invisible men. When you can't see yourself in the mirror, you lose sight of who you are, I guess. You start doing things and there's no one around to see, so there's no one around to hold you accountable. Like I said, Harry was hunting monsters, and maybe he was liking it too much.

Didn't take too long before he decided he might like to try some easier prey. We had to put old Harry in the ground after that.

I stopped one of the meat golem waitresses. She was taller than me by a good stretch, and pretty in an oddly catlike sort of way. Her large, slanted eyes were mismatched: the right was so black it looked purple, and the left was a clear, nearly colorless silver. A line of stitches ran diagonally over the bridge of her prominent nose. Her skin was patchwork: some pieces were green, others ivory, others gray. She wore her black hair long and in victory rolls. Like all meat golem women, she had a pair of silver streaks running up from her temples; these were pinned up behind her head, giving her a halo. She had a nice pair of legs. I wondered who they'd belonged to originally.

"Uh, hi. Hyuck, hyuck. I'm looking for an invisible man?"

The meat golem raised her eyebrows in exasperation, then pointed at her mouth.

"Oh, right. Sorry." For some reason, meat golem women couldn't talk. The men could, but they weren't exactly famous raconteurs.

I reached into the pocket of my clown suit and she flinched. It was just my wallet. I showed her, but her posture stayed tense. I fished out a couple bucks and handed it over. "Can you point me in the right direction?"

She glanced around, then took the money and tucked it into her bustier. Looked like there was a lot of room in there, and then I realized I was staring at a meat golem's chest. I nearly apologized, but she took my arm in one iron grip. Meat golems were strong, and that included this one. Must be a great second line of security. Get past the ogre at the door and meet the army of ladies ready to pull your arms off like a kid with a housefly.

She dragged me through the swinging doors on the other side of the club and I found myself in the kitchen. The first thing I saw was a raccoon stirring a giant pot of soup. Smelled pretty good, kind of halfway between lobster and some kind of wood. The soup, not the raccoon. I didn't smell him.

"I'm sorry, sir, are you...Jane?"

I turned to find a rotund woman regarding both me and the meat golem. Her face was pleasant, creased with wrinkles, and even though she was confused, a good-natured smile lit the room. She wore a food-splattered apron over her lumpy dress. Based on the raccoon and the way I had the urge to hug her, I was going to guess she was a witch, and the mother of her coven.

The meat golem—Jane, I guess—pointed at me, then pointed at the witch. She nodded as if to herself, turned around, and pushed through the swinging doors to the club.

"We don't get many clowns in here, but I suppose if Jane vouches for you, you must be okay. Wyeth Wyrd." She didn't offer a hand. Either because she was a cook and didn't want clown makeup in her soup, or because I was a clown.

"Nick...uh...Nick Laughington."

"First name could have used some work, dearie. Now what can I do for you? If it's a complaint about the food not being sweet enough..."

"Nothing like that, ma'am. Uh, hyuck, hyuck. Right. No, I'm wondering if you get any invisible men in this place."

"Oh, sure, from time to time. Some of them even get dressed up, if you can believe that. The Nocturnist is a place to see and be seen, so you'd think they might not go for that. But they do. Sometimes they do."

"Any invisible men in particular?"

"How would I know?"

"Right."

I wasn't sure if I should be flattered that Moon and Garou thought I could work some kind of magic finding a man no one could identify except by sniffing a hanky they kept at headquarters.

"Uh, thank you for your time, Miss Wyrd."

"Missus," she corrected with a demure curtsy.

"That too."

I went through the door Jane had disappeared through and found a hubbub. Dulcinea Ramos was finished singing and Capriccio Español hadn't started up another tune. The audience was too busy being enraptured. The Gobfather, flanked by his three diminutive enforcers, was heading for the front door. Following them, four meat golems—Jane too, I noticed—were carrying the lattice egg on poles like footmen carrying a queen. Dulcinea, standing stoic in her flowing gown, was the focus of every monster in the room. They were devouring her with their eyes, wishing they could get a little more literal with that devouring.

That's what this was. The Gobfather was showing off his pet meatstick, one so pretty every monster who saw her had to have her. As I followed them out the door, I wasn't sure if I was still looking for Bosch or if I couldn't stand to let Songbird out of my sight.

Maybe it was the get-up, but I wasn't all that different from them after all.

THREE

Thursday, October 27, 1955
Moments later

Running in clown shoes isn't easy. You rarely see killer clowns running, unless it's part of a gag. If they're after you, they can just appear wherever they like. Clowns were some of the more powerful monsters out there, able to do nearly anything that struck them as funny. Knowing their sense of humor, that was a pretty long and chilling list.

Me, I was just running for a cab. There was one up the street, disgorging a crawling eye and a shapely mummy. I didn't want to miss it, because we had a shortage of cabs in the City of Devils. Every kind of monster under the sun, but don't try to find a simple taxi.

I slid into the back seat.

"Brains," said the driver. He was a zombie, naturally, and in an advanced state of decay.

"Wait here for a minute."

"Brains," he told me, and flipped the fare. I'd be billing that to the LAPD.

In front of the club, now half a block behind me, a carriage had been waiting for the Gobfather. It was missing the actual car part. The meat golems were in the process of fitting the egg in place. The Songbird would go through Hollywood like that, on display for any monster who happened to look. A team of four gigantic stags—the kinds of beasts they were pulling out of the La Brea tar pits—were harnessed to the front.

A moment later, the team came clattering down Sunset Boulevard. Flux was driving, the Gobfather posed regally next to him, surveying Hollywood like a king checking out his new digs. Murk and Sawbones hung off either side of the strange vehicle, but neither one blocked the view into the egg. Songbird stood; there was no place to sit down in there. She was, after all, meant to be seen, not comfortable.

"Follow that carriage," I said to the zombie.

"Brains?"

"You see another one? Uh...hyuck, hyuck."

The hack driver gave me a muttered "Brains" and followed. The carriage wasn't going fast, and I encouraged the driver to hang back. Wouldn't do to let the mob boss know he had a tail. Not that they were looking for one. Perils of arrogance.

This whole thing was a show. First introducing Songbird to the crowd at the Nocturnist, now this trip into West Hollywood. Mobsters liked to flaunt their power, and from everything I heard, sidhe were the same way. It was why they were actors, politicians, and the like. They wanted to be seen. A sidhe mob boss was inevitable, and one who chose Hollywood? Well, that was a match made in hell.

The carriage crawled west, and we stayed a couple hundred feet behind it. This thing wasn't going to be easy to lose, even accounting for the wealth of strange traffic in the city. The farther we went, the buildings got thinner and the plant growth thicker. West Hollywood was a lot less urban than its next-door neighbor, every edifice featuring a thick garden. The carriage pulled into a driveway right by a pink neon sign advertising THE PIXIE RING.

"Right here."

"Brains."

I checked the meter and paid the driver his money, getting out a few doors down from the sign. Once I got a little closer, I figured the place was supposed to be a restaurant, one of those outdoor cafés. Situated in a garden, the tables were all at different levels, giving each one a sense of privacy, with stone paths leading between them. Trees stood all around, their living branches woven together, forming the framework of a ceiling. Small lights shone from these at irregular intervals. The garden itself was filled with fragrant flowers, plus the occasional man-eating plant. I'd have to keep an eye on those.

The Gobfather was being led to a table on the top terrace, against the slope that formed the back wall of the bistro. He had the best view of the place and the street beyond. Dulcinea was right next to him, freed from her egg for the first time that I'd seen. The three enforcers were close by.

As the Gobfather passed, one of the other diners, a pumpkinhead in what was otherwise a fetching evening gown, started to transform. Normally, pumpkinheads were the size and shape of slender human beings, albeit with green skin and a jack-o-lantern for a head. Get them riled up and they grew to the size of ogres, sprouted three-foot thorns, and generally tried to kill whatever had set them off. In this case, it was merely the sight of the Gobfather that did it, but she quickly got herself under control.

Pumpkinheads were supposedly spirits of vengeance. If there was one thing that made them lose control, it was someone who had hurt an innocent. I wasn't surprised the Gobfather qualified, but to scare a pumpkinhead into backing down, without even noticing she had changed, well, that set my nerves jangling.

The waitstaff was a mixture of killer vegetables and banshees. I looked over the clientele and saw what I expected: goblins, trolls, a few phantoms. I blinked when I saw a face I recognized. My secretary's favorite star, Audrey Hepburn, the sidhe princess of Hollywood, was dining at a table, accompanied only by a stag with a rack of antlers bigger than the sofa in my living room. I had to tell Ser—my secretary, Serendipity Sargasso—that I'd seen Miss Hepburn out and about.

A killer carrot tottered up to me as I entered the garden. "Table for one?" it asked in its peculiar buzzing voice.

"Yes, please. Uh, hyuck, hyuck."

The carrot paused, and the thing didn't have eyes to speak of, but I could feel it giving me a once-over. Finally: "Right this way."

It took me to a table at a lower level of the garden. The table was made of living wood, woven together into an approximate table shape. The chairs were also wooden, but weren't planted into the ground. The furniture reminded me of a chair I'd seen in a monkey khan's office once, although these were a lot smaller.

I had a decent view of the Gobfather's table, and for the first time I really took in the restaurant. It was cop proof. The realization hit me all at once as everything I'd seen but hadn't really noticed resolved into crystal. The indigo flowers blooming in great clumps all around the edges? That was wolfsbane. Mirrors hanging from trees gave a pleasant silvery moonlight to the bistro, but they were also reflective. Same with the pools of still water placed all about. No doppelganger undercover man could get close. I didn't know what they had for the invisible men on the force, but it had to be something.

No wonder the cops needed a human to tail this guy.

Yeah, I was finally safe from the cops. Also, any backup wasn't going to be able to do much. No, I was stuck in here. Trapped. Dressed as a clown.

"Sir, I must apologize."

I jumped. The buzzing voice belonged to the killer carrot. My waiter.

"Uh, what?"

"We don't have any candy on the menu. If you wish to find another establishment that might cater to your palate, I assure you, the Pixie Ring will not be offended."

"Uh, no. A salad will be fine. Hyuck, hyuck." I winced internally, wondering if I'd just set him off by ordering a bowl of his pals.

"The salads are exclusively vegetable. We don't have jellybeans or malt balls or Zagnut bars. We don't even have Bebop Cola."

"Do you have rye?"

"Yes?"

"That'll do. Um, hyuck. Want a balloon?"

"No, thank you, sir."

"Suit yourself."

The killer carrot shuffled off. I hadn't expected to get that kind of treatment, but really, I should have known better. For most humans, monsters just look like monsters. A big mass of the folks in charge. It's easy to miss that they have clear distinctions. You don't find vampires mopping floors or mummies driving cabs. That's work for zombies, ghosts, blobs, headless horsemen, and the like. Just because clowns were monsters didn't mean they were welcome at every monster joint.

Me, I had more experience with monsters than most. Socially, even. They all had little names for each other, the way humans used to do for different skin colors. Hell, I'd used those names, too, even if I didn't mean anything by it, before there was one of those names for me. Before I knew they stung. For monsters, gill-men were fishies, sirens were sea hags, vampires were leeches, werewolves were doggies, sidhe were elves. Humans lumped monsters under one heading, "snatchers," but monsters had so many more ways to hate each other.

The killer carrot brought me my salad and rye, and I watched the Gobfather, Songbird, and the three goblins eating. About halfway through their meal, Audrey Hepburn rode her stag sidesaddle out onto the street. Ser was never going to believe I saw her.

I was watching Serendipity's—and if I was going to be honest, my— favorite movie starlet gracefully exit when a pop and a poof pulled my attention back to the Gobfather. A human silhouette in a cloud of white struggled in panic against the swirling dust, near the edge of the garden about ten feet from the Gobfather's table. I knew what it was instantly. We had used them back in the Night War: flour bombs. Place them on the perimeter and let an invisible man blunder into them.

Boom: now he's covered in flour, dust, powdered concrete. Anything that'll stick.

It did more than make them visible; it made them panic. I had flour bombs on tripwires around my home. Most human houses did. Monsters, though, were always squeamish about using each other's weaknesses and fears, maybe knowing that once they started, it would be inevitable that another monster would do the same to them.

I stood, knocking my chair backward into a carnivorous seed pod. I wasn't sure what I was doing, but sometimes my reflexes moved faster than my brain. I didn't have time to do much of anything, though. Sawbones got up, and using the trick I'd seen in the picture, snapped his fingers. A flame played over the greenish-gray flesh of his hands. Then he threw the flame onto the invisible man.

The keening wail coming from the burning man filled the air. The killer vegetables and the phantoms ran immediately at the sight of the inferno. Couldn't blame them for that.

I charged up the slope of the garden, pushing past a goblin couple doing nothing more than gawking. I pulled the seltzer bottle from my clown costume—and it was filled with actual water, which I had learned at the station much to my relief—and I hosed down the invisible man. He was already still, only visible by the incomplete halo of fire and flour on his body.

He was dead before I'd gotten there, killed by the invisible man's weakness. I glanced over at the Gobfather's table. All five of them regarded me, the Gobfather with disinterest, the goblins with suspicion, and Songbird with frightened curiosity. Sawbones chuckled, his voice muffled beneath the gas mask. I turned back to the dead man.

Well, at least I could tell Moon and Garou that I'd found Bosch.

Four

Friday, October 28, 1955
After midnight

I was out front when the cops finally arrived. Nobody wanted to bother the clown, even after he had put out a fire rather than starting one he thought was funny. Moon and Garou were there with the first of the uniformed officers. This was technically a job for the Hollywood Sheriff, but I wasn't going to get involved in a jurisdictional dispute. I didn't have the best relationship with them anyway, since I'd been partly responsible for the last sheriff getting his ticket punched by a gremlin bent on revenge.

Long story.

The sheriff's deputies arrived around the same time. They were wearing their wolf forms—and these were honest-to-god wolves, albeit big ones—their howls a pretty good approximation for sirens. There was some beef between the wolfmen of the LAPD and the werewolves of the sheriff's departments. They never explained it to outsiders, and I never asked. As they arrived, the werewolves changed into their human forms: hairy, bearded men with badges tattooed over their hearts, and looking ready to throw down with the uniformed LAPD wolves.

"Stand down, deputies," Moon rasped. "This is an LAPD operation."

"You're out of your jurisdiction," a naked deputy shouted back.

"So's your mother," Garou told him.

I didn't think it would be prudent to point out that made no sense. It apparently worked on the deputies, at least long enough for the uniformed wolfmen to take over the argument. Moon and Garou walked up to me and in unison flinched when the smell of wolfsbane hit them.

"Evening, detectives," I said, not bothering to get up from my seat.

"What do you got, Moss?"

I pointed up the slope to where Bosch's body lay. The Gobfather's group had stuck around, but that might have been that they weren't done eating yet. They placidly watched the gathering cops, untouchable.

"Nice joint," Garou said, scowling. "Trust an elf to pick 'em."

"What did you see?" Moon asked me.

"Audrey Hepburn."

"Audrey Hepburn?"

"You know, she's a movie star? Really pretty. Rides a deer."

"What did you see about the *body*?"

"Oh. Mab and his cronies were tucking into dinner, and I hear a pop. I was looking away at the time. I look back and I see an invisible man caught in a flour bomb. One of the goblins lit him up. I tried to put out the fire, but the invisible man was dead by the time I got up there."

The wolfmen exchanged scowls. They didn't want to go up there, what with the wolfsbane, but they didn't have much of a choice. I didn't know what it felt like for them, but I always imagined it was like having a stone in your boot there was no way to find, no matter how hard you looked.

"C'mon, Moss. Let's go."

"There's a lot of wolfsbane between here and there."

"Then I guess you're doing some gardening on the way, aren't you?" Garou said.

I obediently got up and led them up the path. Whenever I got close to a wolfsbane plant, I yanked it up by the roots and tossed it away. Every time

I did, I heard a buzz of dismay from the killer vegetables assembled below.

As we approached, the goblins stood up, forming a protective cordon in front of the Gobfather. Mab stayed sitting, leaning back in his chair and regarding us like a bug he'd found in his soup. Songbird was nervous, eyes Disney-wide and slender body trembling. It was hard not to imagine holding her, but I did my best.

"Which one of you is responsible for this?" Garou demanded.

Sawbones stepped forward. His face was unreadable under the gas mask, the lenses over the eyes white in the light. He spoke:

> *The glass man came hence,*
> *A hungry dagger raised.*
> *Burned him up in self-defense,*
> *His body roundly blazed.*
> *My innocence I reaffirm,*
> *His hostility I maintain.*
> *My attorney will confirm,*
> *Esquire, Doug U. Larvane.*

"Can't stand goblins," Moon muttered, moving off toward the dead guy. I didn't blame him. The rhyming thing could get a little tiring.

"Larvane? That parasite?" Garou growled.

"I trust my associate has answered your questions?" Mab said to the two detectives.

"Yeah, not exactly—"

"Got a dagger here," Moon said. "We'll need to take it to the lab, but it looks like iron to me."

Cold iron was how you killed sidhe, goblins, and, come to think of it, doppelgangers too. I didn't think the last applied in this situation, but it was interesting. Had Bosch gone so far as to try to bump the Gobfather off? If so, Sawbones might have been a thug, but he was a thug acting in self-defense as he said. Or rhymed.

"You stay there," Garou said, jabbing a finger in the general direction of the Gobfather.

I followed him over to the corpse. Moon gestured at a thick growth of bushes. There was, in fact, a dagger back there, not too dissimilar from the one tucked under my right armpit.

"Is it Bosch?" Garou asked.

Moon squatted down by the half-visible corpse. His knees popped like champagne corks. He sniffed the body, then pulled the packet with the hanky from his jacket. He broke the plastic and had a sniff.

"Yeah, it's him."

He stood up with difficulty, and handed it over to Garou. His partner sniffed the hanky, then the body. "Goddamn it. It's him."

Garou stood up and turned to me. His eyes flashed yellow, and his voice deepened and grew rougher. His face darkened with the fur sprouting from it. "You couldn't move faster? Keep that goblin from lighting him up? Stop Bosch from bringing a knife to a firefight?"

"Settle down, Lou. We hired him to find Bosch. He found Bosch."

Garou whirled on his partner, breathing heavily. Slowly, the wolf features bled away. I was grateful to Moon. Sure, I was armed with silver, but there was no way I was going to shoot a cop. Especially not in front of two different law enforcement organizations. At the bottom of the garden, the nude sheriff's deputies were still arguing with the uniformed wolfmen at the cordon. They hadn't broken it.

I knew it was in my best interests to keep my mouth shut. I should have absolutely nothing to say here. But something was bothering me. Something didn't seem right. So I talked when there was no earthly reason I should have said a word.

"Bosch was an experienced cop," I said.

Garou turned back to me, the wolf only barely beneath the surface. "What of it?"

Moon stepped forward, putting a hand on his partner's arm. "What are you thinking, Moss?"

"He was experienced. The file said he was turned back in what, '51?"

"Get to the point."

"He had to have seen flour bombs. We used them all the time back in the Night War—"

That's all I got out of my mouth before Garou was on top of me, fully changed, snarling his coffee breath right in my face, mitts wadding up in my clown costume, and making me certain I was about to be food for a bunch of wolves. I think Garou was trying to say something, but he was beyond speech. He had turned the entirety of himself over to the raging monster right under his skin. And if he killed me, well, there was no way a human's death was going to bring down an LAPD detective.

Moon yanked Garou back, interposing his formidable bulk between me and his partner. Moon had changed as well, now covered with gray fur. "It's all water under the bridge, Lou. War's over."

The two wolfmen locked eyes. I don't think anybody made a sound as we all waited for the two detectives to tear each other apart. No way Moon would survive that, no matter how much I may have wanted him to. Three guesses as to who Garou would come after next.

Finally, Garou nodded. Moon kept a hand on Garou's chest but the other cop was no longer pushing at it, trying to get at human meat.

"Bosch was experienced, but you know invisible men. They can lose it. He probably got excited. Lost sight of what he could and couldn't do. Got Mab in his sights and took a shot," Moon said.

"Yeah," I said, not taking my eyes off Garou. It was hard to think of anything other than not getting myself killed.

The two detectives moved past me, turning their attention on the Gobfather and his party.

"We running in the little one?" Garou said.

"You have to ask? The mug offed a cop," Moon said.

"He's not going to do more than an hour of time. And we have to deal with that expensive lawyer of his."

"Least he has to pay Larvane."

"Sawbones, assume the position. You're under arrest."

Your accusations I'll defeat,
Your charges I'll deny.
Hard of hearing? I'll repeat:
Your frame-up's gone awry.
So throw me in your steel cage,
Clap iron 'round my wrists;
Know you've provoked a goblin's rage
And that you've made the list.

"You tryin' to say somethin', hob?" Garou snarled, making a lunge at the little monster. Moon held his partner back, and the goblin never flinched. Just regarded the wolfman through those blank gas mask lenses.

"Cute poem, hob, but you're coming with us," Moon said, slapping the cuffs on Sawbones.

"Officers, I believe we have complied with your demands. If there's nothing else, we'll be going," the Gobfather said.

"Detectives," growled Garou, but it took him a second to avenge the slight in the face of the regal disinterest of the sidhe.

"Of course. My apologies." There was no way Mab meant a single word.

Moon and Garou frog-marched Sawbones down to the street with me following. Behind us, Mab, Songbird, and his remaining goblins were taking their time descending. Showing the cops they would leave at their own speed.

A shiny navy blue Packard pulled up at the cordon. I recognized the wolfman who stepped out of the driver's seat. His picture was in the papers every morning. The hero cop Los Angeles was famous for. This was Hunter Moore, the leader of the Wolf Pack. When he started barking orders at the deputies, they backed off. The jurisdiction debate was officially over.

Moon and Garou met Moore at the street, handing Sawbones off to a uniformed cop, and in close tones took their boss through what had happened. When they were finished, his steely gaze fell on me.

Moore was difficult to stand up to. Tall and lean, he had the silhouette of a gunfighter. That's more or less what he was. One of those lawmen from another time somehow transported to modern day. Of course, he was a wolfman, unlike any of those Old West sheriffs. He wore a spotless gray suit with a fedora set at a rakish angle. His face was long and craggy, and with that squint, I felt rather than saw his eyes.

"So this is the one you wanted to hire to find Bosch?"

"Sir, he did find Bosch," Moon said, and coughed. "I mean, strictly speaking." Moore didn't twitch. He kept the lead weight of his attention on me.

"Not what I had in mind," he said. "But I'll take it. Pay the man, Detective Garou."

Garou glared at me rather than his boss, but peeled off a couple bills from a slender roll and handed them over. It wasn't quite what I should have been getting for the job, but I knew better than to kick.

Abruptly, I was the last thing on Moore's mind. The Gobfather and his group glided down the path.

"Good evening, Detective Moore," Mab said. "So sorry I couldn't help you tonight."

Moore watched the mob boss. A strange vibration shook my tissues. Took me a minute to realize Moore was growling so deeply it couldn't be consciously heard.

"Knew hiring you was a mistake, Moss," Garou said as he put his cash away.

"Yeah, wish you'd figured that out before you had me go out at night."

"A wolfman could have made it to Bosch before he was killed."

"A wolfman wouldn't have made it into that restaurant at all."

Garou's lip curled. "I should turn you for that. See what it's like for us."

"We *are* pretty close to a lot of wolfsbane, aren't we?"

Garou stuck a finger into my chest. "Keep it up. Sooner or later Phil won't be around to keep me off of you. Then getting changed is going to be the least of your worries."

"This, um, this might be a bad time to ask, but can I get a ride home?"

Garou stepped back, then in a louder voice said, "Find your own way home, meatstick."

I jumped. All eyes were on me now. The werewolves, the wolfmen, the looky-loos, the goblins, the Gobfather. Songbird, too, but unlike the frankly predatory stares of the others, I saw fear and sadness in her eyes. Then the Gobfather swept her away, going for his carriage.

I was going to need a cab ride all the way back to Watts. Looked like I wasn't going to make anything from this job after all. Now I just had to make it home without getting turned.

FIVE

Friday, October 28, 1955
Closer to sunrise than sunset

Looking the way I do, I never thought I'd have many admirers. I'm on the short side, and I've been nicknamed "weasel" so many times I figure the resemblance is uncanny. I tend to sweat and stutter when I get nervous, which is almost all the time. That's not to say I've never had company of the female variety—it's just that I always had to work for it.

All of that changed when the world did. Put me in a room with a bunch of monsters and I'm the prettiest girl at the ball. Only instead of a dance, these things want to slap some tentacles on me. Maybe give me a nice sunlight allergy while they're at it. I'm a potential child for them, because that's how monsters make more of themselves.

Most monsters will get some...ideas...if they figure out you're human after dark. When the Fair Game Law says it's okay to turn you. That's just lust, though. They're not looking to marry. When a monster really wants to turn someone, it's for some quality that person has, or some shared history. Every human ends up attracting admirers. The regular visitors to your house at night who prowl around and hope you forgot to ward some part it. If they can get in, they're allowed to turn you or anything else they've a mind to do, and it's all legal. So long as it happens between sundown and sunup. That's California state law for you.

When I arrived home to Juniper Street in Watts, I had to navigate my particular group of admirers. Sam Haine the pumpkinhead waited patiently on my front lawn, nervously fiddling with his tie. Mira Mirra the doppelganger, and my secretary's smitten roommate, stayed closer to the street. She was afraid of Sam after they'd tangled a month or two ago, but they'd since accepted one another, more or less. Lastly, the glowing eyes of Lurkimer Closett the bogeyman peered from under my house, looking like a cartoon monster in a dark room.

Fortunately, or maybe unfortunately, I'd gotten used to sneaking into my home after dark and I managed without Sam, Mira, or Lurkimer being any the wiser. I went into the bathroom, jumped when I saw a clown in the mirror, and got to work scrubbing the makeup off my face. I had a bit of makeup remover on hand, since it was the best way to drop a clown. They are, after all, only makeup.

The following day I came into my office to find my secretary, Serendipity Sargasso, taking an emery board to her claws. Ser is a siren, and she's quite particular about that term, which means she's a fish girl. Her skin is blue with thick yellow stripes, her hair is greenish black, her fingers and toes are webbed and clawed. The gills on her neck have a habit of popping out whenever she gets surprised or embarrassed. She sees the surface world through saltwater-filled goggles: she can't see properly through air.

She's a monster, but she had proven to me time and again I could trust her.

"Morning, Nick!" Her eyes are huge in those goggles. "You look terrible. Did you sleep?"

"Almost half the night."

"What happened with the police? That job they wanted you to do?"

"It's what kept me out so late. I found the guy. He was dead, though."

"That's great! And terrible."

I sighed, pouring myself a cup of what Ser inaccurately called coffee from the pot. I swear, it always tasted a little fishy. "You're never going to guess who I saw at the Pixie Ring last night."

"How did you get into the Pixie Ring?" she demanded.

"I don't know. I was wearing a clown suit."

"Oh, that explains it. Who did you see?"

"Audrey Hepburn."

"No!" Ser's jaw fell open, displaying more needle-sharp teeth than should be in a pretty girl's head.

"Yep. She was riding a, whaddyacallit, stag."

"You saw Pippin too?"

"The stag has a name?"

"Of course the stag has a name. It's hers. Did you get me an autograph? You had to get me an autograph."

"I'm sorry," I said, opening the door to my tiny office and leaning on the jamb.

"Why didn't you get me one?"

"I didn't want to be turned!"

Ser blew a raspberry. "I don't think Miss Hepburn would be interested in turning you."

"She wasn't who I was worried about."

I stifled a yawn and looked into my office. Next to the reception room—which was small, but could at least fit five people if everyone was standing and didn't mind getting friendly—my office was a closet. Piles of papers hid most of my desk, filing cabinets leaned in like movie heavies. The window looked out over Flower Street, and on the second story where I was, it was at least a decent view. With how cramped and stuffy it could get in the summer, I was grateful the weather was turning to winter. Didn't get cold in Los Angeles, but it got cooler, and that was enough.

I sighed, wondering what I was going to do with my day.

The front door jangled open. I put on a solemn face, ready to greet a person who was missing a loved one, but what I saw brought me to a screeching halt. It wasn't a human. It was a phantom.

I tensed. My whistle was already in my hand.

He looked young, but with phantoms it's tough to tell. They always look like they have too little skin stretched over their skulls. His black hair was slicked back from a widow's peak, and with his buggy, lidless eyes he looked as surprised to see me as I was to see him. He wore a double-breasted suit and carried an instrument case.

Maybe the Gobfather had phantom enforcers. I wouldn't put it past him. When it came to fiendishly inventive violence, the only thing that topped clowns was phantoms. Sure, phantoms got their little crushes, but at least you didn't have to deal with clowns.

"Can I help—" I started.

"Billy!" Ser said, bouncing up from her desk. She crossed the room and gave him a peck on the cheek. "What are you doing here?"

"On my way to rehearsal, couldn't get you out of my mind, baby. Thought I'd stop by."

"Oh, you." Serendipity blushed blue. Well, deeper blue.

"What's going on right now?" I asked, still not sold on putting the whistle away. One discordant note and the phantom would be on his knees crying uncle.

"Nick, this is my boyfriend, Billy. Billy Bounce. Billy, this is my boss, Nick Moss."

He stuck out a hand pale as cheesecloth. "Pleased to make your acquaintance, Mr. Moss. You want tickets to the show?"

No way I was shaking a phantom's hand. "Show? What show?"

"Billy plays trumpet at the Ninth Circle Downtown." Ser turned to Billy. "Nick's human. He doesn't like to go out after dark."

"Oh!" Billy said, probably trying to blink but having lost the ability when he turned. He took his hand back, flexing it in confusion. "I'm hip. No offense intended, Mr. Moss. Didn't know there were any human dicks left in town."

I was too annoyed with a phantom in my office to quibble about terminology.

"Nick's the last one," Ser said with a trace of pride.

"How's the detective game?"

"Mostly I just look for people who've been kidnapped by monsters and turned against their will," I told him.

"Oh."

"Now if you'll excuse us, this is a place of business."

Ser sighed, rolling her eyes. The goggles made that an epic gesture of exasperation. "Come on, Billy, I'll see you off."

She escorted her beau out the door with a backwards glare at me. A phantom. Ser could do a lot better than a phantom. Really, any monster would have been better. I didn't have much against...I thought about it, landed on witches, and figured that wasn't Ser's cup of tea. In the old days, I'd never have considered anything like that, outside of a few suggestive postcards I saw in France, but now both monsters and humans took a much more cavalier attitude toward that sort of thing. None of my business anyway.

The door clattered, and I readied myself for a thorough grilling of Serendipity over this Billy Bounce character, but it wasn't Serendipity who filled the doorframe.

He was a Mexican kid barely out of his teens. The undershirt he wore instead of anything proper showed off a pair of muscled arms crawling with a variety of tattoos. Some of these were symbols—a cross, an evil eye: literal wards etched into his skin. Others were more ominous, like the line of hash marks on his right forearm. His hair was done up in a high pompadour, glistening with oil, and he wore the overconfident mustache of a person who'd just gained the ability to grow one. His jeans were stained with dirt and motor oil, and he wore a heavy pair of steel-toed boots perfect for stomping people into the earth.

I had only met him once, but he was difficult to forget.

"Jaime Alvarez? What can I do for you?"

He rubbed his eyes, suddenly self-conscious. Last time I saw him, he was in a place of power, with the rest of his gang. Jaime was a member of the Normandie Knights, those bogeymen Garou was convinced were responsible for the Monster Slayer killings. From my perspective, they were a bunch of confused kids who didn't know the Night War was over.

"Wasn't sure you'd remember me," he muttered.

"Maybe I wouldn't. You want to step into my office?"

"Sure."

I nodded and snaked my way behind my desk. Jaime followed, shutting the door behind us and sitting down.

"How's Corrina?" I asked. We'd met because I was looking for Corrina Lacks, his girlfriend.

"She dropped me."

"Sorry to hear that." I wasn't really all that sorry. Corrina was a college girl, and she had as good a life ahead of her as any human could expect. Jaime was a no-account hood in the words of Corrina's mother, and I had yet to arrive at another opinion.

"She said I was going nowhere fast. That's how she put it. I got no job. I got no future. Sooner or later, some monster is going to catch me napping. Or some cop is going to decide he don't need no reason to take me down, and I'll hang in my cell."

"Cops cracking down on the Knights?"

"Always." He swallowed. "But yeah. It's been worse lately."

I thought of the Monster Slayer board. I wondered how many of those were in different stations through the city. Made sense they'd be going after the Knights worse than usual.

"Did someone go missing?" I prompted.

"After you came up to El Castillo," he started, naming the small bluff where the Knights liked to loiter, "I asked around about you. Talked to some of the old timers. Heard some stories. I already know what you did for Corrina." Jealousy was a spike in his voice, but I pretended not to hear it. "I saw what you were doing and I thought I should be doing it too."

"You want to be a detective?"

He met my eyes, nodding. "In the books and in the movies, the guy always has, like, an assistant."

I thought about it. A lot of detective work ended up being sitting in one spot, staring at a place or a person. Having someone else to do that would help. A lot.

"Listen, Jaime, I don't get paid on the regular. If there's a case, I can use you. I can even pay you, but this isn't what you'd call stable." It was more stable now that people regularly went missing, but I didn't want to get Jaime's blood up with a comment like that.

The front door clattered. Either we had a client or Serendipity was back.

"Sure, whatever you can do."

"Okay then," I said, taking his hand. "Welcome aboard."

If this was just his way of getting Corrina back, well, in the scheme of things it was probably the best thing he could do with his time. Or maybe I was just susceptible to flattery.

"One thing—" I started as Jaime opened the door.

"Snatcher!" Jaime shouted.

Serendipity screamed.

I grabbed Jaime. The kid was as strong as an ox, but confusion kept him from committing to a direction. "That'd be it. Jaime, calm down. This is Serendipity Sargasso. My secretary."

Ser was behind her desk, one hand over her heart. She was calming down, but her gills were fully out, giving her an Elizabethan collar. Jaime stood in the doorway, baffled. He was unarmed, but still ready to fight. I would have admired that if the person he was ready to fight wasn't my secretary.

"New client?" Ser asked.

"New employee. Meet Jaime Alvarez, my legman."

Ser stood up, her gills retracting into the slits on the side of her neck. She extended a webbed hand. "Charmed."

"Yeah," Jaime said, stalking over to the one chair we kept on hand for clients.

I was beginning to see how this could blow up in my face. Ser and I shared a look as she took her hand back. "And you, Nick. You should be nicer to Billy."

"I was plenty nice," I said.

"You were—" but she got cut off.

A tiny woman came through the door, with the sad, guardedly hopeful look of a client. I put on my most professional face for her. "Hello, ma'am. I'm Nick Moss. What can I do for you?"

She spoke in a thick Chinese accent. "My husband has been taken. Help, please."

I'd heard the story a hundred times. I hoped I could end it better for this woman.

Six

Friday, November 25, 1955
Almost quitting time

Serendipity, sweetheart that she was, spent the next month trying to get Jaime to like her. I was pretty sure that the friendliness was stranger to Jaime than any kind of outright hostility. Monsters were the other side in a desperate war for survival. They weren't friendly young women who brought you doughnuts and told you you looked like Clark Gable.

I shouldn't have been worried about paying Jaime, either. We had a steady stream of cases all through November. With his help, I wrapped a few up quicker than I otherwise would have, and was even able to double up without a drop in quality. Jaime was still getting used to our lousy success rate. I tried to tell him it had jumped ever since he joined up. It had, too. Now instead of one in ten, we brought home one in five.

Serendipity was still with that Billy. I found out I had an unlikely ally in my dislike of the trumpeter: her parents. Sirens and gill-men lived together in big clans, and the Sargasso family was one of the larger ones in the Southland. Understandably, they wanted to see Ser with a gill-man, not some phantom hipster. That was when I knew the battle was lost. There was nothing a woman loved more than a man her parents didn't like.

It was early afternoon on a Friday, and Jaime and I had just wrapped up a case. We determined, that yes, the Henderson boy was in fact a robot now. I was in my office wondering if I should stick around. Ser was at her desk, probably vibrating with the desire to go someplace and get discovered in showbiz. Jaime had taken up his usual position in the one chair we had in case a client had to wait, studiously working on a crossword puzzle. The kid loved those things. Never know it to look at him.

The day was over. I had a place to be, and there was no need to keep either of them in the office. "Okay, go home," I said going to the doorway of my office.

"Still got a couple hours," Jaime said. "We could get another client."

"Sad fact of the business, kid. Monsters like to take people over the weekend. If we're not doing something by now on Friday, we're not going to."

Serendipity was already up, flashing her terrifying grin. Jaime shuddered. She still gave him the heebie-jeebies. He really didn't like it when she sang.

"And where are you going to be discovered this evening?" I asked her.

"I'm going to see Billy play tonight." She paused, her gills extending a few inches past the slits: her equivalent of a slight blush. "And if there just so happens to be a director in the crowd, well, that's not something I can control."

"Knock 'em dead," I said, shaking my head.

She paused briefly. "You boys have fun."

Jaime flinched, and Ser pretended not to notice. Then she was out the door.

Jaime stood up, and gave me the most dubious of dubious looks. "You sure, boss?"

"Get out of here. See you Monday."

Jaime touched his forehead in what he probably thought was a salute and headed out the door.

I went home. It was early enough in the day that the monsters hadn't gathered around the houses yet. It could have almost been a neighborhood before the war, so long as you ignored all the more permanent wards still affixed to the sides of houses or hanging from eaves. Unless we were just a very religious community who happened to like wind chimes and the occasional booby trap.

I changed my shirt. November or not, I could still sweat through one, and I didn't know to what kind of classy joint Mickey was going to take me for that late lunch he'd promised. I checked my jacket for my various tools. I didn't have to, just something I did before I left the house, an ingrained habit that would keep me alive. Small pockets were sewn into the lining, and vials were in each, filled with a variety of substances that could kill or frighten a monster: salt, speckled mushrooms, makeup remover, wolfsbane. Other pockets held tools to do the same: a small mirror, a whistle, a flashlight. My two main weapons, a cross-shaped cold iron dagger and my .32 revolver, stayed in two different shoulder holsters. I had permits for all of it, and believe me, I carried those at all times. If a cop caught me without them, I was in dutch. Or if he didn't care, I at least wanted a fighting chance.

Not that I was expecting trouble, but it never hurt.

I left the house and locked up, then turned around right as my friend Will Hammond was jogging across the street toward me. Will was dressed in his sewer worker's coveralls, and I was grateful that they didn't look wet. Meant he'd smell more or less fine.

"Hey there, Nick."

"Will. What can I do for you?"

"Haven't talked to you since Thanksgiving. Did you enjoy yourself?"

I'd had Thanksgiving dinner over at the Hammond place the week before. I had been planning on a TV dinner and some *Gunsmoke*, but I'd take a pity invitation if it meant a home-cooked meal any day. Will had a nice family. The kind you were supposed to want, with a pretty wife and two good sons. Will had gone through the hell of the Night War with them, and a man who could keep that many people safe was one to be reckoned with. I only met Will at the very end of things, and by then he was a formidable fighter. Now he was a family man. And I was going to meet a gangster for lunch.

"Thought that was obvious after how much I ate. You thank Esther for me, will you?"

"She was happy to do it."

"For the invitation, I mean."

"Yeah," Will said, and the look on his face said he was caught. "Listen, you remember Arnetta?"

Arnetta was Esther's cousin. Pretty as a picture, too. "Uh, yeah. She was nice."

Will sighed. "Nice like you'd like to see her again? Nice like she had a piece of broccoli in her teeth and now you can't stop seeing it?"

I laughed. "I don't know, she was nice. She didn't really say much. Wait, did Esther put you up to this? Is Esther matchmaking?"

"A little bit. She's not wrong, though, Nick. It's fine to look at monsters every now and again, but you have to be realistic."

"Realistic?"

"That witch you were sweet on." Will held up his hands to placate me. "Believe me, I got nothing against that. A man's gonna look and maybe a man's gonna get sugar where he can find it. But you and she both know monsters and humans don't mix. Not like that."

"You're probably right."

"Should I tell Esther to call Arnetta?"

"No, don't do that. Nothing against Arnetta or anything. I'm not really looking to start anything just now, and a girl like Arnetta deserves a man who will be in with his whole heart."

"Girl like Arnetta won't be around forever."

"I know that, too."

Will looked me over. "You on a case?"

"Going to meet an old friend of ours."

"Who?"

"Mickey Cohen."

Will kept a hold of his expression, but he was fighting surprise. "You watch yourself, Nick. Even back then, Mickey was trouble. I don't want to know what he is now that he sleeps at night."

I got into my Ford and drove north and east into Boyle Heights where Mickey lived. Will's words were rattling around in my head. *Monsters and humans don't mix.* He was right, of course. Didn't stop me from being hung up on a witch.

It would be difficult not to get hung up on a lady like Hexene, although she would no doubt object to being called a lady. She was brave, pugnacious, and smart. Before the war, it would have surprised me to find those qualities in a woman, but when you've fought off werewolves back-to-back with a woman, that kind of prejudice goes away. Will was right about one thing: Hexene and I never were together. We never even had a moment. No, the last thing I did for Hexene was fail her.

Maybe that's really why I was hung up.

My job is mostly failure. Looked at it from most standards, so was my life. There weren't a lot of choices for humans anymore.

Except maybe for what Mickey found.

In Los Angeles, there were a lot of large homes. Built in the early studio boom when land was endless, they came in every style you could think of and a few they had to make up. Nowadays, if they were for humans, the big ones had been chopped up and walled off into apartments. When I pulled up in front of the two-story Craftsman in Boyle Heights, I was momentarily surprised that Mickey would live with anyone.

I quickly found out that he didn't. That place was his. It wasn't big by the old definition of the word. Or really the modern one, either, since I'd seen the digs of crawling eyes, doppelgangers, and even giants. But for a human, it was impossibly large. I bet there were at least three bedrooms in the place, and a bathroom on each floor.

I knocked on the front door and it opened to Florence Fantasma, Mickey's ghost girlfriend. I'd only met her in passing, and hadn't spoken to her since, other than briefly on the phone, so this was my first real look. She had a round face and a curvy body, but the whole thing was perforated by gunshots. Her legs grew more insubstantial as they went toward the floor, leaving her to float a half a foot above the carpet.

"Miss Fantasma? Nick Moss."

"Yes, Mickey said you would be coming over." She sounded like she was trying to smother a Mexican accent, and had gone too far trying to imitate Mickey's movie-gangster swagger. "Please, come in. And call me Flo."

I walked past the ghost. A full vial of holy water sat right in the small of my back. Florence wasn't acting like most ghosts. They ate fear, and so tended to compulsively try to frighten people.

"You want something to eat while you wait?"

"Uh...how long will I be waiting?"

"Mickey just got into the shower."

I grinned. Mickey had spent most of the Night War complaining about how he couldn't bathe. He was probably enjoying himself. These days, everyone had the things they missed, and we all had the tendency to overindulge once we got the chance. I know I ate my weight in pastrami after the Treaty got inked.

"I don't think I'll have time."

"I'll fix you something," she said, and faded from sight before I could protest.

I had a seat in Mickey's living room. The furniture might have been a bit threadbare, but it was all working. The walls didn't have any holes, which was more than you could say for my place. I settled down on Mickey's sofa. A picture window gave me a nice view of the tree-shaded street. This was beginning to feel almost homey.

Florence reappeared, clutching a glass of lemonade and a bowl of potato chips. Neither one had spiders or maggots or anything else to scare me in it. The lemonade she handed over, the chips she put on the coffee table. I thanked her and she went off to see how Mickey was progressing.

It took Mickey well over three hours. How any shower could take more than a few minutes was beyond me. It was like Mickey was finding new areas of himself that desperately needed to be cleaned and recleaned. He'd always hated getting dirty, but maybe there was more to it than that. The more I thought about it, the more a ghost lady made a strange kind of sense. He could have a pretty woman on his arm without having to touch anyone or anything. I couldn't imagine being close to a monster that long and her not even trying to turn him. That was the advantage of being close to a witch; she'd never turn a man. She couldn't.

"Hey, Flo? You mind if I ask you something?" I asked the ghost as she was bringing me another glass of lemonade.

The ghost cocked her head expectantly. I thought I saw some confusion in her dead eyes, as though none of Mickey's friends ever asked her. "Sure."

"I know, uh...mixed relationships happen. I've just never seen one up close."

"Oh!" she said. "Mickey and I have been an item for a time."

"Right. What's a girl like you doing with a fella like him exactly?"

The room dropped a couple degrees along with the expression on her face. "A girl likes to feel safe."

I nodded, regretting my burst of curiosity. I'd offended her and still had no idea what was going on there. "I can understand that," I said, and I was sincere.

The room returned to its previous temperature. "It's a big, bad world, isn't it?"

"Bigger and badder every day."

One hour in, and there was a knock at the door. Florence opened it to reveal Johnny Stompanato. I got up to greet him, and he took my hand, but his eyes held nothing but contempt.

"John," I said. "Good to see you."

"I'm sorry. I've forgotten your name."

"Nick. Nick Moss."

"Nick, Mick, no wonder I got it mixed up."

"Yeah, no wonder."

Two hours in, Florence offered us some ice cream. I took her up on it, but Johnny didn't, and she returned with a scoop of chocolate and a scoop of vanilla in a bowl. The spoon was gold. I had to laugh. Silver flatware was hard to come by these days, and trust Mickey to buy gold rather than get the tin that most people made do with.

Mickey sauntered in around four in the afternoon in a shiny gray suit. His skin was white with powder, and it trailed off him in summery puffs. A tiepin in the shape of his initials sparkled from his chest.

"Nick Moss," he said, smiling and nodding happily. "Good to see you. Flo get you some ice cream?"

"She did." Apparently that was a normal thing. "Thanks. Nice spoon."

Mickey laughed. "You noticed? Of course you did. Always had those eagle eyes and that spaniel nose. My little way to show people I'm pulling in the cash. Can't move out of a human neighborhood, 'cause they won't let me, so I gotta show it off in other ways."

"Should you be talking like this?" Johnny asked.

"Cool your jets. I been in a foxhole with the weasel here."

"We're, ah...we're not still calling me that, are we?"

Mickey's grin got wider. "If the shoe fits, boychik. Flo? Flo, where are you?"

Florence faded in next to Mickey. I jumped and was the only one to do so. I guess they were used to it.

"Flo, honey. You meet us at the Nocturnist later, okay? When your shift's over."

"Will do, Mick."

"Don't forget to bring along some of your friends."

"I won't."

He didn't kiss her on the way out. Yeah, she was the perfect girl for Mickey.

It was getting late, and with the days even shorter than usual, I was antsy. Being out after dark didn't have much appeal. I'd have begged off then and there, but the truth was, I wanted to see Mickey. For all his character flaws, he had been a damn good friend under some very weird circumstances.

We piled into a blue Cadillac. It was maybe ten years old, and had a few dents here and there, but it was a real Caddy, and it still moved. Johnny drove, while Mickey insisted I sit in the backseat with him. Since Johnny was, well, Johnny, I went with it.

Mickey took us over to the outskirts of Chinatown. I thought he had a hankering for some chop suey, which didn't sound half bad to me, but we pulled up outside an aging stucco building calling itself the Eastside Market.

"I remember you said you like pastrami," Mickey told me. "Best in the city. You ever been here?"

I shook my head.

"Then let's get you fixed up."

The market was dark, with a few tables set in front of a deli counter. One of the tables had already been taken over: Jack Whalen and Rob Sampson, Mickey's two palookas I met at the Nocturnist before. Both of them had empty baskets in front of them with a crumpled-up piece of butcher paper inside; they'd finished their sandwiches a while ago, waiting for Mickey to arrive.

Mickey greeted them, then reminded them of my existence. "Siddown, Nick. Romeo!" he called.

A small Italian man peered up over the counter. "That you, Mr. Cohen?"

"Two pastramis and a meatball."

"Right away, Mr. Cohen!" And the little man busied himself behind the counter.

I sat down and realized I was at a table with four gangsters. Real ones. There's a look a man gets in his eyes when he's killed someone. You can see it in fellas who've been to war. Usually, it goes away after a few years, when the war turns into something you have the occasional nightmare about. These four had that look all the time, like their eyes were chips of flint held upright in their sockets.

"Where'd you find this weasel?" Rob Sampson wanted to know.

Mickey broke out laughing. "I told you, Nick! I told you!"

"You a cop?" Big Jack asked me.

"No. They, uh, they don't take humans."

"He's a friend of Mickey's from way back," Johnny said, supplying a verbal eyeroll even if he wouldn't dare to do it physically. Not in front of Mickey.

"Nick may not be much to look at, but he's faster than a rattlesnake and twice as mean. Ain't ya, Nick?"

"Sure?"

The gangsters laughed.

"Let me tell youse all a story." Mickey said *youse* whenever he could manage it, which was most times. "Me and Nick and our old pal Izzy, we was a group of us in, what, '50?"

"Yeah, about that, I think. That or '49," I said.

"Or '49," Mickey agreed amiably. Between words, his lips returned to their natural purse, so that he always seemed to be tasting lemons. "So it was the three of us, and maybe a half dozen civilians. Jan the Polack, only she only *looked* like a civilian, the Ramirez sisters, old man Righetti, and what was it, the Brooks family."

"We didn't meet the Brookses until '52."

"You sure?"

"Pretty sure," I told him.

"Doesn't really matter, because other than Izzy, me, Nick, and that Polack, there wasn't anybody to do the fightin', and our group was getting smaller by the night. We was trying to live in Griffith Park, figuring most everyone is going to leave us alone. Well, then a pack of werewolves get the scent on us. And you know them, wolves damn near the size of Shetland ponies."

Romeo, the man in the kitchen, brought out baskets filled with sandwiches as big as cats. The pastrami was drenched in red sauce and packed into a crumbly roll. He put cardboard cups of iced tea next to those, then another basket of chips in the middle of the table. Mickey gave Romeo a grateful nod, then dug in. He told the rest of his story around mouthfuls of pastrami. I didn't have to understand it, though. I'd been there.

"Well, these werewolves was giving us hell. Howling through the night, tracking us, just waiting for us to let the old guard down. Izzy, he has this single-shot deer rifle, been in his family since the days of Lincoln. I got my tommy and my .45, but ammo's as scarce as a hooker in church. Nick, he's packing this German Luger. I gave him hell for that one. Jewboy like me don't need to see a kraut gun, you know?"

Mickey grinned. He always loved it when I told him I took it off a dead kraut.

"Nick's got cartridges, though. And one night—this is maybe a week after these things started following us. We're staying up all night, we're hoping, we're praying. We're sure they're just playing with us now. Well, Nick's had enough. It's like he got replaced. Suddenly he's ice cold, like nothing I seen. He says, 'Hey, Mick. I'm going to go have a word with those wolves.' And that's it. That's all he says. Then he walks away from the fire, and he's gone. I thought he was fit to cut out paper dolls."

Mickey laughed again. I didn't. He was right. I'd snapped a little. A week of no sleep, of being hunted? That'll do it to a fella.

"Yeah, so I think Nick here is going out to die. I tell Izzy and the Polack we got to keep the eyes peeled and we're down one man. But then I hear a gunshot. And believe you me, I know what a Luger sounds like when she's barking. Funny thing is, I love that sound now. A kraut gun has something to say, and the only word it knows is hope.

"So Nick's gun snaps. Just once. And I know, for sure, that he's not panicked. Nick shoots a lot? He hits nothing. He shoots once? Something's dead. So I think, *Okay, Nick got one. That's one less, I guess.* I figure the wolves got on him then, tore him up some, or they turn him and soon Nick will be a small weaselly wolf trying to bite our ankles."

The gangsters laughed, but neither Jack nor Rob were looking at me like a figure of fun anymore.

"Then I hear that kraut gun speak. *Snap.* Just like that. This time, I hear the wolf crying out. First like a wolf, then like a man. He's calling for help. A minute or so later? *Snap snap.* Then nothing. Except that one wolf, crying and crying."

Mickey shook his head.

"When I hear rustling, I start wondering if one got away. But no, it's Nick coming out of the dark. He's dirty—well, dirtier; we were all filthy as farmhands in those days—but he's fine. I ask him what happened. You remember what you told me, Nick?"

I nodded, because I still felt guilty about it from time to time.

Mickey went on, though. No way he was giving up the floor, even to the man who did it. "Nick tells me he was hunting the wolves, then he figures why look for them when he can get them to come to him. So he shoots one of them in the guts. Most painful place you can get it. And Nick waits for the rest of the pack. He croaks them both, and then leaves. I ask him, I say, 'You left that one alive?' And Nick shrugs and says, 'Ammo's hard to come by.'"

Mickey slapped the table and roared with laughter. Jack and Rob joined in, and soon so was Johnny, but his was brittle, faking it to fit in.

"Ammo's hard to come by," Jack said, shaking his head.

"That's cold. Ice cold," Rob said with real admiration.

"You remember the war," I muttered. "Lot of terrible stuff."

The pastrami tasted like roofing material. I choked it down anyway and tried to pretend that was as fun a memory for me as it was for Mickey.

When Mickey was done with the sandwich, he vanished into the men's room for a good ten minutes.

"Hey, Nick," Jack said. "How'd the Mick wash his hands back in the war?"

"He didn't. Used to bellyache about it all the time, too."

Jack and Rob burst out laughing.

"You shouldn't talk about Mickey like that." Johnny was glowering at all three of us.

"Don't be sore," Jack said.

"The boss has his quirks, same as anybody," Rob said.

Mickey came out of the bathroom, his hands red and shining from the thorough scrubbing he'd just given them.

"Okay, boys. Now for a night on the town," he said.

They were nodding. I looked from face to face. Not a sliver of fear on any of them.

So I spoke up. "A night on the town? You think that's a good idea?"

"Sure, why not?"

"The Fair Game Law? Monsters crawling the streets who can do anything they want to us?"

Mickey laughed. The other gangsters exchanged amused glances.

"You armed, Nick?"

"Yeah. Silver, cold iron, you name it."

"Then what are you worried about?"

I thought I could give Mickey a list, but it wasn't like it was going to change anybody's mind.

SEVEN

Friday, November 25, 1955
After sundown

Johnny drove the Cadillac, and Jack and Rob followed in a car that could have been a twin of my old Ford Coupe. We drove into Hollywood, or right around there, where the streets were seedy and none of the tourists ever came. Some of the buildings were still marked from the Night War, and one place had been bombed nearly flat. Johnny pulled the Caddy into a big parking lot around a blocky gymnasium with bullet-pocked walls. The lit sign advertised A FULL FIGHT CARD! No names, though, and I took that for what it was worth.

I checked the lot for motorcycles. This part of Hollywood was Howler turf, a gang of phantoms I'd had some trouble with. I had won the first round, but I wasn't looking forward to a second. I didn't see a single one of their bikes, so I breathed a little easier. Until I remembered it was after sundown in Hollywood and I was about to wander into a building where a bunch of monsters already had their blood up.

I was beginning to regret not saying anything.

We got out, and the other four straightened their jackets. All of them were lumpy with weapons and so was I. That was supposed to keep us safe.

The zombie at the door selling tickets didn't stop us. He didn't even say "Brains" at us as he watched us go past with his remaining eye.

We stepped inside and the scent hit me. That had changed, too. Not everyone stank the same way, or in the same amounts. Martians got a chemical scent, like Listerine, ghouls smelled like rot, and vampires didn't sweat at all. Blood was the same way, and that had been shed here almost as much as sweat. These varied aromas sank into the ring, the planks, the floor, and the walls, permeating the gym with a faint and muddled miasma.

The gym was one large room with a small office, some locker rooms, and restrooms off to one side. The ring was right in the middle of the room, though instead of ropes, the place was fenced in. The Marquess of Queensberry was a forward-thinking sort, but he never planned on people up and growing tentacles. Like every other aspect of life after the Night War, the sweet science had some changing to do. The old weight classes were the first to go. Underground human fights still used them, mostly, unless the poor slob was up against a monster. For the official, sanctioned bouts, they'd had to get a little more elastic.

In the middle of the ring, a killer potato rolled in a circle, its collection of eyes pointed skyward at its opponent, a human fly buzzing in and out of range. The human fly would come in, pepper the potato with jabs, then zip out before the vegetable could get its vines on him.

It looked like the fly was trying to knock the potato out. I didn't have the first clue as to how that was done. Seemed like the fly was in the same boat.

"Nothing like the fights, huh?" Mickey said, puffing up his chest. "You know, I taught Nick everything he knows."

"You box?" Rob asked.

"Not professionally."

Mickey wasn't telling the truth. I'd learned how to fight in the service. It's true Mickey had taught me some tricks, but he was the first to admit he was never much of a prizefighter. The scars on his face were mementos of some of the worst beatings he had taken.

"Jack, why don't you get us some popcorn. C'mon, boys," he said to the rest of us, leading us through the crowd to a bare few feet of bench. Some of the monsters reacted as we went by, giving us looks like a hound dog sighting a biscuit.

I sat down and ended up next to Johnny. Just my luck.

"You were in the service," Johnny said.

Wasn't sure how this was going to end in an insult, but I had faith Johnny would find a way. "Yeah, Army. Fought in Europe."

Johnny laughed. "You boys in the European theater were lucky. In the Pacific, we saw things you can't even dream of."

I didn't know what to say, but Mickey spoke up. "You two make nice, Johnny. Both of youse fought, and both of youse should have a whole chest fulla medals. But you ask me? A jewboy never had nothing to fear from no Jap. Nick was putting Hitler's mugs six feet under, and he has the gun to prove it."

Jack came back and handed out paper bags of popcorn, then plopped himself down between me and Johnny. I'd seen my cat do the same thing: that was where he was sitting and that was the long and short of it.

The potato knocked the human fly out by grabbing him with the vines and hammering him into the mat. Like I said, the rules had changed. Then it was time for the main match. A bug-eyed monster came into the ring, and bellowed out names and records. It was Hurok the Facemasher in one corner, and Stone Chin in the other. Ogre on troll.

Hurok carried his usual club, and Stone Chin hefted a hammer with a head the size of Big Jack Whalen. Some weight classes allowed weapons. That had been a change when no one could figure out how to tell this one ogre to leave the skullcrusher at home. Supposedly the ogre it happened to was actually named Skullcrusher, but that sounds like a wooden nickel to me.

The fight was nothing special. Mickey fought at featherweight, and the one thing he did impress on me was an appreciation for the lighter weight classes. Most casual fight fans, they like the behemoths throwing leather like Old Testament curses. Nowadays, those behemoths could be upwards of fifty feet tall. There's only so much punishment a skull can take, and if one of those hits connect, the fight's over. I'd rather watch the chess match between a couple fellas too small to turn the lights out on each other.

Stone Chin turned out to be optimistically named. The Facemasher pasted him in round one, and Chin went down, counting stars. He took the full ten count, and by the looks of things, would lay there until someone came in with construction equipment to move him. Facemasher celebrated in the ring while Chin's trainers, a pair of goblins, tried to get their man to rise with a combination of water and dirty limericks.

Mickey sighed. "Stone chin but a glass jaw," he said with a shrug. "Let's go, boys."

We got up and joined the monsters shuffling for the exit. From time to time, a monster would look over at us and their eyes would light up. Before they could do anything, another would grab them and whisper. Their eyes would flicker to Mickey, and they'd move away.

For the first time since night was off limits, I felt powerful. Maybe this was a shadow of what Mickey felt.

Mickey stopped, and the rest of us did as well, fanning out around him. Funny how fellas started moving like a pack of wolves so easily. Facing us was a group of four ghosts, all glowing softly.

The one in the lead looked vaguely familiar, though I'd never seen him before. He wore a pencil-thin mustache on his round face, and otherwise was built like a fire hydrant. His zoot suit was perforated with bullets, like the rest of him.

Floating next to him was a severed head. No idea where the rest of the body went. I wondered if that was its own ghost somewhere. The head was in pretty bad shape, too, leaking ectoplasm from the stump of a neck, and blackish blood from the eyes. His expression was that of a man in the midst of the worst indigestion of his life.

On the lead's other side was a woman, or what remained of one. Her skin was burned away in sloughs, the little bit of hair left on her head in white wisps. Whatever she had looked like before she had been shoved into an oven was a mystery.

The last was an old man, blindfolded and gagged. He crouched next to the others like an animal, his fingernails long and clawlike.

"Hello there, Hector," Mickey said. "Didn't think to see you so far from Spookstreet. You gotta be as weak as a kitten out here in Hollywood."

Spookstreet was a part of Westlake. True to the name, the ghosts had taken it over. It was like a haunted house, but several blocks wide. Humans didn't go there much, or if they did, they didn't come back. Ghosts, the more powerful ones, could stray reasonably far from where their remains were, but the farther they went, the more power they lost. Mickey was digging at this Hector.

"I see a new face there. Going kind of small for new muscle."

"Where are my manners?" Mickey said. "Nick, meet Hector Plasm, head spook of the Spookstreet Specters. That's the Huntington Head, Marie Fury, and Old Rend." The Specters were famous, a street gang composed entirely of ghosts.

"Nick, huh? I'll keep an eye on you," Hector said. Only it was the Head keeping the eye on me, as it floated over and started dripping clear ghost-mucous on my shoe.

"This is no place for a lady," Mickey said to Marie. "Or you."

"Come on down to Spookstreet, Cohen. We'll show you where we belong," Marie shot back.

Old Rend scratched the floor. A chill chased itself up my spine.

"You want I should clear them out?" Jack asked.

"Nah, Jack. They know. *Our* powers don't get any worse no matter how far we get from home. Burning sage still works the same. Holy water still works the same." Mickey paused. "And we got both."

Hector was silent, watching Mickey with all the rage he could muster. When it came to ghosts, that was a lot. Finally he said, "Fight's over. Let's blow."

He turned and floated away, and one by one, his ghosts followed. The last was Old Rend, who continued to scratch the floor before scuttling off after the others.

"Never seen a gang so desperate they'll go for dames," Mickey said with a laugh.

I tried to laugh along, but really, *not* allowing dames was the dumb move. No need to divide ourselves in half after the world chopped us up into tiny groups.

"Hey, Mickey. How do you know that guy?" I asked.

Mickey laughed again, and the others joined him. "He's Flo's brother. They died in the same—" and here he mimed using a tommy gun to hose someone down with lead. "Still can't stomach his baby sister shacking up with a meatstick."

I wondered if that was really the line Hector was drawing.

EIGHT

Friday, November 25, 1955
A little later

I figured after watching an ogre give a troll brain damage and nearly starting a rumble with a haunted house, we'd be done with the evening. Nope. Mickey took us to the Nocturnist. Once, I had never imagined going in, and this would be my second time in as many months.

We parked both cars on Sunset and walked to the club. I could feel the gazes of passing monsters crawling over me. Unlike when I was in my clown get-up, they knew I was human. Knew we all were. They didn't go for us, because they also knew what Mickey and the others were. Hell, what they thought I was. As far as they were concerned, I was one of Mickey's button men. Made me walk a little straighter.

The ogre bouncer glowered at us as we came into the foyer.

"Evening, Hargoth," Mickey said, peeling a bill off a roll and brazenly stuffing it into the ogre's pocket.

The huge monster watched him do it, a thick strand of saliva like mucilage dangling from one tusk. Even the classiest of ogres couldn't fight the drool forever.

"G'wan," the ogre rumbled. He didn't open the door for us. Probably his last bit of disrespect even if he was forced to let a bunch of humans into the club.

We went into the Nocturnist, and under the watchful gazes of the wolves in their enclosures, I sidled up to Mickey. "What gives?"

"How do you mean, Nicholas?"

"That ogre didn't even try to eat us."

Mickey cackled. "Hargoth the Bonechewer knows what's good for him." He opened his jacket, showing off the .45 automatic that looked comically large on such a small man. "Rabbi blessed my heater. Johnny's got a switchblade blessed by a priest. You got something too, right?"

I nodded. My cold iron dagger had gotten the business from Ephraim Olson, a Mormon I knew briefly right at the outset of the Night War. Back then, we figured the hand of God might help out against monsters. We were right in a few cases.

"There you have it. He doesn't want to let meatsticks in, but what's he gonna do? Every monster in the joint knows we can turn the lights out on 'em. We don't start nothing, but they know we can. Keeps 'em on their leashes, right where they need to be."

Rob Sampson laughed. "They know. Boy, they know."

With Johnny in the lead—he was eager about something—we entered the club proper. Johnny broke into a wide grin when he saw a handsome man in a light suit sitting alone in a booth. He gave a continental wave to Johnny. I recognized the fella immediately, although the last time I'd seen him, he was playing Vampiro on the big screen. Yeah, the character was just a cheap Zorro knock-off, but you couldn't have a movie about a human being heroic. No, Vampiro was fighting greedy human landowners in the days before monsters and such could live freely.

The man was the actor Turner Coates, and like most doppelganger movie stars out on the town, he was wearing the face of his most famous character. With the swarthy good looks and athletic physique, that's probably what I would have picked if I had the choice.

Coates got up as Johnny approached, and the two men embraced. Then they kissed.

You saw that kind of thing from time to time, especially now that the monsters didn't seem to care what kind of plumbing you had. Hell, I knew a couple fellas in the service who were that way, though they didn't exactly advertise it. It was still a little shocking to see out in the open. I was probably old-fashioned.

Mickey shook his head. "I don't get it."

"Lots of ladies in the world," Jack said philosophically. "All shapes and sizes. Shame to give up so quick."

"He ain't giving up," Rob said. "He's, you know, acey-deucy."

Johnny came over with Turner Coates, and I'll be honest, it was a thrill to see Vampiro up close. Ser would be jealous. So would Gary and Phil Hammond. They *loved* Vampiro, much to their father's chagrin.

"Mickey, so good to see you," Coates said. He was even using Vampiro's almost Spanish nobility accent.

"How's tricks, Turner?"

"Started shooting the new Vampiro picture."

"Oh yeah?" I said. I didn't realize I was going to sound that thrilled. Okay, so maybe I liked Vampiro as much as Gary and Phil. Maybe I had been the one who took them to the last one.

"A new employee, Mickey?"

"An old friend. Nick Moss, meet Turner Coates."

"I'm a fan," I said as I shook his hand. "*The Coffin of Vampiro* is one of my favorites."

"So nice to meet a fan," Coates said, abruptly bored with the interaction. "Would you gentlemen like to join me?"

"Sure thing, Turner."

He led us over to a big booth. The seats were red leather, and the table black lacquered wood. We spread out, with Johnny and Turner in the middle. The two of them leaned into one another, speaking in low tones like a couple of schoolboys. I didn't want to know what they were saying, and I doubted it was very nice.

I scanned the crowd. No Gobfather tonight. I spotted the meat golem who had helped me out that night, though. Carrying trays around the room, looking preternaturally self-possessed. *Jane.* The name popped right into my head before I could consciously think it. I found my eyes following her around the room whenever I looked up.

"There she is," Mickey said with pleasure. I jumped, thinking he was going to call me out for eye-frisking a meat golem.

Mickey, though, was looking in the direction of the door. Four ghosts floated in, all of them in short dresses, showing off ectoplasmic legs—well, leg in the case of the one who had been cut up. They were heavily made up, their hair nearly solid with styling.

Mickey, Jack, and Rob stood up. I followed suit.

"Ladies," Mickey said. "You look ravishing." He leaned in and kissed the air an inch from Florence's glowing cheek. Yeah, she was the perfect girl for Mickey. "Gents, I'd like to introduce you to some of Flo's friends from Bawdy Bags."

Rob and Jack greeted the new ghosts. Counting them up, it was easy to see what Mickey had in mind. The ghosts paired off with each of us, and one was coming my way. She was pretty and all, but she was carrying her head in a transparent hat box.

"Aren't you cute?" she asked me.

"Uh, my mother always thought so."

"Hattie Box," she said, extending a glowing hand.

I took it as best I could, and when my fingers passed through her flesh, a hideous chill worked its way through me. "Nick Moss."

"Buy a girl a drink, Nick?"

"Sure, what do, uh...do ghosts drink?"

She giggled, and the group of us settled into the booth.

"Say," Mickey said, addressing Hattie. Florence leaned over and whispered into his ear. "Hattie? You got a good friend of mine there. You treat him right. That there is Nick..." Mickey broke into a grin, "Nick the Stick, you got me? He's killed more monsters than fire."

I expected her to shrink away, but she didn't. The look in her eyes, well, I'd seen it before. Not on a real woman in some time, but on a monster right before they tried something.

Hattie leaned closer. "Well, if that's not the mummy's bandages."

I tried to talk to Hattie, but my attention kept wandering to Jane. She was circulating, taking orders and coming back with drinks and food. We had our own meat golem waitress, and she did the same. Hattie and the ghosts ordered something called a haunting, and when it came back it just looked like a glass of smoke. We humans had whiskey, except Mickey, who ordered ginger ale, and the doppelganger, who wanted a martini. I think that last was more a reflection of taste than species.

I was a little disappointed that our waitress wasn't Jane. If nothing else, I wanted to thank her, or have her see me when I wasn't dressed as a clown. Or know that I was here and unafraid. Not that I *was* unafraid, but I thought I was doing a good job of faking it. Believe me, I knew exactly where my holy water was, and if Coates tried anything, he was getting six inches of cold iron through the heart. I had a lighter to frighten off meat golems (and kill phantoms and invisible men if it came to it), but that wasn't on my mind as I watched Jane. She was only a couple tables over, putting full tumblers, a bowl of frogs, and a miniature TV on a table in front of some monsters. I kept my eyes on the tops of her stitched-up stems where they disappeared into her yellow satin shorts.

"Nick? Ain't that right? Nick?"

I blinked and turned to Mickey. He'd been talking, I guess, and I was intended to respond. "You said it, Mick," I said, and guiltily glanced at Jane.

Mickey broke into a grin as he followed my gaze. "Oh, so that's it. You're dizzy for a skin-dolly. Not my cuppa tea, but to each his own."

"No, I just..." I swallowed the rest of my whiskey and coughed as it tried to dissolve my neck. "Need another round," I croaked.

Jack chuckled. Rob and Johnny were barely paying attention, both wrapped up in their monster dates. Hattie was miffed; her head rolled its eyes over at her body like they were in cahoots. They kind of were.

"Hey! Miss!" Mickey waved at Jane. Took him a couple times, and he ignored me hissing at him to stop.

Jane came over and paused, an expectant look on her patchwork face.

"Yeah, so my pal here Nick wanted to say hi."

Jane turned to me, and a flicker passed behind her mismatched eyes. Meat golems could fly off the handle from time to time, and with their strength, that could be dangerous.

"Sorry," I said. "Hi. I was hoping I could have another whiskey."

Jane nodded and was about to leave, when Mickey stopped her.

"Nick here's just being shy. What's your name, skin-dolly?"

I sucked in air. Mickey didn't know what he was doing. You didn't call a meat golem that if you wanted to keep your limbs all attached to your body.

"Jane. Her name's Jane," I said, struggling out of the booth. I had to pass through Hattie, and she squealed. *I know how you feel, sister.*

"My friend here likes you, Jane. Can't imagine why. He's a killer, you know. Back in the war, I mean. Nothin' a lady—well, a buncha ladies, I s'pose—needs to worry her pretty little head over."

Jane's hands clenched, and the pen in them snapped in half, just like a bone. If Mickey noticed, he didn't care. He was just waiting for Jane to sit down, like the invitation had been engraved or something.

"Nick never killed no skin-dollies I know of. Has a pelt of everything else. Leeches, doggies, fishies, you name it, and—"

I laughed. It was the phoniest sound I'd ever made, and that included my attempts to mimic werewolf howling. "Mickey, you card. Uh, April Fool's, Jane."

She looked at me, the rage still boiling behind her eyes.

"Except in November to make it more unexpected."

The confusion got through her anger and she didn't exactly calm, but she was at least not ready to murder everyone at the table. Maybe Mickey really was trying to bait her.

I touched Jane's elbow and tried to lead her away. She snatched her arm back, but she did follow me. When we were a good twenty feet away, I said, "Listen, I'm really sorry. He's...well, you know." She glanced from Mickey back to me. There wasn't any hint of softening in her eyes. I didn't blame her. I deserved it and worse.

"I just wanted to thank you for the other night." She frowned, but it was at least in confusion. "I was dressed as a clown. You brought me to your witch friend. Look, you tried to help me and I wanted to thank you. I didn't know I was going to drag you into, um, into that."

Jane didn't give me a nod or a shake of the head. She turned on her heel and walked away. Last time I'd see her, I imagined. Probably for the best, for all concerned.

I came back to the table, my face hot. "Sorry about that," I said to Hattie. She ignored me, continuing her discussion with Big Jack.

Mickey grinned wolfishly. "So you work things out?"

"Thanks, Mick," I told him, and he caught my meaning.

Mickey laughed. "I did you a favor. Skin-dollies are cut-up corpses. You know what can fester in there?"

"Yeah, you're a regular saint."

Conversation died all around the club. Didn't surprise me to see why. The Gobfather and his three goblins—guess Sawbones wasn't boasting when he said he'd beat the rap—strode into the room. The real attention was being paid to the Songbird, Dulcinea Ramos, four meat golems carrying her gilded cage. The group went to a table front and center, so that the entire club could see them.

Mickey glanced at the Gobfather once, then turned to his ginger ale. Mickey once told me and Izzy he didn't drink. We didn't believe him until Izzy scrounged up a couple bottles of suds from a looted market. We were going to split them three ways, but Mickey begged off. Turning a beer down in the Night War? Yeah, Mickey didn't touch the stuff.

as flammable as an invisible man. When that's your silver lining, it might be time to look into some better clouds.

As I got closer, Songbird nodded. I nodded back, and she nodded again, this time more emphatically. I realized then she wasn't nodding, she was pointing. And there, on the floor, glittering only slightly in the carpet, was a hotel key. I walked by and picked it up, shoving it in my pocket. I straightened, and that's when I felt it.

The Gobfather was staring at me. Nothing like sidhe were supposed to exist in the world. There had been legends of them for hundreds or maybe thousands of years in the old country, and that's how the gaze felt. Heavy with years and contempt. This was a man noticing the bit of dirt on his shoe and wondering if he should brush it off. And in this scenario, I was the smudge of filth.

From far away, you could pretend sidhe were human. Sure, they were inhumanly slender, but that's the kind of thing you can ignore, or even appreciate if that's your preference. Closer, and their alien traits started to get more obvious. The pointy ears were a dead giveaway, but their facial features, too, were off. Their eyes were a bit too big, their cheekbones too sharp, their skin too smooth. They were like a poet's idea of what humanity should be, but in all the rhyming he'd left off the details.

The owl on the Gobfather's shoulder shrugged its shoulders and opened one saturnine eye. The Gobfather was as still as a statue.

"Evening, uh, sir," I croaked at him.

The Gobfather's head turned away, smoothly as on greased ball bearings. I'd ceased to exist.

Fine by me. I scurried away and had a look at the key. It was from the Hollywood Roosevelt Hotel, Room 237. I kept it in my palm, turning it over and over, as though to reassure myself it was real. The rest of the evening passed in a blur. The other fellas were more interested in their monsters than in me, and for that I was grateful. Mickey offered me a ride home, but I told him I'd take the red car.

"Getting used to the night life, huh?" Mickey said with a grin. He knew the hooks were in. Just had to let me play on the line for a little while.

"I guess so."

"If I was fast as you, maybe I'd be out alone, too."

**Titanio Mab,
the Gobfather**

Nine

Friday, November 25, 1955
Deep into the night

This was maybe the stupidest thing I'd ever done, and believe me, I'd done some stupid things. Things that should have gotten me tossed in the booby hatch. This, though, going to the Roosevelt Hotel? This could be a trap from the Gobfather, maybe some misguided blame for what happened with Bosch. Or it could be what it looked like, which was me making time with a mob boss's moll.

Or it could be she needed help. Just as dumb, but I couldn't turn her down.

I went past the ghoul at the front desk and up to room 237. Hotel rooms were marginally safe. All you had to do was have a receipt or a key and they counted as holy ground, which was the same as being home. Didn't stop monsters from occasionally "forgetting" and taking humans anyway. I'd been hired to find more than one person who vanished from a perfectly paid-for hotel room. That was the last thing on my mind as I paced back and forth in the room.

When another key crunched into the lock, I turned. I didn't pull a weapon; filling a hand with the wrong thing was worse than an empty one. My right hand twitched, though. Sidhe or goblins coming through that door both asked for cold iron, and if this was a setup—and how could it not be?—they would be the ones checking the trap.

The door opened, and in a rush of satin, Songbird came in. I realized I'd been thinking of her that way. Not her name, what Mab had taken to calling her. The name she gained in her cage. She turned to me, back pressed against the door. I couldn't quite believe it was her. Women that beautiful belonged on another plane. And this was human beauty.

"I didn't think you'd come," she said. Her accent was soft, the kind you'd hear in the Mexican neighborhoods where the locals had been around since it was actually part of Mexico.

"I, uh...I didn't think so either."

"Thank you." She took a few steps toward me, then paused, suddenly demure. Her joints were stiff with fear, but she was fighting it. She probably got good at not showing that kind of thing off in front of monsters.

"What's..." I cleared my throat. "What's this about?"

She moved past me, on a wash of cinnamon, to the window. "You're human. I saw you at the Pixie Ring." She finished the thought with a shudder. She touched the curtain and peeked out to the street.

"Are you on the run?" I asked her.

"If I was?"

"Maybe I can help."

She smiled, and I knew what it was like for the sun to shine only for me.

"You like to help women, Mr. Moss?"

"How did you know my name?"

"Not hard to find out. The last human detective. There's poetry there."

"I don't know. Nothing rhymes."

"I've heard of you. They say you found a girl at the bottom of the ocean."

"One time."

"And now you're one of Mickey Cohen's."

"That might be...overstating."

"Sounds like I'm the safest girl in town."

"That's definitely overstating."

"It's close enough for me."

She took a step toward me. Then another. That was the sun all right, and it was heating me up. I felt myself sweating through the shirt. I cursed inwardly. Couldn't even be kind of suave.

Didn't matter. She pulled me close, and I was breathing her breath. "It's been a long time since I touched another human."

She didn't talk much after that. Wasn't much to say. It felt like a dream when it was going on, and when I woke up alone in the bed the next morning, I was nearly sure of it. Except the pillow still smelled like her.

TEN

Monday, November 28, 1955
Bright and early

And then he took me up to the Hollywoodland sign, and the whole city was spread out like stars." Serendipity paused to sigh. I hid my distaste by taking a bite of doughnut. Of all the kinds of monsters there were, she had to be making time with a phantom. Only a matter of time before he went insane and built some kind of elaborate deathtrap. Then who's on the hook for the whole thing? Her boss. Me.

At least Jaime wasn't in. As much as I disliked phantoms, Jaime felt that way and worse about every last variety of monster. Still, meant I had to hear about her perfect date with Billy Bounce with no one to share a long-suffering eyeroll. All I could think about was my one night with Songbird. I knew it would be the only night. Those things were never long term.

Ser was probably my closest friend these days, which had to be the saddest and strangest fact of my life. I didn't want to kiss and tell exactly, and I didn't want to brag, but I kind of wanted her to know. Only, if it started floating around that I had gotten biblical with the Gobfather's moll, my life expectancy would have to be measured with a stopwatch.

Sometimes the universe listens to what you're thinking about and it decides to give you the opposite of what you wanted. Just to let you know that it only cares about you enough to hope that your life is measurably worse.

The front door burst inward, and three figures, all about three to four feet tall, tottered in. I knew them, of course: Flux, Murk, and Sawbones, the Gobfather's three top enforcers.

Flux bared a mouthful of shiny black teeth. "Deliver to our claws, the meatstick known as Moss."

"Huh?" Ser said.

They hadn't pulled weapons, but I knew Sawbones didn't have to. Chances were Flux and Murk had nasty tricks, too.

"I'm Moss," I said, ready to skin my dagger and see how fast these three were.

Murk wiggled his pig snout. "We're here to hire...wait, no. That's wrong. Sorry, let me start again...we're here to engage...no, damn it."

"We haven't the time for you to find the rhyme," Flux said.

"I'll get the hang of it!" Murk promised. "I'll be like a pig in sh—" He glanced at Ser, and color rose to his flabby cheeks. "Sorry, miss."

"Oh, think nothing of it," Ser said blithely.

"You want to hire me?" I asked them. "Uh, right this way, I guess?"

I led them into my cramped office and took a seat behind the desk. Flux, the tallest of the three, took one chair, and Murk, the fat one, took the other. This left Sawbones to pace my paper-covered office. I resolved to finish this up quickly before he got bored.

"What seems to be the problem?"

Sawbones rhymed:

> *A girl vanished from her cage*
> *Leaving neither hair nor trace.*
> *A human dick we will engage*
> *And that one will take up the chase.*

"Why me?"

"Asked Baskerville, asked Gevaudan, said Nick Moss is the only one," Flux said.

"Yeah, you come, uh, highly recommend..." Murk slapped his forehead. "Think, Murk! Nothing rhymes with 'recommended'!"

"You'll get the hang of it," I said.

Murk brightened, showing off the boarlike tusks coming from his lower jaw. "You think so? I'm going to...go? No, I have to stay. What am I doing?"

"Look, fellas, I don't want you to get the wrong idea," I said, tensing for one of them to explode into violence. I didn't imagine monsters took disappointment well. "I find missing people, it's true. But I don't find them for monsters who just want to turn them. I'm sorry."

"Songbird is a treasure. She lives for Mab's pleasure," Flux said.

"Yeah, she's not going to be turned. Uh...maybe...burned?"

I nodded to him. Those rhymed. And around Sawbones, possibly accurate.

Sawbones, his voice muffled by the gas mask, rhymed:

> *Songbird, the maiden fair,*
> *Abducted from the goblin's lair,*
> *Her tender flesh a siren's song.*
> *Without us, she won't last long.*

"Yeah, I kind of got that from the way she was paraded around...uh, not that it's my business and all."

"At the Pixie Ring you drew near, seems you have a policeman's ear," Flux said.

"Well, uh, kind of. I've done favors for the wolves on occasion. They run me in just as much."

The goblins looked at each other, nodding happily.

"You're perfect!" Murk crowed, then fell silent, probably trying to come up with a rhyme for "perfect."

"Well, uh, I guess that's okay then." I quoted them the monster rate—double my normal rates—and they didn't attack me. "When was the last time you saw her?"

"Friday night to the Chateau Marmont she returned, we went to bed, unconcerned."

"After midnight," Murk added helpfully. "Uh, we had quite a fright?"

I didn't nod to Murk, because I was frozen in place. I tried to swallow, but my throat was dry as a bone in the Sahara. I knew where Songbird was a few hours after she went missing. In my arms.

Murk handed over a card. "Call us anytime," he said. "Thanks for your time! Oh, god. I can't rhyme time with time, can I?"

Flux looked just as disgusted with Murk as the newbie goblin looked with himself. They rose and shuffled out the door. I was only too happy to see them go.

I followed them to the door of my office. Right as they got to the front door, it opened, revealing Jaime on the other side, holding a cardboard pastry box. Jaime swore in Spanish—I'd gotten to know enough of the language to know when he was doing it, although not what he was saying—but he didn't give an inch.

The goblins fanned out as much as they could and calmly waited. Jaime stared at them, every muscle and tendon in his body stiffened and ready to snap. If Jaime went for it, there was a good chance he'd end up dead, and then a ginned-up gangster or two would turn on the rest of us. Even if everything came up for us, I'd have three goblins to dispose of and their boss knowing exactly where their last stop had been.

"Hey, Jaime, what do you have there?" My voice was shrill, but it got his attention.

"I brought *pandulces*," he said.

As though he suddenly realized what was happening, he stepped aside. The three goblins filed out, with only Murk stopping.

"*Pandulces*, you say? Uh, um. Can I have one? Er, pray?"

Jaime, stunned by the request, opened the box and handed over a shell-shaped piece of bread. Murk stuffed it into his mouth and chewed, dropping a snowfall of powdered sugar and dough. He gave a muffled "thank you" to Jaime and followed his friends out the door.

"What was that?" Jaime asked.

"Clients," I said.

"You need me to tail somebody?"

"No. I'm sorry, I have to start on this."

I ran out the door. If the goblins tracked Dulcinea's next movements to me, I was a dead man. I needed to find where she'd gotten to, and fast.

ELEVEN

Monday, November 28, 1955
Morning

Being a detective is like trying to tell a story when you're completely powerless to write anything. You only know a few of the characters, and you maybe know where they were at some point, but never truly why. You're trying to fill in gaps that might be impossible to define, and if you fail, then someone gets away with it. "It" being something suitably heinous.

As I drove to the Hollywood Roosevelt Hotel, I tried to think of what Songbird might have wanted. She knew I was human because she'd heard Garou call me a meatstick. Humans don't leave the house unarmed, and they never leave after dark. Maybe she had wanted a weapon.

I took inventory automatically whenever I got home. Just something I did. Only problem was, I did it so much, it was autopilot. See what was low, fill it up, if I was close to out, add it to the apothecary list on the fridge door. The big stuff, the gun, dagger, whistle, and so on, got cleaned and checked. I couldn't remember a specific inventory, even one taking place a couple days ago. As far as I knew, nothing had been missing or strangely low. I would have noticed that.

She'd probably been waiting to see me again to slip me the key and do whatever escape she had planned. She'd also seen me with the wolves, so maybe she thought I could handle myself. Didn't explain why she'd vanished before the fight could happen. Didn't explain anything. She had been frightened of something that night, and she had come to me.

I should have asked.

I should have asked *more.*

But as soon as she was on me, soon as I felt her mouth on mine...well, that went out the window. It had been a little bit of time for me. Years, even. Times I had even thought that part of my life was in the rearview. Didn't excuse me. I was a heel, and that was for sure.

If she was scared, why not stay? If I was good enough to protect her for a time, surely I was good enough to protect her for a little longer. None of it added up and it pointed nowhere.

I pulled up at the Hollywood Roosevelt. The concierge was a devil, all red skin and horns, his face locked in a dismissive sneer. I hated dealing with devils, but if people liked it, then you wouldn't have that saying.

"Hiya," I told him. "Listen, I was hoping I could have a look in room 237."

"Room 237? What do you want in there for?" The devil grinned, showing me far too many teeth.

"Just need to have a look around. I misplaced my wedding ring."

"Sir, we're not in the practice of letting people into rooms. Bad for business."

"How about if you rent me the room? Say for twenty minutes?"

I peeled off a couple bills. He was no longer looking at me. The money was his whole world.

"Everything is, of course, negotiable," he said, licking his lips. His tongue was forked.

I slapped the money down on the desk. "Twenty minutes."

"Ten," he said.

"The time isn't...oh, never mind. Ten."

"Wait! I'll sell you twenty for—"

"Thanks, pal," I said, leaning over the desk and snatching the key from where it hung on a pegboard. "I'll get this back to you."

"Don't disturb anything!" The devil called after me as the elevator doors closed. The zombie elevator attendant took me to the second floor, told me "Brains," and let me off. I found room 237 and unlocked it.

It was stupid to think any kind of evidence of our rendezvous would remain. It had been cleaned at least once since then, any sign of us long gone. I poked around, knowing I wasn't going to find a thing, and I wasn't disappointed. No one would ever know Songbird had been in that room. She had simply been erased. The fate of so many humans over the past couple of years.

I emerged, and hunted up and down the halls until I found what I was looking for. The maid cart was in the hallway next to an open door. I stopped by it, and called inside, "Pardon me? May I speak with you?"

A second later, a greenish-gray shape, glowing softly, appeared in the hall. She was a young woman, and looked like she had gotten the raw end of a disagreement with a lawnmower. "Yes?" she asked.

"Do you have maids who work overnight here?"

"Oh yes, of course, sir." She called me sir. Probably thought I was a wolfman. She glanced around. "You know ogres," she confided.

"Yeah, a few. Do you know who was on duty late Friday and early Saturday?"

"Say, what's this all about?"

"A young woman went missing."

"Woman? Human?"

"Yeah," I said.

She shrugged. "Stick around. She'll appear here sooner or later with some new wounds and she'll go to work with the rest of us."

I shuddered at how casually she said it. "Yeah, I'm, uh, I'm sort of hoping it doesn't come to that."

"Suit yourself," she said.

I went around the hotel, talking to the staff. The devil concierge tried to pump me for more cash, but it was obvious he knew nothing. He wasn't even on duty Friday night. The zombies were pointless to talk to, as no matter how much they inflected "Brains," it didn't mean much. The maids, though—the maids were helpful. They bounced me around for a while until I found a woman who was a little more than a selection of parts, and not much of those, either.

"Oh, you're looking for Chopped Mary," she said. "She was on duty, and if there was a room on the lower floors that needed her, she'd have been there."

"Thank you, ma'am. Do you know where I can find her?"

"Well, you can come back here after dark."

"What if I'd rather not?"

"She lives over in Spookstreet. Don't know any more than that, sorry to say."

"I appreciate your help." I turned to go, but had to stop. "Say, if it's not rude, what happened to you?"

"Danced with a bear."

"That didn't sound like a bad idea to you?"

"Sure it does. Now. Never know how dumb a thing is until after it bites you."

Twelve

Monday, November 28, 1955
A little while later

Spookstreet was not a place a man like me went willingly. And by "a man like me," I meant still breathing. Not dripping ectoplasm everywhere and covered in spectral wounds. There were lots of ghosts in the city, and that was where they concentrated, building upon each other. It was also Specter territory, and I didn't really fancy another run-in with them. Besides, the lead was as thin as it could be. If I was lucky, Chopped Mary saw what, exactly?

I sighed and drove back to the office. I could spend some time thinking over what I learned. Maybe try to find another way in. There had to be something. Or maybe there wasn't. People disappeared every day, and the Gobfather had made certain that nearly the entire population of Los Angeles wanted Songbird for their very own.

I parked my car on Flower Street, still lost in thought. My office was up ahead, right above the laundry where I got my suits washed. Maybe Ser or Jaime could shed some light on something I wasn't seeing, but that would mean explaining it to them.

I didn't see them coming. One second I was walking, the next second I was tasting the paint job on the hood of a Buick. My arm was wrenched behind me, and a rough hand was digging in my jacket.

"You don't move a muscle, meatstick," Detective Garou snarled in my ear.

"Of all the goddamn things, Moss," Moon said nearby. His mouth sounded full. I was absolutely positive he had just stolen some kind of pastry from my office. He'd done it before.

Garou's hand came out of my jacket, holding my .32. He turned it over, then sniffed it once. "Silver," he said wincing in pain. He handed it over to Moon, who wrapped it in a handkerchief. It was hard not to panic, what with me already picturing them planting that gun somewhere.

"What the hell is going on?" I demanded, but the words were mashed.

"You talk all you want," Garou said. "You *sing*. And I get my wish, you in the clink with a bunch of monsters who are gonna *love* you."

"Hang on, jail? What's—"

Handcuffs squeezed my wrists. My hands were going to sleep inside a minute. Garou didn't give a damn. He yanked me hard off the hood and my shoulders protested. He opened the door of the Buick and threw me in the back. They drove me to 77th Street. This time, when Garou shoved me through the station, I was a suspect rather than whatever it was I had been last time. Now the cops gazed at me in open suspicion and sullen violence. Wasn't like I had a sudden camaraderie with the people arrested, either. Just as much hostility there.

Garou continued opening doors with my face and giving me a smack whenever I slowed down. He yanked open the door to a featureless sweatbox and threw me inside. Just a table, two chairs on either side. An interrogation room. At least someone would get to ask a few questions. Probably not me, though.

Garou shoved me into the chair, then kicked the leg out from under me, because that's the nice kind of guy he is. He loomed over me, looking like he was ready to stomp my face in. I wasn't getting to any wolfsbane with my hands cuffed behind me. Not that I could feel them anymore.

"That's enough, Lou," Moon rasped, but there wasn't much feeling in it.

Garou's eyes flashed yellow, then returned to their natural brown. He nodded, but kept looking me over like he wanted to bury my bones in the yard.

I got up nice and careful, showing these two I didn't mean any harm. Moon I could trust not to fly off the handle, but Garou was a seething mass of lupine rage. There were a lot of bad feelings after the Night War, and in some ways the Treaty was the worst thing that could have happened. Left wounds to fester.

"So am I under arrest here?" I asked.

"We gotta arrest you for something, meatstick?" Garou snarled.

"Not yet," Moon said. "We'll see how you do."

"If I'm not under arrest, how about you take these cuffs off?"

"Like I said, we'll see how you do."

I knew that if I started whining about how I couldn't feel my hands, that'd just guarantee the cuffs would stay on. That's how bullies worked. Moon might have been a friendlier face than Garou, but I didn't believe for a second they were cut from different cloth. They both wore badges, after all.

I waited for them to talk. Not much else I could do. I tried to fend off the image of my hands getting purple and swollen.

Both detectives tried to bore holes in my face with their attention. "Dulcinea Ramos is dead," Moon rasped.

"What?"

"You heard me, Moss," Moon said.

"How? What happened?"

This time, they exchanged a look. Moon's was placating, almost a *look, it's not him*, right into the implacable rage billowing from Garou. Moon produced some pictures from his jacket and slid them over one by one.

It was Songbird, Dulcinea Ramos, dead. She was on a hillside by the side of a road, lying face down. Bullet holes perforated her back. My stomach wanted to turn over. I forced myself to look. Something in the photo would speak to me. Some kind of clue would point to whoever did this to her.

Whoever she had been afraid of that night.

"It's a damn shame. Pretty girl like her," Moon said.

"Why'd you do it, you son of a bitch? You try something? Take advantage, she runs and you plug her?" A grin rippled over Garou's lips.

"Why me? Lot of people in this city and you're dragging me in?"

"You telling us you have an alibi?" Moon asked. "Spill it and we'll let you go."

"When?" I croaked.

"Start on Friday and go until now."

"Why me?" I asked instead, not really wanting to cop to having seen her.

"Seems she checked into the Hollywood Roosevelt, and who should meet her there, but..." Moon opened a notebook and flipped through some pages, then read what was written there, "a short man, hairy, kind of looked like a weasel."

"That could be anybody," I said.

Moon laughed. "Sure, but until then it's you."

"We got you," Garou growled, this time close enough to smell his breath. I flinched. I had to; I was unarmed, and they might have me.

"Was she shot with silver bullets?" I asked.

"Why?" Moon said

"You have my gun. Unless she was shot with .32 caliber silver bullets, it wasn't me. I don't carry anything else. From a firearm perspective, I mean."

"You got a reason to pack silver, meatstick?"

I didn't point out the obvious, that Garou was reason enough to carry as much silver as you could. Mostly because the wolf was coming out and if it did all the way, I wasn't confident enough that anyone could or even would stop him.

"Jesus, Lou, keep your shirt on. You keep at this and Moss is going to wet himself."

Garou leaned back, but the wolf-stink hung in the air like a promise.

"Who kills a choice piece of bait like Dulcinea there?" Moon asked the air. "Look at her. Half the monsters in town wanted to turn her. She was made to be a vampire, a doppelganger. Hell, I see a picture of her and I'm thinking she's just right for law enforcement. And that's it, right there, she was *known*. Everyone in town knew she was the prettiest dame around, and knew she was human. She was out after dark outside of that cage? She was getting turned."

Now Moon addressed me. "Humans knew, too. Knew she was making time with monsters. Not the most popular of pastimes for you people. Some human, maybe one who knew a thing or two about killing from the Night War. Maybe got used to killing humans in the Day War. Sound like anybody you know?"

I thought maybe a derisive laugh would work here, but nothing came out. So I managed a squeak at the end. "That's your theory?"

"And it's a good one," Moon said. "And we know just when you saw her first."

"You hired me to do that. I was working for the cops!"

Moon shrugged. "I don't think that'll come out in court. Do you, Lou?"

"No, Phil. Not even a little."

I swallowed. "I want my lawyer."

Moon laughed, and this time Garou joined him. "You want a lawyer? Lou, he wants a lawyer!"

"Oh, that's rich. That's really rich."

"Hell of a time to get a sense of humor, Moss."

"It's no joke," I told them. I tried to put every last bit of spine I had left into the demand. "You two know I've worked for some pretty powerful people. People who might think they owe me a favor or two. So you know I have a lawyer, and you know what'll happen if you keep up with this railroading." I swallowed. "So yeah, I want my lawyer."

Garou changed then, the fur bursting from his skin, the teeth sharpening and pushing up from his jaw. When he grabbed my lapel, tearing it partly off, his hands were twisted, his fingernails curved into yellow claws. "You get what we say you get," he told me in his best wolfman voice.

If that had been the last thing I saw, I wouldn't have been surprised in the slightest. I'd only known Garou for a few months, but he'd been looking for an excuse to do something terrible to me for every second. Looked like he'd finally found it. This was the one and only time he'd care about the murder of a human.

"Who's your lawyer?" Moon's voice cut right through the fear.

Garou turned around, confusion on his bestial mug. "What?"

"Bud Thirst," I said, naming the one and only lawyer I knew who might be willing to do me a favor.

"Never heard of him," Moon said.

"He's real. I didn't just, um, make him up or anything. Call the law firm of Tepes, Tepes, Tepes, and the Impaler."

Garou dropped me back into the chair as he changed back. The apelike muscle mass in his arms and shoulders vanished. He looked like he had just been slightly deflated.

Moon sighed. "Let's get this leech on the phone, shall we? Stick around, Moss."

Moon undid the cuffs, and I had the momentary relief of sensation in my hands, followed by the feeling of a million glass spiders tapdancing all over them. Then he recuffed my right hand and slapped the other bracelet around the table leg. I wasn't going anywhere.

Garou gave me a smack on the way out. It was the nicest thing he'd done all day. Then they left me in the box. I wasn't sure how long. Felt like hours. I did a little mental math. It was still morning when they picked me up, so I had some time before it was after dark. Really, the only thing that kept track was the increasingly loud rumble of my stomach.

They'd call Thirst. Moon and Garou weren't the types to completely ignore that. They'd take their sweet time doing it, though. Let me stew. I didn't believe they really thought I did it, but that wouldn't stop them from throwing the book at me. They wanted to lock someone up, and I was a convenient patsy. I was going to have to think fast, or hope Thirst could work some legal magic.

I focused on the room. There wasn't much to see. The walls were off-white, the ceiling tiled with perforated squares. The table was steel and bolted to the floor. The chairs were the cheap kind they sold to schools and other places that didn't care much for comfort. No weapons to speak of. No way out.

All I had to look at were the pictures of Songbird on the table. So I looked. I couldn't pretend we had some profound emotional connection. We didn't know each other. Not really. She'd needed something from me that night, and she knew how to buy it. She knew my price the same way she knew it was the price for anyone who ever laid eyes on her.

The pictures gave me nothing new. Shot to death. Four bullets in the back, and she pitched over into the dirt. Monsters still used guns. Well, some did. Using a gun on *her* didn't make any sense. Moon was right about that. No one would have missed the chance to turn her. That was the power the Gobfather was holding over everyone. A human button man added up. Perfectly.

The door finally opened, and either it had been hours or that featureless box was starting to play tricks on my head. Moon was holding the door open, his bulk partially eclipsing the opening. With his salmon-colored blazer, he looked like a giant eraser.

A vampire squeezed past him. He was the perfect image of a vampire, too, wearing an old-style tux, complete with a medal around his neck and a cape with a high collar. His skin was stark white, though close up it was obvious a lot of that was caked-on makeup. The widow's peak was also flimflam; the beginnings of stubble around it said it had been shaved into his hairline. I didn't care a bit for all of that, because this was the first friendly face I'd seen: my lawyer, Bud Thirst.

"Nick! Vhat is going on?" Bud spoke in an elaborate Transylvanian accent. It was put on, but then, no human had ever spoken like that a day in his life. Vampires liked to appear the part. It was a status thing for them. Bud wasn't very good at it. His thick southern drawl was always trying to fight its way out from under those Eastern European consonants.

"I got pinched. I needed a lawyer."

Bud held a finger up to the police. "Vun moment, gentlebeings." He slid into the chair next to me and hissed in his drawl, "Nick, I do *family law.*"

"You what? I thought you were a lawyer."

"I *am* a lawyer. There's a lot of different kinds, you know."

"But you know what to do when people get arrested, right? Families still get arrested?"

"Not that kind of family law! When someone gets turned, you know, you add them to the new...there are lots of new laws! It's a good specialty!"

"I'm really glad your career path is working out, Bud."

"I'm sorry! I didn't know what was happening."

"Are you ladies done?" Garou asked.

He and Moon watched from the other side of the table. From the looks on their faces, they hated Bud only slightly less than they hated me. Vampires and wolfmen were on the opposite sides of law enforcement. Explained why they never got along.

"No, ve are not done!" Bud said, the hokey vampire schtick back on. "Remove the manacles from my client at vunce! I can smell his blood from here. His delicious, delicious blood."

"Please don't do that," I whispered.

"Sorry," he whispered back.

Moon sighed, but he did get up and take the cuffs off, pocketing them. I was finally able to sit up straight. My back gave a solid crack as I did so. Then I glanced over and Bud was staring at my right hand and licking his lips.

"Bud? You mind?" I said, nodding to the wolfmen.

"Not really," he said, still staring.

"Okay, knock it off, you two," Moon said. He jabbed his finger on the photos. "Now, Moss, you going to admit to killing Ramos? We have enough without a confession, but you know, that'd make the judge go easy on you."

Bud's eyes got huge as he noticed the pictures for the first time. "You killed someone?" he gasped at me.

I massaged the bridge of my nose. "I'd like to waive my right to a lawyer. Or at least this one."

"Nick, you didn't tell me...he didn't tell me he killed someone!" This last was directed at the wolves.

Garou pulled Bud out of his seat and shoved him out the door. "You heard the meatstick. Get the hell out."

"I'm not an accom—" Bud got out before Garou slammed the door in his face.

"Smart move, Moss," Moon said. "Lawyers make us real antsy. We're liable to take it harder on you."

"Harder than this?"

"You bleeding yet?" Garou asked.

"Right, yeah. Okay." I gathered myself. The hours I'd had alone with the pictures helped focus me. I addressed Moon. He was the reasonable party. "Moon, you have to know I didn't do this."

Garou scoffed, but Moon held up a hand. "I don't know that. I know you fought in both wars. You told me yourself you killed krauts."

"Yeah, krauts, not real people." I swallowed. "That didn't...that sounded bad. Come on, fellas. One or both of you had to be in the service. You know, the same as I do, that punching a ticket for a man trying to punch yours is a lot different than plugging some poor girl in the back."

"Go on," Moon said after he gave me a little time.

"When did this happen?"

"We found her on Sunday," Moon said finally. "Coroner said she could have been lying there since early Saturday."

"Could have been Saturday night?"

Moon shrugged.

"We can say it was whenever we want," Garou told me.

"Where were you?" Moon asked.

"I was home all weekend. You can ask people in my neighborhood. They'll tell you."

"What about nighttime?" Garou demanded.

"I don't go out at night," I said. It was so natural I didn't realize it was a lie until it was already hanging in the air between us.

"Yeah, you do," Moon said. "I should know. I saw you."

"Okay, okay. I don't go out at night unless I'm being paid." Also a lie. Another one I didn't catch. "Was she killed at night?"

I looked at the picture. It was one of the many winding roads in Los Angeles, going up and over a hill. It was in black and white, but my mind's eye provided the yellow for the dying cattails she had collapsed into. I picked one up that showed the elbow of the road, and pointed at the asphalt.

"What street is this? Where is it? It's some place where gunshots in the daylight would be noticed, right? If it happened late enough it might have passed, right? That's what you're saying?"

"You were with her Friday night?" Moon asked.

I swallowed again. My throat was dry. No way I could lie now. "Yeah. Well, early Saturday morning."

"So you do go out at night," Garou said.

"We weren't exactly *out*."

"Don't have to ask what you two were doing, I suppose," Moon said. My face grew hot, but I didn't look away.

"Your witness...she was a maid at the Hollywood Roosevelt. Then she knows the two of us left at different times. Song...uh, Dulcinea left in the middle of the night. I left in the morning."

Moon gave a nearly imperceptible nod. They were shaking the tree, but it was clear if nothing fell out, then they'd take me.

"Add it up, Moon. You want the one that did it, right? You put us together, but you also know she left me intact. You have the bullets in her, and I'm guessing they're not .32 silver."

"What are you saying?"

I pointed to the door. "You remember that task force outside? You have a killer hunting monsters in this city. Your Monster Slayer. You think a fella like me, who you thought enough of to hire for police business, has enough motive to kill her for making time with monsters? What's a bona fide nut going to think?”

Moon sat back in his chair. I expected Garou to protest, to whine that Moon was listening to me, but when I had a look at the younger cop, he was frowning over what I’d said.

“All right then, Moss,” Moon said.

“What?”

“We’re cutting you loose.”

I stood up, waiting for Garou to remember who he was and do something terrible. He rubbed his pockmarked cheeks, still lost in thought.

“Whether it’s the Slayer or not, you better hope we find someone,” Moon said philosophically. “Because if we don’t, you’re still the best fit.”

I was so eager to get out of there I barely noticed the threat. I stopped at the door.

“My gun?”

“We need to test your gun,” Garou said. He almost sounded reasonable, but he was just taking a silver weapon out of my hands.

I left the police station with my head down, walking as fast as I could without breaking into a run. I couldn’t quite read what they were getting at. Like they wanted me to do their jobs for them again, but the threats were real. The cops on one side and the Gobfather on the other. All trying to squeeze me for everything they could get.

Mickey’s offer was starting to look better and better.

Thirteen

Tuesday, November 29, 1955
First thing in the morning

The Luger's weight was like coming home. I hadn't worn the thing since the Night War ended in March of '53. The pistol should have felt strange and different, a link to a time that should stay gone. The truth was, the .32 was the one that never felt quite right. The .32 had never killed. The Luger had planted both men and wolfmen in the ground. It knew me. It had saved me. And for everyone else, it was a cobra sore at the world and looking for revenge.

The Luger was a killer. Wearing it again made me feel like one, too. And I thought those days were over.

It was going to be no help on the errand I had to run that day, but I liked having it on me. I had to tell my clients that the person they wanted me to find was found, and not in the condition they wanted either. I was going to get to see how goblin mobsters took disappointment. Not very well would be my guess.

The dagger was under the other arm, ready to be used if it came to it. The vial in my jacket was freshly full of speckled mushrooms. One of those could send a goblin into paroxysms of terror. I had to reassure myself they were both there twice before leaving the house.

The card Murk had given me was for a business. "Redcaps," with an address was in Hollywood. I took my heap from the office to the address. The place was a haberdashery, and despite the name, not everything in the wide glass window was red. Looked like they had every design of hat under the sun, from your normal fedoras to wide-brimmed cowboy hats to caps that had to be made for the misshapen heads of a menagerie of monsters.

I went through the front door and nothing jingled. The store was empty, with hats on racks along both walls and in the center breaking up the floor. The air was heavy with the scents of leather, silk, and felt. Mirrors stood in corners, though these had curtains that could cover them. Good manners should a doppelganger customer come in.

Murk sat on a high stool behind the counter in the back. His narrow eyes lit up as he saw me, his wet pig nose wiggling in recognition.

"Mr. Moss! So good to see you. Has there been movement...on...oh, no, I lost it. Damn it!"

"It'll come to you," I said, hoping to keep him talking longer. The more we bumped gums, the longer before I had to disappoint him. "Say, why do goblins rhyme?"

Murk shrugged. "Why do werewolves piss on trees?"

He had a point there.

"Boys? The dick's here! He...uh...he smells...queer?" He mouthed a *sorry* at me.

A second later, Flux and Sawbones emerged from the back. These two were so much more unnerving than Murk. It wasn't just the pig-goblin's sunnier outlook, but his altogether more pleasant features. Flux's exaggerated but still human looks seemed designed to make a fella nervous, and he looked like he was suffering from every skin disease there was. His stringy black hair hung from a distended skull, and his black-on-black eyes could convey only hate. Sawbones, with his creepy gas mask, was somehow even worse. No expression, just the faint hissing of his breath through tubes.

Sawbones rhymed:

> *Sent to find an errant bird,*
> *Pledged upon his solemn word*
> *Our vassal to us returned.*
> *Yet mine eyes be concerned*
> *When they see hands a-bare*
> *Clutching not the maiden fair.*

While Murk remained perched on his stool and Flux paused behind the counter, Sawbones kept coming. He was the shortest of the three goblins, but I had to fight not to take a step back. The lenses of his mask were blank, his breath rasping in and out.

"My associate is right. Is the Songbird still in flight?" Flux asked. He rubbed his hands together and I noticed each finger had an extra knuckle.

"Uh...no. Not exactly. I have some bad news. Maybe you should all sit down."

Murk checked the stool as though he wasn't certain he was sitting down. Flux didn't move. Sawbones walked past me, snapping his fingers every now and then. I flinched each time, expecting an explosion of flame.

"I'm sorry to be the one to tell you this, but Songbird...Miss Ramos... is dead."

"Dead? How?" Murk sounded surprised, but not exactly horribly so.

> *Did she perish in a gout of flame?*
> *Or fail at a phantom's game?*
> *Was she quarry for a gang of men?*
> *Did she wander into the ogre's den?*
> *Trip and fall into a sewer drain?*
> *Have a zombie eat her brain?*

Flux sucked on a tooth while Sawbones listed off options one by one.

"Uh...she was shot. In the back."

"A meatstick's tool, the gun. Never have any fun," Flux said. The other two goblins laughed appreciatively.

"I wanted to warn you. The cops already braced me. They'll be sniffing around soon enough."

"That's nice of you," Murk said, then cursed when he somehow couldn't think of a rhyme for "you." He cursed again when he couldn't rhyme the first curse.

> *A meatstick cut her short,*
> *A meatstick now here stands.*
> *We need no proper court!*
> *Justice is in our hands.*

Sawbones snapped his fingers and a flame played along the gray-green palm of his hand. It reflected in the lenses of his mask, a shimmering golden blade.

"Sawbones, hold the fire, the shop is not a pyre," Flux said.

"Yeah. I know I have to mop it up," Murk said. Then he thought about what might rhyme. He was still thinking.

"Fellas, I didn't do a thing," I told them. My hands were clear of me, but they were ready to grab for the mushrooms.

"Tell your story," Flux said. "Before the shop gets gory."

Sawbones chuckled hollowly behind his mask.

"There's no story. The cops knew I had been hired to find her because I was sniffing around. Like I do." It was a lie, but I couldn't tell them why the cops really settled on me. That wouldn't go over well at all. "They found her on Sunday. She'd been shot in the back, like I said. But not by me."

Flux opened his mouth, but he was about to speak to Sawbones, not me. An order to finish me off in a flash of orange fire.

"Wait, you can be sure it wasn't me because I only carry silver bullets. Whatever got her wasn't silver. Or it wasn't the right caliber. It didn't match my gun. So not only was I not there, I didn't even have the right tool."

"He says he's only using silver, and...wait...I think there has to be something."

> *Take the span of ages as time*
> *For silver there is no real rhyme.*

Murk looked to Flux, who nodded sadly. "That's awful," Murk moaned. He sounded more broken up over that than Songbird's death. "Are there other words?" he asked in horror.

Flux nodded again.

"Which ones?"

"Make me break the sacred rules? Have me join you amongst the fools?"

"Oh, sorry."

"We have to tell the boss. He will be quite cross."

Murk shuddered. Sawbones clapped his hand shut over the flame. When he opened it again, the fire was gone.

> *Meatstick, meatstick, fly away home,*
> *I still want to burn you;*
> *Hide behind a thousand wards*
> *Or one of us will turn you.*

"Right. Yes. I just thought I should tell you." I scurried to the door. Maybe it was the proximity to freedom that made me brave, but I stopped and turned around. "Also, that was a day I worked the c—"

"For failing your hired task, you'll get no cash. Your payment ends with not being burned to ash."

"The special. Okay then."

"Moss?"

Murk threw me a hat. It was a felt fedora, gray with a black band. Pretty nice. Nicer than anything I owned anyway, which, while a low bar, was still a bar.

"Thanks," I said, holding up the hat. I emerged into the sun, grateful that I didn't have to deal with goblins anymore.

Fourteen

Tuesday, November 29, 1955
After lunch

Mickey worked out of an ice cream shop on Figueroa. The storefront was a white fake adobe building, with a few multicolored dots painted around the edges to give it some zazz. Made me think of clowns. I glanced around superstitiously, thinking one might want payback for my ill-advised game of dress-up. There were none on the street at the time, just a few zombies shambling toward the red car line and muttering "Brains" at each other.

Talk to enough zombies, and you could kind of understand what they were trying to say. Or you were just assuming they were saying what you wanted them to. I wondered if the zombies had a deeper understanding of what that one word meant when they spat it back and forth. The quickest way to find out would be to become a zombie myself. I was going to let that remain a question unanswered.

The name of the place was "Carousel Ice Cream," written in a fancy script that looked like a delicate garden fence. The shop was small, and the wide window in front showed all of it. A counter ran along one wall with barely enough room for five stools. Customers would be rubbing shoulders while they slurped down their sundaes. Two tables sat on the other side of the place, and these were occupied. The floor was checkered linoleum, and the decor was clean and modern.

I walked in and a bell jingled. I had to smile. Bell like that would send phantoms running, and it was a clear sign a business catered to people only. I'm sure if the cops told Mickey to take it down, Mickey would play innocent and tell them it was there when he bought the place.

Mickey sat at a table with Big Jack Whalen, both of them in shirtsleeves. Once again, I was struck with the size difference between the two men. Mickey was shorter than me, and either he had grown a couple inches since the Night War or he was wearing lifts. If Jack got any bigger, people were going to start thinking he was an ogre. He was basically a wall with arms and legs. Both of them had glass bowls sitting in front of them, partway full of melted ice cream and a topping or two. I was beginning to see how Mickey had gotten rounder than when I'd remembered him.

"Nick!" Mickey said, getting up happily. "How are you doing?"

He didn't offer to shake hands, but I didn't take it personally. I didn't want him washing his mitts raw for fifteen minutes afterwards.

"Thought I'd stop by. How's tricks, Jack?"

"Another day," Whalen said philosophically.

"Let me get you a sundae," Mickey said. "No, I'm getting a memory. You're a banana split man."

I wasn't especially, but I didn't want to make Mickey feel bad. "That's right."

Mickey snapped his fingers and went behind the counter. He put on an apron and began building a dessert. I could barely see him behind the counter. He was mostly a bobbing head, his thinning black hair slicked down over his skull.

"Hey, Mickey, why'd you call your joint Carousel?"

"I dunno. I liked the sound of it. You know, classy and such, but let the kids know it's for them. Like a real carousel, you know?"

"Why not Ice Cream Cohen's?"

Mickey was still and went dead silent. Then, a softly muttered, "Damn it." Mickey started moving again after that, and quickly was coming around the corner with a banana split. He set it down at the table and waved me to my seat.

Mickey Cohen could make a good banana split, I'll tell you that. Chocolate, vanilla, and strawberry ice cream, a little hot fudge, nuts, whipped cream, a cherry, and of course the bananas. He might have missed his vocation. Or at least, he should concentrate on this rather than being a gangster.

"So really, Nick. What brings you here?"

I talked around the ice cream. Mickey's lemon-pursed lips widened in a smile when he saw how much I was enjoying it. "A job. Well, kind of."

"A job?"

"Yeah. I was hired...you know Mab's girlfriend?"

"The Songbird? She's a dish, and no never mind."

Big Jack nodded. "Prettiest girl I ever seen, and I been to Oklahoma."

I didn't know what that was supposed to mean, and I didn't ask. "Her, yeah. The goblins, you know the ones."

"Dick, Prick, and Schmuck, sure."

"Close enough. They hired me to find her."

"She's missing?"

"She's dead. Shot."

Mickey frowned. "If they croaked her, why'd they hire you to find her?"

"Because they didn't do it."

Mickey watched me. "You're thinking youse should find who bumped her off, huh? This is like with youse finding people during the war. Finding them now, too. Nick the Stick, a crusader."

"No, not a crusader. But I'd like to know."

Mickey shrugged. "Who knows? In a week, no one will remember who she was."

"What do you mean? Everyone knew who she was."

"Sure, but inside a week, Mab'll have a new one. Just as pretty, too. She'll be a dancer or an artist or something. They all are. Dunno where he finds 'em."

"Maybe he has a tree. Where they grow like fruit," Jack said. "A fairy grove."

Mickey blinked. "Yeah, that's probably it," he said, shaking his head. "Listen, Nick, I'm glad you stopped by."

"Me too," I said, my mouth full.

"You like it? Good. There's more where that came from. What I actually wanted to offer you is a job."

"Who's missing?"

"Nobody. Not that kind of a job."

"Mickey..."

He held up a hand. "It's an easy job that pays well."

Jack nodded. "A good job."

I looked from face to face. I felt a little ridiculous, sitting in an ice cream parlor. No matter the surroundings, these were two dangerous men. Men who thought I belonged in the same company as them.

"What kind of job?" I asked.

"I'll call in a couple days and I'll give you all the information you need."

"Okay. I'll look at it. No promises."

"No promises," Mickey agreed, but he knew he had me on the hook. Mickey was smart enough not to push me too far. He just needed that first little step.

I finished the banana split. It tasted just as good at the end as it did at the beginning. Somehow, I thought Mickey's promises should have turned it rancid.

"What are you doing with the rest of the day?" Mickey asked.

"I was going home early. Make sure I have enough wolfsbane out."

Neither one of us had to elaborate. Everyone in the city knew when the full moons were. Both werewolves and wolfmen went crazy on those nights. They'd attack anyone who was out, human or monster, and they loved mixing it up with each other. And because they were the law, there were never any repercussions. On the night of the full moon, everyone, even monsters, stayed indoors and listened to the howling.

"How do you deal with the cops, Mickey?"

He grinned. "Dealing with cops, a silver dollar will take you further than a silver bullet."

"I guess so."

I arrived home as the first howls split the late afternoon. The wolves were already out hunting. They were breaking the law, but who was going to tell that to the cops?

FIFTEEN

Thursday, December 1, 1955
Mid-morning

etting money from a ghoul" wasn't a saying, though it sounded like maybe it should have been. Not that ghouls had a reputation for pinching pennies. No, they were too busy eating corpses and feuding with their unsettlingly large extended families. I had no experience, but something told me Thanksgiving at a ghoul household was the most dangerous place in the world to be.

Lucky for me, Mickey wasn't sending me on Thanksgiving. Wasn't even sending me to a residence as near as I could tell. He told me to get his money from a ghoul that owed him.

Mickey called me at the office that morning, and I headed over to Carousel. There, he introduced me to his dog, Mickey Junior, a burrito of a bulldog who spent most of his time begging for ice cream. Mickey always liked dogs. He used to talk about his pooch Toughie, also a bulldog, back in the war. The rest of us would talk about friends or girlfriends or husbands we'd lost, and Mickey would start getting poetic about Toughie.

He barely mentioned his wife LaVonne, other than to say she was a clown or a vampire or something. That's how little he talked about her; I can't remember what kind of monster she was turned into. And I bet if you asked him, he'd have trouble remembering too.

Mickey offered me a sundae, but it was a little early for ice cream. He ended up giving Mickey Junior the beginnings of what he was making me. Then Mickey got down to the point.

"This ghoul, she owns a funeral parlor in Eagle Rock. She's also got a yen for the horses."

"Mickey, I'm not a legbreaker."

He laughed. "If I wanted her leg broken, I'd be sending Jack."

I had to give him that. Jack could probably break a leg with a veiled threat. "What do you want?"

"I want you to ask her for the money. If she gets frisky, I want you to work some of your old Nick magic."

I wish I had to ask him what that meant. Back in the war I'd been johnny-on-the-spot with whatever we needed. Wolfmen? I'd already have the wolfsbane. Phantoms? What do you know, I had some windchimes. Martians? I'd be hauling over little Aggie Brooks and her latest head cold. That started with reflexes from the Day War, but the thing about krauts is you only ever needed bullets and guns. Wasn't like you could scare them off with a pinch of salt or a bright light. I always knew what to bring—sometimes before we knew what we were facing—and I seldom got it wrong.

"You want me to pull roses on her?"

"You have them, don't you?"

I showed them. A couple dried buds and petals in a vial.

Mickey grinned. "You see how quick that came out? Like Lash LaRue."

"Just a nervous disposition."

"You might fool some fellas with that aw-shucks demeanor, Stick, but not me."

So Mickey sent me to the La Bete Funeral Home with instructions to get the five hundred dollars the proprietress had lost on the ponies. I hadn't been to the track since the war. The horses were never my favorite. They hadn't changed too much since the Night War, it's just now none of the jockeys had heads and the horses left flaming hoofprints. I could understand the appeal.

I didn't know who would willingly go to a funeral home run by ghouls. It's like putting foxes in charge of the henhouse, if the hens were the mortal remains of your loved ones. The ghouls volunteered for it, proving they were no dummies, and everyone went with it. Me, I didn't imagine too many people would care where I went, and I wouldn't be around to care whether or not my bones ended up lining a ghoul's belly.

I pulled up outside the funeral home. It looked like a literal home, an airy and angled Craftsman on the corner of a main street. The front door was unlocked, so I let myself in. The atmosphere was death in all its forms. The air was close, the walls were dark, and thick carpet was a glutton for footfalls. A small room displaying a few different coffins opened up out of the main hall. All the other doors were closed. I was worried I was going to have to go looking when I heard a disconcertingly sunny voice.

"Good morning, sir. Are you bereaved?"

I looked to the top of the stairs. She was a ghoul all right, with a complexion too gray to properly be called porcelain and purplish-black circles under her eyes. Those, though, were striking, bright blue and nearly glowing. Her smile was nice, so long as you didn't mind a little mold around the gums. She was dressed in a tight black gown with a section of white lace at her throat, like the lining of a coffin.

"Purvissa La Bete?" I asked.

She descended the staircase like she was floating an inch or two off the ground. Considering her gown swallowed up her feet, it's possible she was.

"Yes," she said, flashing a nervous graveyard smile. "Do we know each other?"

"Not as such. You know my, ah, well, my employer, I suppose you'd say."

She reached the bottom of the staircase, and was only a few feet away from me. Her perfume, a combination of formaldehyde, old posies, and rot, enveloped me like an amorous martian.

"And who is your employer? We have no viewings scheduled today."

"Oh, he's not deceased. He's pretty healthy. I mean, he could stand not to eat so much ice cream probably, but you try living so close to your food. Oh, I guess you kind of do."

Her teeth vanished. "Why are you here?" Her tone was as flat as her smile had become.

"Mickey Cohen sent me," I said.

Fear hit her first, then it was gone, smothered under a more benign surprise. "Oh. Well, how can I help you?"

"Mickey says you owe him five hundred bucks."

"Five hundred? Oh no. It was four...something. Four hundred and something."

"I'm sure he's charging you interest. And are you telling me you don't know how much you owe *Mickey Cohen*? I don't want to tell you what's what, but that's the kind of money management that gets you in dutch with dangerous men."

"Mister..."

"Moss," I said, then kicked myself for telling her.

"I don't want to get in trouble with gangsters." She touched my chest.

"Um. I'm not actually a gangster. I'm literally a friend of Mickey's, and, uh, it's not important. Could you take your hand back?"

"No."

"Miss La Bete?"

"Purvissa," she purred, stepping closer. She was kind of pretty, in a sort of funerary way. Her breath smelled like the grave. Probably an actual grave out back.

"Purvissa. I'm trying to be as reasonable as I can be under the circumstances. It's really in your best interests to give me the money. If I go back to Mickey empty-handed, he's not going to forget the debt. He's going to tack on another C-note or two, and he's going to send another pal of his over here to get it. That other pal is about three of me, and I don't think I have to tell you what he does to get money."

"Well, Mr. Moss..."

She trailed off, and I blurted "Nick." *God, I'm stupid.*

"Nick," she said, showing her teeth again. "I'm certain there's something I can do for you, and perhaps you can speak with Mickey on my behalf. It's not that I don't *have* the money, it's just that I have so many other bills at the moment that it would be a dreadful inconvenience."

"You have the money? Go get it. Trust me, this is the nice visit. This is the visit you want."

She traced along the lapel of my olive green suit. It really was the ugliest suit I owned. I only kept it because it reminded me of my uniform in the service.

"Are you certain?" She whispered. Her breath over my ear was like the lonely wind over tombstones, complete with corpse-stink.

"Miss La Bete."

"Purvissa."

"Get the money. I'm not kidding around here."

"You know, you're beginning to bore me. I try to make this more interesting for the both of us, and you just stand there, stuttering and sweating and twitching."

"I'm not, uh...I'm not...well, I'm not twitching."

"Nick Moss. Wouldn't even have to change that name if I turned you. Maybe Nicodemus Moss...yes, that sounds just like a ghoul name to me. Or Nicodemus La Bete if you prefer. My last husband left me. He's buried under the house with my feelings."

I blanched. "Okay, sister. Time to knock it off. Get the money."

"You're being rude."

"I'm trying to—"

I don't know where she got the knife. She was probably holding it the whole time. It was long and slender, with a twisty blade. It looked like something rajas might use to solve the odd succession crisis. She was almost on top of me, and the way her teeth were snapping, I got the impression she didn't mind some fresh meat every now and again.

Like Mickey said, though, I knew what I needed. The roses were out and in the palm of my hand before either me or Purvissa could blink. She took one look at the roses and scurried back, dropping the blade. It buried itself point down, going right through the carpet and into the floor beneath. It was always a little funny the first time you saw a ghoul lose their mind at the sight of a rose, but then you remember that's why we put flowers on graves in the first place.

Purvissa cowered away from me, trying to crawl into the wall behind her. All she was facing were a couple petals. A second before, I had been a plaything for her. Someone to put off, tease, and if she wanted to, take me and turn me. Nothing I could do then, a lifetime ago. Now I was ten feet tall. Didn't matter that Mickey sent short nothing me instead of Big Jack. The effect was entirely the same.

"Please! Put them away! I beg you!" she shrieked.

"Are you going to get the money?"

"Yes! I promise! You have my word."

"Okay. Just remember I can get these whenever I want." I put the roses back in the vial and transferred that to my jacket. They weren't in great shape. I'd need to get new ones, but that was why every house on the block had a rose bush. "All gone," I said.

Purvissa opened one eye and regarded me. When I showed her empty hands, she got to her feet and smoothed out the dress over her cadaverous form. "Well, then," she said, miffed. "If you'll allow me to go to my safe and return."

"Uh-uh, I'm keeping you in sight." I yanked the dagger from the floor. "And I'm keeping this for the time being."

"I have a hundred of those," she said, but from the longing way she looked at her blade, I could tell it was her favorite.

I followed her up the stairs and into an office. Like everything else, it was dark colors, and the shades on the windows were drawn. It gave a sense of closeness. Probably good for grieving people, or maybe she just liked the dark.

She went to a painting of herself gazing imperiously down over the office and swung it aside, revealing a safe. She glared back at me as though I was going to look over her shoulder at the combination, then shielded it with her hands as she opened up the safe. A few spins later, she counted out a couple small piles of money and handed them over. Her hand lingered on mine before she drew it back. She regarded me with fear, but underneath, I saw the same spark that had been there when she was trying to sweet-talk me.

I counted it quickly. The money was all there.

"Thank you. And if you want some free advice—"

"It's hardly free."

"Well, if you want it, stop playing the ponies. Or at least, stop borrowing money to do it."

"Will I see you again?" she asked.

I didn't answer her. There wasn't a good one. Instead I left the funeral home and drove back to Carousel. Mickey wasn't there; some kid was behind the counter, and there was no way I was giving him the money. I went to Mickey's house instead, and Florence opened the door.

"Hello, Nick," she said.

I almost asked about Hattie, but I figured neither one of us was fooling anyone. "Hi, Flo. Is Mickey around?"

The ghost cast her eyes upstairs. "He's in the shower."

"Right," I said, fishing the money out of my pocket. "Give this to him. He can pay me later."

Florence accepted the money and set it on an end table. She didn't look even remotely surprised by it.

I almost turned to go, but something stopped me. "Say, Flo, do you know a maid at the Hollywood Roosevelt by the name of Chopped Mary? Lives, or, er, haunts around Spookstreet?"

Florence thought about it and shook her head. "I don't think so."

"Yeah, it's stupid. Sorry to bother you."

"No bother. If you're looking for someone on Spookstreet, you should talk to my brother."

"Your brother?"

"His name is—"

"Hector Plasm. Yeah, we met at the fights the other night. Why would he know?"

"Hector knows everyone on Spookstreet. If you have to find this Chopped Mary, he knows her." Flo rattled off an address on Shatto Place. "That's Spook Central."

"That name sounds ominous."

"It's the headquarters of the Spookstreet Specters," she said. "Hector haunts the attic. I'd be careful if you go there, though. They don't like humans as much as I do."

"Of course not."

SIXTEEN

Thursday, December 1, 1955
Around noon

I n the City of Devils, houses no longer looked haunted; they *were* haunted. The three stories of crumbling Victorian finery Florence directed me to looked like it was going for the blue ribbon in a haunted house contest. I bet even the rats and spiders in there had their own ghosts. Spook Central was hell on earth on the outside. Couldn't even imagine what it was like on the inside.

So of course I needed to get to the attic.

I set a foot on the staircase leading to the porch. The house was slightly translucent and glowed a faint greenish-gray. It was probable that the lot was technically vacant, that the building was created by the ghosts haunting it. Get enough ghosts together and they made a thing to haunt out of their own fears and needs. Ghosts were a lot like paper wasps, except they worked in nightmares.

The stair didn't give under my weight. Don't know why I felt it should, since I'd been on a ghost ship before, and it was just as seaworthy as the scow

I took over to England during the war. I climbed the steps quickly. The door was wooden, with a large window set into it. The window was dusty, and periodically, something crawled over the other side on too many legs.

I raised my fist to knock and the door opened with a sepulchral creak. I had everything I needed to deal with ghosts on my person, but I wanted to play nice. Having one gang mad at me was more than enough. I put one foot over the threshold and called out. "Anybody home?"

The laughter that responded was deep and booming, and had a nice "I'd like to see you dead" edge to it.

Ghosts.

"I'm here to see Hector? I'm an acquaintance of his sister's?"

The laughter strung out, getting farther away, like a fishing lure made out of murder. It was working, so who was I to judge? The door opened into a short hallway. Everything was at once partly transparent and dusty. The dust, and the cobwebs lacing every corner, and the rats skittering through the dark, were probably manifestations of the will of the ghosts. Simple stuff like that wasn't off the table. The ghosts wanted this place to be creepy, so it was creepy. I never liked haunted houses, even back when they didn't have real ghosts in them.

I moved quickly inside, looking for a staircase that would take me closer to the attic.

The laughter resolved into a voice, only one room away. "If it isn't Mickey Cohen's little friend."

"Uh...hi?"

I was in the central hall with doorways open all around. A staircase with a broken banister led up to the second floor. The rooms around me were mostly bare, save for a few shelves and some furniture, all getting ready to fall apart. A rusty tricycle sat right in front of the foot of the stairs. You know, for a dead kid.

The voice came from the room on the other side of the stairs. "Shouldn'ta come here, Mickey's friend." The voice grew closer. I stepped to the left, getting a better angle.

It was a severed head, floating about six feet off the ground, dripping blood and snotlike ectoplasm. The Huntington Head, if memory served. His eyes were popping out of his skull, and he talked like he only had the most rudimentary control of his tongue. All in all, he looked surprised at being only a head. In his defense, that would have surprised me too.

"This has nothing to do with Mickey," I told him.

"Pull the other one, meatstick," the Head told me. "Oh, you can't, because I don't have them." The laughter started up again.

"I don't want any trouble."

"You walked into Spook Central. A man doesn't do that unless trouble's all he's looking for."

"I'm just trying to talk to Hector."

"Lean on him? You think your sad little human mob is muscling into Spookstreet? Oh, I have something else to show you. So much."

Maybe I was still feeling big from what happened with Purvissa. Maybe I didn't like the look on his face. I pulled the vial of holy water from my jacket and showed it to him. "I said I don't want trouble. I didn't say I couldn't handle it."

The Head vanished in a cloying mist. My path to the stairs was free. I went for it. Before I put one foot on the stairs, a clomping sound came from the top of them. Despite myself, I jumped back.

A shadowy shape descended going faster and faster as he got to me, his footsteps disappearing into a rattle by the time he hit the bottom. Then the shape too was mist. I cursed myself for flinching. Ghosts dealt mostly in illusions, but the more you reacted, the more you believed, the better they did. A ghost could scare a person to death, and when they did, they'd successfully made another one of themselves, the new ghost's form in whatever shape it believed itself to be in death. Usually whatever scared it the most.

"I'm a private investigator!" I called out. Then muttered, "It's Nick the Dick, not Nick the Stick." No one responded to that one. The Head was clear on what he thought of my story. I could only hope Hector was more reasonable than his flunky.

I forced myself onto the stairs. This time there was no shadowy shape. Don't use the same trick twice. Probably a ghost truism there. I'd take it.

The wallpaper, which until then I had taken to be a series of oddly symmetrical water stains, began to writhe. These were easy to ignore, but I moved faster when I started to see faces form next to me, all silently crying out.

The second floor was darker than the first. It was the middle of the day. Might as well have been the witching hour. The windows had to have been almost entirely blacked out. I suppressed a shiver as I got to the top; it was an icebox up here. Worse, a persistent smell wormed into me. A smell I knew well from a decade before. It was death.

"Hello there, meatstick." The voice cracked like crusty bread, and underneath, it was pure molasses. It was coming from the opposite end of the hallway, where the next flight of stairs went to the third floor. In the deep shadows pooling there like cobwebs made of tar, I could only see a vague silhouette.

"Hello, uh, ma'am."

"You can call me Marie, if you want."

Marie Fury, the woman burned by the sun. I'd seen what happened when someone got the wrong end of a flamethrower. Marie was worse. Somehow, the remnants of her humanity made her worse.

"You can call me Nick," I said, trying my best to be friendly. Maybe she was more reasonable than the Huntington Head had been.

"What's one of Mickey Cohen's boys doing in Spook Central, I wonder?"

"I'm not one of Mickey's boys. We just know each other from the Nigh...from way back. I'm not here for him, not here because of him."

"I heard what you told the Head," Marie said.

"Yeah?" I was getting closer, step by step. Not trying to move fast enough to make her nervous. Kind of funny, me trying not to make a ghost nervous, but that was one of the realities of the world.

"I don't believe you either."

"Why would I be here otherwise?"

"Oh, who knows? Maybe you as dumb as you look?"

"Or maybe I just want to ask Hector if he can point me to a local for a quick conversation."

The silhouette moved, and caught a tiny sliver of light that had somehow bled into the hallway, a lambent splash over the hideous geography of her ruined body. I shuddered.

"What do you see when you close your eyes?" she mused. "I know you. All you men who were the right color got to go to war. You got a gun, too. Got to shoot back. Not like that here. Not like that for us."

"You don't look like you were killed around these parts," I said.

"Wasn't. Believe me, I've seen what you men will do."

The smell of blood grew stronger. Memories, ones I'd rather not have to deal with, fought inward. With the smell came the sounds. I wasn't walking on old wooden planks getting ready to crumble. Now I was splashing in half an inch of liquid, each step sending another blast of that meaty aroma into my senses. More shadows joined Marie, these scattered along the floor. They had the disturbing geometry of bodies, when the cruelty of murder had stripped away identity.

It wasn't quite right, and I think that's what kept me going forward. See, murder, the kind Marie understood, was personal. Even when they said it was nothing personal—and they nearly always did—it was. The bullets, the blades, the ropes, they were for *you*. Might be a reason bigger than you, something you did, something you were, but they were for you. It was murder and there was only the one address.

War was different. War was a factory of slaughter. Didn't matter who it was; they just threw men at it. Throw enough, and the war stops. They could have saved us all a lot of time if they had just shot us in our home countries and then called it when one country cried uncle.

The bodies she was showing me still had some kind of shape. They weren't pulverized. They weren't the cast-offs of a factory.

"Mmmhmm, meatstick. You like what you're seeing?"

I stepped over a pile of bodies. I felt like an idiot; at best, they'd have the consistency of pudding, but I did it anyway.

"Hector's up this way, right?"

I passed Marie and climbed the stairs.

"Keep walking," she told me. "This is as nice as we get. Up there, it's just a dream you can't wake up from."

The scent receded, to be replaced with the burnished smell of old leather. The atmosphere on the third floor was closer than the second, and the light even harder to find. I could only make out rough shapes and hope the layout was the same: another open hallway leading around to the next flight of stairs. I put a hand out and touched the wall. It was solid up here, or maybe I had just drifted into some other place where the ghosts got to determine what was real and what wasn't.

There was one missing from the night of the fights. Old Rend, they'd called him. He was one of those monsters everyone liked to pretend didn't exist: the ones who were obviously from a time before 1945. The agreed-on fiction, when the monsters came into our world, starting with the ones from legends or the silver screen. Then they got stranger from there.

Why the monsters felt the need to keep with the '45 lie was beyond me. They were in charge. We had a monster president, officially, since '52. Even though the first one was assassinated, they had a spare with the VP. They could tell us that monsters came out of cereal boxes, and what's the human population going to do? Hide in our houses more? Already had that cold.

Old Rend looked like one of those stories about the old loony bins. The ones where people were thrown before there was any kind of thought to cure or even care. Dungeons for the poor. And believe you me, go in combat, or even meet a clown and live to tell the tale, you start to learn that the line between sanity and its evil twin is a whole lot thinner than most people believe. Maybe he had been a normal man at one time, driven into insanity by a place like that.

And I decided to come over to his place. This entire plan was sounding dumber and dumber. I'd even be willing to run past Marie and the Head, put up with the mocking laughter that would come my way. The thing was, Hector could find Chopped Mary, and she might have a clue as to what happened to Songbird. Another link on the chain back to the bare roadside where she'd been filled with lead and daylight.

clickclickclickclick

The sound didn't come from any specific direction. It was out there, in the dark. I couldn't tell if it was because of the echoes, but it came from everywhere at once. It sounded like spiders looked like they should sound, if they were the size of terriers. Could Old Rend climb on walls and ceilings? Why not? He was a ghost. He didn't even have a body, strictly speaking.

I started for the next flight of stairs. It was tough, as my legs were as wobbly as old Jello. It wasn't all that far a distance to go. Just around the side of the stairwell, make a quick turn, and there it would be.

...but I was on the top floor. My eyes adjusted enough to the gloom right as I'd made the realization. There was no extra flight of stairs. It was a hallway with doors on either side. Attic access was going to be a little more difficult.

"Excuse me, um...do I call you Rend? Is that right?"

clickclickclickclick

I don't know what I was expecting. Old Rend was gagged by one of the leather belts that wrapped his body. Another one covered his eyes. He wasn't going to respond. I raised my voice and tried to address someone I hoped was a bit more reasonable.

"Hector? Can you hear me? I need to ask you something!"

No response other than some cruel laughter filtering up from Marie and the Head.

Then, in the hall in front of me, I barely made out a shape. Skinny as an insect and with the same kind of toylike flexibility. He was crouched on the floor, one of his clawlike nails tapping the floor. I tried to read it like Morse Code, but unless Rend was trying to tell me AOEWENESBLERM, I could probably forget about it.

Come to think of it, it was worse if he was sending that my way.

"Hi. I don't suppose you're going to believe me when I tell you I'm just here to ask Hector a question, are you?"

clickclickclickclick

Or, possibly, ZUMRF.

"That's not too helpful."

The weird, hunched-over ghost charged me, and I dove through the nearest door. Maybe it was because he looked solid enough and I thought wood would stop him. Of course, he wasn't solid, and the door wasn't wood. It just looked that way, probably because this place could have used a single working light or open window somewhere in it.

I was in another room I could barely see, and now the clicking of Rend's nails on the floors (and maybe walls or ceilings) was all around. I didn't have a destination in mind. I was just trying to get away from the maddening sounds of Rend's pursuit. The rooms beyond the hallway were a maze. There didn't seem like there could be so many, but they were impossible to see, and this was a haunted house. There were as many as the ghosts wanted, or needed in the recesses of their psyches.

The only thing I could hear was my steadily more panicked breathing and the clicking of Old Rend's nails. Unless it was vitally important that I know ERKLUWFLAP.

When something hit my face, I struck outward. Then I scolded myself. I had holy water. Rend had made me forget I had a way to destroy him the instant I wanted. I went for it and readied myself to give the ghost a splash. Something brushed my face again. I caught it. A cord, going to the ceiling.

The attic.

With Rend's maddening clicking growing louder, I hauled it open and scampered up. The clicking stayed below, but grew faster, more desperate. Hungrier.

The attic was not large. It terminated in a stained glass spiderweb at the end, throwing a patchwork rainbow onto the boards. In the splash of light sat a ghost. His head was bowed, his elbows resting on his knees.

Bullets had made Swiss cheese of him, leaking black blood over his zoot suit. It was Hector Plasm, leader of the Spookstreet Specters.

"You can put the holy water away," Hector said, without looking up.

"You're willing to talk?" I asked as I put the vial back in my jacket.

"Anybody who runs the gauntlet gets a word. Never seen a meatstick do it before."

"Yeah, I'm, um, tenacious."

"Like a cockroach."

"Not even a weasel? Ouch. I wanted to tell you, I'm not here for...a hit or anything like that."

Hector finally looked up. His eyes were pits of darkness. Bullet holes, actually, but the light of his soul was inside of them now, and when he looked at me, it was like staring into a whirlpool made entirely out of the afterlife. "If I thought for one second you were here to kill me, you never would have made it past the first floor."

I swallowed. The way he said it, with such chilling finality, loosened the old bowels. "I believe you."

"Good."

"I know you and Mickey don't really get along. Is that because he's your sister's beau?" The look Hector gave me said it would be best if I never spoke on that subject again. Or at all. "Right," I said instead. "I should probably get to the point."

"I think so."

"There's a maid at the Hollywood Roosevelt by the name of Chopped Mary. I'm told she lives in your neighborhood. I want to talk to her."

"Looking for a ghost girlfriend like your friend Mickey?"

"Nothing like that. My intentions are honorable. Not that I'm talking marriage at all! This isn't romantic. Not even a little. There was this witch I was hung up on and now that's not...I'll stop."

"That might be best. What do you want Mary for?"

"Just want to ask her a few questions."

"What kinds of questions?"

I fumbled in my suit and found a business card. I realized I was probably going to have to get Jaime some. And a PI license. Now wasn't the time to think about it. I offered a card to Hector, but he didn't move.

"I'm a detective. Private."

"Doesn't answer my question."

I put the card away. "Mary might have seen something."

"Something like what? Something that Mickey did? She's a witness."

"Nothing like that. No, nothing at all. She might have seen something that has nothing to do with Mickey. Unless Florence told him, he doesn't even know I'm here."

"Florence sent you?"

"Yeah. I asked about Mary and she told me to find you."

Hector nodded, considering. "Who hired you?"

"Uh, nobody. Well, the Gobfather did, but that contract is discharged, in the sense that the missing party was found."

"What are you blathering about?"

"There was a murder."

"Mary saw who did it?"

"Maybe. I don't know unless I talk to her."

"I don't like this."

"I don't mean any harm. I give you my word on that. Just need a word with her, that's all."

Hector considered. "I'll have her brought here, and I chaperone the whole thing."

"Fine by me."

"Then pull up some floor."

I did as he asked, and slowly, the ghosts of Spook Central emerged from the trapdoor to gather in the attic. Me, I got to feel their attention crawling all over me, and hope the one ghost I actually wanted to speak to would hurry up and get here.

SEVENTEEN

Thursday, December 1, 1955
An hour later

It takes a special kind of life to look forward to the arrival of a ghost. I never thought I'd have that particular kind, either, but I did. Took some time, but finally the Huntington Head escorted Chopped Mary up into the attic. She wasn't lightly named either. Every joint on her had been severed, the only thing linking them appeared to be blood flowing through nothing. She was chilling, but she was also dead and moving around. So it came with the territory.

Hector had kept his place beneath the stained glass, while Marie and Rend went to stand by him. The other ghosts in the room, and there were a lot, crowded to the sides and behind me. They were either Specters themselves, or they were close enough to stay in Specter HQ. Either way, I wasn't going to try anything, which was likely the entire point to their presence.

When Chopped Mary arrived, I bounced up to my feet. Some of the ghosts tensed, ready to throw down, but I wasn't there to fight.

"Chopped Mary?" I asked.

"Yes?" She was frightened. That much was plain. I could imagine. She'd just been brought up to a gang's inner sanctum to talk with someone who was allegedly so dangerous he couldn't be talked to anywhere else. I didn't have the first clue how to put a ghost at ease, either.

"Nick Moss. Private detective."

"How do you do, Mr. Moss?"

"I was hoping to ask you a few questions?"

Mary glanced around the room. I caught Hector give her the slightest nod. "Oh...okay," she stammered.

"You're a maid at the Hollywood Roosevelt Hotel, correct?"

"I am."

"And you were working the night of November 25? It was a Friday?"

"Yes."

"Did you see anything on that night? Anything out of the ordinary?"

Another glance to Hector. Another subtle nod.

Chopped Mary gathered herself. "I was on the second floor. We had an ogre guest and you know ogres..."

I had to nod. I had guessed ogres weren't ideal guests, but this was the second time I'd heard it from a maid, and it was in the same hushed, almost religious tones. This must be the horror stories they tell each other. Considering the few ogres' dens I'd gone into, I had to agree. "Yeah."

"I saw a human," she blurted. "A very pretty human. She burst out of her room. She was beautiful, like some kind of princess from a storybook."

"Did you recognize her?"

Mary shook her head. "Who was she?"

"A powerful monster's girlfriend."

"Oh."

"What happened then? Did you follow her?"

"Oh no. I got right back to work."

"It's okay. I'm not your boss."

"I followed her."

I nodded again. "And then?"

"She went out the side exit on Orange. I was thinking she was in a lot of danger. She could be turned."

I didn't bring up the obvious, that Mary already had it on her mind to turn Songbird. We both knew it, but it didn't need to be mentioned.

"By the time I got out to the street, she was already in a car. It turned around, went north, and turned right on Hollywood Boulevard."

"Was she driving?"

"No, she was in the passenger seat."

"Did you see the driver?"

She flinched at my eagerness. "No, I'm sorry. I didn't."

I should have known it wouldn't be that easy. "How about the car?"

"It was blue, I think? It might have been gray. Or black."

"Oh, good."

"It was so late at night it was kind of early in the morning, so the light was strange," she said defensively.

"What kind of car was it?"

"I don't know. It was a car? Kind of normal."

"How many doors?"

"Two or four, definitely."

I resisted the urge to cradle my head in my hands. "Can you think of anything else?"

Mary shook her head. "Sorry."

"Thanks for your time, Mary. Thanks, Hector, for your help."

I turned to go.

"Let me show you out," the Huntington Head said.

"I can find my own way, thanks."

I was at the trapdoor before Hector finally spoke. "What are you looking into?" he asked.

"Nothing, I guess."

"The girl, she was murdered?"

I nodded. "Shot in the back."

"Just because she was shot doesn't mean you might not get to talk to her. After all, you can talk to me."

Eighteen

Wednesday, December 14, 1955
Late afternoon

Ten hours, knee deep in saltwater, with who knows what crawling around on my feet, staring at an old outflow pipe, and you know what I got?" Jaime demanded.

"Nothing?" I ventured.

"A cold," he said, and punctuated it with a sneeze.

Serendipity covered her mouth. "Don't sneeze on me! I don't want to get sick. Billy's taking me out on Friday."

"I told you to pick up hip waders," I said.

"Where am I going to afford hip waders?" he asked.

"You could borrow mine?"

"How am I supposed to fit into anything you wear?"

Ser laughed.

"You too?" I shook my head. "Surrounded by Judases. Did you see anything at least?"

"Man, I saw a lobster as big as a baby. And like a big baby. A real fat one."

Ser brightened. "Where, exactly?"

"Ser, we can't send you to the place we're staking out. That might inform the gill-man that we know he has David Rubinowitz, and if he knows someone is looking for him, he might step things up and turn the kid."

Ser folded her arms in a huff. A tiny fish swam though the water in her goggles.

"So what do you want me to do, boss?" Jaime asked, sniffing.

"I want you to get some hip waders. You can bill me for them. Tomorrow, first thing, I want you back out on that mudflat, watching that outflow pipe. If the gill-man is turning David, he'll bring him out to open water. It's some kind of religious thing."

"Dedication to Dagon," Ser said, still in her huff. Serendipity followed the weird watery faith of the gill-men and the sirens, but she wasn't fanatic about it. Got her in some trouble with her folks, who were far more serious about honoring the creatures from the deep who would eventually emerge and devour the surface world. It sounded strange to me, but no stranger than anything we humans went about believing.

"Right, the Dedication to Dragon."

"Dagon."

"What'd I say?"

"Dragon."

"Right, him."

Ser gave a theatrical sigh and collapsed deeper into her squeaking chair.

I turned back to Jaime and caught him smiling. He put back on the mad dog face he'd worn with the Normandie Knights. "You got your marching orders, kid."

"Yeah, yeah."

"And while you're at it, get some long-sleeved shirts. I can't have you showing your anti-monster tattoos to the world."

Sometimes I doubted that Jaime had ever seen a shirt with buttons on it. For him, undershirts were more than enough. Jaime muttered something in Spanish and left, waving over his shoulder. I leaned against the doorjamb between my office and the front room. A tiny Christmas tree stood next to Ser's aquarium, more evidence she wasn't taking her ostensible Dagonist faith as seriously as the rest of the Sargassos might have liked.

It was late in the afternoon. We'd close up in a little while. With things as slow as they were, Ser would have normally asked to leave early, but she had been less gung-ho ever since a producer said she was old. Now most of her time was spent with that phantom of hers.

Songbird flitted through my thoughts. They weren't romantic. Whatever we had, love was never on the table. No, it was failure. She hadn't wanted me to protect her for a second longer than I had been with her, but still, she left in the middle of the night. She left, and she died. I couldn't have prevented that, but I could find who did it.

The wolves hadn't bothered me since the first interrogation. Maybe they'd solve it. I doubted it, though. Their reasoning held water, but I didn't like it. Something was wrong and there was no way to see it. Maybe if Mary had seen something useful, but she hadn't. I needed to move on. Save the people I could, like David Rubinowitz, who probably didn't want to spend the rest of his life talking to fish.

The front door opened, and Johnny Stompanato stepped into the offices of Moss Investigations. "Whoa, Mickey said this place was small, but I didn't think he meant it was a matchbox," he said.

"What do you want, Johnny?"

"What's eating you, shamus?"

"Sorry. To what do I owe the illustrious presence of—"

"Well, hello there, miss. Name's John Steele."

"Steele?" I asked the air. I turned to Ser, certain she wasn't going to fall for this jiggery pokery.

No such luck. She giggled, her gills frilling from her neck. "Serendipity Sargasso," she said.

He kissed her hand. It's a wonder he didn't leave an oil slick. "Beautiful name for a beautiful lady," he murmured.

"So, uh, Johnny. You didn't come here to moon over my secretary, did you?"

He didn't break eye contact with Ser. "Call it a side benefit." He finally turned back to me. "Mickey said to come by and pick you up."

"What for?"

Johnny grinned. "You think we're taking you for a ride?"

"Wait, are you?"

The grin became a laugh. "You are a nervous little man. I'll never know what Mickey sees there. We're going for a night out, Moss. Drinks and dinner at the Nocturnist."

"The Nocturnist," Ser squealed. "I've never been!"

"Now that, my dear, is a crime," Johnny said.

"Right, so let's go? Ser, can you close up the office?" I said.

"Maybe I should call you," Johnny said.

"Maybe I'll answer," Ser said, batting water-magnified eyes at the gangster.

"Maybe you talk it over with Billy Bounce," I suggested. Ser shot me a glare that, were the legends true, might turn me to stone.

"C'mon, Moss. Let's go." Ser kept the death ray on me until I was out the door. "Sea hag for a secretary," Johnny said, as we piled into an aging Ford.

"They prefer 'siren.'"

"She's no hag, I'll give her that. Never pegged you for a fella who'd work with a monster."

"How do you mean?"

"Oh, the way Mickey talks about you. The way I hear about you. Nick Moss, war hero. Fought in Europe, fought in Los Angeles. A killer through-and-through, only now he finds missing kids. Doesn't sound like the kind of fella who'd let a monster anywhere close."

"She works for cheap, for one thing. It's hard for a human secretary to handle the kind of pain most clients are in. And she keeps me from being turned by any monster who walks in."

Johnny watched the road. Finally, he muttered, "Yeah, that can be tough."

I didn't want to pry. Mostly because I didn't like Johnny and this might make him seem less bad. I could only figure he was talking about his time alone with Turner Coates or whatever monster beaus he'd had in the past. I couldn't imagine Coates was the first.

We arrived at Mickey's house and Florence let us in. The dog, Mickey Junior sat nearby, gazing suspiciously at the ghost floating in the living room. Mickey was in the shower, and I didn't know how long that meant we'd be waiting. Johnny settled into the couch and I took a seat in an easy chair.

"My brother mentioned you came by to see him," Florence said.

"Hector? What did he say exactly?"

"Something about how you were looking into a murder? I didn't know you did that."

"I don't. I wasn't hired or anything. I just thought I might have owed the murdered girl something."

"A man is the sum of his debts," Mickey said. He stood in the doorway, clean and freshly powdered. "Of course, you gotta know who you owe and who you don't."

Mickey's tone never changed, but I knew him. The temperature dropped ten degrees, same as if a mad ghost were trying to make an example of us. I was standing at the doorway of a C-47, looking out over a field of exploding flak. One way or another, I was going to have to jump. I just had to make sure I didn't hit anything on the way down.

"Who don't I owe?" I asked.

"This broad," Mickey said. "I know she was whistle bait, but she was Mab's girl. Way I see it, if he wants a pound of flesh for it, he's the one balancing the scales."

I sighed, realizing only then I was holding my breath. "You're probably right. Doesn't matter anyway. I hit a dead end."

"Hector said it didn't look like you got what you came for," Florence said.

Mickey burst out laughing and Johnny joined him. "You went to Hector? Oh, Nick, you did all you had to and more. Where did you find Hector?"

I squirmed in my chair. "Spook Central."

That only made Mickey and Johnny laugh harder. Mickey wiped away some tears. "Yeah, you did more than you *ever* have to. Besides, that's old news. Wolves pinched a human for it."

"Who?"

"Some human, like I said. Doesn't matter."

"You think Mab will get to him in the slammer?"

Mickey shrugged. "Nah. I mean, don't get me wrong, Mab wants someone in the clink offed, that fella's pushing daisies by noon. But I don't think he'll care."

"Yeah," I muttered. I was hot. Mab didn't care about Songbird enough to go after the guy who did it. And worse, the wolves had been right all along. It was a human way to kill someone, and the motive was there for anyone who cared to look. I needed to forget about it. Enjoy myself.

I put on a smile, but I'm sure it looked feral. "Let's have some fun then."

Mickey clapped his hands, a small cloud of powder exploding from them like a cartoon had just taken off running. "Now you're talking!"

We were out the door shortly afterwards, with Mickey admonishing Florence to show up later with some of the other girls from her work. Didn't take much detective work to figure out what kind of joint that was. Mickey's taste in ladies hadn't changed, except for the whole ghost thing, and that was only because back then, Mickey hadn't known about ghosts yet.

We met Jack and Rob at a restaurant on the border of Chinatown. They welcomed Mickey like he was family, and a Chinese man I took to be the owner joined us. Mickey introduced him as Wong, and before long, it was clear he was another member of Mickey's human-only mob. We stuffed ourselves on dumplings and chicken feet, and the tea got my nerves buzzing right up through my skin.

Wong joined us when we left. We piled into Mickey's Caddy, and there was more than enough room, especially with small fellas like me and Wong. It was after dark and I scarcely cared. All six of us clinked softly as we walked. All six of us carried weapons on our belts or under our arms. All six of us were ready for any monster who tried to come at us. And the monsters knew it.

I'll admit it: I liked it. I wasn't exactly one of Mickey's guys...or maybe I was. I didn't really know. I'd done a job for him. He'd paid me for it, and the money was good. An easier wad of cash I hadn't earned in a long time. There was no crying family begging me to find their little boy or little girl. No one I was letting down. No life I was changing when everything inevitably went FUBAR.

Right now, David Rubinowitz was probably chest deep in water somewhere getting taught how to be a gill-man before he changed. There was nothing I could do about that. But put fear into some monsters of the human race, I could do that, and line my pockets the whole time.

We went into the Nocturnist and the bouncer, Hargoth the Bonechewer, gave us the stinkeye. This time I grinned at him. He blinked when he saw it, but he didn't do anything. Not with six blessed weapons waiting for an excuse. He waved us in.

Capriccio Español and his orchestra were in the middle of a jazz number. A phantom on a sax played us in. The song wasn't about us, it wasn't for us, but it felt like it was. We were the ones being watched. Six humans who had the nerves to walk into a den of drunk monsters.

We took a booth and spread out. Tonight, Johnny's beau Turner Coates wasn't around. Wong asked where he was, and I had to admit, another evening in the presence of Vampiro would be something. Johnny said Coates was shooting, so he was on the prowl. The fellas laughed at that.

I settled in. When our meat golem waitress stopped by, Mickey ordered five Cuba Libres and a ginger ale. I found myself hunting for Jane, and I saw her, delivering champagne flutes to a table of mummies. It was a shame how things turned out, but that's the way it went. Not like there was a future there.

I picked up my glass and raised it to Mickey. He caught my eye and grinned back, raising his ginger ale. He had me. At least at that moment, he had me.

It was maybe an hour later, in the middle of our second—in Jack's case fourth—round that the Gobfather arrived. Nyx Nocturne, the vampire who ran the place, went to one meat golem and whispered in her ear. She then gathered three others and they went out the front door. A moment later the Gobfather entered with Flux, Murk, and Sawbones arrayed around them. The goblins were strutting, which was ridiculous, until I realized I had probably looked exactly the same way. Following them were the meat golems, carrying the gilded egg. The shape behind the slender, vinelike bars was Songbird.

I blinked. It couldn't be. Songbird was dead. But the silhouette was identical. Slender but obviously female, a rare kind of perfection unseen outside of poetry. The white satin dress and elbow gloves were Songbird's. But then the girl inside turned her head, revealing shimmering red hair.

That was kick in the gut. Hexene's pugnacious face flashed in front of me. It wasn't Hexene. By any objective meter, the woman in the egg was more beautiful than the witch, but as far as I was concerned, she couldn't hold a candle to Hexene. No, it was someone else. Someone I didn't know. Someone Mab had used to simply replace the dead Songbird. Used her up, and when she was thrown away, wasted no time in getting a brand-new one. The passing of a goldfish was treated with more respect.

My stomach flopped over. What gave the Gobfather the right to treat people like that? And what were these girls thinking, letting themselves be used in this way? Before Songbird there was a litany of others. All vanished. And now, one killed.

"What's eating you?" Mickey asked.

I shook my head. "Nothing important."

Mickey followed my gaze. "Gobfather. Yeah, I know. But the enemy of my enemy and all that."

"What do you mean?"

"The Bellum mob owns everything in this town. Anybody carving up that pie is something like a friend."

"Mab isn't going to give you anything."

"No, but it's easier to take from Mab than Bellum." Mickey took a gulp of ginger ale. "Well, it couldn't be any harder, anyway."

"I'm not going to do anything."

"Good. Because you were sitting there, and youse got this look in your eye. It's a look I seen before, right before youse walked into the dark after them werewolves."

"Don't worry. I'm not...that's not me."

"It's still you, Stick. If it wasn't, you think you'd be sitting there?"

I didn't have time to figure exactly at whose feet he was laying blame. I caught what was going on first only as movement. A quick predator stride. By the time I had focused, they were already halfway across the Nocturnist and heading for the Gobfather's table.

Zombies.

A group of them, eight or ten, all dressed in pinstriped suits or nice skirts and blouses. A dull flicker of metal in their hands said cold iron. They moved at a fast clip, their shambles making it look like they were perpetually falling horizontally. The one in the lead was a grinning skull, his lips and eyelids rotted away. He was wearing an old steel collar, a speaker at his throat. I knew him. He was an enforcer for Sarah Bellum by the name of Mr. de Kay.

A murmur followed them like a wake, growing louder as they drew closer to Mab and his men. The sidhe and goblins weren't paying attention. Instead, they were accepting drinks from their waitress, who I noted with mounting horror, was Jane. They didn't see the zombies until the walking corpses were right on top of them.

I popped up from my seat. Behind me, Mickey called out that it was none of our business. He'd seen it. Of course he had. I didn't move any closer, but I had a better view.

The zombies hissed "Brains" as they raised their dull iron daggers.

They were after the Gobfather. The daggers fell, and the Gobfather darted aside, grabbing the cage and tipping it over. It crashed to the floor, crushing two zombies underneath, and the new Songbird screamed. The daggers whistled inches from the Gobfather, or so I thought. When he staggered back, lines of red had appeared along his white suit.

The Gobfather scurried away. And that's what it was. He was scurrying, like an animal. His unearthly grace had abandoned him, and I was seeing a man—a monster—in desperate fear for his life. All for some cold iron. I had enough salt to discourage any zombies from getting close, and if they insisted, well, a silver bullet through the head would do the job.

This was still in the slivers of time between seconds. Sawbones snapped his fingers. Boom. Might as well have been nothing else in the room. The flame leapt out of his palm. With a flick of his wrist, he tossed it at the table. It caught the cocktails Jane had recently placed on the table in its hungry tendrils. A yellow-orange flash and an angry *whoosh*, and the table was blazing. A zombie staggered backwards, waving a flaming arm. Jane was caught too, the fire climbing her legs.

I sprinted for the fray.

Murk picked up a haunch of lamb from an overloaded plate in front of him and bludgeoned one of the zombies. The Bellum enforcer staggered under the hit, and she turned, ready to perforate the piglike goblin.

Flux cackled in hysterical glee and spat on one of the zombies. The wad of greenish phlegm stuck to the corpse's cheek and hissed as it dissolved the paperlike flesh. The zombie didn't even seem to notice.

The Gobfather had opened the cage and was hauling the frightened girl from inside. Her white dress was stained now—blood or wine, it was impossible to tell, and both had been spilled. De Kay and another zombie were still in pursuit, the others stymied by the explosion of flame and the sudden violence of the three goblins.

The heat of the fire blistered my skin. The ravenous flames spread from the table, consuming whatever they touched. Explosions marked contact with other drinks. *What the hell were they serving here, anyway?* Flame was one of the most common monster weaknesses and could do the trick on most of them if you kept them in one spot long enough. The phantoms, mummies, and meat golems had panicked and run. All except Jane. Her stockings on fire, she was on the floor, desperately trying to crawl away from her own body.

I yanked a tablecloth from a table as I passed, spilling drinks and the odd bowl of soup, and jumped down next to Jane. This was the most dangerous part. Meat golems could hit like a truck, and panicked ones weren't likely to be choosy about whose face they rearranged. I threw the cloth over her legs and smothered the fire, the whole time being convinced I was one second away from getting my jaw broken.

I pulled the cloth away from her legs when I had chased the last flame from them. Didn't look like any permanent damage was done. She was smoking a little, her fishnets had charred holes in them, and a few of her stitches had melted, but other than that, she was fine. Unlike other monsters, meat golems were only *frightened* of fire. Electricity was the real killer with them.

"Are you okay?" I asked her. She stared at me in mute incomprehension. Of all the legs in all the world, it had to be hers on fire.

I never got a response. Not even a nod. Wasn't her fault; she was stunned. I was yanked to my feet from behind, then spun around to face my attacker.

Mr. de Kay stared down at me. Without the eyelids, you might think he'd look surprised. Not really. He always looked insane and angry. "Brains," he said. He didn't have lips, so it came out "Hrains," but I knew what he meant.

A voice came crackling out of the speaker at his throat, deep and butter-smooth, belonging to LA's biggest crime boss. "Mr. Moss. Fancy meeting you here."

I tried to think of something funny to say, but my internal monologue was screaming in terror.

"Brains," de Kay said.

"Mr. de Kay, would you please bring Mr. Moss with you?" Sarah Bellum asked her enforcer.

De Kay dragged me out of the Nocturnist along with the surviving zombies, now in full retreat. There were only three left, the others burned, dissolved, or clubbed to death with mutton. As for the Gobfather, he was wounded but alive. He held the limp body of his Songbird replacement. She had been stabbed half a dozen times.

He'd been using her as a shield.

Nineteen

Wednesday, December 14, 1955
A few minutes later

Sitting next to one zombie is one zombie too many. Sandwiched between two of them, with a third driving the Cadillac you were all in, was much worse. The stink of decay permeated every part of the car, and they saw no need to crack a window.

Mr. de Kay drove, and he wasn't talking other than for the occasional "Brains." De Kay's voice was exactly how I'd always imagined Death's. He never spoke above a whisper, but he never had to. He got the point across, namely that he would like to see your brains, by force if necessary.

I recognized the zombie on my left. The bite marks on his still-meaty flesh were covered in a greenish mold. He was in better shape than the other two zombies in the car, but that was because none of his bones were exposed. He still looked like a dead man, down to the haunted stare in his milky eyes.

The zombie on my right was a woman, and she was missing the skin on the left side of her face. It was just gone, the edges ragged with teethmarks.

She still had an eye in the bony socket of her skull, and perversely it had retained its lifelike green color, while the eye in her good side was covered in death's own cataract.

I didn't have to do a lot of guessing to figure why I was being taken for a ride. I had encountered Sarah Bellum through her man de Kay. She had been making a move on the hotel casino on Catalina Island and had tried to enlist my help to off the head of security. I'd agreed, then reneged, mostly because I'm bad at making decisions. This had to be the fruits of that.

They'd threatened to turn me, and at this point, that was looking like the optimistic ending. They hadn't relieved me of my gun or salt, so I could mount a defense. I knew I could beat one of them on the draw. Maybe two. Not three, though. And I'd learned the hard way Bellum's enforcers wore steel-plated fedoras, so any shot was going to have to take that into account.

Other than grabbing me, though, they hadn't done anything else. I was content, at least for the moment, to see where they were going with this.

They were going to Beverly Hills. We found ourselves on the wide streets of LA's royalty, then turned into a gated complex. The house was a gigantic Spanish-style villa, shielded by palms and copses of banana trees. It looked like the kind of hacienda that should have a commanding view of the ocean. The gate shut behind us as de Kay parked on a stone roundabout in front of the house.

"Brains," he said, and got out of the car.

The moldy-faced zombie hauled me out of the car and the half-faced zombie joined us, one on either side. They kept hold of either armpit while de Kay led us into the mansion. The floors were old Spanish tile, the walls painted an off-white shade. Plants bloomed in alcoves. There was a time when I would have thought this would be out of place for a monster, but the truth was, they had different tastes. Mobsters, though, seemed to like the island life. Maybe it was a subconscious thing, living in a place that felt like the freedom they'd have when they fled or retired.

The zombies took me down a long hall ending in a pair of double doors. De Kay opened them, revealing what was probably a ballroom at one time.

It wasn't anymore. For one thing, the windows were covered with armored bulkheads from Naval ships. A bank of televisions showed a variety of images. Some displayed idyllic natural vistas while others were showing bumpy images of the city. One of them, I determined after I saw my own face, was originating somewhere on Mr. de Kay. A pair of Browning .50 caliber machine guns turned on automated turrets and tracked me as I entered, and the television screen caught my look of stark terror as I noticed this.

The center of the room was a massive machine. The television screens and the machine guns were only the edges of it. *Like eyes and hands,* I thought. The base was silvery metal, multicolored lights, and beeping readouts. The top was a glass tank filled with bubbling liquid. Inside was a large brain, a few tentacles writhing listlessly underneath like the tethers of a zeppelin. This was a brainiac, and it wasn't hard to guess which one: Sarah Bellum, the most powerful gangster on the west coast.

"Good evening, Mr. Moss," she said. Her voice was louder in here, coming from speakers all around me. It was probably designed to make me feel small. It worked.

"Good evening, Miss Bellum."

"It's nice to see you. I trust you remember Mr. de Kay."

"Brains," de Kay threatened.

"Um, yeah. Likewise."

"I'd like to introduce my other two associates, Bracken Mold and Aida Parrish."

"Hi. Hi."

"Brains."

"Brains."

The machine guns were leveled at me, and moved whenever I so much as twitched. I decided not to twitch so much.

"Imagine my surprise when I send my boys to the Nocturnist to deliver a message, and they find you. I thought you were bold before for violating Catalina's no humans law, but to go out at night? That's rare courage in a human."

"Thanks?"

"It just goes to show I was right about you."

I looked around the room. Maybe I was nervous, but I swear the two Brownings tracked even that movement.

"You're a busy man," Bellum said, "so let me get to the point." Lights on the base of the contraption below her tank flashed along with the syllables. Brainiacs needed that sort of thing to live at all. The ones of more modest means went for these mass-produced carts that could get them around. Oldsmobile made a popular model called a Brainwave that was supposed to be affordable, according to the billboards.

Bellum paused, and in the silence, punctuated only by the whirring of the motors in the gun turrets, I couldn't help but perk up my ears to listen.

"You owe me."

"Um, well. About Kong. I didn't think it was the best idea to go after—"

"Forget the ape. He's not going anywhere. We'd rather talk about more immediate issues."

"The Gobfather," I said.

"The elf has been a persistent thorn in my side, yes."

"More than that. Your botched hit reeks of desperation." I blinked. "Not that desperation is a bad thing."

"No, you are correct, Mr. Moss. We attempted to remove the elf forcibly and we failed."

I glanced around at the zombies. They had the decency to look ashamed, muttering "Brains" and looking at their feet.

"I can see how you would have thought that would have worked," I said. "Eight gunmen...okay, daggermen? And sidhe are powerful, but not *that* powerful. Especially when they're away from nature. Maybe if your boys got a foot closer, or the goblins spotted you a second later, this would've turned out different."

"Exactly." Bellum didn't betray many emotions in her voice, but she couldn't hide her pride.

"Of course, it's never going to work again."

"You're telling me things I already know, Mr. Moss."

I swallowed, giving the machine guns another side eye. "Sorry. So why do I think you have another plan already?"

"You are correct. As much as I would like to pretend the underworld is a simple chessboard, it isn't. Pieces move unpredictably, such as finding a man who owes me a debt in the very location of a setback."

"If you want me to off the Gobfather for you...I can't do it. You have professional button men. I'm just a detective. I find people for a living."

"Yes, Mr. Moss. I know. After our broken deal on Catalina Island, I must admit I didn't think of you very much. You are human, and humans have very little ability to effect change one way or the other."

"Thank you?"

"It is merely a statement of fact. You see how quickly you lost the planet? Eight short years was all it took. Oh, there are still pockets of humanity who have decided to hold out, but that is only a matter of time."

I'd heard the rumors. Every human had. Free human states. Sometimes they were in Europe, but more often they were in Asia or South America. Somewhere where geography and superstition combined to make the perfect monster fighters. There was a time when I dreamed of living in a place like that. Officially, the monsters denied any such places existed, and I had chalked it up to wishful thinking. This was the first time I'd ever heard a monster confirm it. I tried not to let that show on my face when I nodded.

"I looked into you after Catalina, just to find out who you were. Then I put such knowledge away for a rainy day. Can you feel it, Mr. Moss? It's raining in Los Angeles."

"It's that, or someone's pissing on me."

Bellum laughed. Whatever machine made her voice did a good job, because she sounded like an aging nightclub singer, her voice deepened with hundreds of hours of whiskey and smoke, caught unawares by a pleasant joke.

"Oh, Mr. Moss, I can see turning you would be a waste. As much as I rely on my soldiers, they are somewhat limited from a conversational standpoint."

"And they can't dance."

"When I saw you in the club, I realized you were the one person in the world who could perhaps assist me in a task I had thought impossible."

"Oh?"

"You see, there is someone in Los Angeles I wish to locate. Someone I have tried to find. With all my resources, with all of my zombies, I came up empty. You, however, find people for a living. And this time, you have no clock ticking down to an inevitable turning. This individual is useful regardless of her present state of being."

"Who is this?" I asked, though I was beginning to have an inkling.

"I want you to find the only woman who has ever escaped the elf."

"Someone escaped?"

"Yes, about six months ago. One of the elf's young ladies. He collects them, you know. All incomparable beauties, so I'm told. I have no real appreciation for such anymore. They are paraded around the city for a time, then, without warning, are never seen again. Another appears after that, and the cycle begins anew."

I burned, thinking about the poor girl who had been killed in the attack.

"One of these young women escaped. Shortly thereafter, she vanished."

"How do you know it wasn't because he caught her again?"

"I don't, but I do know if she is there to be found, you are the one to do it. Humans take care of their own, and there are places a human can go that my men cannot."

Bellum had a point there. "Who is she?"

"All of the elf's women are artists of some kind. Writers, painters, musicians. This one was a dancer. He called her the Golden Swan, but her human name was Liling Lam."

I made her spell it.

"What happens to the girls who don't escape?"

"I never thought about it. Why?"

"No reason," I said, and fought the chill crawling up my spine. "What do you want Miss Lam for?"

"That is my business. Will you find her or not?"

"I need to know. I won't serve anyone up to be turned or killed."

"I know about your moral code, Mr. Moss. I assure you, with me, she is as safe as safe can be."

"I have your word on that?"

Bellum laughed again, full and throaty, despite the complete absence of a throat. "That you would value my word inspires me to value it as well. Of course, you have my word. Miss Lam is far too important to kill or condemn to life as a zombie."

"All right, Miss Bellum. I guess I work for you now."

TWENTY

Thursday, December 15, 1955
Morning

Janina Rakoczy used up all of her imagination on killing monsters. That was the only explanation I had for what she chose to call her butcher shop, which stood on the corner of Grandee and Century in Watts. The sign was fading red lettering on white, and it said simply, BUTCHER SHOP, followed by a pig with a cleaver buried in its back, presumably for the benefit of any illiterates.

Janina, who Mickey had always referred to as "Jan the Polack," because either he never saw the look in her eyes when she sharpened her blades or because he didn't care, was a friend from the Night War. One of the few I saw regularly, too, since she was who sold me my meat. She was also someone who might know where I could start looking for this Golden Swan.

As Janina's shop was close to home, it was my first stop of the day, before even going into the office. Getting home the previous night had been a challenge. Bellum had been nice enough to give me a lift back to my car, which was at the office, and then I went home, terrified the whole time a cop would pull me over and decide now was the time to change the meatstick. Maybe it was because I was brazenly out at night, but no one came for me.

Actually getting in was a mite more difficult. My usual admirers were arrayed about the property, each staking out a separate corner. *Their* territory on *my* property. I parked a street over, went up the alley running behind my house, and climbed the fence.

Lurkimer Closett happened to be back there, and he made a swipe from under my tiny back porch. I dodged him and made it inside. He screamed and cursed, but there wasn't much he could do about it. I had flashlights and teddy bears, and no bogeyman was going to brave that kind of danger.

I lay in bed later, staring at the ceiling and trying to come up with a way to find a person even Sarah Bellum couldn't. Janina was my best bet.

The human underground existed. The monsters were hysterical about it, and a lot of the HUMAC hearings were focused around that fear. The Treaty said they couldn't do anything about crimes that had happened up until March 21, 1953, but anything after was fair game, no pun intended. The mistake most monsters made was that they thought of the underground as this giant monolithic thing. A single organization, probably headed up by President Truman. As if he were still alive.

The truth was, there were more organizations than zombies. The Normandie Knights could be considered one, but they were more in the freelance violence business. For all I knew, the Monster Slayer was another organization masking its activities as a single killer. Hell, you could consider the Democratic-Republican Party a member of the underground, if only because it was impossible to be a human politician without their support.

Not that a human was getting elected anywhere, but we liked to make the effort and run somebody. There were four major monster parties, so maybe the vote would get split enough to put a human in the top spot. Or at least that was the thinking. Of course, for that to work, the monsters would have to stop coming up with new ways to deny humans the vote. The poll tax was alive and well, and in all forty-eight states.

Janina Rakoczy had enough rage in her that she was never going to fully assimilate. Those stories Mickey told about me were all true, but Janina was as bad or worse than me. She hailed from Poland, and got out of there under Hitler's nose. She didn't talk about it much, but I knew she'd seen much worse than I ever would, and she was going to take it out on the world. In some ways, the Night War might have been a good thing. At least she was giving it to something that deserved it.

I went into BUTCHER SHOP and rang the bell on the counter. Janina came out of the back. She was probably intended to be fat, but war and privation had ensured nothing would ever stick to her bones. She was stocky, but also reedy, and I knew from experience she had the kind of strength usually reserved for lumberjacks and stevedores. She wore a bloody apron over a simple dress and sweater. Her blond hair was going to gray, all collected in a tail. Her tiny, wrinkled face looked like the midpoint between a porcelain doll and an angry potato. She clutched a cleaver in her right hand and a knife in the other. I tried not to take that personally.

"Nick," she said in her thick Polish accent. "Bologna? Or is today the day you treat yourself to ham?"

"No meat today, Janina. I was wondering if you could help me."

She slammed the cleaver into a wooden chopping block. I jumped. "What do you want?"

I glanced around. We were the only ones in the shop, and there wasn't much reason for monsters to go get meat in Watts. They wouldn't be coming down until sunset.

"I was wondering if you were still friendly with anyone in the underground." I whispered the last word, and she scowled.

"Why does Nick Moss want to know about something like that? He is not a man who still fights. He is a man who took the Treaty home and sleeps under it like a blanket."

"It's not like that, Janina."

"No? If it were not, you would have nothing to ask me. You would already know."

"Okay, I guess that's true."

"I have also heard you work for snatchers."

I didn't like that word. Of course, the reason I didn't like that word was because I knew some monsters I wouldn't want to call that. Ones I even considered friends. I must have winced, because Janina reacted to something she saw in my face.

"Yes, I see this is true."

"No, it's not...wait, yes. I've worked for a few monsters."

"So why would I talk to you?"

"I never help them find anyone to be turned. Never to be killed."

"How do you know?"

"They mostly want to find other monsters. The only time a monster had me find someone, I returned the girl to her family. As far as I know, she's still human."

Janina gestured with the knife. The blade was slick with fat and blood. "As far as you know."

"Most of my clients are human. Humans who hire me to find people who have been taken by monsters."

"Why are you asking me now?"

"I'm looking for someone and you might help."

"Pfah," she said, turning around to head into the back.

"Janina, please. You know me."

"I think I know you. Now I am not so sure."

"You know me. We fought together in the Night War, you and me. You've saved my life too many times to count and I've done the same for you."

She raised an eyebrow, waiting for me to get to the point.

"You know I'm not going to let anyone get taken or turned." I didn't add the part that it was seldom my choice. Janina didn't need to hear about my abysmal success rate. That would turn anyone into a pessimist.

She watched me, sucking on a tooth. Finally: "Who is this person you seek?"

"Her name is Liling Lam."

"I do not know her," Janina said after some thought. I cursed inwardly. "Why, is she missing?"

"She escaped a monster. A sidhe gangster they call the Gobfather."

"I think I like this girl." Janina considered. "When did she escape?"

"About six months ago."

"And if you find her, there is no turning? No killing?"

"You have my word. The word of the fella who shared a foxhole with you."

"Yes, I like *that* Nick Moss. I would like him back one day." She thought some more. "Very well. I do not know this girl, but there is someone who might. Six months, you say. Yes, there is someone who might have helped her run. Helped her hide. His name is Raymond Cole, and he owns a human-only nightclub in Frogtown, at the end of Riverdale Avenue."

"Thanks, Janina."

"I tell this to my Nick Moss. If the other hears it..." She trailed off, yanking the cleaver from the block, her clear blue eyes never leaving mine.

"There is no other Nick Moss. I can promise you that."

"There is, but I think he is weak." She ran the blades over each other. "Yes, quite weak."

I got to the door when she spoke again.

"This club, Last Night, does not open until a half hour before sundown."

"I thought you said it's humans-only?"

"Yes. They barricade themselves inside and pretend it is their last night. It is a joke, I think. Do you get it? They do what takes them, and the doors open at sunrise." She shook her head. "I do not understand such people."

"Neither do I. Thanks, Janina."

She didn't nod. She just watched me, vanishing behind the counter as I moved away. I wish I didn't know what she meant by the two Nick Mosses, and I hoped she was right about the status of one of them. I didn't think I could look myself in the mirror if it were anybody else.

Flux, Murk,
and Sawbones

Twenty-One

Thursday, December 15, 1955
Not long after lunch

When I walked into my office, my secretary was holding her goggles under the water of the aquarium. Below, a lobster waved its claws at her, a warning to stay away if she knew what was good for her. I noted with some relief it wasn't the size of a baby and thus not the one Jaime mentioned.

"Ser?"

"Sorry, I had a mishap," she said, turning around and squinting at me. She couldn't see a single thing without those goggles. She leaned over and got them over her head, the seals meeting flush with her skin. Now she could look through a layer of seawater and see the world.

"Hiya, Nick," she said with a smile she probably intended to be winsome, but had too many death-teeth to work.

"Hiya, Ser. What happened?"

"Siren problems," she said.

"You're in a good mood."

"It's a lovely day, isn't it?"

"I just missed Billy, didn't I?"

Her gills popped right out of her neck, a sudden crimson collar telling me I'd got it in one. "Um, no."

"Okay," I said, heading into my office.

"You just missed Jaime. Billy left when Jaime came in. Because, you know."

I knew. The only question was whether Jaime made any explicit threats or Billy had decided that he didn't stand a chance against a Knight if he lost his cool.

"Did Jaime have anything to say?"

"He wanted to give you an update. He was wearing the hip waders, but he still doesn't own anything with sleeves."

"One battle at a time, I guess."

"He said he saw the gill-man come out of the mudflat, but it wasn't the pipe we thought he was using. So Jaime's looking for another way in. He thinks he has it narrowed down, but he's not sure. He stuck around for the gill-man to come back."

"Where was he?"

"Grocery store. Came back with everything in watertight plastic, and then went under. Jaime did his best to follow, but couldn't without tipping him that he was being watched. Jaime wanted to go home for fresh socks and batteries for his flashlight. He stopped by to let us know, so now I'm telling you and now everyone knows everything they need to know."

She plopped into her chair. The metal springs groaned.

"Thanks, Ser. Now get out of here."

"Really?"

"I'm staying put until the end of the day. If anyone comes in, I can handle it."

"Thanks, Nick!" She bounced up and was out the door so fast, I was momentarily surprised she didn't leave a Serendipity-shaped hole.

I settled down in my office with the door open, ready to kill some time. I had a paper and a pulp magazine, and a whole lot of nothing on my mind. Not until I talked to Raymond Cole at his after-sunset party.

The phone rang in the late afternoon. I frowned at it, wondering who could possibly have something to say. "Moss Investigations," I said.

"That you, Stick?"

"Yeah, it's me, Mickey. How are you?"

"How am I? How are *you*? You're the one got dragged out of the joint by a zombie. I thought youse was a goner for sure."

"No, they just wanted to hire me to find somebody."

"Hell of a way to hire a fella."

"You're telling me. Say, Mickey, you know anyone by the name of Liling Lam?"

"That a broad? I still got trouble with the Chinese names. Never can tell one way or the other."

"She's a lady, yeah."

"Never heard of her. Sorry. Listen, I just wanted to make sure youse weren't hungry for brains."

"Just egg salad."

Mickey laughed. "Good, good. Well, you wrap this thing up, and you and me will do the town."

"Now you're talking," I told him.

We said our goodbyes. An hour later I got my jacket and was ready to go to Last Night. I could hope the name of the place wasn't prophetic.

TWENTY-TWO

Thursday, December 15, 1955
Forty-five minutes before sundown

Last Night had no sign. Didn't need one either. It was like the old saying from back in the service: at chow time you follow the crowds. Monsters probably had something similar, though no doubt horrifying. I started getting them in ones and twos as I drove into Frogtown, a tiny neighborhood squashed between Elysian Park and the LA River. First a martian, then a couple of vampires under their parasols, then a gremlin flivver coughing through the air and looking like it would plow into Riverdale Avenue at any second, then a family of ghouls walking hand-in-hand up the sidewalk.

I pulled into a space about a block from the end of Riverdale and got out. The monsters coming down the street gave me a once over. I pulled my jacket closer over me, as though that were the problem. I was still armed, but without Mickey and the others it wasn't the same. Now I was just a lone human. Monster bait.

Last Night was a converted warehouse at the very end of the block.

The monsters were gathering around it as I got to the door. A group of gill-men and sirens pulled themselves out of the LA River, regarding me with fishy eyes. I looked away as quick as I could.

The building was a brown box covered in wards and charms. More had been painted onto the surface of the walls. Those looked more like warnings than anything that would actually repel a vampire or witch. Halfway between tribal markings and functional warding.

The woman at the door was six feet tall with a shaved head. Half her face was given over to nasty scars, looking like she'd been practicing dentistry for sharks. She was leaning on a staff-sized cattleprod carved with crosses and wrapped in tape, and I knew instantly she had used it more than once. I wasn't even positive she was a woman until she spoke.

"Human?" she asked me.

"Yeah, of course."

"We'll see."

She waved me inside, and I saw what she meant. A short hallway led into the rest of the club, like the first chamber of a castle where attackers could be corralled. I had to cross every ward there was. Lines of allward, salt, chicken blood (well, I assumed it was chicken), potassium, and sand formed a series of barriers. A collection of holy symbols, evil eye charms, horseshoes, optical illusions, mirrors, ceremonial masks, and the odd gold coin were tacked to the walls. Cages containing cats, roosters, and mice were spaced evenly, the animals apparently quite used to strange people passing them. Torches burned at regular intervals accompanied by clumps of smoking sage, as well as naked wires occasionally sparking with malice. Opera music sounded through the hall, alternating with shrill, discordant notes. Beanstalks, roses, speckled mushrooms, and wolfsbane grew wild and healthy in pots. Bright lights flashed on and off, haloing me, then plunging me into darkness. Spiders worked busily at webs. Feathers hung from the ceiling.

What surprised me was that some of the things present weren't just for fears. They were weaknesses. This place was prepared to kill. Eager for it.

When I got to the end of the hall and the club opened up around me, I saw that was the theme. Medieval weaponry hung on the walls, and loosely, like they were intended to come down. Functional rather than decorative. Some of them had the dull blades of cold iron, others were tarnished silver. I was certain more than a few were regular steel and had been blessed. There were also cattleprods, buckets of water, and more torches. There were more plants than I would have expected in such a scuzzy joint, but they were all the same functional varietals I'd seen in the hallway. Wherever there wasn't a weapon to be used on a monster, there was a symbol or object there to frighten them off. It might have been the most fortified place I'd ever seen.

Not like anything since '53.

The right side of the room was a stage, and there didn't look to be much of a backstage, judging by the band drinking in plain sight while they plugged in their instruments. In front of them was a dance floor, I suppose, but it was just a section of wooden floor worn buttery smooth by feet. Tables were haphazardly scattered around the room with variable numbers of chairs. The bar was on the left side, and if the Last Night was a castle, that was the keep. The bar was heavy oak, and half the bottles were filled with non-liquids I had no doubt were for monsters. The two-handed sword hanging behind it was dinged up with use.

The place was almost entirely full. The air crackled with electricity, and that wasn't from the cattleprods. The people had the bright and filmy eyes of couples in love. They talked too loud. Their movements were jittery. They were waiting for their Last Night.

The man behind the bar was huge. His forearms were the size of my thighs, and I don't think he ever made it through a single door without stooping. His skin was deep brown but almost completely unlined, and his short hair was the color of cold iron. He dressed like a lumberjack, with a checked shirt tucked into blue jeans, and all of it looked like it might explode off of him if he twitched the wrong way. This had to be Raymond Cole.

He went to the inner door and let the bouncer in, then turned to the crowd.

"Ladies and gentlemen, sundown is upon us. Anybody wants to go, now's the time, but you got a gauntlet to run." He waited, but no one moved. "Then these doors are shut until sunup. Time to act like it's your last night on this sweet earth."

A cheer went up from the crowd. Cole and the bouncer shut the door and threw a bar across it like this was a real castle door. A second later, and a howl went up from outside, and the monsters started pounding on the door and walls. I tensed, my hand wanting to go into my jacket for something, but there were too many calls. It was impossible to know what to pull.

Cole smiled. "They keep knockin'. Now go on, enjoy yourselves." He went back behind the bar, while the bouncer leaned against the wall, supremely unconcerned with the monsters outside.

The band started up shortly afterwards. Their music was a bit like some of the stuff the younger phantoms were doing, but it was harder, louder, and far more discordant than anything a phantom could stand. I grew up with Glenn Miller, Perry Como, and Bing Crosby. This was a little tough to take, but the people loved it, doing something that was part dancing, part acrobatics, and part fistfighting. The band had their hair cut short and their clothes were tight. That was an old Night War fashion— harder for monsters to grab what's not there—but they were too young to have done too much fighting in that one. The styles were patchwork too, like what we had in the war, when any item of clothing had to be repaired so much eventually it wasn't the same garment anymore. Holy symbols dripped from their necks, rosaries wrapped their hands like brass knuckles, and every one of them carried at least one weapon.

I turned my attention back to Cole, even as the music hammered at my head. The bar was a press of people all ordering their first drinks of the night. This wasn't a cocktail joint or even beer. No, everything was straight hooch, and poured to the brim. I worked my way to the front, and finally Cole got to me.

"What can I get you, friend?"

"Raymond Cole?" I asked.

"Who's asking?"

"Nick Moss," I said, sliding a card over the bar.

Cole picked it up and squinted at it. "Now I know there's no doggie gets through my wards, but this says you're a dick."

"I'm a detective, yeah. And I'm human."

"What a world we live in." He poured a drink for someone without looking and palmed the cash they slapped on the bar. "Can I get you something, or was you trying to impress?"

"I need to have a quick word with you."

Cole looked up and down the bar. "Tell you what, Moss. You sit over yonder and I'll come on over when it cools off a bit."

He poured me a whiskey that was more liquor than I normally drink in a week and handed it over.

"Okay then."

He nodded and got back to work. I went to the table he indicated. A nearby torch haloed me in light. The blistering heat brought me back to the other night when Sawbones had tried to burn down the Nocturnist. Here, the monsters weren't running. They were trying to get in. And chaos found a home here, too.

The dancing spilled out over the floor. The air blazed with the acrid scent of reefer, and I watched a man against one wall painstakingly prepare a syringe of something before launching it into his arm. People threw drinks back like their insides were on fire and they wanted them to blaze hotter. Others cuddled, petted, necked, and in some cases looked like they were only inches from the big deed. Men with women, but also men with men, and women with women, and in arrangements of twos, threes, and fours. Sometimes a couple or group would get up and head into a back room. People lingered in the doorway, watching the action.

I hadn't seen this kind of abandon since the war. That's what these folks were after. That feeling that we were all about to die, and dying was the happy ending. I was the only one in the joint not enjoying himself—hell, even the bouncer had a drink—so maybe it was me. I didn't mind my existence. Janina was right. I had been sleeping under the Treaty. I wasn't in any kind of underground, but I also wasn't doing this. Truth was, I wasn't doing anything. Was this what was normal? Was this what we were now? Maybe people had changed too much. Maybe I just didn't get humans anymore.

"Now what did you want to ask me, friend?" Cole boomed. I'd watched him get closer; hard to sneak around when you're built like a piece of geography.

"I wanted to talk about someone," I said, motioning to the chair on the other side of the table. I wanted to keep this quiet, but it was impossible to be heard without shouting.

Cole grunted as he sat.

"This place is jumping for a Thursday," I said.

"Jumping every night. Not a lot of jobs in this town for us. Frees up some time for everything else. You, though, you look like you just got back from a funeral."

"Different kind of place. What with the weapons on the walls and the palooka at the door."

"That palooka is my wife."

"Oh!" I said, swallowing. I glanced back at the bouncer. She was watching us, her pale eyes narrowed. "She's very beautiful."

Cole smiled. "She's a hatchet-faced mug. But there ain't no one in the world better to have at your side. I watched her cut the heads off six ogres, one at a time. Chop, chop, chop, chop, chop, chop. One swing each, with that there *zweihander* I got behind the bar. I saw that, thought to myself, 'That's the lady for me.'"

"That's very romantic."

"You damn right. Now I know you didn't come up in here to ask about Darlene."

"No. I wanted to talk about Liling Lam."

Cole watched me like he was using his eyes to strip layers of skin off me one at a time. "Not a name I was expecting on finding in your mouth."

"It's a name you know. Janina Rakoczy said you could help me track her down."

He shook his head. "Nobody can help with that, friend. Nobody."

"Because they don't know or don't want her found?"

"Pick."

"A message then?"

"What kind of message?"

"That card I gave you. If you can get it to her and ask her to contact me."

Cole fished my card out of his breast pocket and looked at it again. "Why do I want to do that?"

I handed him a twenty. That hurt, but this was paying off a debt to a gangster, so I'd handle it. "That's just to pass the message. All she has to do is call me in the office. That's it."

He took the bill and pocketed it with the card. "I'll get the message to her, but whether she calls or not is her business."

"Her business."

He rose from the chair with another grunt. "Long night, friend. Maybe try to enjoy yourself. Drink a little, dance a little, maybe talk to one of these dames or gents who might like a gainfully employed man."

"Maybe I will," I said, knowing I wouldn't.

He knew it too by the way he looked at me. He returned to his place behind the bar. I stayed in my chair, sipping my whiskey and watching the people. Over the course of the night, three women and one man asked me to dance and I told them all the same thing: I had a bum knee, but they should enjoy themselves. I listened to the howling of the monsters outside and wondered which of us were the real crazy ones.

Dumb question. It was the world.

TWENTY-THREE

Tuesday, December 20, 1955
Daytime

I have a canned speech I give to new clients when they want me to find their kid. I tell them nine times out of ten the happy ending is that little Susie likes being a fish girl now. I consoled myself that I wouldn't have to offer something like that to the Rubinowitz family, as David was a fish *boy*. Jaime found the kid, but found him too late. He wanted to give the gill-man a good beating for it, but David had been taken in the nighttime. No law had been broken, and if Jaime had gone after the gill-man, he'd be the one sent to the big house.

That was the job.

Two small gifts nestled under Ser's tree, one for me and one for Jaime. She was still doing her best to win the kid over. He no longer tensed whenever she looked at him, so things were going well. She hated the evil eye ward tattooed on his right shoulder, but she was polite enough not to mention it. I'd caught her shying away whenever he turned that arm toward her. Luckily, he had gotten his first shirts with buttons on them. They were short-sleeved, but I was calling that a victory. Sure, it was winter, but it was also Los Angeles. Jaime had a light jacket.

He was out of the office at the moment. He had been beating himself up over David Rubinowitz since it happened. He still took the losses hard. Sometimes I wished I still took them that way. Eventually he'd get callouses on his soul and he wouldn't worry so much. Wasn't like I could tell him he should be happy about feeling that way. In the meantime, he could work the case we'd gotten, tailing an ogre back to her cave to see if she'd taken Alberto Campos of Monterey Park. I was grateful to the kid. I hated doing that kind of legwork, but he just volunteered for it.

I was at my desk, avoiding filing investigation reports. My door was open, and Serendipity was in the front of the office reading *Look.*

And then I was on a beach. All nice and stretched out in the sun. The light on the water was blinding. I put an ice-cold bottle of Coke to my lips—shame they no longer made that stuff—and listened to the laughter in the water and...

"Ser!" I called. "Are you singing?"

"Sorry," she said, and I was back. Sirens. There was a term they had for that, when they started singing and sent you somewhere else. "Christmas carols. My mother would have guppies if she heard me."

"I bet. They have Dagonist carols?"

"Oh, sure. They're really more like hymns, though. None of them sound right out of water. You need the different acoustics."

"Sounds like something to hear."

"You wouldn't like them. Most humans who hear them call them 'sanity-blasting.'"

"Oh."

"Yeah, I don't know what it is. They're just songs about invoking an ancient power beneath the waves who will one day awaken and consume the world in...okay, I can hear it now."

"What kind of religion is this?"

"Traditional," she said blithely. "At least, that's what my folks say."

I didn't know what to say to that. The phone saved me. Ser picked it up after the first ring and in her best operator voice said, "Moss Investigations."

"Phone call, Nick," she informed me a moment later, transferring it to my line.

I hit the button and picked up. "This is Nick Moss."

"Mr. Moss?" The voice had a faint accent, but I couldn't identify what it was. The vowels were long, the consonants soft. "I understand you wish to talk to me."

"Miss—"

"Do not say my name. If you wish to speak with me, we will do so face to face. Meet me at the La Brea Tar Pits."

"Now?"

"Now, Mr. Moss."

"I'll be there as soon as I can."

I hung up the phone and went into the outer office, grabbing my overcoat off the rack. Unlike Jaime, I liked a little extra, because you never could be sure when the weather would turn on you.

"What's going on?"

"I have a meeting to get to."

"Will you be back?"

"I don't know. Maybe. You can close up at five."

She nodded. "Be safe, Nick."

"As houses."

I drove west into Hancock Park. The La Brea Tar Pits, located right off Wilshire, were the kind of place that made you think that maybe monsters weren't such a new invention after all. They'd been pulling beasts from the sticky black tar ever since there had been a Los Angeles. Before, the goal had been to exhibit them, maybe learn a little about what the earth had been like before humans. Now, the mad scientists had taken over. They were trying to bring those monsters back.

The tar pits were a series of ponds, all shining with a layer of water on top of the tar. You could smell it though, like a thirsty engine running on a summer day. Smaller sinkholes opened up, and more than one pair of pants had been ruined by suddenly dropping an unsuspecting visitor into one.

A machine, looking something like a metal hippopotamus, dipped head-like construction equipment into the main lake and made a sucking sound. Frothing water and tar shot into the device, likely to be sifted, strained, and sorted. Nearby, a mad scientist in a white lab coat cackled. A saber-toothed tiger reclined on the ground next to him like a bored housecat. It looked up at the scientist, blinked a couple times, and thumped back to earth. Cats will be cats, no matter what the era.

A few other structures stood near the mechanical hippo, looking like a military bivouac. A crew of zombies in one of the open tents sorted stained bones, occasionally remarking "Brains" to one another. Two robots patrolled the edges of the park, never stepping off the sidewalks, their death rays a clear threat to anyone who would attempt to horn in on this mad scientist's work. This had to be a plum place for those maniacs.

"Mr. Moss?"

I turned. She had been completely silent in her approach. By this point, I had seen two of the Gobfather's women. No amount of beauty should have stunned me, but the sight of Liling Lam reached right into my lungs and yanked out whatever air I had. Her skin was porcelain, burnished with gold highlights. Her brown eyes were large and flecked with the same tawny gold. She was dressed simply, but she had a dancer's figure, with long legs and elegant curves. Her hair was glossy and black, and reached her shoulders.

"Hrmghv," I said thoughtfully.

"I'm sorry?"

"Yes. Sorry. I'm Nick Moss."

"Liling Lam," she said.

"The Golden Swan."

Her expression turned to stone. "Don't call me that. That was Mab's name for me. It was not something I called myself."

"Sorry. Miss Lam."

She pulled her coat closer around her narrow form. "What did you want to speak to me about, Mr. Moss?"

"I was hired to find you."

She didn't exactly tense. It was more like the opposite. Her body uncoiled, ready to fight or run. Veterans had that reaction to potential danger. Any girl who'd escaped the Gobfather probably had a bit of steel in her. Liling Lam might have more than I had anticipated.

I held my hands out to placate her. "It's what I do. I'm a private detective. Most of my business is missing persons."

"I'm not _missing_," she said. "There's no one looking."

I didn't have to ask to know she didn't have a family. The look in her eyes said it all. I figured I should be honest. If she decided to run, she had about ten years and five inches of leg to outpace me with.

"Do you know the name Sarah Bellum?"

"Of course. Mab hated her. They were in the same business."

"Exactly. She hired me to find you."

"Why?" she asked, but she wasn't quite asking. She had a reason in mind, probably saw it laid out right in front of her.

I said it anyway, just so she knew I was on the level. "Mab's had a lot of girlfriends, but only one who ever escaped. That makes you valuable to someone who might like to bump the Gobfather off."

A smile quirked at her lips. "She said this?"

"I was reading between the lines. She gave me her word that she didn't want to turn or kill you, and before you say it, yeah, I know. Word of a crime boss isn't what you'd call ironclad. The way she said it, it felt like she had something else in mind and turning you never entered her head. Or, you know, brain...tissues."

"You have my attention, Mr. Moss."

"Can I ask you something? How did you escape?"

"It would take a long while to explain, and I don't know how much of it would make sense."

"I assume it wasn't easy."

"No, Mr. Moss, it was not. Sidhe are quite powerful. But I was lucky in one regard. Mab is a creature of habit."

"Oh?"

"Yes. Once Mab left me for the night, I had time to slip out. My absence would not be noticed until after dawn."

I thought of Songbird, fleeing in the dead of night, only to vanish before sunrise. "Can I ask you something else?"

She glanced around, taking note of the position of the two robots, the mad scientist, and the saber-toothed tiger, then gave me a curt nod.

"Do you know anything about Song...about Dulcinea Ramos?"

"One of the girls after me."

"Yes, her."

"I never met her, if that's what you want to know."

"No, I think you two had something in common. She was killed recently."

"I read about it in the papers." Small wonder that she might keep tabs on news about the Gobfather.

"What the papers didn't mention was that she was trying to escape at the time. Like you did."

Liling frowned for the first time, and it vanished just as quickly. She shifted her posture, once again checking where the nearest monsters were. "How do you know?"

"She...I know. Trust me, I know."

"The paper said she was shot. Was that true?"

"As far as I know, yes."

"Mab never would have shot her. We always had more importance than that. Bullet holes would ruin our perfect beauty." She said the last with an angry lilt. Really, "perfect beauty" was the first phrase that even came close to describing her or Dulcinea.

"They arrested someone for it. A human."

"There were those who hated us for what we were. Traitors. There were worse names."

I'd heard a couple of those names on occasion. Mixed marriages weren't common, but they did happen, and no one understood it. It was one thing for different kinds of monsters to pair off and I was sure a mummy and a zombie tying the knot would result in some consternation, but monsters and humans? Like Will Hammond said, we didn't mix. Not in that way.

"Yeah, I know. I wasn't asking about that. I was asking about why she ran. It wasn't the cage. It wasn't the attention. Something happened, and you're the only person on earth who might know what."

Liling swallowed. She was unraveling, just slightly. The porcelain doll façade beginning to spiderweb. "She probably found the Gallery of Angels."

A chill rode those words right up into my spine. "What's that?"

"Mab promises you that you will be turned. That's why we were selected. Our art, our beauty, that was going to be preserved. We would get to be sidhe. The pinnacle of monsterhood. I know what you're thinking. I can see it in your eyes. 'If all the girls are turned, then where are they? Why do they vanish?' I thought the same thing, but only after a time. In the beginning, when Mab takes you in...you're the only one in the world. You don't know what it's like with the sidhe. They're pure spirit. Pure magic."

"Yeah, they're lookers all right."

"It's not that." Color rose into her cheeks, and I swear, my knees wobbled. "It's not *just* that. Yes, the sidhe are more beautiful than any human could ever be, but everything they touch...it's like starlight." She sighed. "You can't understand. Not unless one of them takes you."

"Love?" I asked her.

She shook her head. "I don't think they can. They're missing a piece of their souls. They can't love. Can't make art. They just live."

"And you wanted to be that?"

"I remember the time before the Night War. For a Chinese girl, there weren't many choices."

I coughed. "Right. So what happened? What made you know for certain?"

"I found the Gallery. Mab's former...paramours. All of them preserved in time. Perfect beauty forever."

The chill was back, and it brought friends. I hadn't felt anything like it since I spent that miserable winter in '44 freezing in Belgium. This was targeted, right at the center of what made me human. I didn't want to ask the question bubbling to my lips, but I couldn't stop myself.

"Dead or alive?"

Liling met my eyes. She was utterly flat behind them. She lost a piece of her soul, too, maybe the same one as Mab, and if you looked into her eyes at the right angle, you could see it, broken and jagged.

"These words don't really apply, Mr. Moss."

TWENTY-FOUR

Thursday, December 15, 1955
An hour or so later

eviathans looked like Mother Nature had gotten fed up with people ever venturing into the sea and decided to do something about it. They were a bit like giant whales, though there were definite shark parts, but they also had clumps of tentacles and partial shells. They carried entire schools of fish, coral reefs, and in one case a real functioning island nation on them. There were, supposedly, only seven of them alive at any one time, and if you asked me, that was seven too many. Not that I was advocating genocide or anything, it's just that when the most terrifying parts of the Bible decide to become a reality, well, I'm against it.

I had never seen a leviathan in person. Every now and again, you see them on television. They're the kings and queens of the seas, and act like real, actual monarchs. The one with the island on his back is the only one who has actual human (and monster) subjects who might get hurt if he does something crazy like submerging. The rest of them rule over fish and crabs and so on. Still, they'll give press conferences. *Look* Magazine interviewed King Humboldt (he's the local King of the North Pacific), and Ser couldn't stop talking about the time she'd seen him.

Some wiseguy had decided to build Neptune's Kingdom to look like a leviathan, and the scary thing was it was actually a leviathan in miniature. Two city blocks and this thing was tiny. The entrance was the main mouth, and the rest of the aquarium extended into the different parts—neighborhoods—of the sea monster.

I had called Bellum from a phone booth a few blocks from the Tar Pits while Liling waited close by. With me acting as a go-between, the two agreed on Neptune's Kingdom as a meeting place. Big enough that Liling felt safe, but with all that glass, to say nothing of what was behind the glass, there wouldn't be any shooting from Bellum's men.

I hadn't been to Neptune's Kingdom before. Humans were allowed, but not exactly encouraged. The gill-man who took our tickets stared at the both of us for a long time before letting us in. It's also possible he was falling in love with Liling a little bit. I could hardly blame him for that.

The walls were sculpted with windows into huge aquariums. The ones by the door contained fairly normal fish. There was the explosion of color of a coral reef in one. In another, bright orange fish danced through the reaching stalks of kelp. Dolphins frolicked in still another, while sharks prowled through a great cylinder, never slowing or stopping. As we went further into the aquarium, the collection got stranger and stranger. These were the creations of the mad scientists. Some of them were for use in the Night War, others were just...something a mad scientist made. That was the problem with the first part of the name. Tended to overwhelm the second.

Crabs the size of sedans clattered across a sea floor, while something that looked like a cross between an alligator and a seal but was the size of a city bus swam overhead. A swarm of creatures that looked like spiked barber's poles twirled through another tank, giving off streams of bubbles. Fish who walked on stilts plied another. Then there was a reef that was actually a gigantic fish, only revealing itself when it gulped down a tuna that was swimming by.

Then it got *really* strange. We found de Kay, Mold, and Parrish in a room of swirling blue, viewing glass in the walls and ceiling. The creatures in those looked like nothing I had ever seen before: something like shrimp or lobsters, but lean and aerodynamic, covered in whirring flippers and sharp spines.

The zombies were all nattily dressed, de Kay and Mold in pinstriped suits, Parrish in similar but with a skirt. The bulges under their jackets said all three were armed, though I wondered if it was pistols or cold iron. De Kay's collar let us know the most important person was present.

Liling did not tense when she saw the zombies. It took me a while to spot, probably because I had been mooning over her since we'd met, but Liling was armed, too. Not as much as me, but she had something on her. I was willing to bet she never went anywhere without a supply of speckled mushrooms.

"Brains," said all three of the zombies.

"Mr. Moss," Bellum said, her deep voice crackling from de Kay's speaker. "And Miss Lam. It is a distinct pleasure to meet you."

"Likewise, Miss Bellum."

"How much has Mr. Moss told you?"

A creature I had no word for swam by behind the zombies. Every now and again, I was reminded just how strange the world had gotten.

"He merely said you wished to talk to me."

"I apologize if that caused you undue distress, but I value discretion in my employees."

I squirmed at being referred to so casually as an employee there. I wanted to say I was only there to wipe away a debt no sane person would say I incurred, but I held my tongue.

"Then there is more," Liling said.

"Mab and I are...competitors. While I would much prefer the markets he has cornered, he would rather violence spill over into our streets. This city was better off when I was the only such presence and I would like to return it to that state. I would like to engage Mab in a frank discussion of the future."

"You wish to assassinate him."

"Yes," the speaker crackled.

"Brains," de Kay whispered. He was apparently fond of this plan as well.

"You are the only person who has ever escaped Mab's clutches. You could tell me about his security, and, of course, you will be well compensated for any information you give."

"That might be a problem."

"I can afford to pay you quite a bit."

"That is not quite it. Mab lives on the fourth floor of the Chateau Marmont."

"Yes, I know."

"What you don't know is what the presence of a sidhe has done to it. I can't give you instructions on how to get through it. I would have to lead you. Otherwise, you would be lost. You would never stand a chance."

"Then add a zero to your asking price, Miss Lam. I wish to impress upon you that the amount of money scarcely matters. If Mab is eliminated, my coffers will overflow. Name your price."

She did. I let out a low whistle. I couldn't help it. Bracken Mold caught my eye and nodded, muttering, "Brains."

He wasn't wrong.

"Done," Bellum said.

"Not quite," Liling said.

"Miss Lam, I am not unlimited in my patience or even my generosity."

"I have one stipulation. Mr. Moss has to come along."

"What?" I asked.

"Why?" Bellum asked.

"Brains?" Mold wanted to know.

"I will not go into the Chateau Marmont without another human with me. I don't mean to cause offense, but I can't trust monsters."

"Why him?" Bellum asked.

"He's been honorable in his dealings so far."

"Very well. Mr. Moss?"

"Wait, hang on. You told me to track down a missing girl. I did that. That's my job. But you're talking about..." I dropped my voice, even though the chamber was empty except for a scarecrow staring wistfully through the glass, "...an assassination!"

"We know exactly what we're discussing," Bellum said. "I should also remind you that I'm not talking about an upstanding citizen. I'm not talking about a human. I'm talking about an elf who preys on pretty young humans like no other monster. I'm talking about performing a favor for the people of Los Angeles."

"Miss Bellum—"

"The debt you want to clear, Mr. Moss...if you come, it's discharged. Forgiven. If you don't, we might decide you serve better as a warning to others than an employee in good standing. Am I understood?"

"Uh...yes. Yes, you are."

I was beginning to wonder if I was ever going to be out from under Bellum's thumb. Or nerves, or what have you. She could always declare the debt unpaid, and what was I going to do? The only thing I knew for certain was at the moment, I couldn't say no.

"We'll go on—" Bellum started.

"May I make a suggestion?" Liling asked.

"Of course. That is why you're here."

"The 25th is a sidhe holiday."

"Christmas?" I asked.

"Close enough. If there is a day Mab will not be ready, it is that one."

"Very well then. Christmas Day."

Twenty-Five

Christmas Day, 1955
After presents, before caroling

For a swanky place like the Chateau Marmont, the service elevator wasn't much to look at. An oblong box with tire stains on the linoleum floor and cheap wood paneling sent a message no zombie would miss: nobody who will see this matters, so it can look like hell. This group was the kind of riffraff the management would have thrown out on the streets had they been the wiser. Zombies, even hotel staff and gangsters, had a sense of solidarity with each other, bolstered with some sawbucks pressed from one rotting hand to another.

I rode up in the service elevator with Liling Lam and the six zombies chaperoning us on the world's worst date. Liling had told me to wear my overcoat for some reason, and I was already sweating inside it. I carried my normal arsenal inside my jacket, along with some extra mushrooms. When you know your opponent, it's a good idea to prepare in advance.

The zombies had done the same. All of them had cold iron daggers clutched in their unfeeling hands, except for Parrish, who carried a pair of hatchets. Liling had insisted on a dagger of her own, and though Bellum didn't bother to hide the amusement in her voice, she had given her one. It was the smallest of the bunch, barely worth the name, but I imagined it would get the job done if she stuck it in the right spot.

Liling shifted from foot to foot, her knuckles white around the dagger. She was dressed all in white, sweater, pants, boots, and overcoat. She stood out against the rest of us in our pinstripes, grays, olive greens, and navy blues. I was going to have to keep an eye on her. I was the combat veteran here, after all. I'd fought and I'd killed. The zombies were the same, but I'd be lying if I said I cared one way or the other for them. Liling would not have been there had I not found her and she'd wanted me along as a bodyguard, so I was going to do it.

She had gotten us through the back of the Chateau Marmont, though the kitchen. Like most hotels, the staff was almost entirely ghosts and zombies. Monsters had a hierarchy. Made being turned into something like a sidhe that much more attractive. I understood maybe a bit of what Liling had meant when she told me about her seduction, but the truth was, I didn't even want that. I wanted to stay as I was. Wasn't much to look at, maybe, but it was me. I wanted to know the weasel in the mirror.

We got to the service elevator without incident and hit the button for the fourth floor. The zombies muttered "Brains" at one another, and I could only imagine that was them reiterating the plan. Or it was a compulsion. De Kay wore his collar and speaker, but Bellum was silent, at least for the time being. I wondered if a brainiac could wait with bated breath, seeing as they didn't have lungs. They liked to portray themselves as pure reason, but Bellum had shown a capacity for anger and spite. I could imagine she was looking forward to Mab doing his best impression of Julius Caesar.

The doors opened and a frigid draft rushed into the box. This was because the doors didn't open into a hotel's hallway. It opened into a forest covered in a fresh blanket of snow. Some of the trees were bare and clawlike, others were evergreen. They reached into a sky at twilight, one that looked close enough to touch. Iridescent petals fell from the sky from no clear source. When they touched the snow, they vanished into nothing. The forest was alive, too. Shapes moved in the shadows beyond clear vision. Stags with giant racks of antlers, white owls flapping silently through the boughs. Other shapes too, lean and predatory.

"Brains!" Mold exclaimed.

"You said it," I muttered.

"This is why I told you to wear a coat," Liling said, stepping out onto the snow. It was soft and fluffy, like no real snow ever could be, but colder than a devil's heart.

We followed her out of the elevator. The forest was dense, with only slight gaps bridged by impassably thick thorny brambles. There was no path I could see. Liling moved toward what looked like a solid wall of wood and frigid rock.

"This way."

"Brains," whispered de Kay.

"He's right," I told her. "There's no passage there."

"This is why you needed me," she said as she stepped between the trees and vanished.

I ran to where she was, feeling my eyes bugging out of my head. Liling stepped back into view.

"See?"

She showed us that the trees only looked flush next to each other. It took an act of faith to step between them, but once I did, the way was clear.

"The sidhe have a way of beguiling you," she said.

"Brains," Parrish said, twirling one hatchet in her bony hand.

"Where are we going?" I asked.

Liling pointed to a smudge of light against the horizon. "There."

"Looks far off."

"Then we should walk quickly."

"You sound like my C.O.," I mumbled.

I hadn't been in many forests over my life, and most of those were in Europe, and usually in the process of exploding all around me. So I didn't have the best frame of reference. Far as I was concerned, a proper forest should be in the middle of a kraut artillery barrage. All I knew about this one was that it looked staged. Like if I could walk behind the trees, I'd find a wall painted with shadows of trees like the wall of the Nocturnist, lights, and some zombie stagehands boredly telling each other "Brains." But the longer I walked through the winter chill, through the constantly falling petals, the more I was realizing that this place, despite the blatant artifice, was real.

The sky never changed, hanging right at the verge of sunset. The terrain was uneven, though there was almost always a clear path Liling led us along. Occasionally, it would fork and branch, but she never hesitated to pick the route. It gave me some confidence in where we were going. Of course, it was equally possible she was entirely lost and didn't want to let a contingent of zombie gangsters know.

A frozen river ran from our right down into a valley. A valley, on the fourth floor of a hotel in Hollywood. Best not think about it too closely. Or the fact that there were fish in the river, frozen solid in the ice.

I sidled up next to her, and murmured, "You know where you're going, right?"

"Of course."

"Great. How?"

"If I did not, then I never would have escaped at all."

A hooting wail echoed through the woods.

"What's that?" I asked, trying not to betray my nervousness.

"I don't know. There are *things* out there. You will only ever see them in the distance. Their shadows or their tracks."

"So they don't get close. That's good."

"Or they kill all of those they get close to."

The ululation came again. I shuddered. "You're not much of a people person, are you, Miss Lam?"

"I am a person!" she said, eyes flashing.

"It's...that's not what I was saying."

She crossed the river easily, like a deer over the slick rocks poking out of the ice. I followed her and quickly learned that she only made it *look* easy. I jumped onto a rock, teetered, wobbled, and caught myself. Then repeated it three times before making it to the other side. That was when I realized that the zombies weren't going to do as well as I did.

They ignored the rocks, crossing the jagged ice of the river. The water had frozen mid-rapid, in the blink of an eye. Like the breath of winter had hit the land all at once. Cresting waves and eddies were now blades, shredding the pantlegs and ankles of the zombies. They didn't feel a thing, but on the other side, Mold looked down at his ruined suit, and complained.

"Brains," he said.

"Brains," Parrish responded, yanking her hatchets out of her belt, where she'd tucked them for the crossing.

"Brains," de Kay told the two of them, and they nodded sheepishly.

What just happened? I wanted to ask them, but I didn't. I already knew what they'd tell me.

The other three zombies, who I'm certain could be introduced to me as Brains, Brains, and Brains, made it across the water and the eight of us continued our trek. Liling led us up a short, rocky rise on the bank of the river and up into a wider section of woods. That might have been the first time I felt despair.

The paths opened up like the tentacles of an octopus, every one of them sticky with gloom. As I was looking from path to path, wondering which Liling would direct us to, I noticed her attention wasn't on them. She was staring into the treeline above us. At owls. Hundreds of owls. They perched on the grasping branches, so thick they looked at first like lumps of snow. Then one would ruffle its feathers, blink its big, liquid eyes, or turn its head like it was on casters, and it would be revealed as a living creature. And like a ripple, those around it, those around the next, and the next, until it was more birds than I had ever seen, more owls than I thought existed in the world.

Watching us.

"Mab knows we're here," Liling whispered.

"Maybe we should come back later?" I ventured.

It sounded like someone was chopping wood, but the rhythm was all wrong. A single chop, then a long pause, then one on the heels of another too quickly for a good swing. Close too. I turned, confused rather than afraid.

An arrow stuck out of Brains One's chest, then another sprouted from his neck and then a third from his skull. It was the third one that sent him falling. He did it slowly, collapsing into the cottony snow over the course of three or four days. The world took its sweet time. Everything slowed to a crawl and you got to watch, in grotesque detail, your buddies getting chewed to bits by kraut machine guns.

I turned again, too slow, and arrows sprouted from the zombies like beanstalks. Parrish raised an arm to block her head, and got two arrows sticking from her forearm for her trouble. An arrow stuck from de Kay's chest, and I watched another spark as it broke and bounced off his steel collar. It left a black smear behind as it went: the arrowheads had been rubbed in poison.

The goblins surfaced, snow falling off them like sand. They held bows, crossbows, blowguns, and slingshots. All filled the air with missiles. It was not the first time I had been utterly convinced I was a dead man, but there was not much to dissuade me from the impression. Not with poisoned death raining all around. I regretted that I'd pulled Liling into all of this, that she had escaped once and had been lured back only to become a pincushion for the goblins.

I felt myself moving, but it wasn't my idea. I had been yanked nearly off the ground, and spun away from the falling arrows. Impacts ran through whatever had me, and up into my body. Then I was tumbling down a snowy slope, every impact throwing white puffs into the air. I didn't know how long I fell. Could have been half a second, might have been years. I kept rolling and rolling until I stopped, opening my eyes. Above me, a few branches scratched at the twilight.

"Brains," moaned Mold.

He hauled me to my feet. Arrows stuck out all over his body, though none from his head. The felt of his fedora had been nicked away in places, revealing the steel underneath. Bet he was grateful for that.

"Brains," Mold insisted, pointing up to the ridge we had tumbled from.

Goblins crested it like a greasy wave. Goblins I knew. Flux, Murk, and Sawbones, all armed with outdated weaponry, and they had seen us. I could go for my pistol, but I had no idea what silver bullets were going to do to goblins. Now wasn't the time to find out, with arrows thudding into the trees around us.

"Brains!" Mold shouted, grabbing me and shoving me down the path.

It wasn't any closer to the center, but we had no choice. We were just going to have to flee and hope for the best.

Twenty-Six

Christmas Day
Seconds later

I could have shaved with the last arrow. It went right past my cheek and buried itself into the snow ahead of me. I hopped over it and continued, while the arrows sliced the air around me to ribbons.

Mold was not fast. That was the worst part of zombies. He shambled, which meant he fell forward and depended on his legs to catch him. It also meant he moved at a relatively constant pace. I kept him between me and the arrows—at his insistence, assuming I understood what "Brains" meant in that context—but I wanted to haul him forward. I wanted to throw him into a wheelbarrow, really. We could have gotten a good clip going.

Fortunately, the goblins weren't doing too much better. Flux was the tallest at four feet, and Sawbones could not have been an inch over three. So what was knee-deep snow for Mold and me was a waist-deep hazard for the goblins. Alone, I might have been able to leave them in the dust, but with Mold, the best we could do was keep barely ahead of them.

My breath was a constant fog in front of my face while my lungs burned with every frigid gasp. The path snaked around in loops, occasionally branching out around us. There wasn't much I could do within sight of the goblins. I needed to get far enough ahead of them, and then there might be a chance.

"Mold," I gasped.

"Brains?" he said. His voice was distorted since an arrow had torn through his neck. It dripped poison and zombie pus down the front of his suit.

"I need you to move faster."

"Brains."

"I know. But we have to lose these fellas or we're done for. Eventually one of them is going to get lucky and either knock that steel lid off your head or sneak in underneath it."

"Brains," he sighed.

"Yeah, so you need to speed up, dead man."

"Brains!"

Fire sparked in Mold's milky eyes, and he gave it the old college try. He didn't move his legs so much as he tipped himself over even further. He was pretty much just falling now, his limbs flailing to keep up. It would have been funny if there weren't still poisoned arrows falling from the sky. I put on another burst of speed. Back in the service, it wouldn't have been a problem. I'd run Currahee Mountain every goddamn day in Basic, and sometimes twice. But this was thirteen years and a thousand doughnuts later.

I'd be damned if a zombie was going to outrun me, though.

The terrain had leveled out somewhat, and paths either climbed up and over rises, or dipped into small dells and even valleys. I picked the lower path whenever there was an option; I didn't want to get silhouetted over a rise and give the hobs a nice fat target. Mold could get hit all he wanted, what with his blood no longer flowing, but I was betting the poison would put an end to me.

The arrows, or lessening thereof, were my first warning. They receded behind me first, no longer falling around me and into Mold, but into the path behind us. Then the sounds of the impacts against trees and rocks grew faint. Then they stopped altogether, the goblins likely hoarding their ammo until they had another clean shot. I risked a glance behind us right after a turn, and the goblins were well out of sight. There were two paths, one rocky one going up and over a rise, the kind of path I'd been studiously avoiding. Then there was a path going into a low area, covered in snow and shaded by trees.

Mold headed for the low path, but I caught him.

"Wait," I said.

I didn't have a lot of time. The goblins would be moving even faster now that they were no longer trying to air out our insides. I grabbed a rock from the higher path and bowled it down the low path, tearing up the fresh snow as it went.

"Come on," I said to Mold, and ran up the rocky path.

As I reached the top, I could hear the goblins rhyming at each other as they closed in. I won't repeat what they said, but it must be harder to rhyme the word "hunt" than I thought.

Mold struggled with the slope. He couldn't fall upward, no matter how hard he tried. I grabbed him by the lapel and hauled up upward, nearly throwing him bodily up and over the slope. I followed him right as Flux appeared around the bend.

I froze staring up at the icicles hanging from the trees like wind chimes. The earth might as well have been a block of ice, but I stayed there, back against it, completely motionless.

Man and zombie will not escape,
the path is bare.
I'll wear their skin as a cape,
the tracks are there.

I listened as the goblins went down the false trail, then turned to Mold, who was leaning against a tree nearby. I shot him a grin. He smiled back.

I got to my feet and went down the slope. We needed to move for a bit before we could rest. I needed one. My legs were rubbery and my lungs freezer-burned. Mold looked like a porcupine, and kept catching the ends of arrows on trees. I was going to have to pluck him like a chicken if we were going to keep up any kind of respectable speed.

We made it past several trail intersections, and this time I alternated going up and down, while trying to keep going in the general direction Liling had shown me was our eventual destination.

Liling. I had lost sight of her as soon as the arrows started falling. If anyone could have gotten out of there, it was her. She was the only one who had, after all. I hoped she'd made it back to the elevator and gotten free. Otherwise, she was yet another woman who had depended on me and gotten nothing but pain in return.

Eventually, Mold said "Brains," and put a hand on my shoulder. He pointed to a rock.

"You're right," I said, and sat.

Mold tried to sit, and only then realized he had several arrows in his legs. He tore them out one by one, casting them into the snow with contempt. The last one he held up, noting the black goo dripping from the arrowhead. "Brains," he said.

"Poison," I confirmed. "Thanks."

"Brains," Mold said, turning his attention to the arrows sticking from his body.

"You move pretty fast," I told him. "Were you in the service?"

"Brains," he said as an arrow snapped off in his hands. The arrowhead was still buried inside him. He shrugged and moved to the next one. "Brains?"

"Army. Airborne. I was in Europe."

"Brains."

I settled back on the rock, catching my breath as I huddled in my coat. Mold continued the task of making himself look less like a rotting pincushion. I owed the fella my life. That was going to be a hard debt to repay. Even harder to come to terms with. Bellum was the one who forced me into this place, but Mold had saved my hide.

"Brains?" Mold asked.

"Get to that light Miss Lam said we were looking for, I guess."

"Brains."

"Who knows?" Wouldn't break my heart if a bunch of dead gangsters got the push off, but Liling...I wasn't ready to consider that. Not yet.

"Brains."

"Yeah, we...hush." I cocked my head to listen, then dropped off the rock and rolled. An arrow hit the stone where I had been sitting and broke in half.

The goblins emerged from around a bend.

"Intruders, we have you cold," said Flux. "You'll die for being so bold."

A volley of arrows arced from them, two hitting Mold and the third perforating the ground next to me. Mold turned around, and I swear he looked frustrated with two new arrows sticking out of him right after he'd just been plucked. He began to shamble, and a second later I was on my feet and running.

"How many arrows do they *have*?" I muttered.

"Brains," he said.

We ran. This time, there was less hope. Before, we were trying to get away. The goblins had shown us that wasn't going to be possible. They knew this maze. We didn't. They could hunt us at their leisure, and they only had to get lucky. I pulled the vial of mushrooms from my jacket. I dropped one in the path as I ran.

Murk yelped as he saw it. "Mushroom! Er...it makes my heart go foom?"

"Many forks has the path! Block one and you feel our wrath!" Flux called.

The goblins vanished, and I thought it was bravado until the three of them emerged from our left a few minutes later, unleashing a sheet of arrows that nearly claimed us.

"Nowhere to run, nowhere to hide, I'll eat your organs fried!" Flux told me.

Charming.

I grabbed Mold and yanked him down the path as the arrows thudded into him. Still, none of them had found the tiny bit of brain between his hat and his neck, though they were getting a lot closer. I tried the mushroom trick several more times, but it never worked. Block the rear, and they came around the side. Block the sides, and they were ahead of us. The only way would be to surround ourselves, and then they could take us apart with arrows. And besides, I had extra mushrooms with me, but not an infinite supply.

"We have to do something," I said to Mold as we staggered through the snow.

"Brains."

"I don't know. We can't fight them if they stay away with their bows."

Mold glanced behind us. "Brains?"

"No. If you charge, they have a clean shot at your eyes. They only have to get lucky once, and by my count, they're due. Once you close, that's when Sawbones lights you up, Flux dissolves you, or Murk finally reveals whatever magic trick he can pull out of his snout."

"Brains."

"Yeah, well, I been in worse situations."

"Brains?"

"I can't think of them right now."

"Brains."

"Run faster."

He listened to me, as well as he could. We ran because we had no other options. We could only put distance between us and them. I kept my eyes open as we ran, hoping for something, anything to turn the tables on our pursuers. While I would have liked a Sherman tank, or better yet a kraut Tiger, I'd have gone for nearly anything. I found it in the form of a cave.

We had just turned a corner, and the path opened into a small clearing. The cave was nearly hidden against the slope, the black opening partly hidden by drifts of snow and freezing gray rocks. It was easy to miss, but I had to hope the goblins' knowledge of this place would work against them.

I shoved Mold into the snow and he fell back with a puff. He fought to rise, rage flashing through his milky eyes.

"Shh!" I told him. "Hide under the snow."

"Brains," he muttered dubiously, but started to push the snow around him. I ran to the cave, then backtracked, carefully putting my feet in the footsteps I'd left in the snow. Now there was a clean track right to the mouth of the cave.

Then I wrapped myself in my coat and burrowed into the fluffy snow.

The goblins stepped into the clearing seconds after I was hidden. It wasn't the best job, and most of my face was uncovered, but any subsequent movement was going to pull their attention right to me. So I had to stay as still as I could while the chill seeped into my bones and the three goblins, arrows nocked on bowstrings, stalked into view. Flux was in the lead, his evil face set in its customary grimace. Sawbones was next, wheezing through his gas mask. Murk was last, huffing and puffing. They paused, and Murk put his hands on his knees as he caught his breath.

Flux swept the clearing with his black gaze.

"You think we're going to catch them soon?" Murk asked, too tired to even beat himself up for not rhyming.

Sawbones rhymed testily at the piggish goblin:

> *Foolish goblin, you're to blame*
> *For lack of breath, for endless girth.*
> *You're the Gobfather's secret shame*
> *As you waddle upon his cursed earth.*
> *Meatstick and corpse, trapped in our maze*
> *Cannot conceal their heavy tread.*
> *They beg for my angry blaze*
> *And with jam we'll eat their bones like bread.*

Murk scuffed the snow with his foot.

Flux, though, scarcely noticed. He had spotted the bait. Whether or not he was going to take it was another matter. He glanced from cave mouth to the end of the trail I left him, where I was hidden, and not very well. I didn't know how long I could remain there, either. Not with the snow doing its best to turn me into an icicle. I had thought Bastogne was as worse as it ever got, dug into a foxhole in the dead of Belgian winter with only a coat to protect me. And I was one of the luckier ones: lot of the fellas didn't have much more than their uniforms to keep the frost at bay. It was the one time I was positive that if there was a God—and I had my doubts even before the monsters rose—He knew of me and wanted me to suffer. Personally.

But all that time, I'd had snow falling on top of me. I wasn't burrowed into it...well, like a rabbit hiding from a fox. I wished I hadn't come up with that particular comparison. It was exactly right. Only there were three foxes, they were armed with poison arrows, they all had deadly magic tricks, and worst of all, a compulsion for bad poetry.

"Hark, see yonder trail?" Flux whispered to his men. "Frightened tracks betray the tale."

Sawbones nodded. He was carrying a complex-looking crossbow, and he began to crank a lever, drawing the string back. His glassy lenses remained focused on the cave mouth as he placed an arrow on the device.

"Huh?" Murk asked, squinting at the clearing. "What are we looking at?"

Goblin, goblin—

Flux cut Sawbones off with a raised fist. He was intent on the path, though whether it was the cave mouth or the apparent origin of the steps, where I was buried, was impossible to tell. Was it too much to hope that goblins had real eyes, rather than those wet, black orbs? Crawling eyes had perfectly nice eyes. Well, *were* perfectly nice eyes. And three feet across. Of course, there's no way I could have hoped to fool a crawling eye with this ruse. They'd spot it in a second.

Flux stepped closer. I wanted his steps to crunch on the snow, but they didn't. They moved it aside soundlessly, another layer of phoniness that made the whole place surreal, like a dream. Sawbones followed, sweeping his head back and forth, the crossbow held steady. Murk waddled forward, and when he was partway into the clearing, he gasped and pointed at the tracks. He nearly said something, but Flux held his hand up and the pig-goblin went silent.

Three arrows. One would be enough, especially at this range, when I was making the best target in the world. I had to keep quiet, which wasn't a problem. I had to keep still, and there I was running into some difficulties. My body wanted to shiver, needed to shiver. I had every muscle tied in knots, and they were beginning to swell and burn. No matter what happened, if I turned into a mass of charley horses, this plan wasn't going to work.

The goblins got closer. Close enough that I could see the black poison dripping from the scarred tips of their arrows. Flux paused at the line of tracks. Fifty-fifty. Either he went for the cave, or he found me. My face was there to be seen, amongst a few rocks and brambles pushing up through the snow. Nothing to see here, hob. Move along.

Flux turned to the cave, trotting quickly to the opening.

"Inside, brothers, and catch our quarry, with arrows, venom, and acid we harry."

Flux disappeared inside, followed by Sawbones. Murk paused at the entrance. *Go. Move,* I thought at him. *Go into the cave.*

Murk squinted, his piggy snout twitching. *Could he smell me from there?* I waited. Waited for him to catch my scent and call the others back. They'd have me in a second then. Murk could probably do it himself, and then Mold would be dead. Mold, who saved my life even when he hadn't had to. Who I forced into this stupid plan because I thought we had no other options. We should have run. Kept running. Longer legs and zombie endurance. We could have gotten away. Give us a long enough race, and we'd have done it.

Murk chewed his lip.

"Outside passing gas?" Flux demanded, his voice echoing from the inside. "Move your spacious ass!"

Murk squinted.

Listen to him, Murk. Just go. I started wondering if I could make it there and get the dagger through his heart before he brought me down with an arrow. Charging, I'd be the perfect target. And there was the matter of my cramping body. Maybe when I'd first hidden I had a shot. Not now. Definitely not now.

Finally, Murk shrugged and ducked into the cave.

I burst out of the snow. Mold struggled to free himself. I couldn't imagine what the cold had done to his dead joints. For all I know, he had spent the time freezing solid. I staggered to the front of the cave. My legs were stiffer than Mold's had been, and moving them was agony, but I did it anyway.

"Brains!" Mold called, pointing up the trail.

"Not yet," I told him.

I sprinkled out the last of my mushrooms, making a nice line along the edge of the cave.

Then I threw myself flat. I might have heard a faint whistle, or seen a gleam against an arrowhead, or just knew what to expect. Didn't matter. I kissed the earth. Three arrows whizzed overhead, disappearing into the fluffy snow. I rolled aside to the edge of the cave, and when the next volley came, it was purely rage.

"Meatstick, what have you done? Trapped us in a web you've spun!" Flux shouted.

"Enjoy the cave, boys," I said, trying to keep the shivering from my voice. "I'm sure you'll get out eventually."

The goblins kept up their howling. Two of them managed to do it in rhyme.

I got up and dusted myself off. The snow wasn't wet, I found with some relief. Freezing, sure, but not wet. It hadn't melted and got into my clothes. That was the real killer. So I was going to warm up, given some time.

"Brains!" said Mold, clapping me on the back.

"Yeah. Mold and Moss, what a team, right?"

Twenty-Seven

Christmas Day
Some time later

The essential problem with mazes is right there in the name. You have a goal in mind; in this case, it was the light on the hillside. Heading directly toward it was possible, but pretty soon the path would be looping away, backtracking, and going in pointless circles. "Toward" didn't mean much in a maze. That was the whole point.

Not that I'd known I was in a maze when I agreed to this cockamamie mission. I thought I'd be going into a suite of rooms. Liling would point at the right one, and the zombies would go in there and poke a couple new holes in the Gobfather. I thought, absolute strangest thing I'd see was maybe the Gobfather's stag had a room of his own. Bed, maybe. Doe pinup on the wall. Whatever it was they liked for mints on the pillow. Instead, I got this forest that shouldn't exist.

Bellum had shanghaied me but good. She wasn't risking a thing. Sure, she sent in her favorite zombies, but I had to imagine to her they were as replaceable as hankies. Certainly the two humans she sent along with them were. Or more to the point, she wouldn't even care enough to replace us if we bought the farm.

I clung to the thought of Liling backtracking her way out of this place. I couldn't think of the alternative, that she was pincushioned with goblin arrows, or worse, taken prisoner again. If I fell into those thoughts, I didn't think I'd have the strength to move.

I wasn't certain how long Mold and I had been walking. It never went from dusk to full night, though. I started wondering if time was moving outside, or if the Gobfather was that strong. The existence of this place said he was plenty powerful. Whether it was a portal to somewhere else or he had transformed the fourth floor of the Chateau Marmont into this, it was a level of power I wasn't comfortable dwelling on. Knowing that sidhe were among the most powerful monsters was one thing, but finding out the extent? When you were already under that power? Well, that was something else entirely.

Mold didn't have much to say on the subject. You can probably guess his take.

The petals kept falling from the sky, though what they were was a mystery. They caught the light on occasion, exploding into scintillating color, then would tumble, and were as insubstantial as smoke. They were like crystal, if it was only fleetingly in solid form. Catch one, and it dissolved. Let it fall, and it joined the piles of white we waded through.

The pathways, which had been narrow, snaking trails between impassable rocks and forest, stopped at a rise. It could have been a mound of snow for all I knew, collected by whatever forces worked in this place. No trees grew from the top, and the surface was entirely smooth with no rocks poking up like islands. It was different, though, and I was of the opinion that in this situation, different was good.

I glanced over at Mold. "Brains," he said with a resigned shrug.

I trudged forward, expecting the ground to stay flat. If it was solid snow, I could let Mold try to make it through, assuming he was game. We didn't have to. The ground rose, and soon we were both hiking up the steep slope. It was only about three times the height of a man, so at least it wasn't that long of a hike. What we saw at the top stopped me in my tracks.

The ridge formed a ring, broken in two places. Behind us, the mazelike forest stretched out into infinity. Ahead, more forest, but broken by a lake that shone like crystal. Inside the ring, forming a concentric circle, were statues mounted on stone platforms. Only I already knew they weren't exactly statues.

The shapes were of beautiful women, all of them of the same rarefied perfection of Dulcinea or Liling, and of every race of person I could imagine. The clothes stretched back through the ages, from gowns to togas, and in one case entirely in her birthday suit. Each one caught in a pose of art: painting at an easel, singing with hands clasped, writing longhand at a desk, frozen in the middle of a dance. They were in the cleanly explored lines of the kinds of statues you only saw in museums, but they were partly transparent, as though made of glass, or possibly ice.

This was the Gallery of Angels. The place Liling and probably Dulcinea found when they realized they'd never be turned. How many others had done the same thing? The clothes implied this stretched long into the past, but who knew? Could have been how Mab dressed them before...this. Whatever it was he did.

These weren't statues. These were the remains of real, living girls. He'd killed them for some art gallery. I was shaking now, and it wasn't the cold. I turned to Mold, hoping he hadn't seen me, but he was staring at the clearing.

"Brains," he whispered in horror.

He'd gotten it too. He understood, and was stunned with the rampant cruelty on display. I hadn't expected a monster, much less a gangster, to care about this, but he did. Mold had already proven he was a cut above most monsters or gangsters. This was just more evidence in his favor.

I picked my way down the slope. There was no choice in it for me; I had to see this place for what it was. See what Mab had done. Maybe to get my blood up for the inevitable showdown. Maybe I needed to see what was on the table. I couldn't imagine what Liling or Dulcinea had felt when they found this place. I saw horror, sure. They saw betrayal.

They had fantasized about living the rest of their lives—maybe forever—as inhumanly gorgeous magical beings. Then one day they saw all the other girls who heard the same promise. Now, all dead.

Or I hoped dead.

Now I really was shuddering, but it was revulsion and fear more than anger. To hope all these women were dead, for that to be the happiest ending available, well, I wanted to collapse right there. I'd seen some pretty terrible things the krauts had done, but the silver lining there was, I only saw them because the krauts were losing. We had them beat. Evil popped out of its cage and we soundly kicked its head in.

Then the Night War happened and I got to learn that evil got a lot weirder. As bad as things were, there were some monsters who weren't so bad. And maybe I'd gotten used to that. I'd forgotten there were a lot of monsters worth the name. No matter how pretty Titanio Mab was on the outside, and he was plenty pretty, he was uglier than sin on the inside.

Mold followed me down the slope, gazing at the statues as he went. It was easy to be lost in their beauty, unearthly in their material but the epitome of earthiness in their form. Easy to appreciate them as nothing but statues. I knew, and don't ask me how, but I knew, that was how Mab thought of them. Even before he transformed them. They were potential art. Ready to be preserved.

A new admiration for Liling and Dulcinea struck me. The kind of bravery it took to run was staggering. Dulcinea had tried it one way and she'd failed. Liling had succeeded. Another twinge of guilt twisted in my belly. I'd brought her here. Maybe got her killed.

A petal landed in my hand. For a second, it was a tiny rose every color of the rainbow. Then it vanished.

"Mr. Moss?"

I turned, my hand going for my dagger. Liling stood at the crest of another slope. Wrapped in white, she looked born to this place. Relief washed over me.

"Miss Lam!"

I waved her over. A moment later, de Kay and Parrish crested the slope behind her and followed her into the Gallery of Angels. The three zombies moaned "Brains" at each other, which was probably them getting caught up on business. I liked Mold just fine, but it was nice to talk to someone who had more in the way of a vocabulary. And if I'm being honest, it was nice to talk to someone who looked like Liling.

"Are you okay?" I asked.

"Yes. Goblins are tenacious," she said.

"Where are the others?"

"We got separated. When the goblins ambushed us, I ran, and these two ended up with me. How did you survive?"

"Same," I said.

She nodded. "We should count ourselves lucky."

I wanted to gripe about her loose definition of the word, but she was right. Three dead after this fiasco was a small price to pay. Mab felt like a god, and here we were invading Eden.

"So how about we turn around? Let's go back through the forest. Get to the elevator."

"Mr. Moss, what about this place makes you think it conforms to that kind of logic?"

"Um...nothing?"

"We are already inside the maze. Were we to turn back, we would only wander until we starved to death."

"The goblins might kill us first," I said, just to get a point in.

"They might kill *you*," she said. "Mab has another fate in mind for me."

The guilt hit me like a physical blow. I didn't understand what she had at stake until I saw the Gallery for myself. Now I knew. She was risking a kind of horror I couldn't even understand.

"So what do we do?" I asked.

"The only way out is to get there," she said, pointing at the light on the hillside. We were closer, and a vague shape had resolved itself against the backdrop of snow and trees. A house, maybe, blazing with firelight.

"You said Mab knew we were here. Won't he be waiting for us there?"

"Undoubtedly. His realm, his rules."

"That's not filling me with confidence."

"I was not put on this earth to give you confidence, Mr. Moss."

She left me sputtering in the snow, moving across the Gallery toward the exit on the far side. The zombies fell in behind her, one by one. Mold was fifteen feet away when he paused, turning to me.

"Brains?"

"Yeah, probably," I told him.

He nodded, and the two of us followed Liling for the end of the maze. Sometimes the only choice the world gave you was a bad one. Liling was far too young to have absorbed that lesson, but it felt like she'd gotten it more thoroughly than I ever could.

Twenty-Eight

Christmas Day
A little while later

"Mirror Lake," Liling said, gesturing at the lake I'd glimpsed from the top of the slope.

It was a good name for the place. The water was like a literal mirror, cut out irregularly and laid flat. Not a single eddy, not the slightest bit of movement. The whole thing was roughly hourglass-shaped, a single arching bridge spanning the pinched middle of the lake. "Pinched" was a relative term, too. The bridge looked to be about half a football field from end to end.

Nothing marked the lake, but I knew enough of this place to be certain there was something beneath that calm surface. Something mean.

"So, what, we go around?"

It looked clear enough, with a wide path going around the shore. The forest opened up in a few places, leading back into the maze of trees. A stone wall poked from the brambles on the far side. I felt a little relief, what with something man-, or rather *sidhe*-made, instead of trees. It also meant Mab was closer.

"Going around won't work," Liling said.

"What happens?"

"You go around and around and never get anywhere."

"That's...confusing."

"That's this place."

"Yeah, I'm beginning to get that."

"If we wish to progress, we have to cross the bridge."

"Brains," de Kay whispered.

"Brains," Parrish agreed.

"Yeah, it doesn't look that hard," I said.

"It is more dangerous than it looks. Mirror Lake feeds on the people that cross it. If you look down, you'll be caught by your own beauty. You'll never move again."

I snorted. "Look at me. Look at them. I don't think it's going to be a problem."

"It doesn't matter what you look like. You could be the most hideous creature ever imagined, and the lake will show you beauty you have never seen. You will be ensnared. Just don't look down."

She was serious, and I understood her trepidation. If I looked like her, I'd probably spend a lot of time with mirrors.

I glanced at the zombies. "Everyone got that? No one looks down."

"Brains."

"Brains."

"Brains?"

"You neither, Mold."

"Brains."

I looked to Liling. "Lead on."

She gave me a dubious look, but nodded, leading the way to the bridge. It was a deep brownish red, looking a bit like cherry wood, a graceful arch over the lake. The surface of the wood was unmarked, as though this bridge had been erected yesterday, and carved by a craftsman who spent a good thirty years doing nothing but building really pretty bridges to span frozen lakes in elf-controlled worlds. Poles spaced out regularly held lanterns, and these glowed so softly they weren't illuminating much beyond the air around them. In the velvety blues of the coming evening, I could see just fine.

Which was part of the problem. Skeletons were scattered over the wood, their bleached bones highlighted against the red surface. Hopefully most of those were fake, but I wasn't going to investigate it too closely or I might start screaming and never stop. The sheer number of skeletons on this bridge meant every other step would be over a grinning skull, or skirting a collection of bones leaning over the railing.

After a great deal of thought, I turned to Liling and said, "Uh..."

"Yes?"

"That's a lot of bones."

"What are you trying to ask me?"

"Those aren't real, are they?"

"The lake is quite dangerous, Mr. Moss. Did you not hear me?"

I pointed at my mug.

"Yes, even for you."

I shuddered. I was finished with all of this sidhe magic. Had you asked me a day ago who were the biggest threats to humans out of the monsters, I'd have said mad scientists, or wolfmen, or monkey khans, or maybe even brainiacs or martians. I wouldn't have even thought of the sidhe. I would have said they were too rare to cause much trouble. Sure, they could control animals, but that was just Disney stuff, getting birds to dress them and so on. Nothing to be scared of.

Now? Now I was thinking the sidhe had to go. Even that Audrey Hepburn, and wouldn't that break Serendipity's heart. I wasn't going to go out and do anything, mind, but this was a bunch of monsters sitting on an atom bomb's worth of power, and we all knew what those could do.

While I was quailing from the boneyard, Liling stepped onto the bridge, her head held high. De Kay, Parrish, and finally Mold shambled after her, all three holding their weapons in hand. I went last.

I did my best not to look at the skeletons too closely. The bones were unnerving precisely because I wasn't used to them. I'd seen bodies, but most of them still had skin on them. I had gotten used to the more horrifying parts of death, and yet something as simple as bones—well, to be fair, a lot of bones—could get under my skin.

And for what? If Liling was being serious, it was for looking into the water. Maybe they were all lookers?

I wasn't going to take chances. Listening to Liling had worked out so far, and she was the only one who knew what she was talking about when it came to this place. I kept my eyes glued on the rocky wall across the other shore. Watch that get bigger and bigger and forget about this danger underfoot.

Surprisingly enough for a fella with my dim view on luck, it was working. Mirrors weren't a big temptation with me. I already knew what'd be looking back. Nothing much.

We were almost halfway across when the lake stopped playing fair. A roar echoed across the water, coming up from directly below. It sounded like someone had glued the worst parts of a crocodile to the meanest parts of a hippo, then shot the thing full of whatever mad scientists used to make animals bigger than God intended. I pictured the monster breaching the surface, bellowing. I rushed to the railing, knocking the skull and most of the shoulders of a skeleton into the water. The zombies were joining me, ready to see what we were facing.

"Don't look!" Liling shouted.

It was enough to catch all of us, but Parrish spoke for the group. "Brains?"

"The lake will try to trick you. Don't look down. No matter what you hear, you can't look into the water."

"Let's run," I said. "If it's going to start that, maybe if we...you're shaking your head."

"It will not work. If you run, you will fall, and these boards are far enough apart to see through—don't look!"

"Sorry. You keep saying that, and it's sort of a suggestion."

The lake roared again. I shut my eyes, the shivers taking over. That roar, well, I knew it. I'd never forget it, either, and though I'd exorcized some of my fears, enough remained, a tarry residue that could cling to an experience and turn it into terror. The roar was the war cry of a monkey khan, fifty feet of cheesed-off gorilla who liked to eat people like popcorn. The first time I'd seen one, he knocked in the wall of a baseball stadium, reaching that massive mitt of his in to kill and eat a friend of mine.

Joke's on you, lake. Kong can't swim.

With that thought, I set off again after the others. The lake kept it up, too. I think it was calling to each of us in turn. Plucking stuff out of our minds. Sometimes it was speaking Chinese in the voice of an older man, then a young woman. Once it was Sarah Bellum's coffee-and-cigarettes purr, exhorting each zombie in turn to fetch her from the water. Another time it was a crying child, then a man speaking in Spanish, then a woman crying for Ricky to come home. The zombies scarcely reacted.

For me, it pulled out the guilt. Dulcinea Ramos was the first, begging me for help. She was drowning, see, and I was the only one who could help. It gave me others too, reaching back into my life for a parade of all those I'd let down. Those I'd known in the Night War. Those I'd failed to find. I was getting less tempted to look down and thinking more about how I could possibly burn down a body of water.

The lake went silent as I stepped onto the snow. The zombies all verified they were doing fine, or else they really were commenting on brains.

"That was the first test of three," Liling said.

"Three? What?"

"There are always three. I thought you knew that."

"What was the forest back there? With the goblins?"

Liling shrugged. "An introduction?"

"That's swell. What's next?"

She pointed at the rock wall. "The Maze of Lies."

"That sounds pleasant."

"It's not," she said. Liling might not have been up on sarcasm.

"What is it?"

"Exactly as it sounds."

"Great. So we go the opposite way we think and we'll get to where... you're shaking your head again."

"The best lies carry elements of truth. The Maze of Lies is the same way. Mindlessly believing the opposite of what your senses tell you is no better than obeying them slavishly. You should follow me."

"Show us the way, fearless leader."

The wall was made of rocks piled on top of one another, collections of fluffy snow here and there on the parts irregularly jutting outward. It reminded me of some of those I'd seen in the English countryside that locals would tell me went back to Roman times. At the time, I figured they were having a little fun with a Yank whose idea of ancient history was last Wednesday. Now I wasn't so sure.

This wall was a lot taller than those; they tended to reach about the waist and had gaps where they'd partially collapsed. This was in fine shape, and twice as tall as me.

Liling walked along the wall, her hand playing through the air about a foot from the rocks. Finally, she stopped. I knew enough at this point not to be shocked when she stepped through what looked, from my vantage point, to be solid. I went ahead and followed, and I was in the maze.

I can say with absolute certainty, we never would have made it through the maze without Liling. Probably not the lake, either, but the maze definitely would have claimed us. The skeletons lying around said as much, and though they weren't as densely packed, there were more of them. It was incredible to think Liling had made it through these tests, not only on her first go-round, but all alone. There was more to her than she was letting on, and I was grateful for all of it.

"People want to believe lies," Liling said. "That is what makes them so seductive." She gestured through one of the turns. Beyond, still enclosed in the stone walls comprising the maze, was an idyllic garden. A banquet was laid out in the center, but my stomach turned when I saw what was on the menu. Fresh brains.

"Brains!" Mold said.

I grabbed him. "Don't."

"Mr. Moss is correct, Mr. Mold." Mold looked disappointed. "You want to believe. Trust the maze, and you will wander in circles. You will learn nothing."

We walked past the banquet, and Mold hung his head. I didn't blame him. I was getting a little hungry myself, but nothing on earth was going to get me to eat brains. We passed other pathways, some promising an exit, others food, booze, companionship. She took us down the darkest paths, where old thorny vines grew wild. It was impossible to get down these without drawing blood.

A gap in the path, barely two feet across, came up. I picked up a bit of speed to hop it. Liling caught me.

"Don't tell me," I said.

"It's farther than it looks," she said. She broke off a section of thorny vine, opening a few more holes in her palms, then tossed it underhand. Not much of a throw, but it should have easily made it across.

It arced downward, and seemed to pass through the snow-covered flagstones on the other side. Then my brain caught up to what my eyes were telling me: she was right, it was much farther to the other side. What looked like two feet was more than twenty, everything meticulously arranged to appear close enough to hop.

She pointed into the crevasse. "More than one person was fooled."

I peered down. She wasn't wrong. The pile of bones spoke more eloquently of the dangers than anything else could.

"We took the wrong path," she said.

"Wait, you're lost?"

She shook her head with such certainty I trusted her. "It is always tempting to believe the lie. Even after you know it for what it is."

She took us back to the last turn, and this time picked a path that barely was worth the name. We were forced to crawl. Thorns turned my hands to ribbons and sliced into my cheeks. The blood turned icy. When we emerged on the other side, Liling nodded. "We are close."

"Brains," Mold muttered. The thorns had managed to make him uglier. No mean feat.

A few more twists and turns, and we emerged. The walls fell away behind us. Ahead, the snowy ground sloped upward, evergreens bursting upward. The lights on the hill were almost near enough to touch.

"There," Liling said. "The last test."

TWENTY-NINE

Christmas Day
Seconds later

I had seen the chateau before. 1944 in Carentan, a little while after the landing. It was this gorgeous old manor that had probably been around when they were curing headaches amongst the aristocracy via amputation. It had been shot up some, and judging by the sandbags and broken windows, the krauts had been using the lower floors as a machine gun nest. They had abandoned the position by the time we got there, no doubt deciding discretion was the better part of valor.

My squad spent the night in the chateau. I'd been fighting more or less since my boots touched the ground the night before D-Day. When I wasn't fighting, I was worried about fighting. You never knew when a stand of bushes was going to reveal a kraut machine gun or one of their panzers that squealed like a hurt dog and hit like a thunderbolt.

Well, that night in the chateau, I wasn't worried. I bunked in the front room with the rest of the squad, and it was the usual. The fellas farting and talking and telling the same dirty jokes we'd been telling since Basic. Me, I just lay there, looking up at the ceiling. In America, you don't pay attention to ceilings much, but in Europe, they put some thought into them. They had a starry sky painted up there, framed with this gold wainscoting. I was just some kid from Santa Monica. I didn't know from anything, but it looked mighty fine to me. Peaceful. Almost hopeful. This kind of stuff had to be all over France when the krauts rolled in.

Don't know why, but staring up at it, knowing the krauts hadn't destroyed it, meant something. I thought the world was FUBAR, but there were places, here and there, where it wasn't so bad. Little bits of beauty, of purity, untouched by evil. I had the best sleep of the war, the best sleep of the next nine years, in that room. We left the chateau the next morning. Seeing that old building, a little scarred up from the fighting, but standing proudly in the blooming dawn, was something I instantly knew I'd never forget.

And here it was, inside Mab's strange place. Out of the corner of my eyes, I saw skyscrapers, their windows shedding light, but when I looked, it was snow, and trees.

"This is the City of Dreams," Liling said. "The most dangerous test of them all."

"I know this place."

Liling stared at the chateau, her own eyes filled with the sweet nostalgia I felt. "We all do."

"You were in Carentan?"

"I don't know what that means. I am not seeing whatever it is you are. Each of us sees somewhere different. It is from your memory, or your dreams. Someplace you return to when you need it. A place you felt at peace."

"Yeah. I've dreamed of this place more than once."

"There is the danger. This place *wants* you. As much as you want it. It will want to keep you."

"You know something? I'm beginning to rethink my decision of coming along with you."

"I am sorry, Mr. Moss. There was no way I would trust six zombies."

"Brains!" Parrish said, and she sounded offended.

"It was before I knew you," Liling said.

"Brains," Parrish mumbled.

"Is Mab in there?" I asked Liling.

"It is Mab's home. Yes."

"Great. Then we follow you like before...and I am getting very tired of you shaking your head at me."

"I'm sorry, but in this case, we can't. This place, whatever it is to you, is your own. You have to travel it alone, and to get through you will have to leave something of yourself behind and bring something of yourself along."

"I don't know what that means."

"It is as close as I can get to explaining. Hopefully, you'll understand what I mean when the time comes." She set her shoulders and prepared to set off for the front door, then she paused. "If you see an animal, follow it."

"Aren't those Mab's?"

"Maybe. Maybe not. You'll know the difference."

"Do you have any useful instructions?"

"Brains," Mold agreed.

"I might do better in my first language. Do any of you speak Cantonese?"

I exchanged a frustrated look with the zombies.

"Then do the best with what I've told you," she said. "Now hurry up. Mab awaits."

Liling was the first up the slope. I wondered what she saw. What the zombies saw. What Mab saw. I didn't understand this place, and doubted that I ever would. Liling was talking in riddles, but this whole place was a riddle. I was asking her to explain the inexplicable. I had to hope that I could glean enough of what she said to react properly. Otherwise I'd be joining the bones I was certain littered the interior.

Liling opened the front door of the chateau and went inside. I followed her, and for a moment, I even saw her standing in the foyer of the old building. Then she was gone. The house shook, a snowfall of dust coming down. I ducked, reflexively trying to pull the helmet that wasn't there down over my ears. I ended up cramming my hat nearly flat. Felt wasn't going to do a thing against shrapnel.

The pounding started up again. We hadn't been shelled in the chateau. I turned around to warn the zombies, maybe catch sight of Liling, wherever she had gone, but the door was shut and I was alone. Outside, through the broken windows, the French countryside disappeared into the night. It was summer, as it had been when I'd stayed here. Occasionally, a flash from a nearby explosion would light everything around. The artillery hammered, throwing up gouts of soil or blasting trees to smithereens with each hit.

I cursed. I thought my kraut fighting days were done. I pulled the Luger from my coat. In a pinch, silver bullets would do for krauts.

I went from room to room in the chateau, hunting for my squad, for anyone, really. I checked the room with the starry ceiling where we'd spent the night. It was empty, save for the abandoned kraut sandbags piled by the windows. The rest of the downstairs was empty as well, and outside, the artillery was getting closer than I generally prefer. Each hit rattled the entire chateau and threatened to dump me on my ass. My ears whined after every blast, only stopping when the next one boomed loud enough to drown out even my thoughts.

I wasn't panicking. Not yet. But I was getting close. Being shelled is one of the worst things a person can live through. The heavens sound like they're falling, and you're getting showered with dirt and pieces of your bunkies. And that's the good part. They say you don't hear the one that kills you, so in those brief periods when you can only hear the tinny emptiness between your ears, you're certain that's it. A single shell could easily crack this house open like an egg, and I'd be the last to know.

Absurdly, my mind kept going back to that ceiling. The shell that would obliterate it from the face of the earth. That was a crime. Worse than taking me.

I ran through the house, looking for something, anything that might help me. The shells thundered outside, getting closer. Now the chateau shuddered like a human being tensing before being hit. I ran through the looted dining room and into the kitchen.

The back door to the kitchen burst open and krauts flooded into the room. Their uniforms were mixed. I saw some war-weary *Wehrmacht* in there, but their leader was a spit-shined SS bastard. He looked like he was dressed for a parade. He held a Luger on me, and the rest of the squad bristled with gewehr rifles and MP submachine guns.

"Where are you going, American?" He spoke English with the kind of kraut accent that made you want to punch him on general principle.

"Um, well, I think I'm a little lost? The war ended ten years ago."

The Germans shared a genial laugh about that. There's something about people laughing in German that's more ominous than any other language. Then again, that could be just because, on the balance, krauts have tried to kill me more than anyone else.

"Ended? No, American, it's only just begun." The commander laughed warmly with his men. Well, it was warmly from their perspective, probably. "I think we can find a place for you." He barked something in German and the soldiers flooded around me. I didn't go for my pistol, but neither did they. It hardly mattered.

They weren't hustling me anywhere. Several of them kept me glued to the spot with their guns, while the others started setting things at my feet.

Rocks.

Specifically, the same kind of stone that had made up the Maze of Lies. Sort of beige, but a touch of red in the places where it shined wetly. They stacked them with confidence, *clack-clack-clack*, one on top of another, forming a five-foot circle around me never more than a single stone thick. They looked like they should topple over, but they never did. The rocks stuck together or were balanced so perfectly it didn't matter. They were making an impenetrable wall without mortar, or even regularly shaped stones.

The wall was up to my knees when I looked up, ready to try to reason with the krauts. These weren't real Germans, after all. This was some kind of hallucination the Gobfather made. But when I finally tore my eyes off those rocks, the krauts were gone. So was the kitchen for that matter. And the chateau. And the artillery.

Outside the ring of stones now piled up around me was darkness.

It wasn't the pitch black of a basement, but rather the permeable gloom of night. Shapes moved around out there, and they brought with them hideously familiar sounds. The hiss of a tentacle over concrete. The giggle of a clown when he sees his prey. The clicking of metallic limbs and the sparking of bizarre machinery.

I tensed to run. But there was nowhere to go. *Clack-clack-clack* went the stones at my feet. I only caught glimpses of what stacked them now. Claws, tentacles, furry mitts, pale human hands, a glove with straw poking from the edges, tiny three-fingered talons. Once, an apelike hand the size of a Model T. Every kind of limb I'd ever seen on the end of a monster, adding to the wall, stone by stone.

I couldn't move, either. Not with the monsters out there. They would be waiting. It was too dark to know what I needed, or I would fight them. I was all alone. No backup. No friends.

Then they started talking.

"Hey there, meatstick," something hissed.

"You're looking good enough to eat," said something else in a bad Transylvanian accent.

"Where are you going? You want a friend?" asked an animalistic snarl.

"Don't be frightened. I could take care of you." The words sounded like they were coming through mud.

"Me want you. Me take you. You mine now," rumbled another voice.

"Brains."

The sounds pounded in on me. Every one made me smaller. Pushed me inward. I didn't want to show anything. Didn't want them to see. The words made me want to be somewhere else, some*thing* else. Chase me out of my skin. Let me leave everything behind.

But I couldn't. The leering tones never stopped, and with each one, *clack*, another stone fell into place. They were on the other side of the rising wall, but I didn't feel any safer. They weren't keeping me safe. They were locking me up. The words tumbled over each other, the last come-on not even finished before the next was echoing over the clacking of the stones.

The wall rose to my waist, to my chest, to my eyes.

Artillery boomed. The voices weren't silent, either. They rode the hammering of the guns. The booming had once sent me into a foxhole, now this as well. Then the sky lit up with the explosions, and in flashbulb seconds, I saw the crowd around me. Monsters, every kind, stretching back into the distance. All with the same grin on their faces.

No, all with the same *face*. Under clown makeup, furred and fanged as a wolfman, or lipless and quivering as a martian, I saw the same features I did whenever I looked in a mirror.

The monsters, me, after my change. Each time that I had failed to fight it off. There I was, my skin running like wax. There I was, with green scales and gills. There I was, a wobbling mound of pink protoplasm.

Didn't stop them. I fell to my knees as the wall piled up. I tried to stop out the sounds, but it didn't work. They slithered through my fingers and into my ears.

I don't know when I heard it first. It kind of bled into the other sounds, and by the time I understood it, it felt like it had been there all along. A voice, calling my name softly. "Nick. Nick. Nick." Sweetly. Warm as a baby's blanket.

I opened my eyes. Hexene Candlemas stood beside me. Hexene was always pretty, though only the most smitten would call her boyish and freckled face beautiful. Normally her mass of curly red hair was trying to escape her head in every direction at once. Now, it had been corralled under a tiara. She wore a ball gown, but like her normal style of dress, it looked like it had been made entirely from old Amish quilts. The witch held out one hand to me, as though to help me up. Her fingernails had always been short, nearly bitten to the quick, but now she had long and elegant nails, each painted a different color.

"Hi, Nick."

"Hexene?"

I got to my feet. My rational mind knew Hexene wasn't here. She'd left town, and the way she acted, she wasn't coming back. There was no earthly way she was in this place. But she was. I couldn't explain it. Hexene's scent, like rosemary, filled my senses. And the look in her bright green eyes, well, when a lady looks at you like that, you do whatever she asks and thank her for the privilege.

"It's me," she said.

"What are you doing here?"

"I sensed you needed my help, so here I am."

"Why are you dressed for the cotillion?"

I expected her to scowl. Maybe to hit me. She smiled instead. "You can't come to a sidhe's home underdressed."

"I guess that was my first mistake. So how do we get out of here?"

"Is that what you want?"

"Yeah, why? What were you thinking?"

She shrugged, looking shyly away. "We could leave. Or we could stay."

I swallowed. "We?"

She nodded, her eyes meeting mine and shining with her own inner light. "We."

"Are you serious?"

She nodded.

"But what about your powers? You said you left to get them back."

"They don't matter. I missed you too much. I want to be with you, Nick."

"Yeah," I said. I didn't have much strength to say anything more. I had never wanted to believe anything so badly. But it was wrong. Hexene never would have given up. Not even for me. That was one of the things that made her irresistible. I'd rather she was out there doing what she had to do, than cutting a piece out of herself for me.

Because that wouldn't be her anymore.

Maybe it was that revelation that made me notice, or maybe it was simple movement drawing my eye. A weasel scrambled along the edges of the stone wall, sniffing at a piece, then moving on, sniffing again. I dropped to a crouch to regard the creature. It rose up on its hind legs, looking like a cross between a snake and a bear, and regarded me right back with beady black eyes.

"Hello there," I said to it.

It squeaked.

"Nick?" Hexene said. "What are you doing?"

I ignored her. "So, Mr. Weasel. You wouldn't happen to know the way out, would you?"

The weasel squeaked again and fell back to his tiny paws. He probed the edges a few more times, then he disappeared, like a shadow had gulped him up. Then he emerged from what I now saw was a hole in the rocks, squeaking. Just like the way Liling seemed to walk through walls in this place. I had to grin as I followed. Somehow it was big enough for me, even though it only looked like a rabbit's burrow a moment ago.

"Nick! Didn't you hear me! I said we could be together! Nick! Don't go!"

I followed the weasel—well, I couldn't see it, so I followed the squeaking—down the tunnel. Behind me, Hexene continued to call, saying all the things I wanted to hear but knew she would never say. She might say them to someone, but not to me. The weasel was more trustworthy as it busily hopped along ahead of me.

As the tunnel continued on, I started noticing I was crawling higher and higher. At first, I was on my belly like a grunt advancing on a machine gun nest. Then I was on hands and knees like a baby. Pretty soon I just stood up, cautiously at first, certain I was about to ring my bells on a stone ceiling. No hit ever came. I was standing just fine, wondering how long I had been crawling like an idiot, when I felt something on my leg and heard the squeaking.

I reached into my jacket and fished out the flashlight. Forgotten that thing was in there, especially since I wasn't fighting gremlins or gill-men. Sure enough, it was the weasel hanging onto the leg of my trousers, giving me a look that asked, *Are you done?*

"Yeah, I'm done."

The weasel squeaked and scampered down the tunnel. The walls and the floor were more stones like the ones that had been stacked to trap me in the first place. I knelt down and put my eye up to one of the small gaps in the stone, shining my light out of it.

I saw a field of pearls. A rainbow sky shining down on them, while misshapen humans frolicked about. The ground was perpendicular to me, and the vertigo nearly made me throw up. I made a mental note not to look too closely into any sidhe magic. I stood up and followed the weasel, who was watching me impatiently with his beady eyes.

After a short time, I started to see a light up ahead. It was gentle and gold, with the smeary quality of old lanterns. I picked up the pace, and pretty soon the weasel as well, since it was obvious where we were going. The tunnel ended in a pair of baroque doors, the light bleeding from underneath and in between.

I opened them up and emerged into a powdered-wig ballroom.

"Lord Nicholas Albert Moss of Santa Monica," boomed a voice next to me. I jumped and turned to find a masked servant standing by the door.

"I'm not a lord," I told him, but he didn't respond.

He might not have been real. The mask was ornate like everything else in the room, and between that and his George Washington wig, I didn't see any actual skin. The rest of the outfit fit the look: gloves, filly shirt, vest, breeches, hose, and buckled shoes.

He wasn't the one out of place. I was. The women wore Marie Antoinette hairdos and ball gowns so big they each had their own telephone exchange. The men were in fancier-looking versions of what the servants had on. Everyone wore masks. Sometimes, one of their features slipped into view, and they were all made up heavily. Skin was whiter than flour, beauty marks like greasepaint, lips wet and red like blood. They twirled and bowed around the dance floor at the center of the ballroom.

Only I got it all wrong. The women were showing off cleavage as was the style back then. The first girl I looked at, I figured she didn't have much up top. That had never bothered me. Then I noticed it wasn't just her. It was every woman. And the breasts were on the men. I put it together after that.

I looked down at my suit, now grimy and wrinkled from the trip through the forest and the tunnel. I really was out of place.

I looked around, wondering what the next test was. The people were probably more figments of Mab's imagination, and I saw no goblins. Nothing was trying to make a Poe character out of me for once. That was enough to make a fella relax.

Until I saw the Gobfather. Titanio Mab danced through the couples, taking one of them for a quick spin before depositing them with a new partner. Mab's eyes, big and slanted, were locked on me the whole time. I'd seen that same look when my cat stared down a fresh can of tuna.

I don't know why I didn't pull the dagger right then and there. I couldn't. More sidhe magic.

"Mr. Moss, what a pleasant surprise," Mab said, as he arrived at me. He didn't offer his hand. The dancing portion of the evening, at least for now, was over.

"Uh...hi. You know my name?"

"Not until recently. But when you come to my home, my home grows to know you. I am impressed you made it through to find me here."

"Yeah, I'm something all right."

"More than meets the eye, I believe is the term. You *look* like a filthy little weasel man..."

"Hey!"

"...but perhaps there's a heart beating in that narrow chest. Tell me, why do you wish to kill me?"

"Same reason everyone does."

"Oh no. Your zombie friends are here out of duty. You're not."

"Your home can't read that?"

Mab smiled, but there wasn't enough soul inside him to know happiness, let alone show it. "There are limits. Perhaps if you'd stayed in your dream like you were supposed to."

"I'm here about your Gallery."

Mab clapped his hands. His palms were too short or his fingers were too long. Either way, he gave me the heebies. "You saw my Gallery! What did you think?"

"It's monstrous. Evil. Wrong."

"Wrong? Whatever do you mean?" Mab asked, frowning.

"You're killing them. Or preserving them...you're doing something to them I don't quite understand, but I know it's not what they want."

Mab's frown deepened. I'll give this to him, he frowned prettier than most girls. "What do their desires matter?"

"Um...what?"

"They're only human. They live, they die. They never make any sort of mark on this earth, nor anywhere else. Why should their desires influence one such as me?"

"Holy...you're serious, aren't you?"

"Mr. Moss, I am giving these girls a great gift. You have seen them. You know their beauty. Transcendent for a race of beings that is little more than dirt held upright by ego. They die, yes, but they live on as objects of that same perfect beauty. Age never mars them, never diminishes them. They never know the misery of losing pieces of themselves to the years."

"That's their right! They're the ones who get to choose that, not you!"

"Why? I have a much better understanding of what this entails than they. They would make a selfish, emotional choice. I allow them to live on. Forever. The true tragedy is that my Songbird will never join them."

"Her name was Dulcinea."

"The name her parents gave her," Mab said, waving the thought away like a fly.

"Is that why you killed her?" I asked.

"Killed her? Why would I do that?"

"Or had her killed."

"Mr. Moss, you need to start making some sense."

"She was running from you. She didn't want to join that Gallery of yours. She wanted to live a life. Whatever she wanted to do, it would have been hers.

But you couldn't handle it. So you got someone to shoot her for you."

"You wound me, Mr. Moss." Mab actually did look hurt, or as close as he could manage without ever actually feeling any such emotion. "I would never have hurt my Songbird. Had she returned to me, she would have been welcomed. Had I found her, I would have done what was best, and even now she would have her place in the Gallery."

Mab looked upward, as though trying to remember something. "Yes. She was dear to you. I can feel that. No...not dear. There is a different emotion...but she was something to you. If only for a moment. Mr. Moss, you beheld true beauty, and for that, I will allow you to visit my Gallery whenever you wish."

"What? You're not listening to me."

Mab smiled. "I believe we are finished, Mr. Moss. I will not allow you to kill me, but neither do I wish you dead. Not when I see the tiniest shard of myself in—" The words were wrung off.

Mab's eyes widened, and considering the size of those things, it was something to see. His face crumbled into utter astonishment, the first truly honest emotion I'd seen there. Then he looked down at his chest. His white shirt was being pushed outward. Then, around it, a stain spread like a birthmark. The white cloth turned red, grew wet and sticky. The shirt tore away around a point as razor-sharp cold iron was born from his body.

Mab went limp, but he was still being held partially upright. Liling stood behind him, both hands on the handle of her dagger, driving it through the sidhe's back and impaling his heart.

"Hello, *Gobfather*," she snarled in his ear.

He gaped, trying to catch sight of her as the dagger ran him through.

"My Golden Swan," Mab whispered, bright crimson blood falling from his mouth.

"My name is Liling Lam," she said. Then, her face contorted in rage, she twisted the dagger. Mab shuddered once, and the world shattered.

It was like I was a reflection of myself, and the mirror holding me had been broken by a thrown brick. Reality, or whatever the Gobfather's home had been, came away in pieces, and I was flung through the shifting void. Nothing I saw made much sense: slices of a freezing forest, a section of maze, a small pagoda on a smoky hillside, a cemetery in a shady valley.

And then I was flying through the December night in Los Angeles. My body responded like the drill sergeants in Georgia had taught it to. I tucked, rolled, and landed as gently as anyone could expect in a copse of banana trees. I blinked, staring upward at a broken window on the fourth floor of the Chateau Marmont. I was outside, once again in the real world.

Thirty

December 26, 1955
The wee hours of the morning

So what happened to the weasel?" Sam demanded.

Sam Haine was sitting cross-legged on my tiny porch, staring at me with eyes that were little more than triangular holes in a pumpkin. His jagged mouth hung open enough to see the perpetually burning candle in the center of his head. He was dressed in a fancy pinstriped suit, his green fingers steepled together as he listened to what happened to me that evening.

Mira Mirra sat next to him, her legs folded demurely under her. It was a big deal to see the two of them sitting so close together after their last blowout. It was like owning cats, really. Or so Mrs. O'Herlihy from down the street would tell me whenever Muffin and Peanut Butter weren't getting along.

Mira was in a fetching red dress with a white cardigan over her shoulders. Right now, she was wearing her most common pretty face, that of a young woman in her early twenties, with bouncy black hair and bright blue eyes. She looked so familiar, and I didn't know why until I saw that face on a Campbell's Soup ad. I didn't tell Mira, though. She was nice enough to look at this way, and I liked to recognize her when I saw her.

I was sitting just inside my house, my screen door shut and all the wards out, my weapons laid out in front of me. The Luger, the dagger, a whistle, and so on. Behind Sam and Mira, the chaos of Juniper Street unfolded, with robots sparking and shambling over lawns, zombies clawing at windows, and a clumsy killer potato trying unsuccessfully to scale the Mendozas' fence. No rest on Christmas night for the people of Watts.

"I don't know," I told them, taking a pull from my beer. "I don't think there was a weasel at all."

"You said there was a weasel," Mira said, and Sam nodded in agreement.

"You lying to us, meatstick?" The voice belonged to Lurkimer Closett, a bogeyman. He couldn't get up on my porch because the streetlamps would burn his sensitive skin—well, scales, or whatever it was he had—so he was hiding under my porch. He whined when we all decided to have the conversation up here, but I wasn't going outside. These three were on their best behavior, but I wasn't going to trust them without a line of chicken blood, a mirror, and a teddy bear close at hand.

"I'm not lying."

"You should be more polite," Sam scolded Lurkimer. "I'm sorry, Nick. Some monsters have no manners."

"If your feelings are hurt, I could rub your back," Mira said.

I ignored the come-ons. There weren't any bricks here. At least not ones I could see.

"Go to the beach, Lurkimer," I suggested to him. He was always sore I, a mere human, had played him for a sucker when we first met. "Where were we?"

"The weasel," Sam prompted.

Getting home had been a challenge in itself. I only saw Aida Parrish outside the hotel, and she was finding her own way home. The fourth floor of the Chateau Marmont looked like it had just hosted a monkey khan's birthday party, and the howls of the Hollywood Sheriff's Department were closing in. I got out of there. Whatever leverage I had from working for the LAPD did not extend to their rival department. What happened to the others, I had no idea, and other than Liling and Mold, didn't really care one way or the other.

I took a red car back to Watts and sneaked in through my back door. When I peeked out the front window and the three of them, Sam, Mira, and Lurkimer, all started catcalling, I realized I kind of wanted to talk to someone. I had a list in mind of half a dozen other people I'd have preferred to talk to, but beggars couldn't be choosers. After I assured them I wasn't letting them in and showed them a few instruments of their personal destructions, we were able to talk with only Lurkimer getting really spicy.

"I'll eat weasels!" Lurkimer howled. Like all bogeymen, he acted toughest when he was safe. Put your mitts on him and he yelped like a schoolboy in a clown college.

"Hush now," Mira scolded. "Nick. Nicky...please tell us more about weasels. You know, I love pets."

My cat hissed at her lazily from the couch. I reminded myself to get it an extra can of tuna.

"No, I don't think there ever was a weasel. I think most of that was a mirage or something."

"An illusion?" Sam asked.

"Like a movie set," Mira explained, and Sam nodded.

"What did you say? I missed that!" Lurkimer shouted from under the porch, but no one cared to repeat it.

A step pyramid floated over my house, down the street, and kept going, rumbling like the earth took up humming.

"Uh...yeah, actually. Like a movie set."

"Where *were* you?" Sam asked. He wanted to know, but that was also jealousy. He'd wanted to turn me for so long, he didn't like the idea of me stepping out on him. Despite the fact that I had in no way stepped in on him in the first place. I'm not sure that made sense anywhere other than in his head.

The point here is that I didn't tell them where I had been. They didn't need to know I was part of some mob hit. If the wolves came calling, who was going to get pinched? A bunch of zombies with expensive leech lawyers? Or me, who couldn't even afford a batboy fresh out of law school? I was vague. I'd said "sidhe," and there were a handful of those in the southland. They liked pretty people and we had those in spades.

"Like I said, it was on a case," I lied, then put my finger on the lip of the bottle of beer, tipping it back and forth without letting it fall.

Sam took the hint. "Oh. I still don't understand."

"The weasel was me," I explained.

"Like a witch's familiar?" Mira asked.

"Witches have familiars!" Lurkimer shouted.

"Kind of? Except not an animal at all. It was me, but it was outside of me. It, you know, it guided me on a path I couldn't have seen otherwise."

"Oh," said Sam, nodding in comprehension. "I still don't get it." So much for that.

"I learned a lot," I said, finishing off the beer. I stared at the bottle. This was Christmas night...well, wee hours of the morning after Christmas, anyway. I was spending it talking to three monsters who wanted to turn me. I could go for another beer, or I could grab some shuteye and be ready for Monday morning in a couple hours. Of course, it was a little sad that none of the three of them had anything better to do on Christmas either.

"You know, I might be able to understand if you'd let me in," Sam said. "You and I are such good friends and all. I mean, you'd want to tell me."

I yawned, standing up.

"Nicky, I'd be happy to talk to you. You know...after," Mira said, moving her legs so I could get a glimpse of smooth, pale skin.

"Nice try, both of you. I'm gonna get some sleep. Merry Christmas."

They wished me Merry Christmas.

"I'll get you, meatstick!" Lurkimer wailed.

He wasn't going to catch anything but a cold under there. I didn't need to tell him that. I shut the door to the disappointed moans of my visitors and went off to bed. I barely heard the monsters outside as I drifted off. I dreamed, though. I dreamed in colors I couldn't remember.

THIRTY-ONE

New Year's Eve, 1955
Nighttime

Y ou know, when this whole Night War thing happened," Mickey said, sipping his ginger ale, "there were those not prepared. Those who had some issues with breaking bread with a Negro, or a Chinese, or a Jew." He nodded at Rob, Wong, and me with that, but I didn't have the heart to explain to him, for the millionth time, I wasn't Jewish. "Youse come from Boyle Heights, you're already used to it. Youse already know that a man from your neighborhood is a man. A man from somewheres else, is a mug."

He broke out laughing. The next table over, a group of mummies glanced over at us, their eyes momentarily glowing red. They minded their own business pretty quick. I'd heard Mickey's speeches before. He liked to pat himself on the back for being tolerant, and the truth was, for a mob boss, he was basically Jesus.

"Night War happens and now we have to find a new way to live. Some of us was prepared. Some of us was clinging to the old ways. Youse ask me, them others are clinging to the old ways in a new way."

Big Jack Whalen frowned, his rocky face looking like a South Seas idol. "I don't mean to gainsay you, Mick, but I'm plumb lost."

"It's okay, Jackie. See, it's like this. You got the Gobfather, who does he use? Goblins. You got that Bellum broad. Who does she use? Zombies. And that's it. Oh, sure, they got one or two other kinds sorta floatin' around, but mostly it's that. Goblins on one hand, zombies on the other. Monsters finding new ways to separate each other. You ask me, they'd be a lot smarter to use whatever they got. Ogres for muscle maybe, some brainiacs for accounting, maybe a martian for munitions, a gremlin to keep the cars working, a phantom for security. And humans. Oh yeah, a whole gang of humans who go wherever they like. No one's got a working ward to keep a man from where he wants to be."

"Other than locks," Wong said philosophically.

"You can't pick a lock, wiseguy?"

Mickey looked us all over. He was the shortest fella at the table—usually my stock in trade—but he was in charge. Not a one of us was going to say a word against him. He pursed his lips, nodding. In the dim light of the Nocturnist, the crescent scar under his eye looked like a canyon.

"That's what killed this Gobfather," Mickey said finally. "If he even had one ogre on the payroll, you think Bellum's hatchetmen get him?"

The hit on Titanio Mab had been splashed over the front pages of every newspaper in the city. The *Minion* scooped them all, since it was their pictures that ended up being run. Titanio Mab, the Gobfather, found dead by an apparent mob hit. His body had been up on the fourth floor of the Chateau Marmont, and in all the pictures it looked like a normal, ritzy hotel. The Gobfather's death broke whatever spell had been on it. Erased that little bit of wonder, that awful wonder, from the world.

The reaction was mixed. Nobody was too cheesed the Gobfather went to a farm upstate, but it was still more violence in a city getting to be defined by it. Lots of bawling for more police enforcement. Complaints about how the City of Angels was falling to the Devil—but you ask me, that happened ten years ago. All suspicions were falling on Sarah Bellum, but since she was still officially a legitimate businessbeing, they couldn't come right out and say it.

The first day, I had been terrified the wolves would come to my door. If they had, what options did I have, really? I could sell Bellum out and see how long I could last in the big house. Not that I was going to stay human if they put me away. No, humans got turned inside a week if they were lucky. Rumor said it was worse for the humans who didn't get turned.

I couldn't give them Liling even if I wanted to, and believe me, I didn't. She had been cagey enough not to let me see where she laid her head. If the wolves came for me, it was going to be me only.

But they hadn't come, and I was beginning to think they weren't going to. The truly frightening thing was that they knew who was behind it. The Gobfather's murder was going to go as officially unsolved as every other mob hit in the city. If you ask me, the wolves were happy they were going to have to clean up fewer bodies now that one side was well and truly out of the game. If the city really had gotten that corrupt, was there any hope for us?

Or even worse, did it matter to me? Brainiac on one side, wolfmen on the other? Law and outlaw looked an awful lot alike when you were on the bottom.

Mickey took it as a late Chanukah present. The Gobfather was dead. First words out of his mouth when I went to his place. I got to wait a couple hours while he was primping, spending my time petting the bulldog and accepting drinks from Florence. The main group came over one by one: Jack Whalen, Johnny Stompanato, Rob Sampson, Wong Lee. When Mickey was out of the bathroom, he was like a sunny day. Mab was dead. The rackets were wide open. He greeted all of us happily, and we were off to the Nocturnist for an evening out.

"We got everything we need," Mickey was saying. "We just have to be quick, or quicker than zombies. If we ain't that, we might need a new line of work."

The fellas laughed.

I smiled and laughed where I had to, but my mouth was glued shut when it came to information. I didn't tell Mickey I was part of the hit, and

I sure as hell didn't tell him where Bellum was. He'd call me a turncoat if he ever found out, but I was doing him a favor. If Mickey knew where Bellum was hiding out, he'd go there, and those two .50s would chew him to pieces. Wasn't my job to protect Mickey from himself, but he didn't have an angel on his shoulder. I was the closest thing to it.

"You'll all be getting your marching orders soon," Mickey said. He was looking at me.

They all nodded, sharing happy looks at the prospect of slicing up the city like a pie.

"What do you say, Stick?" Mickey asked. "Do you get your marching orders?"

I coughed. "Yeah. Um...I gotta see a man about a horse. Be right back."

Mickey's expression turned to stone. I stood up and went for the men's room. I was going to have to give him some kind of answer. Going to have to decide if this was my life or not. If I was really a private eye or if I was going to become one of Mickey's bagmen. I'd already collected for him. I'd already helped bump off the Gobfather. Maybe I had already decided and I didn't even know it.

Here I was, out at night in a room full of monsters, and no one was going to lay a claw on me.

Jane was serving drinks to a table of monsters. She didn't see me. She looked okay, too. Better than okay. The fire hadn't done anything permanent. That was good to see.

I opened the door to the can, surprising a wolfman on the way out. He was fully furred and he broke into a hungry grin when he slapped eyes on me. I coughed, showing him the butt of the gun under my left armpit. He put two and two together and found it added up to Mickey Cohen. He scurried back to his seat quick as you please.

I took a leak mainly to give me some time, and I tried to pretend I was Mickey when I washed my hands. Get those things squeaky clean, because the longer I spent, the longer I had until I had to answer him.

Because I wanted to say yes.

If I said yes, then that would be nobody looking for the missing. Yeah, there were other snoops in town, but they were monsters, and if you think monsters gave a hoot for missing humans, I have a bridge I'd love to sell you. I'd done my time, though, right? I'd done it and I still wasn't making a dent. I had a replacement in Jaime, too. With Mickey, at least the monsters knew what was what. That wolfman a second ago didn't know me from Adam, and he was scared.

Was this where the weasel was leading me?

The door boomed open.

"Gotcha, meatstick, with your pants down. You're ours, or six feet underground."

Flux, Murk, and Sawbones sauntered into the bathroom. They weren't holding weapons, but they had already proven they didn't need guns or poisoned arrows to ruin someone's day. Ask Anonymous Bosch. As though he was reading my mind, Sawbones kept snapping his fingers, and each time I expected an explosion of bright flame.

"Something I can do for you fellas?" I asked.

Sawbones said:

> *Hold your silver tongue,*
> *Save your sad excuses.*
> *Your fate's as good as hung,*
> *A bill for past abuses.*
> *To zombies you were guide,*
> *To us you're but a bleeder.*
> *You're coming for a ride*
> *For what happ'ned to our leader.*

I went for the mushrooms. I don't know what that says about me, if anything. I went for a way to scare them off rather than the dagger that would end them. Didn't matter one way or the other. I was fast, but I had been woolgathering and there were three of them.

Flux was on me first, planting a fist right in my crotch. I dropped to my knees and Sawbones cracked me in the eye with a left. His hands were small enough that his knuckle made a nice home in my eye socket. My vision went white and blue and purple, the agony hot.

"Quick, get him up!" Murk huffed. "Uh...make up...what rhymes with..."

"The rhymes elude your flabby mind, the meatstick's hands you'd better bind," Flux said.

"Oh. Yeah. Of course, Flux."

I felt my hands being yanked behind my back and rope burning into my wrists. Sawbones yelped.

> *The cursed mushrooms in his coat,*
> *Cold iron 'neath his arm,*
> *Though temptation calls to gloat*
> *With these he does us harm.*
> *Mind his weapons cruel*
> *And his gambits devious.*
> *Bound, he fights no duel*
> *While we hold to plans previous.*

Murk and Flux hauled me to my feet, one goblin under each armpit. Murk drew the short straw as he had his whole life and got the side with the dagger. He yipped periodically as it touched his skin. It would hiss, sending up smoke from his flesh. The mushrooms were in a pocket in a vial in my jacket, and they didn't have to look at them. I was helpless. Sawbones put another couple hits into my stomach, but I couldn't feel a whole lot over the pain in my eye and family jewels.

With Sawbones in the front, they carried me back into the Nocturnist. I wanted to call for Mickey and the fellas, but I didn't have breath or voice to do it with. They might as well have been in Arizona for all the good they did me. None of them even looked in my direction; they were too involved in the fantasy of divvying up the city.

The goblins kicked in the kitchen door and I got a glimpse of that witch who'd helped me earlier. She gasped as we went by, but she didn't stop us, and the goblins didn't acknowledge her. They opened the back door with my face and hurled me down the few concrete steps into the alleyway. I hit the far wall and before I could do anything, I felt a fist, tiny and hard like a ball peen hammer, smack right into my liver.

The hit felt like a hand squeezing a sponge full of agony into my body and I dropped to the ground. My knees smacked into the asphalt, but I barely noticed that whisper of pain, not over the shrieking green flames now chasing one another through my entire form. I didn't get much of a chance to think about it, because Murk threw a knee into my face that toppled me to the floor of the alley. The back of my head hit the filthy surface, and the whole world went swimming.

I stopped counting the hits. I knew they kept coming, though. Fists, feet, maybe a pipe. I wasn't too sure. When I got a little bit of control, I pulled burning arms up to shield my head. It was pointless. This was going to happen until they got bored and Sawbones gave me the Emperor Nero treatment. It was a shame I wouldn't be around to find out which poor human they decided to pin my murder on. Or maybe they'd rule it suicide. *Mr. Moss self-combusted*, the coroner'd say, and everyone would stand around nodding and agreeing that was the most reasonable verdict.

The goblins were rhyming up a storm the whole time, but I didn't hear them too well. Pain can be loud, too. Or maybe that was just panicked blood in my ears, waiting for the flash of orange that meant I was going out for good. So I didn't notice precisely when the rhyming got confused.

Just that they had stopped kicking me. There was no new pain to be had. A greenish shape had thrown one of them against a wall and bounced another off the ground. I heard cracking sounds like old sticks being snapped in half. And a whole sack of cats hissing angrily.

That looked good to me. A nice dream to go out on. I closed my eyes and fell into the black.

Jane Stitch

THIRTY-TWO

New Year's Day, 1956
Sometime before dawn

I opened my eyes, and was immediately surprised I was able to do that. Maybe I'd found the afterlife, but it didn't look like any afterlife I'd ever heard of. A threadbare sofa didn't really say heaven *or* hell. Neither did a fitting dummy, a sewing machine, or a couple Oriental screens. The windows were open, and looked out onto some California oaks, a cold night sky, and the second stories of a few lightly rundown Craftsman houses.

Was the afterlife in East LA?

I tried to sit up, throwing off the afghan that had been pulled over me, and my head gave me a good kick. Felt like I had the worst hangover of my life. I sank back into the couch. The light came from a fancy-looking lamp of carnival glass. The room was colorful, but patchwork. Nothing quite matched anything else, but didn't in an oddly pleasant way.

Heavy footsteps, first on wood, then carpet, let me know I had company. I turned my head and saw a pair of bare feet. Lady's feet, but large for it. As patchwork as the room, too. Sections of flesh were grayish, others green, others ivory, all joined with train tracks of sutures.

Oh, so this *was how I get to go.*

My gaze went up the legs, hoping maybe it would be some kind of joke. That I wasn't in the home of a meat golem. She was wearing a cheap silk robe with a Chinese crane pattern on it, and had a small slate around her neck like a schoolkid from thirty years before. It was Jane, looking down at me with her mismatched eyes. Her hair was down, long and straight, the twin skunk-stripes from her temples tracing the even fall.

I panicked, trying to inch away even as my head felt like it was splitting in two. I reached for the lighter in my jacket and realized only then I wasn't wearing my jacket. Wasn't wearing my gun or my dagger. All three of them were hanging on a hatrack across the room.

Jane held up a hand. I had a quick image of it being stitched together from the corpses of a couple different girls. She corralled a piece of chalk, tied to the slate with a bit of twine, and wrote on its surface. She turned it over and showed me the message.

Calm down. Her handwriting managed to be both precise and pretty, like a typewriter that learned cursive.

"You're going to turn me!"

She rolled her eyes, rubbed the surface of the slate with her palm, and wrote another message. *Why are you not turned yet?*

She had a point.

"You're not going to turn me?" Jane shook her head. "Why am I here?"

You saved me. She rubbed that message away, then wrote another. *Thank you.*

"Oh, uh...my pleasure. Thank you."

My pleasure.

"What happened to the goblins?"

Ran away. She pantomimed fright and waved her hands in the air, then she smiled sheepishly.

I chuckled, and immediately regretted it. "Ow."

Need something?

"Ice?"

Jane nodded and left the room. I tried not to look at her legs, really I did. I felt like a weirdo. She had a pair of stems on her. Sure, they were cobbled together from a couple different ladies, but they were something to see.

She returned with a blue ice bag, and put it on the back of her head before handing it over. I winced when I touched it to my skin. She nodded sympathetically when she saw my reaction. Jane went over to a chair by the window and sat. She then wrote a single word on her slate.

Why?

"The goblins?"

She nodded.

"Oh. I guess I should start at the beginning."

Please.

"Okay. Um...let's see. My name is Nick Moss, but I think you knew that."

Jane Stitch.

"It's nice to meet you for real, Jane. Anyway, I'm a private eye and I mostly find missing people. Occasionally I find missing monsters. Do you remember the..." I faltered. Bringing up the Night War in front of a monster was a crapshoot. It was still pretty sore for a lot of them, but then there were those who got turned after. Or those who never really did much fighting. In the old days, I thought all monsters were monsters. I'd learned since that wasn't the case.

I coughed. "Night War?"

She nodded, and she stared through the wall behind me. I wanted to know the story there, but I didn't know her well enough to ask. We'd saved each other's lives and we were strangers.

"I knew Mickey Cohen from the Night War and I ran into him when I was doing a job for the LAPD. Finding one of their missing detectives. I found him at about the same time as one of those goblins set him on fire."

Jane nodded eagerly, then wrote on her slate. *They're trying to keep you quiet!*

"Uh...no. That beating was an unrelated matter."

She frowned. *Coincidence?*

"Not exactly. It put me in their orbit, though. And I kind of owed someone else a favor, and they gave me a choice. Help them bump someone off, or they could put me in the ground."

Jane wrote a single word, and showed me. *Gobfather?*

I nodded, and she erased it as quickly as she could, glancing around as though there might be someone watching through the windows. There wasn't. Not a single monstrous face appeared in any one of the open portals. Nothing hung from the eaves, either. No tracks of salt, or blood, or anything else crossed them. I felt naked, but there was no one to see but Jane.

Jane's robe had fallen open, revealing a camisole over her chest. I forced myself to look at her eyes, or at the slate. It was difficult, and I was happy there was a blanket over my lap.

"I didn't want to do it, but there was no way around it. I didn't kill him, for whatever that's worth, and I don't think I'll lose any more sleep over it than I do over the krauts whose tickets I punched during the big one."

Day War?

"Army. I jumped out of planes."

She laughed completely silently. It was eerie. *You?*

"Yeah, me. Jumped into France the night before D-Day. Landed on a German, too. Poor fella could not have been more surprised to see me, I'll tell you that."

Goblin revenge?

My mind jumped back to the first track. "Yeah, I guess so. Rough me up and leave me as a warning maybe."

Look out for yourself.

"I know. I don't even quite know what I'm in, just that it's up to my neck. If you weren't there, it'd be up over my head. Like six feet over."

She shrugged, abruptly finding the stitches in her hand very interesting.

"I should count myself lucky. If you're going to get roughed up, there's no better help than a meat golem. Pull the goblins off me, then stitch me up."

Jane turned decidedly green—even the parts of her that weren't green yet.

"Did I say something wrong?"

Her face queasy, she wrote, *Don't like blood.*

"You're a meat golem."

She shrugged, then pointed at the same message again.

"Oh." I glanced around the room, which had already told me what she did. "You're a seamstress?"

She nodded eagerly, then wrote, *Hope to be. Design clothes too.*

"Being a waitress makes ends meet."

She nodded, and shrugged.

"Nothing to be ashamed about."

Wish things were moving quicker for me.

"My secretary says the same thing. She wants to be a big star, but she's in her twenties, and she's a siren, so she's beginning to think it won't happen."

What about you?

"I'm human. I'm doing the best I can now."

And Cohen?

"I don't really know. It's somewhere to go. Don't know if I want to go there yet. Don't know if that's who I am."

She watched me. Finally, she wrote. *When I burned, you put me out.*

"I don't know if that says who I am."

It does.

"I hope so." I did. I wanted to be what Jane saw.

She looked at the floor, her bare feet playing with the edge of the old carpet. We were quiet. I turned to watch the wind ruffle the leaves of the trees outside, only turning back when I heard her chalk whispering over the slate.

Jumped into France. Been to Paris?

"Of course. I was shot in the...uh...in the rear end, the first time. Didn't really get to do the town then."

What's it like?

Thirty-Three

Monday, January 9, 1956
Morning

My body was covered in big patches of yellow where the bruises were healing. I was still aching but nothing was busted permanently. I think the goblins had wanted me to hurt rather than break and had adjusted their beating accordingly. I was crunching aspirin like M&Ms, but I could move around well enough to go into the office. Whatever I ended up deciding about Mickey's offer, I needed to pay the bills in the meantime.

Jaime came through the front door. He was in long sleeves, hiding all the tattoos that weren't on his hands and neck, which was a significant change. He was still in old jeans and his steel-toed stompers, but this was an improvement. A cardboard box was tucked under his arm.

"Looking good, kid," I said.

"Thanks. I brought breakfast."

"You don't have to buy pastries. I don't pay you enough to cover that."

"It's fine. My *tía* runs a bakery." He opened the box, showing off the crumbly shell-shaped Mexican pastries. I was getting a taste for them, too. They weren't quite as sugary as the American doughnut, and I was beginning to think that was a good thing.

I went to grab a pink one.

"Not that one," Jaime said, and I went for a beige one.

Serendipity was quiet behind her desk. She knew Jaime didn't like her, and any pastries weren't going to be to her liking anyway. Something about the change meant she pretty much only ate things with fish on them, in them, or with them. Her favorite snack in the world was a cup of sardines from a place down the street she'd eat like French fries.

"Serendipity, I had my auntie make you one, too," Jaime said.

"What?" She blinked in surprise.

Jaime opened the box for her. "It's the pink one. It has anchovies in it."

"Oh?" She plucked it out of the box and took a bite. I'll admit it, she hid the disgust well, but I saw it plain as day. "It's good! Thank you."

"Yeah, it's fine," Jaime said, clearly eager for this to be finished. As he turned his back to set the box on the small table by the door where the doughnuts usually went, Ser and I looked at each other. She smiled happily; the kid was won over. Jaime slouched the chair on the other side of the door and pulled the mashed book of crosswords from his pocket.

Ser set the *pandulce* on a napkin by her desk. I went into my office and sat. I was still trying to find a position that would irritate the absolute fewest of my bruises when I heard the door open.

"¿Es esta la oficina del detective?" a woman's voice asked.

"Welcome to Moss Investigations," Ser chirped.

"¿Quién es la dama de pescado?" a man's voice asked.

"Ella es la secretaria. Se trata de Investigaciones Moss. Voy a ver si Moss está disponible," Jaime said. A second later he was in my doorway. "We have clients I think, Mr. Moss."

"Send them in. Do they speak English?"

"I don't think so."

"Then stick around."

Jaime nodded and waved to the doorway.

"Por favor entra," he said. "Soy Jaime Alvarez. Este es el detective Moss."

The couple was in their early forties maybe, both people ground down into small and hard nubs by a life of hard work. Their clothes were simple and every piece of them had evidence of having been repaired multiple times.

The man reached out over my desk as I stood. He had the kinds of incidental cuts on his knuckles that said he was used to lifting and carrying. His bowlegged stance agreed with that. "Soy Rudolfo Huerta. Esta es mi esposa, Consuelo."

"Mr. and Mrs. Huerta?" I asked, confident enough in my limited Spanish for that. "I'm Nick Moss. Pleased to meet you. If you'd have a seat, you can explain what happened."

Jaime translated, but the truth was, he barely had to. I'd heard the story enough times. Problem is, everyone who walked through that door thought they were the only ones in the world it had happened to. To them, their story was unique, and uniquely tragic. I'd heard it more times than I ever wanted to, and I was the last hope for them. As usual. I already knew that chances were all I could offer them was confirmation of what they were worried about.

The four of us were crammed in an office that could barely fit two people, and then only if we breathed shallowly.

Their daughter Sofia was missing. She worked at a lunch counter in Boyle Heights. Her coworkers had already told the Huertas she had left at the end of her shift, and went to walk home as she normally did. She never arrived. Now, she vanished around five in the evening, which was iffy at best. It was winter, but the sun wasn't technically down yet. Not that courts would be likely to convict a monster on shaky timing.

At least I had a very small window to look into. I was already planning a nice and short investigation.

"Do you have a photo of your daughter?" I asked.

Jaime translated, and Consuelo fished a bent picture from her purse and handed it over.

I suddenly found it almost impossible to breathe as I stared at the girl in the shot. She was on the Santa Monica pier, looking to the side, wind whipping her long hair out like a flag. The photo was black and white, but I swear the sea was blue and it swelled behind her. A girl that beautiful could do that to you. Beautiful and familiar.

Sofia Huerta could have been Dulcinea's sister. An absolute dead ringer. She had Dulcinea's upturned nose, the large and almond-shaped eyes. Her skin was smooth, on the darker edges of olive. I couldn't even believe she wasn't Dulcinea. This had to be a doppelganger, or some new kind of robot, or a trick by a mad scientist. Maybe an invention of Bellum's, to draw out the last remaining vestiges of the Gobfather's organization.

I looked up into the Huertas' eyes. No. I'd seen that grief and fear enough times, too. I knew when it was real, and it was here. They had lost their daughter, the girl in the picture. I stared at it again. There were differences between her and Dulcinea, but they were subtle. She was a different girl. Only just barely.

I swallowed, my throat dry. "Can I hang onto the picture?"

Jaime translated.

"Claro, claro," Rudolfo said, nodding.

Jaime took over, leaving me bewitched by the picture. He'd heard me do the spiel enough, and he'd be translating it anyway. He spoke to them in rapid Spanish. He might have been consoling them, quoting our fees, or just describing everything in the room in specific detail. It didn't matter, because of the picture. Sofia Huerta meant everything.

"Jaime, I want you to go with the Huertas. Canvass their neighborhood, check along the girl's route home. I also want you sleeping in their living room. Check the monsters who lurk around there at night."

"Okay, boss." Jaime turned to the Huertas and I can only assume he translated.

The couple's grief and fear momentarily melted into confusion, but Rudolfo started nodding.

Jaime escorted the couple out, but not before they pumped my hand, saying "Gracias, gracias," over and over.

Anyone who thanked me was putting the cart before the horse.

Jaime paused in the doorway. Outside, I could hear the Huertas slowly descending the stairs.

"So, boss, I see which one snatched her, you want me to bust a head?"

A squeak and a thump behind me said Serendipity had jumped in her seat.

"Do I ever want that?"

"Way you looked at that picture, I don't know."

I felt Ser's eyes on me then.

"No. I don't think you're going to find a thing."

"Why not?"

"This wasn't done by some monster who hangs around at night, hoping for a busted ward. This was done by someone I know."

Jaime brightened. I could tell that he didn't want to wreck the monsters just because of something he'd seen in me. The picture had gotten him, too. Pretty girl like that would turn anybody into a sap. There'd be fools jumping in front of trains for Sofia her whole life. That'd be her curse.

It was a curse I hoped she'd have a shot at.

"Who, then?" Jaime asked. His right hand dipped into the pockets of his jeans where he kept the cold iron knuckles. The silver ones were in the other pocket.

"Don't know yet."

"Thought you said—"

"I don't know who. I know I've seen him. Somewhere in the last couple months, I slapped eyes on the mug that took her. I just need to know who."

"You still want me with the Huertas?" he asked.

"Yeah. Cover all our bases. You good with that, Alvarez?"

"No problem. Maybe I'll put a little fright into the snatch..." he stopped himself, and his eyes flicked to Serendipity's desk. "Into the monsters around their house."

"You do that."

Jaime nodded and went out the door.

"What's going on, Nick?" Ser asked, nearly whispering.

"You can close the office if you want, Ser," I said, getting my hat and heading for the door.

"No. It's fine. I'll keep it open."

I didn't know what to tell Serendipity. That this girl looked like Dulcinea Ramos, a woman I knew for a night? That whatever vermin had taken Sofia Huerta was probably the same one who had put four bullets into Dulcinea's back? That I might just be looking for a human?

For the first time I could remember, I was worried I might not be bringing back a fish girl. I might be bringing back a corpse.

Thirty-Four

Monday, January 9, 1956
Not long after

It took a special kind of fool to walk into a police station of his own accord, and I was that fool. I stopped at the desk sergeant out front. He looked normal enough, just a heavyset man who could stand getting out of his chair every now and again. He had the wolf buried inside him now, but I could feel it. Pacing behind the bars, glaring at the world and trying to pick which part it was going to tear up first. Maybe I could see it was because I knew he was a wolfman. Or maybe get enough of them together in a pack like this and they started letting their aggression bleed into the air like smog.

"I need to see Detective Moon," I said to him.

"Name?"

"Nick Moss."

"That's a funny name for a wolfman."

"I'm not a...can I see Detective Moon?"

"Sure, I'll go and get him."

The desk sergeant sat there, staring pointedly at me.

"This is a police station, right? How about I report a crime?"

"You here to report a crime then?"

"Not really. Kind of. Will you get Moon for me? He knows me!"

"Sure he does."

"Listen to me! I have information on a murder! Are you getting this through that giant fat head of yours, or should I talk even louder?"

The desk sergeant got up with the inevitability of an avalanche in reverse. There was a lot of him. He was fat, sure, but the ropy lumps under that uniform said there was some muscle in there. And he just kept getting up. This was the biggest wolfman I'd ever seen. There should be a law against making them so big. The smallest thing on him were his eyes, and those were getting smaller and smaller by the second as they turned a shade of red.

"Now you listen here. Maybe you killed—"

"Moss?"

Both of us stopped short like a grenade had been tossed into the space between us. I followed the voice, breaking eye contact with difficulty. Garou stood beyond the desk, a closed file in his hand, frowning at me like I'd shown up at a party I'd never been invited to.

"Uh, hi, Detective. I was looking for your partner."

"What do you want, Moss? I heard you shrieking from across the goddamn station."

"I wasn't shriek...it's not important. I mean, why I'm here is important. The specific sounds I was making—"

Garou sprouted fur over his face and he grew an inch or two. "Get to the point, Moss," he growled.

"I have a lead on a murder. For you. Well, for Moon and you."

The wolf was gone from his face as quickly as it came.

"You know this weasel?" the massive desk sergeant asked.

"Yeah. He's a stoolie."

The sergeant jerked a thumb over his shoulder. "Go on, then." Then he settled back into his chair like an earthquake with hemorrhoids.

I went through the low, swinging door and joined Garou. He sighed. "Come on, meatstick, and make it quick."

"You two busy? I figured after Mab got plugged, you'd have a lighter workload."

"What do you know about that?" he asked, giving me a hard look.

"What's in the papers," I swallowed.

"Yeah, well, they only tell half the story, if that. That elf was keeping the gray matter in check. Now, she thinks she runs this town. I tell you, in the old days, dames knew their place. Now they think just because they're monsters they get a seat at the table. Won't be long till they're wearing slacks and growing mustaches."

"I knew a lady with a mustache."

"What?"

"She was French. Or Belgian. Something like that. I'm not too good on where the actual border was when I was over there. She was maybe a hundred years old or something, but she fed a couple of us. Made this kind of chicken soup. I don't know from French cooking, but that was pretty good."

Garou was staring at me like I'd just asked him to the Spring Cotillion. "What are you babbling about?"

"Just that some women have mustaches already."

"You know, you find a woman at the bottom of the sea, and I start thinking maybe you're not as dumb as you look, but then you open your mouth and I wonder how you dress yourself in the morning."

"Pants, then shoes."

Garou clenched his fists, the fur sprouting from them. He was making me nervous. Problem was, when I'm nervous, I tend to blather a little bit.

"Maybe you think about shutting up," Garou suggested.

I did more than think about it.

We walked through the station, passing by the Monster Slayer task force. I didn't say anything about it, but there looked to be even more wolves on it than before. I couldn't be sure, but it also looked like there were more faces on the wall than there had been last time. The mass killer had kept busy, but he wasn't doing a thing to humans. Not my problem.

We got to the bullpen, where Moon was sitting behind a sloppy desk, eating an even sloppier french-dipped sandwich. He looked up as we approached, smiling when he recognized me. It'd be easy to mistake for affection, but it was closer to amusement.

"Don't tell me you pinched Moss for something."

"Believe me, I'm thinking about making something up." Garou hauled a folding chair over the linoleum floor and pointed at it. "Sit."

I sat, and did my best not to think about that irony.

"Whaddaya want, Moss?" Moon asked, wiping at the corner of his mouth with a napkin. He didn't get the sauce hiding in his jowls.

"Says he wants to report a crime," Garou said, sitting at the desk in front of Moon's. I was now sandwiched between the wolves. Between them, and a bullpen humming with LAPD detectives, my nerves were electric. I could have killed a meat golem with one of them. To make matters worse, I'd forgotten to leave my Luger at home. It was sitting under my arm, loaded with silver, ready to be confiscated and lost the same as they'd done to my .32.

"A crime, huh?" Moon asked.

"Somebody get snatched at sunset?" Garou said, and I supplied the eyeroll his tone implied.

"Not exactly," I said.

"Oh good. Not exactly a crime. You know not-exactly crimes aren't what we do," Moon said, returning to his sandwich.

"Are you two on the Monster Slayer thing?" I asked.

"Nope. Same thing as before." He didn't want to say he was with the Wolf Pack. Maybe it was a big secret or maybe Moon liked to lord those things over me. "All I know is he plants a body every week or so."

"That what you came to talk about?" Garou growled.

"Sorry, no. You remember Dulcinea Ramos?"

The frowns and blank stares answered my question.

"Songbird?"

I got a glimmer of recognition from Moon. Nothing from Garou.

"Mab's girl. The one who got shot? The one you two braced me about?"

"Oh yeah," Moon said.

"Something was fishy," Garou said.

"I know! That's what I'm here to talk about," I said.

"I meant fishy with you."

"Oh."

"Out with it, Moss," Moon said, gesturing with the business end of his sandwich.

"You collared somebody for it?"

"Sure, yeah. Some meatstick didn't like her making time with the elf. What was his name, Lou?"

"Who cares?" Garou said.

"How'd you know it was him?"

"He was a cousin of hers," Moon said, warming up as the memories pushed their way up to the movie screen of his mind. "Maybe second cousin. Anyways, he was writing letters the whole time when she was in Hollywood with the elf. Sort of half lovey-dovey crap, and the other half getting ginned up and calling her things a man shouldn't call a lady."

"Did he have the gun?"

"Don't be stupid," Garou said. "He dropped that thing as soon as he could. We'll probably fish it out of the reservoir in fifty years."

"Could you put him at the scene?"

"He's got no alibi."

"He's also human. Out in the early morning, which means probably at night too."

Moon sighed. "What's this really about? This fella's taken the rap. Sang like his cousin as soon as we got him in here."

I bet he sang. After they beat on him, told him what was going to happen to him in stir, let him stew for a day or two. What they'd almost done to me.

"Okay, what if he didn't do it?"

Garou made a noise. "He confessed. He did it. A jury's going to decide he did it."

"You have the wrong man."

"You don't want to think one of your own kind did this girl in," Garou sneered.

"It was a human," Moon said. "Girl like that shot? Had to be. Nothing else makes sense. What's she got to do with why you're here? If you're just telling us our police work is shoddy, I might let my partner have a conversation with you alone in an interrogation room."

"Might do that anyway," Garou said.

"So you should start telling us what you're doing here."

"About an hour ago, a couple comes into my office. Their daughter's missing," I said.

"My heart's breaking," Garou said. "If she's lucky she's already looking forward to the next full moon."

Now I clenched my hands into fists. "They hire me to find her, and everything's as it always is. Then they show me a photo of the girl."

I pulled the picture out of my pocket, and for a second, both detectives flinched. Just another reminder of how fast I was. Fast enough to plug one of them. They did their best to cover, and I pretended not to notice. It was dangerous to have cops scared of you, but at the same time, it was the only way I had any strength at all. I placed the photo on Moon's desk, right in front of the butcher paper where the mangled remains of his sandwich now rested.

Moon wiped his thick fingers on his pink-and-green suit jacket and picked the picture up, squinting at it.

"She's a dish all right," was the verdict.

Garou got up then and walked around the desk to get a look. Moon handed the photo over. Garou gave a literal wolfwhistle.

"Oh, she's bait," he said.

Moon chuckled. "I'd turn her myself."

"You, old man?"

"Just because a wolf's old don't mean he stops hunting."

"She'd probably be hopeless as a meter maid, but I wouldn't mind watching her try it out."

My stomach was steadily trying to turn inside out.

"Well, Moss," Moon said, "You got your work cut out. There's not a monster in the city who wouldn't want to turn her."

I swallowed the bile in my throat. "Yeah, but doesn't she look familiar?"

"What do you mean?"

"She looks like Dulcinea Ramos."

"Who?"

"The Songbird! Mab's girl!"

"Oh, right." Moon frowned at the picture. Garou was still looking, but the way his eyes were lit up, it was entirely puerile. I should have just brought a French postcard and been done with it.

"I suppose she does look a bit like Ramos," Moon decided.

"They're dead ringers, Moon. I thought I was looking at a doppelganger."

Moon shrugged. "What's your point?"

"My point? Someone kills Dulcinea Ramos and now two months later, a girl who could be her sister just disappears? That's not a coincidence! It can't be."

"That's what coincidence means, Moss. The man who did Ramos is behind bars, where he's staying. This? You ask me, the only crime is she wasn't taken sooner."

"That I didn't get a shot at her," Garou said.

"You wouldn't know what to do with bait like that," Moon told him.

"I know exactly, old man. You got her, you'd be calling me for help inside five minutes."

"Thanks, detectives," I said, standing up. "You've been a real help."

I plucked the photo from Moon's greasy hands and got out of there before I was even more tempted to fill them full of silver.

Thirty-Five

Monday, January 9, 1956
Before lunch

Faces blurred through my mind, changing eye color, hair color, species, how much of their flesh was rotting or stitched together, how much they liked poetry or haunting things. "Someone I'd met relatively recently" did not winnow the pool of suspects down, especially since Moon and Garou were partially right. They were disgusting, but they were a good gauge of how monsters saw women like Dulcinea and Sofia.

They weren't even humans. They were bait.

That meant that anyone who saw Dulcinea was a potential killer. It was the same conundrum that had paralyzed me before. Then I'd given up when I heard they had someone, not realizing they had just picked the nearest human and come up with a story to match him. Maybe if I hadn't been so distracted. Not much of an excuse, but I needed one. Especially since that negligence could mean I'd doomed Sofia Huerta.

There was someone who could help me. Then again, it's possible I just wanted to see her again. Jane had spent more time around Dulcinea than anyone who didn't want me dead, and she might have a few things to say. The thought of talking to Jane about Dulcinea felt wrong. Shameful. I didn't want to plumb those depths too much. I did want to talk to Jane, though.

I pulled up in front of Jane's place in Lincoln Heights. She lived in what had once been a spacious two-story house, but had since been divided up into apartments. Hers was on the upper floor in the front, with an external wooden staircase leading to a screen door. I rapped on the side of it, and as Jane's willowy shadow closed in, my heart started hammering like kraut artillery.

She opened the door for me, breaking into a smile and waving me inside. She was dressed in a pair of high-waisted shorts and a plaid shirt tied at the waist. A handkerchief corralled her hair. A bolt of gray cloth was fed into her sewing machine. Jane picked her slate off a table and wrote a message.

Hi Nick. How's tricks?

"Not great. Do you have time to talk?"

Sure. Can you stand here? She pointed to a stool and set her slate down.

I climbed up on it and she held her arms out, pointing to me. I did as she mimed, and she looked me over. She pushed my arms down, then opened up my jacket, peering at the pockets where I kept my various weapons and wards.

"Oh. That's all for...you know. I have licenses."

She frowned.

I fumbled in my pocket and produced my wallet. The licenses folded out like an accordion. "That's for fire...sorry, and that's for cold iron, silver there, uh...that's just for the gun, there's salt, and so forth and so on."

She picked up the slate and wrote, *That's a lot.*

"Expensive too."

I bet. She wiped that away. *Use them much?*

"Some more than others, I guess. I'd rather not use any of it, but it's not really my choice."

She erased her last message other than the question mark, and tapped it with the chalk. I got her meaning.

"If a monster is coming to turn me or kill me, I'm going to use what he's scared of. Maybe worse, depending. I'm not going out looking for these monsters, either. They make the choice, not me."

I see.

She looked like she wanted to write something else, but didn't know how to phrase whatever it was. I felt guilty for the lighter again. I didn't think I'd use it on Jane, the same reason I'd never use an evil eye charm on Ser. They weren't the only two monsters in the world those were good for, unfortunately.

The hiss of chalk on slate pulled my attention back to Jane.

Happy to see you. Why?

"Why? Oh, why am I here? Yeah, about that."

She set aside the slate and mimed taking my jacket off. I did so and handed it over. She put it on a hanger and hung it on the hatrack, investigating the pockets.

"I wanted to ask you about Dulcinea Ramos." The name caught a frown from Jane. "The Gobfather's girl. Songbird."

She nodded then, picking up her slate and writing a message.

She was murdered. She accented that with a shrug, and I took it as something she had heard.

"I know. That's part of what I want to know."

She shook her head.

"The cops already arrested somebody, but I don't think they got the right guy. How much did you know about her? When she was alive, I mean?"

Not much. We carried her in, we carried her out. Jane thought, then rubbed that out and wrote, *She never ate. Never drank.*

Jane stepped in close to me, laying some bolts of fabric over my shoulder and adjusting how they hung. She smelled like rain and lightning. I focused on Dulcinea and felt like a cad.

"Um...yeah, so...I was thinking, the goblins?"

She looked up from where she was switching out one piece of fabric for another. Her left eye, the bright silver one, was like the moon on a clear winter night.

"The goblins might have been the ones who killed her."

Jane thought about it, then shook her head.

"Why not? Maybe they were jealous. Their leader spending all this time with a human? They resent it, bump her off?"

Jane shook her head more emphatically.

"You're right, that was dumb."

She shook her head, caught herself, then held her index and thumb up. *A little bit,* said the gesture.

I didn't think telling her I was having trouble thinking would help. Two women, a dead human and a live dead girl, grabbing hold of my faculties.

"Dulcinea had a lot of admirers."

Jane nodded, her eyes widening. *A lot,* she was saying.

"Who?"

Jane thought it over and picked up the slate.

Everyone.

"Thanks, wiseguy. Can you narrow it down a little? Think about the ones who never missed one of her performances. Maybe the ones who made a special effort when they knew she was singing. Folks like that."

Jane nodded, thinking. Then she wrote a name.

Nyx Nocturne.

"Your boss." She nodded.

"This doesn't feel like a vampire to me. Sure, with those newfangled umbrellas, they can go out in the daytime, but most of them like to avoid it. Anyone who did this was probably out in the early morning. Tougher to block the sun, too, when it's at an angle like that. Besides, what kind of vampire uses a gun?"

She shrugged.

"Does Miss Nocturne own a gun?"

Jane gave me an *I don't know* shrug.

"I'll call her a long shot. Who else?"

Retinax.

"Sounds like a crawling eye." She nodded. "Studio executive?"

New honcho of Visionary Pictures.

"I, uh...I knew the last guy."

You keep interesting company.

"Tell me about it."

Jane cocked her eyebrow, making her look somewhere between dubious and surprised.

"This doesn't much strike me as a crawling eye thing either. How do crawling eyes bump people off?"

Have their goons do it.

I had to grin. Jane was sharper than a cold iron dagger. She probably would have made a decent detective if she had a mind to it. The cops weren't hiring women, but Beth Gevaudan was a lady PI, and she was supposed to be good. Of course, she was also a werewolf, or maybe a wolfman. Or did they call them wolfwomen? Wolfgirls? I had no idea. In any case, no one wanted a meat golem looking into their affairs.

"Last I saw, crawling eyes used ghosts and headless horsemen."

Invisible men sometimes.

A chill slithered up my spine.

?

"Oh, sorry. This all started...kind of...when the wolves hired me to find a missing invisible man. One of their own, undercover with the Gobfather."

Find him?

"For about five seconds before one of the goblins...you don't want to know," I finished quietly.

Even though I danced around the F-word—that's "fire" when talking to a meat golem— she got the meaning and shuddered.

"I'm not seeing it. A crawling eye has a girl shot? Did this Retinax have a beef with the Gobfather?"

She shrugged.

"Who else?"

Zombie. I think a gangster.

Remembered seeing a zombie that first night, one with patches of green mold sprouting from his decaying face.

"Name's Bracken Mold."

She raised her eyebrows.

"I don't think so. He's a gangster, sure. Works for Sarah Bellum too. But it doesn't jibe with what I know." I wanted to stop, but her expectant look prompted me. "He saved my life for one thing. More important, though, was when we found the Gallery of Angels."

She wrote a question mark and tapped it.

I explained the Gallery of Angels to her as best I could. Her face went from open, to horrified, and finally disgusted. She held up one arm etched with stitches to stop me.

"I know. It's...I don't think there's a word for how awful it is."

She shook her head; that wasn't what she meant. Then she nodded, agreeing with my point, then grabbed her slate. Her fingers were so stiff with anger the chalk squealed once or twice. She started several times, each time rubbing out the few words on there and going back to the beginning.

I know what that is. Not Gallery. I am made. They were too, in a way. The women I was died for this. For me. Those women died for his needs.

I don't want to say I understood what she was saying. Not really. Not the way she did, anyway. I think I got a little bit, and I wanted to spend as much time as it took to learn what she meant about the rest. I'd talked to a lot of monsters in my time, but I'd never heard anything close to what Jane just told me. All monsters came from humans, and most were a one-to-one trade. Transformation. They'd say like a caterpillar to a butterfly, putting humanity at the equivalent of a garbage-eating worm.

Not meat golems. They were like omelets in that it took more than one egg to make one. No, you needed a couple eggs, and mix that with ham and tomatoes and so on. Only each ingredient was a dead person, and a lot of the time, meat golems liked to harvest the tomato right off the vine, not to stretch a metaphor.

Jane's mismatched eyes were downcast, occasionally flicking up to mine. The right one, the purplish one, was deeper than the ocean. It was hard not to fall right in.

"Do you know your..." Father? Creator? I wasn't sure what was polite in this case.

She shook her head, then nodded, then put her palm flat and wobbled it. *Sort of.*

I didn't know how anyone could live like that. Knowing how many people were dead so you were alive. Hell, I wasn't so different. I shifted on the stool.

"There's always a price for any life, I guess. From that kraut I landed on in France. I killed him. Shot him dead where he stood, and because of that, I'm alive. It's more than just him. Go back over my service, and there's more than six corpses between that day and this one here."

Jane stood up straight. With me standing on the footrest, we were about eye to eye. It was getting a little hard to breathe in here. She looked away only briefly to write a message.

That was war.

"The way I see it, the difference was choice. I chose. You didn't get the chance to."

She put her hands at my neck. That was the closest I'd ever let a meat golem get to any vulnerable part of me. You tended to get squirrelly after you'd seen a one of them throttle the life out of someone. She was staring into my eyes, and I looked right back. Outside, a crow called and Jane jumped. Then she was fashioning a collar around my neck, abruptly focused on that.

I coughed and let her work with her cloth while the tension drained out of the room.

"Anybody else?" I asked after a good minute or two.

She frowned, then caught the hanging thread of the conversation we'd been having.

Capriccio Español.

"The band leader at the Nocturnist?"

She nodded.

A phantom. They got crushes that could turn homicidal on a dime. Sure, shooting their beloved was a bit mundane for their tastes, but they had done it before. As long as there was a suitably ironic reason for the act, a phantom could justify any form of violence. If there was one kind of monster I'd never seen much point in, it was a phantom. They combined all the worst features of gill-men, vampires, and clowns.

"Where is he?"

She wrote down a Beverly Hills address. I thanked her and left. I was eager to get to the bottom of this thing and hopefully return Sofia to her parents intact. I also had to leave, because if I stayed much longer, I might try to kiss Jane, and I couldn't imagine a more dangerous hobby than that one.

Thirty-Six

Monday, January 9, 1956
Around lunchtime

Billy Bounce sat on my secretary's desk like a pat of butter with a rancid complexion. When I opened the door and saw him, I nearly took him for the phantom I was about to go see. Billy was twenty years younger—though that was tough to see with the cheesecloth skin and pitted eyes—and he didn't have the Spanish mustache and lacquered hair. He was in his jazz hipster suit, the pantlegs riding high and showing off socks with notes on them. Christmas gifts from Ser; I remembered when she showed them off proudly to me.

Billy had been making eyes at Ser, and she was giving them right back. Keeping in mind that a phantom's peepers looked like a pair of hard-boiled eggs some joker had drawn pupils on and stuck in a pair of pits, and sirens wore thick water-filled goggles to see, well, that was a lot of eye traded back and forth.

"Nick!" Ser squeaked when I came in. The sudden change in expression jogged her lenses, and the saltwater fell down the front of her blouse. "Oh, judas priest," she muttered, trying to fix herself up.

"Afternoon, Mr. Moss," Billy said to me.

"Don't you have a rehearsal to get to?" I snapped.

"An hour or two. Had to stop by and see my best girl."

"So there's more than one, then?"

"Nick," Ser scolded me, dipping her goggles in the saltwater of her fish tank. She leaned over and carefully fitted them over her face.

"I won't keep you long," I said, going into my office. I wanted to make sure my lighter was topped off with fluid. No way I was walking into a phantom's den without being fully armed. Might help to test my whistle while I was at it. Billy would *love* that.

"It's good you're here," Ser said, following me to the doorway. "Mickey Cohen called you."

"Mickey Cohen? The gangster?" Billy asked, excited.

I ignored him. "What about?"

"He wants you to meet him at the Rocket Diner for lunch."

"When did he say? Was he about to get into the shower? Because I still have half a day."

"No, he called early. Right after you left this morning for the Huertas."

"Huh. Then he's probably still there. Where's the Rocket Diner?"

Ser looked at the note in her hand. "Gage and Michigan."

"He didn't happen to say what this was about did he?"

"Nope. He didn't sound mad if that's what you're thinking."

"I don't know what I'm thinking, but that's good to hear."

I filled up my lighter.

"Need your lighter for something?" Ser asked.

"It's not for your boyfriend."

"Better not be," she muttered, going back into the front room.

I left the two of them alone in my office to do god knew what and went to see Mickey. It wouldn't take too long, and I'd rather not test Mickey's patience any more than I already had. We were friends, but I was getting the impression I might be straining that relationship about as far as I could.

The Rocket Diner hadn't been frivolously named. It looked like a rocket ship laid down lengthwise on the street. Round portholes were the windows looking out onto Gage Avenue. The fins on the back threw parallelogram shadows on the pavement. The stairs to the door in the side had even been designed to look like a ladder. Mickey's big blue Cadillac wallowed on the street outside.

I wasn't surprised to see a martian behind the grill when I walked in. Martians were called that because they looked like the Martians Wells described, but they didn't actually come from Mars. They were former humans, the same as anyone else. That they were the spitting image of something a British guy made up fifty-odd years ago was a question no one was keen on answering.

Martians looked a bit like wet balloons made out of cow stomach. The flabby head end had some goggly eyes and a beaky mouth. Where a balloon would have had a string, martians had eight powerful tentacles they could move entirely independent of one another. Most martians wore a variety of equipment to keep from getting sick, as even a common cold could do one in. This ranged from a simple surgical mask all the way up to entire containment suits. This one went with the simple, and considering the state of the restaurant, he didn't need anything else. Every surface fairly gleamed, and other than the food, the most persistent smell was cleaning solution. Back in the service, we were sometimes told to clean something so thoroughly you could eat off it. This was the only place that lived up to that order, and on every last flat surface I could see.

It was well after lunch, so the only people in the place were another martian, a nosferatu waitress, and Mickey's group. He was at a corner table, his back to a wall, with Rob Sampson and Wong Lee sitting across from him. Mickey spotted me first, and the other two turned. Mickey murmured to Wong, who got up and slid in next to his boss, leaving an open spot for me.

"Stick, good to see you," Mickey said. "I was worried youse wasn't gonna get the message. Your secretary said you just left."

"Got hired to find a girl."

"She pretty?"

"Yeah, actually."

"Whoa there, Nick. Don't fall in love with all of 'em!"

Rob and Wong laughed. I managed a weak grin as I slid into the booth. I wasn't sure I wanted to clue Mickey in to what was eating me. Better to keep him in the dark about my connection to Dulcinea and the Gobfather.

"Just trying to find her in the same condition she was misplaced."

"So you're still doing that?"

Jane's face popped into my head when he asked me that. Her strange, patchwork face. "Yeah. I think I am."

"Good," Mickey said.

That was the last thing I expected to come out of his mouth.

"Hey, doll. Come over here and take my friend's order."

The batgirl came over. She was bald, her features rodent-like. Her skin was gray, and she shied away from the portholes. I was wondering why a martian would have a nosferatu in his place, then I put it together. They could control vermin, and that extended to keeping them away. It was why so many nosferatu made a good living as exterminators.

She held the pad in gray hands that looked like angry spiders. "What can I get you?" she asked, her buckteeth tripping over the words.

"Get anything," Mickey said. "Cleanest food in the city, and you can take that to the bank."

I looked the menu over.

"Get him the corned beef on rye," Mickey said.

The nosferatu jotted it down and pinned the order for the chef.

I glanced around the table. None of the three men looked ready to start any violence, and Mickey had already expressed approval at my job. I didn't think he was ready to fit me for a Chicago overcoat, but I didn't *not* think it either.

"So what's on your mind, Mickey?" I asked.

"You notice anything?"

"Is that a new suit? Or, ah, the tiepin?"

Mickey laughed, looking to his guys. "Listen to him! No, nothing I'm wearing, Nick. You notice there might not be as many of us as before."

"How are Johnny and Jack?"

"Johnny? Johnny's fine. Johnny's earning, even if I don't think a man ought to be doing what he does. Jack, though. Jack's who I called you about."

I leaned forward. I didn't like Johnny, but Jack had always been okay. He looked like a big palooka, and he probably was, but with Mickey's friends, he might as well have been a lamb.

"Jack's missing, Nick. I need you to find him."

"I'm sorry. If Jack's gone..." I didn't know how tell him delicately his guy had been bumped off. I didn't have to, because the nosferatu put the plate in front of me. I bought some time by trying the sandwich. It wasn't bad, but it had a weird chemical aftertaste.

"Don't worry, Stick. I'm paying you. I'll pay youse better than you make from other stuff too. I'll put youse on, what's it called when you have a lawyer? Retainer. I'll put youse on retainer. You're finding your lost orphans and so on, but when I need you, you come when you're called. And I need you now. Jackie needs you now."

"I'm really sorry about Jack," I said, and I meant it. "Mickey, if he's gone, I think he's gone-gone. You know?"

"No kidding." Mickey appealed to his fellas. "Can you believe his guy? Tiptoeing like a dowager. Youse find people, so youse can find people ain't breathing anymore. I think maybe that's easier, since they don't move around so good neither."

He kind of had a point. Odds were, Bellum's people had punched his ticket, and the ones that did that usually dumped their prey off a turn on Mulholland. Place was famous as a graveyard for monsters. I didn't relish the idea of driving up there and picking through the trees and shrubs looking for Big Jack Whalen's body, but I'd do it. For Mickey, and for Jack.

"Okay, Mickey. I can have a look around. If I find his body, it's not like I'm going to know who did him in."

"I'm sure we can think of a couple suspects. If Jack's alive, I want to know where he's hiding and why. If he's dead, I want to put his body to rest like he'd have wanted. If he's turned, well, I want to know that too."

Over the course of the lunch, Mickey gave me the information on Jack's last known whereabouts. Mickey still used a lot of euphemisms to talk to me. I wasn't sure if this was because he didn't quite trust me, he didn't want the waitress overhearing when she brought him his third ginger ale, or that was just how Mickey talked about business. Jack was out on "collections."

I listened to some of the names, and here Mickey needed help from his guys, summoning the memories with snapped fingers. A lot were the kinds of names that said monsters, sure, but most of the names were human. That's where Mickey was making his cash. Off humans. The corned beef wasn't so appetizing anymore. I pushed the plate to the side and hoped Mickey wouldn't take it as an insult. He didn't even notice.

"So he had to be nabbed somewhere on there," Mickey finished.

"Yeah, after one, um, collection. Before the next. I got it."

"Great. Get started on that, and there's gold at the end of the rainbow for you." He waved the waitress over and handed her a twenty dollar bill, enough to cover four meals and then some. "Keep the change, cutie."

The nosferatu left us, and we stood, buttoning our jackets. Mickey looked around the diner, pursing his lips and nodding. "I tell you. Say what you want about martians, but them squids can keep a clean house."

I glanced over at the kitchen, but I didn't think the martian heard us. Mickey just loved throwing those slurs around.

We emerged onto the street, the car keys jingling in Wong's hand.

A black Packard barreled down the street, screeching to a stop in front of the Rocket Diner. The shotgun blast sounded like a car backfiring, and Wong fell on his back, the front of his chest a pockmarked mess. The cloud of stinging cordite blew from the Packard's front passenger window. Another black shotgun barrel sprouted from the backseat. Behind it, the face of a rotten corpse, and this sounds a little weird to say, but not one I recognized. Bet if I asked him his name, he'd say "Brains."

I was moving before I made the decision. Had to thank both wars for that one. My body knew gunfire when I heard it, even if it took my brain a little bit to catch up. I also found my Luger in hand, like it had been waiting to squirt lead at the next deserving target. I threw myself behind the front tire of Mickey's Caddy, right in time to hear the second *boom.*

I didn't see the hit, but I saw Mickey spinning to the floor, Rob in front of him, pistol in hand and returning fire. Mickey was moving on the ground, though about as well as you'd expect after stopping some buckshot with his chest.

I popped up from behind the wheel and sent a couple rounds through the windshield of the Packard. Stupid maybe, using silver on zombies, but I didn't even carry lead anymore. If I was going to be dancing with corpses, I might have to start.

The back door of the Packard opened. A lean zombie toting a shotgun and looking for another round stepped out.

"Get Mickey in the car!" I shouted at Rob.

He was ahead of me, picking the keys out of Wong's lifeless fingers.

The zombie stalked around the far side of the car to get a clean shot at Rob, Mickey, and why not, me too. With the street sweeper held at his hip, there wasn't much chance he was going to miss. I shot him twice, pockmarking his sleeves with ragged bullet holes. He wasn't going to stop unless I got lucky with a headshot.

The zombie worked the slide of his shotgun, the abrupt silence on the street punctuated by the hollow sound of the empty shell hitting the pavement.

Rob, the keys in hand, hauled Mickey to his feet. My friend had lost one of his shoes when he was shot, now stumbling along on one stocking foot. He had one arm around Rob's neck, and the taller man was half-crouched to support the much shorter Mickey. Mickey's shirt was sticky and red.

I was impressed, though, when Mickey filled his hand and fired at the incoming zombie. The impacts made the zombie stumble back a half step, a confused look on his rotten mug.

Rob opened the back door and threw Mickey inside.

The shotgun boomed. The back window shattered.

The front door of the Packard opened. It was pure luck I heard that. I whirled and fired until the Luger clicked dry. I don't think I hit much of substance, but the zombie who had been coming out fell backward.

Rob was crazy; he charged the gunman. I thought for certain I was about to see Rob cut in half.

The gunman racked a shell and the shotgun *boomed* again, but it was a second too late. Rob was already on him, and had turned the barrel aside. Pellets raked the back of the Caddy and the Packard. Rob shoved his .45 under the zombie's chin and took the top of his head off, then picked up the shotgun, emptying it at the enemy car.

The Packard started up and squealed off. Rob ran to the front seat of the Caddy.

"You coming?" he shouted at me.

I stepped aside. "Just get him to a hospital!"

Mickey's Caddy left tracks as it burned away. Two bodies lay on the pavement. Wong, on his back, right in front of the restaurant. Never knew what hit him. The gunman crumpled on his side in the street, the top of his head gone. I ran for my car and tried to drive as calmly as I could as the sirens zeroed in on the Rocket Diner.

Thirty-Seven

Monday, January 9, 1956
Shortly after

When you leave a war, you think to yourself that you're done. That's it. The worst thing that can happen to a man has already happened, and you got through it. Those feelings, the fear, the anger, the blinding hatred, that's gone. In the past. But for the ten seconds the attempted hit on Mickey had taken, I was back in the war. I was helpless to stop what was transpiring, sure, but at the same time, I was strong. I was vital. I spat fire at the other side.

It was a familiar bad old feeling, partly because it felt so damn good.

I drove around, my blood humming from the shootout. I pulled over in the parking lot of a hamburger stand and reloaded the pistol, pressing cartridges into the magazine one by one. A human mother walked away from the stand, holding a white paper bag in one hand and the hand of her chubby kid in the other. The kid looked over at me and caught my eye. I didn't see the consuming wonder of childhood there. I saw fear.

Across the lot, a pair of zombies openly watched the mother. A blob rolled after her slowly, probably unaware it was daylight.

She climbed into her car, buckled the kid into his seat, and was out of there quickly. That's what it was being human. Flitting from place to place between ticks of the second hand. I thought about getting out of the car, maybe showing those zombies what it meant to put their eyes where they weren't wanted. A little potassium sprinkled on that blob would settle it down, too. I didn't, though. I didn't need to be the crazy meatstick who got torn up by the cops. Especially when the last thing I'd done was get in a shootout.

Seeing Mickey go down hurt. Whatever he was in life, we'd been together through some of the worst years the world had ever seen. Get out of the Night War, and the deal was you got to live. We were pardoned. The world was going to continue. Today it nearly stopped for Mickey, or maybe it did. I didn't know how bad he got hit, but that was a lot of blood on his suit. He could be dying in a hospital that kept him waiting while monsters filtered in and took his place at the front of the line.

Finding Jack Whalen was that much more pointless. Bellum had him knocked off, and she was angling to do the same to Mickey. Her biggest rival had been taken out. Why not add to the grave? The LAPD wouldn't lose much sleep over Mickey taking a dirt nap.

The Huertas needed me more than Mickey did. I drove to Español's address in Beverly Hills. His digs wouldn't put Croesus to shame, but he was doing okay for a bandleader. The house looked like the architect couldn't decide if he wanted a creepy castle or a Cuban hacienda and had decided to kind of split the difference. Wide, tiled patios existed alongside looming towers with cathedral windows. I parked on the street, not wanting to risk my coupe on any driveway pit traps I might run into.

The driveway was done up in earth-toned bricks, the landscaping a Hollywoodized island theme. Palm trees swayed on narrow trunks, punctuated with ferns and the odd plantain tree. As I approached the door, I started to hear the singing.

As much as I don't like phantoms, I do have to take my hat off to the musical talent. The voice was male and running scales up and down the upper limits of his vocal range. I had to stop there, on the phantom's doorstep, and appreciate what I was hearing. The voice was like stained glass, clear and true, but of so many different vibrant hues, throwing sunlight out in a million rainbows. Yeah, the kid had pipes.

I knocked on the door, a thick wooden portal with a barred window on top. It opened a couple inches, unlocked. I leaned into the gap, but not too far, and called out.

"Hello? I'm here to talk to Mr. Español? The name's Moss!"

The singing didn't stop. A single note faltered, followed by a loud crack. The scales started up even quicker. I pushed the door open and was about to step inside when I paused. I'd gone into more than one phantom's lair during the war, and if there was one thing I learned, it's that you don't put your foot anywhere you haven't checked first. Sure enough, a nearly transparent line of wire was strung across the threshold.

Like an idiot, I had nearly stepped right over it. The floor beyond was covered in more Spanish tile, and maybe someone who wasn't looking might not notice that one of the tiles was a few shades off. I stepped around that one, and I was in the entrance hall of the house. A heavy blade was suspended over the door, ready to pull a Marie Antoinette on anybody who tripped the wire. A staircase spiraled upstairs on my right, and hallways downstairs led off in three directions. A chandelier tinkled and glittered above me. The singing echoed through the house, bouncing around so much it sounded like I was surrounded by a whole choir of angels warming up for their big show.

"Mr. Español?" I called out. "I need to have a word with you."

It was probably because my senses were still fox-sharp from the fight. A creak came from above, followed by a snap, and I knew enough to dive like I was trying to steal home. The crash was too close, coming all around my ears, along with shards of crystal. I got up and saw exactly what I thought: the chandelier had collapsed, and now the frame was skeletal, the sharp bits having all shattered and sprayed the room with shrapnel.

I shook my head and took a circuit around the broken chandelier. Español had to have heard that one. I was about to look around when I heard a zip behind and above me. I barely got my hands up in time. A leather lasso snaked around my neck, and would have tightened to the bone had I not gotten my thumbs in the way. It yanked upward, and I realized with horror that the wielder was standing on the stairs above and was trying to reel me in like a trout.

"You cannot have him, wolfman!" The defiant declaration sported an accent that sounded like it had taken a confused route through Spain, Mexico, Italy, and a few made-up places for good measure.

I tried to explain that I wasn't a wolfman. I was a private investigator.

"Urk."

Yeah. that'd do it.

"You might not meet your end at the hands of my punjab lasso, but you learn to respect it, no?"

"Capriccio? What's going on?" A new voice. Younger, clearer, with a hint of Massachusetts.

"Go upstairs, Joseph. This does not concern you. These are the affairs of monsters!"

"Did you say wolfman? Is this a cop?"

"Look at him, Joseph! What else could he be?"

"He's trying to say something."

I was trying to say "Man," but all that came out was "Haaaah." My face felt like it was three times its normal size, and black crowded in on my vision. My thumbs were the only reason I was still conscious at all, and they were going numb.

"Lies! He speaks lies!" Español said.

"Maybe we should talk to him first. Hear the lies."

"Joseph, he is sent by your family. They do not understand the path you have chosen. The beautiful music you will make when you sing with the voice of the night."

If I could, I would have rolled my eyes, but as they were presently popping out of my skull, that might have gotten ugly.

"Maybe. Maybe not. What if he's just going door to door selling the Watchtower or something?"

"Then he is a slave! But I cannot deny a favor asked so sweetly."

Abruptly, the lasso was gone, and I fell to all fours, gasping and trying to get my face to stop feeling like ants were crawling all over it.

"Well? Speak!" Español demanded.

"Give him a minute," Joseph said.

I stood gingerly. Deep tracks marred the bases of both of my thumbs, and the burn all around my neck said I'd find a matching one in the mirror. I looked up, where both figures stood in the curve of the staircase.

Capriccio Español was in shirtsleeves, dressed all in white like some island potentate. His skin was sallow, the corners of his mouth rotting away. His hair was parted down the middle and slicked to his head, and his pencil-thin mustache and goatee in perfect order. He held a short staff with a leather loop at one end, like he had taken up lacrosse but thought homicide was the most important part of the sport.

Joseph was a young fella in his twenties. He reminded me a bit of Jaime. They had the same pompadour hairstyle, and both of them were convinced that undershirts were quite enough to wear around. No tattoos decorated his dark skin, and his face was open and unscarred. One look at him and I didn't know if he had the psychotic chops to be a proper phantom.

"Speak," Español said, "but know that I will not surrender Joseph without a titanic struggle. You have already lost once, and you shall not win again!"

"Well," I said, choked, and tried again. My voice came back with a little difficulty. "The name's Moss. I'm not here about Joseph. I don't know who he is."

"If you are not here for Joseph, what could you be here for? Are you, perhaps, a fan?" Español warmed up to that, raising an eyebrow as thin as his mustache.

"Not exactly. I mean, I've, uh, I've heard you sing at the Nocturnist, and you're great. One of the best shows I've seen."

"*One* of the best?"

"The best. Sorry. Didn't know what I was saying there." I wasn't going to tell Español this, but I'd take the Salem Sisters over at the Gloom Room or Jungle Jim and the Hepcats at the Isla Calavera over him any day. Hell, I preferred the Disasters if you got right down to it. I'd take him over the racket at Last Night, though. Not that he'd take that as much of a compliment.

"But you are not here for an autograph? To perhaps experience the rhumba of the night?"

"Uh...no."

Español and Joseph shared a confused look. "Then why are you here, Mr...Moss?"

He gave "Moss" a long *O*. I decided I kind of liked it that way.

"I'm here about Dulcinea Ramos."

Español brightened immediately. "Ah yes, the Songbird! It is a tragedy what happened to her."

"She was very young."

"I have not much to do with Titanio Mab. He was an admirer and quite gracious at all times, and I do not like to speak ill of the dead."

A setup like that begged for a *but*.

"But he was a fool."

There we go.

"What do you mean?"

"Songbird was not meant to be human. Her talents were far too pure for such things. Were she made a phantom, given the proper voice of darkness, she too could have made music to endure beyond such petty concerns of morality or mortality."

"So you wanted to turn her?"

"I would not have refused the chance to do so, but there was another I was far more interested in giving the gift. Young Joseph here. He interprets the lyrics far better than Songbird could, and he was not fettered with a sidhe who might have taken my interest as an excuse to hurt me."

"I see."

"I had heard there was an arrest made in her murder, no? A mea..." a glance at Joseph. "A human?"

"Yes."

"Then what is the Los Angeles Police Department doing here?"

"I'm sorry. I didn't mean to give the impression that I was with the police."

"Then who exactly are you, Mr. Moss?"

"I'm a private investigator."

Español paused, trying his best to figure out what a private eye was doing there, apparently investigating a murder. Sometimes people thought we did that sort of thing, but I liked to tell them that was what cops were for. He opened his mouth to say something, but he got out maybe a syllable when the door crashed inward behind me.

I turned, hand going to my jacket. Just outside was an angry mob of humans and a single gill-man. They were dressed in work clothes, carrying a variety of weapons: pipes, baseball bats, chains, and tire irons. Whistles bounced on their necks, and each one had a collection of unlit torches hanging from their belts.

"Look out!" I called to a young woman who was about to trip the wire.

She hit it, but my words made her recoil, and the guillotine blade dropped maybe inches in front of her.

"Joe!" she called. "I came for you!"

Joe rolled his eyes. "I told you, I don't want to marry you!"

"He's got you beguiled!" the young woman called back.

The gill-man hefted the guillotine blade, his prodigious strength allowing him to rip it clean off its tracks and hurl it into the room.

"Joe!" he bubbled. "We can be together too!"

"Not interested, Walter," Joe said.

The group, the young woman in the lead, boiled up the stairs. One, a big blond kid who looked like he should be on a farm lifting tractors, pointed at me. "You!"

"Me?"

"You're not gonna stop us, doggie!"

"I'm not a, oh, Chri—"

My blasphemy was cut short as I ducked under one hamhock mitt. I planted a fist in his gut, but I might as well have socked a battleship. He swung again, this giant haymaker aiming to knock my block off. I stumbled back. On the stairs, Español was locked in combat with the mob, using his punjab lasso as a staff to fend off the gill-man and jilted bride. Joe was behind them, shouting at them to leave him alone.

The farmboy kept coming for me, and pretty soon he'd throw something I couldn't dodge.

"Hey, kid, I'm not a wolfman."

"Yeah, you expect me to believe that?"

"Have I changed yet?"

"You're gonna! Right when I drop my guard."

"Well, then what are you gonna do, huh? Punching a wolfman isn't—" I swallowed the rest when the farmboy skinned a silver letter opener and gave me gap-toothed grin. I probably shouldn't have reminded him.

"Got anything else to say, doggie?"

"Nothing comes to mind."

The farmboy lunged. I reached out, grabbed the first thing my hand closed around and flung it. It was a vase, and it shattered over his head. I don't even think he noticed.

"Criminy, kid, what the hell are you made of?" I muttered.

It hadn't worked, but maybe I hadn't tried something heavy enough. As the farmboy chased me down the hallway, I kept throwing. Decorative plates, artwork, statuary, books. I knocked over pedestals and shelves to get in his way. I tried to talk sense to him. I dodged backward whenever one of those paws swiped the letter opener at me. I didn't duck into any of the rooms we passed, either. No reason to let him corner me. No, I was going until the real estate ran out.

I reached out to a bookcase and flung a copy of *Treasure Island* at the farmboy. He didn't care much for literature, batting that aside with his hand and making the book come apart into fluttering leaves. I reached out for another and pulled. It didn't come free.

I turned. The book was halfway out, and a section of the bookcase had swung aside. A secret passage. That was phantoms for you.

I ducked inside, and the shelf swung shut behind me, leaving me stranded in the dark. Or it would have, had I not been forced to live in a world with monsters. I look out my flashlight—perfect if that gill-man had come at me—and had a look around. I was in a narrow hallway. I felt like it should have been choked in cobwebs and knee-deep in dust, but it wasn't. The place was ship-shape, either through regular use or an understanding maid. I steeled myself to run into a ghost back here.

Farmboy was still making an unholy racket outside, banging on the bookcase. I took the hint and made tracks down the hallway. Before long, the booming stopped. Either I had gone far enough that I couldn't hear him, or he had given up on me and was going to help his friends. Truth be told, I didn't know who I wanted to win there. I'd wandered into that particular movie late, and it was going to end with or without me. I'd pick without me.

The passage bent and my beam splashed up against a doorway. I opened it, revealing a wall of wine casks. A cord for the light brushed my face, and once I was sure it wasn't a spider—which took some flailing and a yelp that might or might not have sounded like a young lady—I pulled on it. The light in here was dim, and unlike the hall outside, the room was dusty. Parts, anyway. A pathway was entirely, obsessively clean. I followed that past a few more shelves of wine and found the end of the trail.

It was a camp.

The corner of this wine cellar had been completely taken over. A bedroll was pressed against the wall, and an empty wine case served as a small table. An electric lamp sat on top of that, next to a notebook. This wasn't the strangest part. That would be the squatter's idea of decor.

Instead of a nice poster of Rita Hayworth were photographs. I knew some of the monsters in them from personal experience, and I recognized others from the papers. Lou Garou and Phil Moon were on there, a shot of each of them. Moon was shoveling a hamburger into his maw. Garou was staring off camera and scowling. I figured something in his field of vision had the temerity to be alive when Garou would rather they weren't. Both pictures were taken when neither wolf was aware of the camera.

There was a shot of Police Chief Alfred Wolfe on there, as well as Hunter Moore, the head of the Wolf Pack. There were other shots of other policemen I didn't know. Some were uniform, others in plainclothes. None of them had any idea a camera had been trained on them.

Most troubling, though, were the red Xs drawn through some of them. One eliminated Garou. Another blocked out Wolfe. It looked like some kind of assassination order, but I'd have heard if Wolfe bought the farm. There would have been a funeral and a parade, and a promise to crack down on something. Take your pick, mob violence, teenage street gangs, humans. Who was I kidding? They'd say humans.

The bedroll, with its single blanket, had been squared away with military precision. I stayed away from sitting or kneeling on it; the last thing I wanted was to leave a trace. I picked up the notebook and leafed through it. Written in cramped but legible handwriting was a log.

MOON
Sept. 9, 1955

0630 Awake
0634 Relieves self
0640 Shower
0703 Arrived at station
0707 Greeted partner
0713 Coffee and doughnut

It went on like that. I paged through it, and found pages labeled GAROU, WOLFE, MOORE, and so on. A detailed log of their daily comings and goings. There was a new entry for each day, though each one tracked a different wolf. It tracked their meals, bathroom habits. Within a few pages I learned that Garou was married but having an affair with a siren chorus girl, Wolfe was looking for a new protégé to turn, and Moore had a hex habit and was getting them from the cook over at the Nocturnist.

I frowned, looking up at the pictures. No X crossed out Hunter Moore. I still wasn't entirely sure what I was looking at and the notebook offered no suggestions. It was clearly written by someone for his own purposes. He wasn't going to explain his reasons. He already knew them.

I put the notebook back as precisely as I could and left, mind spinning.

THIRTY-EIGHT

Monday, January 9, 1956
After dark

The bottle was dusty, but the wine was damned good. I took another pull from the bottle. Mira threw a longing look my way, but whether that was her crush on me or the wine was anybody's guess. The bottle had a French label, and none of the words were in the little bits of French I knew, but apparently they meant "good wine." I'd grabbed it off Español's rack because I'd liked the look of the bottle. Made me feel like a pirate.

Sam and Mira sat on my porch in their usual positions, and every now and again, Lurkimer would bawl about something or other from underneath the house. We mostly ignored him. Sam was wearing a new purple suit and Mira a phantom's face. I didn't have the heart to tell her that for once, I preferred what Sam had on.

"I still don't understand," Mira said.

Sam nodded, the candle in his head flickering.

"Which part?" I asked.

"Songbird," she said, and Sam muttered the name under his breath. Or whatever it was pumpkinheads had for breath. "Why would someone kill her?"

"Well, if I knew that, I could probably tell you who did it."

"What about this human?" Sam asked. "I know it's tough for you, being a human and all, but sometimes you love a human, and you give them chance after chance to become something incredible, and they keep throwing it in your face, night after night, and a guy can get a little hot under the collar."

I took a swig and regarded Sam coolly. "Got something to say?"

Sam didn't answer.

"He's right," Mira said.

Maybe I should have been happy they were finally getting along.

"Okay, why is he right?"

"It's like you said," Lurkimer shouted. "She was a real dish! And I'd like to eat a meal off her!"

On the street, half a dozen monsters turned around and gaped at my house. I burned with embarrassment.

"Lurkimer!" Mira scolded. "Mind your manners."

"Oh, shut it, you dizzy dame. You know if that Songbird showed up and strutted her stuff, you'd be howling like a Tex Avery cartoon, same as Sam and me."

"You speak for yourself, bogey," Sam snitted. "I, for one, am a gentleman. You tell him, Nick. I've been nothing but a gentleman."

"Doesn't mean I'm going to invite you in," I told him.

"Why not? It's not fair I get treated the same as that thing under your porch."

"You got something against bogeymen, you pumpkinheaded freak? We provide valuable services. We keep the undersides of beds totally clean of children. Before us? Kids, just...everywhere. All under beds. And now, do you think people thank us? Closets too. Bogeymen are the best thing that happened to sweaters since mothballs."

Mira sighed. "I'm sorry, Nick. I try to have a romantic evening with you, and these two keep showing up."

"Masher," Sam said, but without much conviction.

"Killing Songbird makes no sense."

"But yet, *Dulcinea* is dead," I said, making sure to emphasize her human name. They didn't hear it, though.

"Didn't the cops catch somebody?" Sam remembered.

"Sure, doesn't mean he did it."

"Of course it does," Mira said.

"Wait," I said, trying to wrap my mind around what Mira had just said. "Are you saying that if the cops arrest somebody, you take for granted they did it?"

Mira nodded. "They wouldn't arrest them otherwise."

Lurkimer howled, "Yeah, they drag you in and you clam up, but still you did it!"

Sam frowned, which was hard to do when your eyes were just triangles cut through the rind of a pumpkin. "Not always. Sometimes, the police are helpless, and you need a spirit of vengeance. Are you telling me, Nick, an innocent man was wronged?"

"Yes! I mean, I think so. Maybe."

Sam didn't hear the rest of it because he was already changing. His greenish skin spouted thorns and he ripped through his fancy purple suit. His body grew to ogre proportions, his fingers transforming into thorny talons, and a long, viney tail whipping back and forth. When a pumpkinhead went to take revenge, this was what it looked like.

Mira squeaked and hurled herself from the porch. Lurkimer swore from the sudden intrusion. Once a pumpkinhead's blood was up, there were only a few monsters who could stand toe-to-toe with one. All the others on the street had scattered.

"Whoa, Sam! Calm down!" I said, not bothering to rise. I had powdered chicken blood over all the ways in. No way Sam was going to eat me.

Although it sure looked like he was thinking about it. He leaned down—he had to—to peer in through the screen door. His features were more jagged, the flame lighting them now a torch. When he spoke, it was with the roar of a bonfire. Heat came from his mouth in shimmering waves. "What innocent suffers?"

"None! Well, possibly one. I don't know! I don't have evidence."

The Sam-monster paused, frowning. He began to shrink, the thorns sinking back into his vine-green skin. His suit was pretty much ruined, now hanging off him in rags.

"I don't always need evidence," he said.

"Yeah, I get that."

Mira peeked up over the side of the porch. "Is it over?" The sibilance of whispers followed her up, and she whispered below the porch as well.

"It's okay. It's okay, right, Sam?" He nodded.

"It's okay," Mira said loudly, though we all knew she was addressing Lurkimer, and climbed back onto the porch, returning to her seat. Her hands and knees were dirty from where she'd been cowering in my flowerbed.

"I wasn't scared of the pumpkinhead," Lurkimer said. "It's that stupid streetlight."

I'm sure we all believed him.

"Are you investigating her death?" Sam asked.

"Dulcinea's? Not really. I mean, nobody's hired me, but there's nobody looking for the killer. Like you said, they got someone, and that's pretty much the end of it."

"If you find the man was innocent and there's a killer free, you have to tell me," Sam said, his voice tight.

"Have to?" The wine was making my lids nice and heavy. Chicken blood or not, I wasn't going to pass out without closing and locking the door first.

"I mean, I'd like you to."

"Oh. Sure, Sam. I did have something I wanted to ask you three about. In Capriccio Español's house, there was this...hidey hole, I guess."

"Hidey hole?" Mira was dubious.

"Yeah, it looked like a squatter found an out-of-the-way spot and bunked down. Like he'd been there for weeks. Is that unusual?"

"Not so much," Lurkimer shouted. "Monsters come and go a lot more freely than humans ever did."

"Especially *some* monsters," Mira said meaningfully. Sam nodded.

"So that's not strange?"

"It's not normal," Mira allowed.

"Sure it is!" Lurkimer said. "I'll sleep anywhere I can. Sure, I spend most of my time under Kong's throne, but I'll go all over the place." Lurkimer Closett was the translator for the fifty-foot ape Kublai Kong out on Catalina Island. Closett was also a bogeyman, which meant he could travel to closets and under beds by some kind of teleportation. "I spent a whole month in Pilar O'Heaven's closet! Oh, you have not lived until you seen a fifty-foot dame put on her bathing suit!"

"Remind me to tell Pilar what you're doing," I said. Pilar was a client, and I wouldn't have minded her stepping on Lurkimer like a bug.

"You'd do that to me?" Lurkimer demanded. "I knew you were a rat from the beginning, but I didn't know you were a sewer rat."

I ignored him. "What kinds of monsters do this?"

Sam and Mira thought about it. "The hard ones to track," Sam said finally.

"Like...oh, come on."

Sam and Mira turned. Gliding across my lawn in a skin-tight gown was Purvissa La Bete. The gray-skinned ghoul who'd I'd extorted for Mickey's money was dolled up for the evening, her makeup making her severe face look downright corpselike.

"Nick Moss?" she asked, peering at the screen door.

"Oh, lord."

Sam and Mira sprang up. "What do you want with Nick?" Sam demanded.

"We were here first," Mira said. Although if that argument worked, she would be gone.

"We need another dame around here like I need a spotlight," Lurkimer whined.

"This is the home of Nick Moss, the investigator?"

"How did you get this address?" Mira demanded, giving me a suspicious glare.

"Little Monster House," Purvissa said. I knew the place. They got addresses from Uncle Sam and sold them to monsters looking for specific people to turn.

"Oh," Mira said, somewhat deflated.

Purvissa took another few steps—that was a guess, since I still hadn't seen her feet—toward he door, and her face lit up. "There you are! Hello, Mr. Moss! Do you remember me? I'm Purvissa La Bete? You had some very...commanding...things to say to me? There were certain...threats?"

Sam whirled. "Nick! What did you do to this lady?"

"Yeah," Mira said, her voice flat. "What did you do?"

"Couple things I wouldn't mind doing," Lurkimer confided to the entire neighborhood.

"Yeah, I remember you. What do you want?"

"Maybe we could have a little chat inside? I'm afraid I've been somewhat...foolish. Perhaps even...bad. I went to the track today."

"What'd you do that for? You're just bleeding money."

"I'd like to bleed something else."

"What does that even mean? No, wait, don't tell me."

"I don't like this," Sam said, shaking his pumpkin head back and forth. "When you started bringing Mira around, I thought that was beneath you. And now with the bogeyman, but a ghoul, too? No, this won't do."

"Especially one who looks like a streetwalker who only works funerals," Mira huffed.

"Thank you!" Purvissa beamed. "I'm so glad someone understands what I'm going for."

"She doesn't have our bond," Sam said. "Our commitment to justice or to the manufacture of quality homemade preserves."

"Sam, for the last time, I don't know the first thing about jams, jellies, preserves, or anything else."

"Chutneys?"

"Those either! I know nothing. At all."

"I could teach you! Oh, the heady nights, Nick. Pursuing wrongdoers! Perfecting this peach cinnamon jam that's got me tied in knots—"

"Aw, baloney," Lurkimer said. "This meatstick you all like so much is a grade A rat. You know what he was doing when I met him? Snooping around someplace wasn't his."

"When I met him, he was watching movies," Mira said, her complexion blooming. "Certain *kinds* of movies."

"That was for a case," I said, but she was already lost in the memory.

I shook my head while the four monsters on my porch kept up with the Nick stories, half of which were made up. They didn't even notice when I shut the door, and I fell asleep to the sounds of them arguing over which of them had the right to bother me when the sun went down.

THIRTY-NINE

Tuesday, January 10, 1956
Morning

Jaime sat across from me in my office, reading from a pocket notebook. A stub of a pencil, barely big enough to keep a golf score with, was tucked behind one ear. His pompadour shone, looking like a wave of crude oil cresting from his forehead. A few tattoos peeked from his collar: a pair of crosses over his jugular and carotid, and a snarling cat at his throat.

He had spent the night at the Huerta house, and his only objection was that Mrs. Huerta wasn't as good a cook as his mom. I hadn't met Mrs. Alvarez yet. I couldn't imagine she was thrilled with me throwing her son into danger night after night. While he was there, he interviewed the monsters who would come close. Those who got *too* close got to see some of the tattoos on his arms, hands, and chest. Those usually convinced them that Jaime was not worth the trouble.

"She's got a jaguar person after her. Go figure." That last was irony. The jaguar people, or balam as they preferred, were just about the best-looking monsters out there. Until they transformed into two hundred pounds of jungle death machine. They tended to want to turn others as good-looking as they.

While a balam wanting to turn Sofia Huerta made perfect sense, it didn't stick with my idea of the same individual killing Dulcinea. Usually, balam didn't actually want anyone dead; they changed accidentally—whenever they got hot and bothered—and the unfortunate object of their attention ended up torn to ribbons.

"Who else?"

"Vampire, of course. Doesn't like the kitty cat either."

"Don't imagine he would."

"She."

I perked up. "Nyx Nocturne?"

Jaime paged through his notes. "Um...Ivana Neck."

"Cute," I said, disappointed, but I didn't think it was going to be that easy.

"She also has a phantom and a coven of witches hanging around."

I wanted to jump at the phantom idea. "It's not Capriccio Español, is it?" knowing damned well it wasn't.

"Angelo Music," he said.

"Half the phantoms in this town have that handle."

"Not everybody is creative," Jaime said philosophically.

I knew better than to ask if he had a name picked out. That was one of the darker party games we humans played from time to time. A lot of folks had a name in their back pocket, and it was usually for one of the more glamorous monsters. Your vampires, your mummies, your sidhe, your giants. No one wanted to face the obvious: they were far more likely to be a zombie, a blob, or some fraction of a meat golem.

"None of those sound likely to me."

Jaime nodded, but I could see the words trying to form on his lips.

"What? Out with it," I told him.

"No, I mean...how do you know none of these took her?"

"Well, for one thing, anyone still hanging around probably didn't do it."

Jaime flushed. Sometimes the obvious stuff didn't occur to people. When he spoke again, he was a little hot. "Okay, that's just the witches and the vampire. We still got a kitty and a goon, and you ask me, either one of them sounds good to me."

I knew it was a goose chase. Jaime couldn't see it. I don't think anyone could quite see it. A pretty girl going missing was the least surprising thing that could possibly happen. Sofia Huerta had been on borrowed time since she turned into a woman. It was crazy of me to think that the only person out there who would take her had done Dulcinea in.

But I knew it. In my bones, I knew every last bit.

It had been worrying in the back of my mind for longer than I knew. I'd been trying to deny it, even going for the longshot of that phantom. But in that list of names Jane gave me, only one of them used a gun.

"It's not them."

Jaime scoffed, shoving the notepad into the pocket of his blue jeans. He hesitated for a fraction of a second and then met my eyes. "You want it to be him."

"I'm sorry?"

"You want it to be the same monster. You want to pay him back what he earned."

I didn't know what to tell the kid. He wasn't entirely wrong. He wasn't entirely right, either. The world was going to let Dulcinea's killer walk. I had been one of the last people she reached out to for help. I gave her what she asked for. In any rational sense, my obligations to her were over.

But they weren't.

And now her killer was going to hurt some other girl. Maybe turn her, maybe kill her. I didn't know what was worse. Finding Sofia turned or finding her with four bullets in her back. I had to make sure neither one happened. That Sofia got the life she was promised and Dulcinea got the justice she deserved.

"Tell you what, kid. You work your angles and I'll work mine."

"This case is mine?"

"Sure. See if this phantom or this balam has her. And use whistles and crosses. I don't want to hear about Angelo Music burning up in a house fire or Whoever the Panther losing a fight with an alley cat."

"Hey, a cat could get into his place."

"I'm not kidding. We don't need the wolves coming down here to pinch you on a murder beef."

"Yeah, yeah. They never got me yet."

"Matter of time, kid. Now, go prove me wrong. Find Sofia."

He popped up out of his chair like he was spring-loaded. A moment later, the front door slammed. He wasn't going to find a thing, but this was decent training. False leads and so on. Or that's what I was telling myself anyway. The more I thought about Español's house and the remaining people I was thinking of, the more I was certain I knew exactly who'd done it. I didn't have to like it, but I did have to see it.

I needed to make a call before I could put any plans into action. I placed the call to Mickey's place, bracing myself for no answer or some bad news.

"Hello?"

"Florence, is that you? It's Nick Moss."

"Nick? How are you?" From the sound of her voice, Florence hadn't been doing much grieving. So that was either good news or a sad indication of the state of her relationship.

"I'm fine. How's Mickey?"

"He's doing well. Would you like to speak with him?"

"Is he in the shower?"

"He's in bed with the dog."

I snorted. Figured. "Yeah, if it's not too much trouble, could you put me on with him?"

"A moment," she said, and she put the phone down.

Another receiver clicked, and Mickey's voice came over the line, sounding dented but serviceable. "That you, Nick?"

"That's me. It's good to hear your voice, Mickey. I thought for sure you were a goner."

Mickey chuckled. "Don't make me laugh. That corpse can't shoot straight. Even with a sweeper, he didn't do more than perforate my spare tire."

"You scared me there for a second."

"The hell I did. I saw youse lettin' 'em have it, just like the old days. I should thank that gray matter, right before I squash her under the tires of my Caddy."

"That's a nice thought."

"I'm proud of you, Stick. They got the drop on us, and we traded 'em man for man. Maybe next time we get the drop on them, things go a little more in our favor."

I didn't have the heart to tell Mickey that Sarah Bellum could afford to trade five for one if she wanted to. Zombies were a lot easier to come by than men, and they were always eager to work their way up in the world.

"Sure thing, Mickey. You just take care of yourself."

"You calling about Jack?"

My brain reached for the association and caught it. "No, sorry. Nothing on Jack yet. I'm telling you, though. We know who did him in. I don't think we need a body."

Mickey's voice grew soft. I hadn't heard this tone from him in a long time. Not since the war, when he'd talk about his old dog, Toughie. While the rest of us would be talking about some girl we'd left behind, Mickey would break in about that old bulldog of his. Mickey probably put that tone away after the war, never let his guys hear it. He was small enough, so had to play bigger than he was. They couldn't hear how things hurt him.

"Jack was my pal," he said. "His body don't get me nothing at all, I just need it."

"Okay, Mickey. I'll do my best."

"That's the only thing I can ask. You know, if it was your body, I'd be leanin' on some other shamus right now."

"Good luck. There's no other human snoop around."

Mickey laughed so hard he nearly busted a gut.

Forty

Tuesday, January 10, 1956
Late in the afternoon

I nearly made a joke about Jane biting some stranger's nails, but I wisely stopped before it came out of my mouth. That had to be an awful thing to say to a meat golem. I'd never have thought of it, not really, not until Jane took me to school on what it meant. That was pain she had to face every day of her life, and I'd be damned if I'd add to it.

I still almost said it, because that meant her nail was in her mouth, and so I was looking at it. Her lips were full but modest, and she had the sly smile of a pinup girl. She showed me that grin when she opened the door and saw it was me on her stoop.

"Hey, Jane. Got some time?"

She nodded and beckoned me in. One of her fitting dummies was half-dressed in a dark gray suit. Looked nice to me. Flattering cut, sleek lines. The woman had talent.

She grabbed her slate, wrote a single word: *Beer?*

"Yeah, please."

She nodded, slipping the slate around her neck and padding off to the kitchen. She was barefoot and bare-legged. The only seams she was showing weren't stockings, but the irregular pattern of stitches over her skin. Jane returned with two bottles of suds still sweaty from the icebox and handed one over.

"Thanks."

She shrugged, but the look on her face was expectant. I read the intent without needing the slate. *What's up?*

"I need your help. Remember Dulcinea Ramos?"

Jane nodded at the name. The only monster so far who did.

"I think I know who killed her, and I think it's the same person who kidnapped another girl. Problem is, I need to get it out of him somehow. I need to get him alone. That's where you come in."

Jane raised an eyebrow as she settled into a chair.

"I want you to seduce him and bring him back here."

Jane hissed. It had been so long since I heard that out of her, I nearly jumped out of my skin. Sounded like she had a cobra stuck in her throat.

"No! No, it's uh, it's not like that. I don't want you to...or, I don't need you to...I mean, you don't have to touch him. Or do anything. At all."

She wrote on her slate. As hot as she was, the words still came out with her machine precision. *I don't have to do anything.*

She tapped *anything* with the chalk.

"Right, I know. I mean, for this favor. I don't need you to do anything. That's not part of the plan. It's just getting him alone, where I can talk to him."

I'm not a joy girl.

"I never thought you were. I swear." I put my hand up, and if she'd brought out a Bible, I'd have sworn on it.

Jane relaxed.

"I don't know how to get this fella alone, and I figure a looker like you, he'd have to be crazy not to follow you home."

Jane looked away, taking a long pull on her beer. Her cheeks were patchwork, but I swear the green parts got greener and the gray parts grayer. Finally, she wrote. *O.K. No hanky panky.*

My heart crawled back down out of my throat. "No hanky panky," I agreed.

She nodded again. I let her gather herself. I hadn't quite realized what it sounded like when I put the plan together in my head. I wondered if Jane got a lot of monsters thinking they could take liberties because she went to work in hotpants and a halter. Probably. I wondered how many hands, claws, and tentacles she'd broken in the process. That was a pleasant thought.

Jane looked up, and she caught my grin. Her mismatched eyes lit up and she wrote a new message on the slate. *Who is the killer?*

"You like this kind of thing?"

What thing?

"Detective work?"

She shrugged, then unfolded those long legs and made her way over to a bookcase. I followed her. She gestured to a shelf that was nothing but beat-up paperbacks, written by Cleave Hunter, Chaz Standard, and a few other of the pulp guys.

"You know, it's not like it is in there."

She nodded.

"Okay. I just sometimes meet people who think I investigate murders and...why are you looking at me like that? Oh, this one time. This is the first time I'm looking into a murder. I'm not even getting paid for it."

Jane gave one of her soundless laughs and brushed past me on the way to her seat. Yeah, she still smelled like rain, and when she was that near, she made my hair stand on end like I was too close to a live wire.

When I turned, she was holding up the slate with only one word. *Why?*

"Why am I looking if I'm not being paid?"

She nodded.

"Because I'm a sap. Because there's nobody left to do it but me. Because this other girl is a dead ringer, and I think if it's not the same fella, then lightning struck twi...sorry, Jane. Wasn't thinking."

She held up a hand, shaking her head. It was okay.

I want to help.

"Now it's my turn. Why?"

A girl is dead. Another girl is missing.

"That's not enough for most people."

It is for me.

"You're a hell of a woman, Jane. Anybody tell you that?"

Her colors went more vibrant, and then she wrote a message. *Who is the killer?* She tapped it again, to let me know I wasn't going to get out of it this time.

"He's a gangster," I told her. "One of Sarah Bellum's hatchet men by the name of Bracken Mold."

A gangster?

"Yeah. He's kind of a friend of mine. Saved my life."

This is exactly like the books.

"Usually it's not," I said, desperate to avoid Jane's excellent point. "Mold hangs around the Nocturnist, so should I meet you there?"

Jane shook her head. *Come with me. Safer for you that way.*

"I'm not going to turn down a big strong meat golem escorting me." She grinned.

Sundown is in an hour, and I have to get ready. Make yourself at home.

I didn't think she meant cover her apartment in wards and then have a conversation with the predators that showed up. Probably meant what it would have before things went crazy. Before a woman like Jane was even possible. I drank my beer and sank into the same couch that had served me well on New Year's. The thing was more comfortable than my bed. Like laying on a cloud made out of marshmallows. Eventually, I got up, selected one of Hunter's books, and settled back to read. It was lurid pulp nonsense, and by chapter three I knew who did it. It was the one human in the book. I wondered if Jane cottoned to that little gimmick.

She came into the living room as the sun was turning her western-facing apartment gold. She was dressed for work, so her legs were wrapped in fishnets, her feet were clomping on another extra few inches of sole, and her hair was done up in stylish victory rolls, highlighting the stripes going up her temple.

Ready?

"You bet," I told her.

She set the slate aside—she wasn't allowed it at work—and we left her apartment. We caught the red car into Hollywood, and I watched the sun set over Sunset. Most people probably assumed we were a wolfman and his meat golem lady doing the town. We didn't get a second glance, save for one from a crawling eye, who could see I was a human at once. He didn't do anything about it. Not with Jane close by, who'd have popped him like a grape.

We got off the car in Hollywood and clomped the short distance to the Nocturnist. Jane took me around the side entrance, where she'd saved me from the three goblins. The alley was dirty, the brick wall on the far side of it stained. She opened the door, and we were in the kitchen, redolent with ant bisque.

"Jane, honey, there you are—" Wyeth Wyrd came around the corner, her apron stained with handprints. A moment later, her raccoon waddled around the pot, also wearing an apron. It wiped its hands and the both of them gave me identical intrigued-but-irritated looks. "You brought someone?"

Jane shook her head and pointed to the door leading into the club proper.

"Well, all right. I can't have some wolf mucking about in my kitchen. No offense, dearie."

"None taken."

She paused, her expression growing keener. "Have we met?"

We had, but I had been dressed as a clown at the time. Monsters took a dim view of trying to pass, so the last thing I was going to do was cop to it.

"I don't think so."

"All right," she said, plainly unconvinced. "Out with you, then."

I obeyed, going into the club. A few early birds were already in seats. The band hadn't entirely assembled, and instead four phantoms were playing something halfway between chamber music and jazz. Each phantom appeared locked in some internal struggle, playing out their theatrical emotions on their own, but the four of them were in perfect harmony. Phantoms, go figure. Whenever they were playing music, or singing songs, or writing books, or anything else, they were fine. Soon as they got free time, it was nothing but death traps and murderous obsessions.

I settled in a table near the back as the crowd filtered in. Jane circulated through the room and occasionally brought me something. A bowl of ant bisque—made from the giant ants out in the Arizona desert, and delicious—some crackers, and cocktails. Didn't charge me, either. I was kicking myself for not bringing her slate. She wasn't allowed to carry it, but I was a customer. I could carry whatever I liked. As much fun as Jane was to look at, she was more fun to talk to. Although, the lady *was* at work.

I watched the monsters instead. Capriccio Español made his debut at eight. He didn't look much worse for wear, so that explained who won that little brouhaha. I wondered how many of the people had made it out intact, and how many had to be cleaned out of the phantom's traps. There wasn't much I could do there, either. Seemed like Joe was with the phantom willingly, and besides, the mob had busted down a door.

Johnny Stompanato came in around nine with his arm around a gorgeous young woman who looked to be smuggling torpedoes in her sweater. Johnny didn't see me, and I wanted to keep it that way. I let myself sink deeper into the shadows collecting all around. Jane might be protecting me, and I was armed to the teeth, but I was still only one man against a room full of monsters.

Trolls couldn't sneak up on anybody. Being twelve feet of semi-elastic stone would do that to you. They sounded like rockslides when they moved, and were about as subtle. I saw the troll coming my way as soon as he made the first move, and I was ready to show him the business end of my blessed dagger.

"Excuse me," he said, when he got to my table.

"Yeah?"

The troll looked familiar. I didn't know any trolls, but this one was ringing bells. The rocks of his face had somehow combined into square-jawed good looks, and the moss on top of his head was cleanly parted.

"Maybe my senses deceive me, but I swear I detect the hint of human on you."

"What's it to you, buddy?"

"If you want some..." He paused, as though putting something together in his mind. His expression dropped. "You're one of Mickey Cohen's guys, aren't you? I'm terribly sorry I bothered you. I didn't know who you were."

"It's fine. Why do I know you?"

"I'm an actor," the troll said nervously.

I snapped my fingers in recognition. The troll flinched. "Rock Hudson?"

"Pleased to meet you. I meant no disrespect, sir," Hudson said, slinking off. Serendipity was going to go green—well, greener—with jealousy when she heard I'd met him.

A few other monsters were looking my way now, but when they saw me notice, abruptly their drinks or the band were much more interesting. I scanned the place looking for Jane. Mold had come in, maybe when I was distracted, and Jane was by his table. She didn't have much up top, but the way she was leaning over, Mold was getting a full view. I was beginning to regret this stupid plan.

Then Jane stood up straight, tucking her ordering pad under the tray. She sauntered away from Mold, giving her hips a sway. I don't know what she said to him, but Mold wasn't looking. Didn't even glance in her direction. What was wrong with him?

She got to my table, moved my cocktail off the napkin, and bent over it, writing a note. I leaned back, glancing around the Nocturnist, because I knew if Jane kept my attention, I'd end up doing something a gentleman ought not do to a lady.

Finished with her note, Jane slid it over and tapped it.

He hate me. Then she scowled and hastily added the *S* where it was missing.

"He doesn't even know you."

Her expression was halfway between annoyed and amused. She took the napkin back and wrote another word.

You.

"Me?"

She tapped the word again. I took that as, *Yeah, you.*

"Wait. You're saying he's not interested in you romantically, but he might be interested in *me*?"

She nodded, tapping *You* again.

"Jane, uh, this is awkward because I don't know what you've been thinking but I'm not like that?"

Me neither. The napkin was getting crowded.

"I don't think he is either."

She shook her head. *Turn.*

"He'd want to turn me." She was right. I didn't want her to be right. "You think I should go over there and seduce the gangster because I've got more of what a zombie's looking for than you do."

She gave such an emphatic nod I worried about the holding power of her neck stitches.

"You also want to see me try to seduce a zombie."

She grinned and nodded.

"Please stop enjoying this."

She shook her head.

"Wish me luck," I said, getting up.

Jane blew me a kiss, and my knees nearly buckled. I walked over to Mold's booth and did my best not to think of the meat golem watching me. What was I even doing there? She was a meat golem. It was one thing to chase a witch who was never chasing back, but she wasn't made of dead girls. Not that any of that mattered when Jane looked at me.

This life would be easier if I weren't such a sap.

"Mind if I join you?" I regretted the line the instant it was out of my mouth.

Mold's milky eyes brightened. "Brains!" he said, gesturing to the seat opposite. "Brains?"

"Can't complain," I said, sliding into the booth.

Mold held up a finger partway covered in fuzzy green plantlife. "Brains?" he said to the room.

Jane clomped over and looked at him expectantly.

"Brains," he said, and Jane nodded, like that made any sense. "Brains?" he said to me.

Jane turned her mismatched attention on me, playing like she'd never seen me before in her life.

"Uh, yeah. I'll take what he's hav...wait, no. I'll take a whiskey." When you see chunks of meat floating in a zombie's cocktail, you reassess your order PDQ. I could only hope those were calf brains seasoning his booze, but I wasn't about to ask. Or let down my guard in this place.

Jane went back to the kitchen to get our orders.

Mold was watching me closely. "Brains?"

"Saw you over here, thought I'd say hi. Haven't seen you since Christmas. Didn't know who got pinched and who didn't."

"Brains," he said sadly. I took that to mean someone did, but I wasn't going to play charades figuring out who.

"Sorry to hear it. We, uh, we delivered all the presents though, huh?"

"Brains!" Mold laughed, slapping the table. I flinched, convinced one of his fingers would pop clean off. His hands had remarkable structural integrity.

"So...uh, what are you doing the rest of the night?"

"Brains," he said with a shrug, looking around the room.

"Because I was thinking—"

I heard Jane coming only because of her heavy heels. She put a round in front of each of us. For my part, I was going to need it. Mold swallowed the last of his old one, chewing on the bits of brain while he set the now-empty glass on Jane's tray.

"Brains," he said, slipping her a buck, but not taking his eyes off me.

It was all I could do not to wither. Jane moved off, but I could see her on my periphery. Her one silver eye was a magnet, and it always looked like it was watching me intently.

"Sure," I said. "So, I was wondering how business was."

"Brains."

"Good to hear. Glad they're taking care of you. It got me thinking, too. How I could be, uh, taken care of. I guess."

"Brains?"

"Well, come on. I'd have to be an idiot not to read the writing on the wall. It says Sarah Bellum, doesn't it?"

"Brains."

"So I was thinking maybe instead of, uh, hanging around here, we, um, we go to your place? Maybe talk about it a bit?"

"Brains?"

"Yep. I am serious as a heart attack."

Mold raised a greenish eyebrow. "Brains?"

"There's whiskey at your place, right? I could use more."

"Brains," he said.

It worked all right. Too well. In five minutes, I was following Mold to his car, leaving Jane .behind at the club. I didn't know what I was going to do if this worked. I knew even less about what to do if it didn't.

FORTY-ONE

Tuesday, January 10, 1956
A short drive later

Mold lived in a modest one-story house in the hills to the east of Hollywood. It was about as far from Bellum's palace as you could get. Don't get me wrong, it was a nice spot, and he had a hell of a view of both glittering lights and the few remaining orange groves. It beat the box I lived in. It's just that for all the glamor gangsters got in the press, you'd think he'd have something more than this.

Mold let me in, shyly muttering "Brains" as he unlocked the door. The same mold that grew on his skin had taken root in the house. The walls were striped with it, and it grew in fluffy clumps on the carpet and wooden floors. Mold flicked on lights as he went, ushering me into a kitchen, where he gestured to a circular wooden table in the corner, with two matching wooden chairs. I sat down and didn't touch any of the knots of mold growing on the furniture.

The kitchen was a lot brighter than I would have expected. Yellow was the main color, on the wallpaper, on the tablecloth, and the tiles, with a few blue accents. Then there was the mold, growing in its haphazard streaks off any surface it could find. I wondered if I stayed put for long enough, if it would germinate in my body too. Turn me into a mass of green and rotten flesh. I turned to look at a tile with a smiling sun on it. It didn't do much to cheer me up.

Mold put two jelly jars on the table and filled each with three fingers of whiskey. I was grateful that the glasses and the bottle, at least, had avoided the plague of mold. I raised the glass to him, he clinked it, and we both drank.

I was beginning to feel like a pig in a room full of ogres.

"Brains," he said.

"I'll tell you, that was the strangest Christmas I ever had."

"Brains?"

"Sure. You think I do something like that every year? Your boss leaned on me to get me there."

"Brains?"

"No, I don't regret it. Not really. That Gobfather was a piece of work."

"Brains."

I tried not to let on that I was watching him. That last "Brains" was so resigned, I knew it meant something more. He was agreeing with me not in the abstract, but about something specific.

"I know you Bellum boys have a lot of reasons to hate the elf. He bumped off a good many of you."

"Brains."

That wasn't it.

"I didn't know what I was walking into. Ever seen anything like that place of his? Me neither. A floor of a hotel turned into some kind of winter wonderland. I tell you, every time you think you've seen it all before, this world of ours throws you a curveball. Like I didn't think I'd owe my life to one of Bellum's enforcers."

"Brains," he said tracing the pattern on the tablecloth with one rotten finger.

"Thanks for that."

Another clink of the glasses. I didn't think I could drink a zombie under the table. Not even when I was still in the service, and we'd drink antifreeze right out of the trucks if that was all we could get. I put the glass to my lips for a long time, but only opened them for a short one. Give him the idea I was drinking long when I wasn't.

"When those hobs were on us, I thought our gooses were cooked. I didn't think we could outrun them on their turf, in two feet of snow. I should be happy they're lousy shots."

"Brains," Mold said, holding up one arm, where he'd had three arrows buried down to the bone.

"Yeah, I have you to thank for that too, I guess. I, uh, I suppose I have a lot to thank you for."

"Brains," he said, staring frankly at me. I was fairly certain I'd given the same look to Jane once or twice. How she didn't club me over the head or crawl out of her skin was beyond me.

"But we got 'em. Locked 'em up and got to the business with the Gobfather. Say, did you see who got him?"

"Brains?" he asked, pointing at me.

"That what Bellum thinks?"

"Brains."

I swallowed. "Yeah, that's right. I snuffed him. He got cocky. And, um, I'm pretty fast."

"Brains?"

"Sure. I mean, I'm still here, right? Not like those girls in the Gallery."

I got the reaction I was looking for. Mold was gone, staring through the table, right back in the snow, in the midst of those beautiful young women, all trapped in the moment of their passions. The sight had cut him back when we were both standing there. At the time, I'd been impressed a zombie had shown that kind of feeling for human girls. Now I wasn't so sure that's what I was seeing.

"Dulcinea Ramos. The Songbird. She was supposed to be there with them."

Mold shuddered, still staring through the table.

"How well did you know her?"

"Brains," he muttered. I didn't need a number. I just needed a *yes*, and that's what he'd given me. I saw his look at the Gallery and he never missed a Songbird performance. That was how monsters were. Obsessed. I had four waiting on my front lawn who taught me that lesson every night.

"You loved her, didn't you? Sure you did. Everyone who saw her loved her at least a little bit. She noticed you, too, didn't she? Only one kind of zombie comes into the Nocturnist, and that's one of Bellum's."

Mold's milky eyes met mine. The panic there, the rage, said I was spinning truth. Once the assumptions were confirmed, then everything else was laid out, plain as the grin on that sun's face.

"Hearing you worked for Sarah Bellum would scare a lot of folks off. Probably scared her, too. But that also made you the safest mug in the joint for someone looking to get out. Bellum would be at least a little bit of a shield. And she saw how you were looking at her. She couldn't miss it."

"Brains."

"Thought so. She wrote you something and it was exactly what you wanted to hear. She wanted away from the elf, and you were the only one who could help her. Then one night at the Nocturnist she caught your eye, and when you went over, you found it on the floor. I don't have to guess about this one. That's how she got the note to me."

"Brains?"

"Yeah, Dulcinea wanted my help, too. The same night she wanted yours. She must have found Mab's Gallery of Angels, and she knew what was waiting for her. She was never getting turned. She was going to live, or die, or whatever happens to those girls. Get turned into art for Mab."

"Brains." The anguish in Mold's voice cut through the words like a cold iron blade.

"She finds the Gallery and she knows she has to get out, right then. She can't wait. She gets in touch with you somehow. Maybe you gave her your number. Maybe she's just that resourceful. She escaped Mab's home, so we know she's a lot more than just a pretty face. She wanted you to meet her somewhere safe with a car, somewhere you won't be seen by the Gobfather's men. Only, on the phone, all you can say is one word. So she gives you a time and place. The Hollywood Roosevelt Hotel, as soon as you could get away. That's why she kept looking out the window. She didn't know when you were coming. She stayed with me, because I was human. I was the one person in the world she could trust not to turn her."

No surprise marred Mold's expression.

"Only when you picked her up, you couldn't control yourself. You'd been fighting the urges since you saw her. All the monsters did, and when Mab paraded her around, he was just fanning the flames. You thought that because she wanted Mab to turn her, she wanted to be turned and any monster would do. Or maybe you didn't care what she thought. Monsters don't always get a choice in the matter, and don't think they need to give one. So you went for it. Tried to clean out her skull with those chompers. You pulled over on that road where she was found and jumped her."

"Brains," he whispered.

I cleared my throat. This was getting hard. I was nearly seeing Dulcinea's final moments. The fear. The shock. The betrayal.

"She fought back, though. She got out of the car and she ran. And if she could make it to the edge of the hill, she might have gotten away. She knew she could outrun a zombie, and you knew it too. But you had something she couldn't outrun. You weren't even thinking about turning her. You just wanted to stop her. So you put four in her back."

"Brains," Mold said, his jaw opening wide as he lunged for me.

"Sorry. I'm fresh out."

The gunshot split the night in half.

Forty-Two

Tuesday, January 10, 1956
The very next second

Bracken Mold was sprawled backward in his chair, the top of his skull scattered through the kitchen. I shot him through the mouth, and on its way out, the bullet had knocked the steel fedora onto the floor, where it had cracked the linoleum with a sharp clang.

Wasn't the first time I'd had to stop an attacking zombie. Normally I'd go for the salt; get a little on their tongues and they'd go lights out. But the Luger had jumped into my hand like it was eager. It knew I was going to kill him as soon as his ragged lips skinned his chipped teeth. Then it told my body. My brain didn't find out until Mold was already on his way to becoming fertilizer.

I tucked the heater back under my arm and tossed the place. The first thing I found was that Mold did have a second story, but it was a lower one, built along the hillside. The upstairs was Mold's kitchen, a small dining room, a bathroom, and a living room, complete with a picture window giving him that stunning view. He kept the house clean, and other than the relentless bright colors, there wasn't much that made it a home.

I took the stairs slowly, keeping my ears pricked for any surprises. I didn't think there would be another monster home, but it never hurt to be cautious. The lower story was small, barely more than a hall with a few doors along it. Bedrooms, I guessed. I started at the end of the hall and found a master bedroom, then a bathroom, then a locked door.

If I had been in a phantom's place, I'd be a lot more cautious. Kick in a locked door there, and you were liable to get burned to a crisp. I knocked on it and listened. No moaning. No one telling me what organ they'd like to munch on.

The door itself was pretty flimsy, too, like it hadn't been intended for much security. Just to get people who might be intimidated by a locked door to walk away. That wasn't me.

I stood back, braced myself, and kicked the thing in. It took two kicks, sure, but the door came open, revealing a dark room. Shadows pooled everywhere. Something inside moved, making tiny, muffled vocalizations. I flicked on a light.

Sofia Huerta was on the floor, bound and gagged. Her eyes were wide and red, her cheeks were wet and her nose was running. When she saw me, she sucked in a deep breath around the cloth Mold had stuck in her mouth. Probably thought I was another monster ready to do what the last one was going to.

I dropped to my knees next to her. "It's okay. My name is Nick Moss. Your parents hired me to find you."

She frowned.

"Oh no. Do you not speak English?"

She said something, but it was all doughy vowels through the gag.

I cut her out of her bonds, and she yanked the gag out of her mouth. "I speak English," she said, and her accent sounded almost exactly like mine.

"Oh. Nice to meet you."

Close up, she didn't look as identical to Dulcinea as I'd thought. Her nose was a little bigger, her lips a little thinner, her eyes a paler brown. Don't get me wrong, she was beautiful, but it would take a lovesick fool to mistake one for the other. Mold had wanted her to be the same girl, but she wasn't. Maybe I needed that reminder too.

"We should get going."

She rubbed her wrists uncertainly. "My legs are all pins and needles."

"Rub some feeling back into them," I told her, getting up. "This place isn't in the middle of the city, but I don't want anyone looking into the gunshot."

"That was you?"

"You thought there was someone else in here?"

"You killed the corpse who took me?"

"Yeah. But keep that under your hat. Or hair. Don't tell anyone."

"The more you talk, the more I doubt you're the man who saved me."

"Just get some blood in your limbs, please?" Her eyebrows reached for the ceiling. "I realize that makes me sound like a vampire. I'm not. We really do need to go."

I didn't wait for her, going to the staircase, half convinced there'd be a monster investigating the gunshot. A silhouette stood at the top. The Luger was in my hand before I knew it. Maybe I was right after all.

"Nick Moss?" asked a voice from the top of the stairs. A voice I knew.

"Liling Lam?"

I took a few stairs and sure enough it was her. Her hair was in a tight bun, and she was dressed head to toe in skintight black, but it was her.

"What are you doing here?" she asked.

"What are *you* doing here?" I countered.

"You shot Bracken Mold."

"Yeah. It was that or let him eat my brains. I made a judgment call."

"Same one I would have made."

"Okay, let's go—eep!" Sofia squeaked as she came around the corner.

"It's okay, she's a friend," I said. Liling didn't deny it. "Do you have a car?"

"No, he kidnapped me," Sofia said.

"Not you, her."

"I didn't walk here," Liling said.

"Can you give us a ride?"

"Where?"

"Anywhere but here."

Liling was silent as she made her decision. Finally, she gave a single nod and turned around.

"Come on," I said to Sofia, and we followed Liling out of Mold's house.

In a sane world, Mold was the criminal. The world had stopped being sane ten—no, eleven now—years ago. In this situation, the only criminal was me. Mold had kidnapped a girl, kept her tied up in his house for a couple days, and that was all fine, assuming he took her when the sun was down. There were times I couldn't believe the Fair Game Law. Worse than that, the Fair Game Law was the improvement. Before it, monsters could take humans at any time.

Liling's car was a Ford that looked ready to fall to pieces at any second. It rattled when she started the engine. Felt like she was ringing a dinner bell. First for the gunshot, then for the getaway. Mold's street stayed quiet.

"Where do you live?" Liling asked.

"Watts," Sofia and I responded in unison.

"I'm not driving to Watts at this hour. The wolves are between us and them. You'll have to stay with me."

Liling didn't turn her headlights on until she got to the base of the hill and there was more traffic to hide in. The bulk of it was cars, but some of the other more exotic conveyances of the city's monsters were represented as well. We pulled up next to a spectral charger at a stoplight, and the creature huffed brimstone and pawed the asphalt. When the light turned green, the horse and his headless rider were off like a shot. Liling was too smart to race them.

She traced the hills back toward Downtown, and at Bunker Hill headed east, into Chinatown. She left Broadway, the main drag of the neighborhood, and headed up into the hills by Elysian Park. Chinatown was defiantly ethnic in a way that no neighborhoods were anymore. In the old days, we humans split up along racial lines because we didn't know what differences really were. Chinatown had those scars, with rooftops that looked like pagodas and signs in their elegant script. After the Night War, Chinatown stayed that way: Chinese. They were welcoming enough to visitors, but only one kind of person lived there.

Kind of made me wonder who were the ones forcing that divide.

Liling drove into the dry hills to the north of the neighborhood, into a maze of roads, half paved, half dirt. No streetlamps twinkled up here, and half the roads were entirely unmarked. The windows of the houses we passed were sullenly dark. The rooftops slumped, and a lot of the walls were chewed up with bullets or dissolved by acid. It had the marks of a neighborhood used by human forces during the Night War, then forgotten about.

No wonder nobody could find Liling.

She was doing her best to hide her house from us even now. The headlights had gone off as soon as she reached up into the hills. She was navigating by starlight, only in Los Angeles, the stars weren't in the sky, they were stretched out over the valleys. I thought of the ceiling back in the chateau in Carentan, where I'd had my last good night's sleep. It was here now. Below me, going out to the horizon. Liling went in circles, scrambling our sense of direction too, and she did it casually, without a glance to either one of us.

I checked on Sofia. Her face was silver with moonlight as she gazed listlessly out the window, massaging the rope burns on her wrists. She'd have scars there. Hell, all three of us did.

I turned around and watched the road. Finally, Liling pulled up in front of a house. There wasn't much to distinguish it from any other, except for one important fact: it was the highest point in the neighborhood. The street approached it on either side with good visibility down both slopes, and it was pressed to the back of a bluff. It was the perfect place to go where no one could approach without her knowing. Like I said. Scars.

She pulled the car into a tiny and half-collapsed garage and turned off the engine. Sofia looked around as she got out, but she wasn't uncertain. Anyone who'd lived through the Night War had slept in worse. And she had to figure anywhere no one was going to tie her up and eat her brains had to count as a step up.

The house itself was barely bigger than the garage. One of the walls had been knocked over, and the whole place was strewn with shattered boards. There wasn't a single ward in sight; this place's only security was in its anonymity.

"I don't mean to gainsay you here, but this isn't exactly safe," I said.

Sofia tensed, grabbing my arm.

"This place is not safe," Liling agreed. She went to the couch, hit a catch beneath it and slid it aside on tracks. Then her quick fingers opened up a trapdoor I could have walked right past and missed. "*This* place is much safer."

The trapdoor revealed a slanted ladder leading into a basement heavy with the muscular scent of earth. The rim was hung with a whole pigeon's-worth of feathers and holy symbols from a half-dozen faiths. Liling went down first, Sofia and I following. Wards were everywhere, in lines, on the dirt walls of this place. Liling shut the trapdoor, and for a second, we were plunged into darkness. Then, with a boom, a spotlight on the other end of the hall haloed us.

I turned around to look at Liling. She was pulling on a cable, and I heard the couch rumbling into place over us.

I had to shake my head. This was a plum to end all plums. I don't know what I'd have done for a place like this back in the war, but it would have been a lot. Whether she'd built this place or found it, I was impressed.

Liling strode past us, disappearing into the bright white light. Ahead, I heard another rumble.

"This way," she said.

I followed with my hand out to make sure I didn't run into anything. When I passed the light, I saw the source of that second rumble. Liling held open a heavy wooden door. A pair of black and white cats sat at the entrance, gazing into a cage filled with mice. A chicken coop stood on the other side. I didn't see the spiders, but I knew they were in here somewhere.

Her security put mine to shame. Not that I could blame her. Liling was once Sofia, just in a nicer cage.

The walls were bolstered with timber, but for the most part everything was dirt. The furniture she had looked to be scavenged, probably from around the neighborhood. Everything was old and threadbare. The whole place smelled of earth. She motioned for us to follow her, then gestured to an open door.

"Take my room."

"I can't do that," Sofia said.

"Don't worry. I don't sleep very much."

I didn't think Sofia would either, but she settled down on the bare mattress Liling used and soon was snoring softly. I didn't know what was worse, that she should lose sleep over what Mold did, or that it was so expected that she didn't lose a wink. I made an effort, slumped against the side of the mattress, but sleep wasn't going to come to me. I was too keyed up. I'd killed someone who had saved my life, and that was definitely a first.

I got up and went into the main room, shutting the door behind me. Sure, felt a little strange to be shutting a door in what amounted to a hole in the ground, but I wasn't a savage. Liling was in the area that served as her kitchen, warming water on a hot plate.

That's not what I was looking at. I was looking at the sword hanging up over her stove. Straight and slender, just like her, its blade nicked from use. It wasn't the only weapon in the room. They were on racks all over the walls. A few guns, a poison sprayer, several medieval relics. They weren't for show, either. They'd been used. All of them. It reminded me of the walls of Last Night.

"Would you like some tea, Mr. Moss?" she asked. Her voice was soft, just shy of a whisper.

I looked into her eyes. Narrow and nearly black, they were inscrutable. No. They weren't. They were flat. The kind of flatness you only saw in soldiers who had been on the front so long they forgot what it was like not to be both hunter and hunted all at once. That's when I knew who she was.

"You're the Monster Slayer," I said.

She watched me, utterly still. Anyone who could do that was far more dangerous than those who wasted energy in twitches. Every move Liling made was deliberate. If she wanted me dead, I wouldn't know it until the blade was sticking out of my chest.

"Yes."

"What are you doing? The Night War is over."

"No, it's not, Mr. Moss. I am surprised that you of all people would not know that."

"What's that supposed to mean?"

"You find people who have been taken by them. You know firsthand what they do. You saw what that corpse was going to do to that girl in there, and you took appropriate measures."

"I did what I had to. Mold wasn't about to give me a choice."

"He wasn't the first you've killed."

"No." Not by a long shot.

"Is that what you tell yourself? That they gave you no choice?"

"I don't go hunting for them. That's a difference."

"You did back in the war, though. Didn't you?"

"Yeah. We all did. Then the Treaty put a stop to all that. We were done. War's over, the monsters are in charge now."

Liling shook her head like I was the slow kid in class. "Nothing about that strikes you as wrong?"

"Right or wrong, it doesn't matter. That's the way it is. That's the way it's going to be."

"If we allow it. Or we can fight back. One at a time."

I'd heard the rhetoric. Who hadn't? The Treaty of St. Louis was a gift. They'd elected a mummy president in '52, mostly because no human was crazy enough to risk the polls in the middle of the war. Well, Raymond James Fish had other ideas, and he assassinated President Rameses III at the inauguration. Burned him up with a Molotov cocktail. Some said that's why the monsters reached out a tentacle of peace. Some said we should have kept fighting. There were even those who said it was all set up by the VP, Vitus Veritas, to get his claws on the White House. But the fact that the monsters were willing to forgive and forget for everything done during the war, well, that was enough. A gift.

Didn't help Raymond James Fish. The president's werewolf security detail made short work of him. The thing was, there were just as many monsters who thought the Treaty was a bad deal.

"You can't be doing this. You're killing monsters, and the minute they find out it's a human, do you know what's going to happen? A crackdown on every last human in the country."

"And then revolution," she said.

"How old are you. Twenty? Twenty-two?"

"Twenty-four."

"Did you forget the Night War? We were losing. Bad. Where were you when Kong came to LA? We never had a chance against him, and it wasn't like we were doing much better against martians, or clowns, or any of the other nightmares. If we start the war again, we're going to lose, and we're not going to get another treaty. We're going to be dreaming of what we've got now."

"We don't have anything now. We have what they give us, and nothing else. We don't have our bodies, we don't have our souls. We live on the crumbs they drop, and we're expected to thank them for it."

I sighed. She wasn't wrong. "You have to stop."

"I won't."

We stared at each other from across the room. I was already wondering if she had a gun on her, and which of us was faster.

Finally, she said, "Are you going to tell the police, then?"

"I can't. Same effect. They're not going to keep it quiet that the Monster Slayer's human. That'll justify every measure they want to use to take the last little bit of what we've got."

"Then you and I will live and let live."

"Just know one thing. If you come for anyone I know—"

"Your meat golem girlfriend."

My face got hotter than the water on the hotplate. "She's not...yeah, her. Or my secretary. If you croak one of my people, you'll find out just how well I did in the Night War."

I could see her weighing each and every one of my words. When she was finished, she nodded. "Very well, Mr. Moss. Now, would you like that tea?"

Sarah Bellum
and Mr. de Kay

Forty-Three

The truth wasn't going to do. I got my story straight with Sofia, since she was going to be the one telling it to her parents. She slept through the conversation with Liling, so at least that wasn't going to have to be dealt with. I woke her after dawn, and Liling directed us to an outdoor staircase that would take us down the hill and to a red car stop. From there, I took us out to Lincoln Heights where I picked up my car from in front of Jane's. It was tempting to go talk to her, but I didn't want to keep Sofia waiting. I might have also wanted to look my best before bothering the meat golem.

The story was that a gill-man had taken Sofia and was hunting around for a siren to turn her. She hadn't seen the monster before, and hopefully wouldn't again. She knew that what I'd done to Mold would only get me in trouble, and possibly her and her parents as well. She wasn't broken up about it, either. There was something hard inside her now. A little bit of her soul had turned gray and calcified. I wish I didn't know the look so well.

Once I was finished there, I went into the office. Ser and Jaime were already in, each one engrossed in the distraction of their choosing, Jaime in his crossword, Serendipity in her glossy magazine.

"Sofia Huerta's home," I said. The night spent awake was beginning to catch up with me. I thought maybe a catnap in my office would put me right.

"What? Who was it?" Jaime asked.

I didn't want to lie to them, but I also didn't want to give them a secret they'd have to keep.

"Doesn't matter. Case's closed and the girl's okay."

"Are *you* okay?" Ser asked.

"A little tired. I was up all night."

"It's been quiet so far today."

"Best news I've gotten. Wake me up if you need me."

I went into my office and shut the door behind me. My jacket came off and hung up on the rack in the corner. I settled back in my chair and put my hat over my eyes and legs up on the desk. I figured the night would come crashing back on me and pull me under to sleep. I was hoping for it. It wouldn't.

I couldn't stop thinking about Liling's crusade. It was madness. The definition of it. The minute she slipped up, she was caught and maybe all of humanity was going to get squashed under a fifty-foot gorilla. It would have been easier if she had been a mad killer. I could dismiss her that way. I kept hearing her over, and over, telling me what they'd taken from us, what they were still taking.

She was the answer to a question I hadn't known I was asking. There were other questions, too, namely that squat in Español's place. The pictures on the wall with the Xs drawn through them. That looked like someone else's problem, but my mind kept worrying at the edges of it. It wouldn't go away. Not until I knew what was going on.

I sighed, sitting up straight. My phone sat on the desk in front of me, taunting. I wasn't going to sleep. Might as well.

I dialed the exchange and got a greeting.

"Detective Moon, please," I told the receptionist.

A moment later, the phone picked up, and Moon cleared his throat with a thunderous rattle. "This is Moon."

"Moon, it's Moss. Don't say my name. I want to talk to you without your partner, okay?"

"Don't tell me he's got your panties in a bunch."

"You willing to talk to me or not?"

"You buy me lunch and I'll talk to you about whatever you want."

"Name the place."

"You know the Moors? It's a cop joint not too far from the station."

"Meet you there at one."

The plan in place, I did manage to drift off for a bit. When I woke up, I went out into the front office, yawning and stretching.

"Sleeping at work?" Ser scolded.

"Perks of being the boss. Where's Jaime?"

"Went to lunch."

I yawned again. "Yeah, okay."

"What about me?"

"Sorry, Ser. Somebody's gotta be in the office, and I'm going out."

"Better be on a case."

"In case you missed it, I just closed one. I'm going to see a man about a horse."

"A ghost horse?"

"A figurative horse."

Ser shook her head. "I don't even know what we're talking about anymore."

"I'm going to leave and pretend you won't be on the phone with that phantom of yours within five minutes."

Ser tried to look innocent, but that was hard when her blood-red gills had popped right out of her neck.

"Real subtle, Ser."

I took a drive over to the Moors. It was mostly a bar with big tables and low lights. Even at lunch, it might as well have been the middle of the night. Instead of fog, the whole place was filled with wood smoke, like I was in the middle of a barbecue. I found Moon in a baby-blue suit near the back, nursing a beer.

"Hey there, Moss," Moon rasped. "What's with the cloak and dagger?"

"Is it so strange I might want to talk to my contact at the LAPD without getting my face ripped off?"

Moon laughed. "I'm your contact? Oh, that's either the saddest or funniest thing I've heard all week."

"Week's still young." I slid into the booth, and gave the waitress a beer order. I had a look at the menu and noticed a theme.

"Lot of meat here."

"Yeah, I love this place."

"No, I mean, a lot of meat here." The place served huge platters of meat. As in, piles of the stuff. On the menu, "chicken" was listed as a vegetable.

"What's the matter?"

"Uh, nothing."

I ordered a hamburger. Moon ordered a full rack of lamb ribs and a side of chicken. A whole chicken. All on me. I had to remind myself that Moon was only nice when stacked up next to his partner.

"So what's got you hot and bothered?"

"Before that, can we talk about Alfred Wolfe?"

"The Chief? What do you want to know about him?"

"Have you ever met him?"

"Sure, once. Shook his hand. He doesn't usually associate with detectives much. He's the head of the whole department."

"He's okay, right?"

"Last I checked. What's rattling around in that weasel head of yours?"

"What about Garou? He okay too?"

"You were just saying you don't want to see Lou, now you're worried about him?"

"He been shot lately, shot at?"

Moon sighed. "Moss, I don't know what you're getting at here, so clue me in."

I glanced around. Nobody was looking our direction, and I wanted to keep it that way. And not just because they were liable to throw me out if anyone sniffed the human on me. "I was out on an...uh...an unrelated matter. Let's call it that."

"Unrelated?"

"Yeah, you know, it's not about this?"

"Really tired of you doing that, Moss."

"Okay. So I'm snooping around, and in point of fact trying not to get my ticket punched by a kid who was bigger than three of me, and I find, well, it's a little weird. Disturbing, even. Bear in mind, this wasn't what I was looking for. You might say I fell right into it."

"Yeah, yeah. I hear you. You were right not to want Garou here for this. He'd already have put you through a wall."

"On this wall, there's pictures. And the pictures are all cops. I see the brass, sure, Wolfe, Sheriff Thorpe. Your boss Moore. But I also see pictures of you and Garou."

Moon frowned. "Pictures? What kinds of pictures?"

"Photographs. The kind where the person in the picture doesn't know they're being taken."

"Sounds like the kinds of pictures you'd take, looking to catch some cheating husband."

"I don't get many of those jobs. You'd be surprised."

"So you found pictures of us," Moon said. He was trying to act like the thought didn't chill him, but it was a bad lie.

"That's not all. Some of the pictures had big red Xs drawn over them in grease pencil."

"And two of those were Wolfe and my partner."

"Exactly."

"And you're thinking that whoever did that is looking to bump them off?"

"What else would they be after?"

"That's not something folks usually do *before* that kind of thing. They don't call their shots like some goofy Babe Ruth before putting the silver to 'em."

"Yeah, but look how things are now. Not every monster is...normal. Wolfmen are reasonable, but phantoms?"

Moon frowned. "Phantoms? You found this at a phantom's flop?"

"Yeah. Capriccio Español. He's the singer at the...you know who he is."

Moon had gone white as a phantom himself. It was like he'd been hit with a full bucket of frosty panic. When he could move his body, he was sliding his bulk out of the booth. "I know who he is. We've had him under investigation for a long time. Thanks for the tip, Moss." He peeled off a couple bills and dropped them on the table, the shock waking his sleeping generosity.

"And have one on me."

He bustled out of the Moors and was gone, the panic coming off him in a wake. I sat in the booth, trying to figure what I'd just seen.

The waitress plopped two plates on the table, one with a hamburger the size of my head, and the other plate invisible under the rack of ribs. I blinked in mute incomprehension.

"Uh...miss?" I asked the waitress. "Do you do doggie bags here? No pun intended."

Forty-Four

The clip was still stacked with silver, but I checked it anyway. Call it nerves. Silver was still legal, same as everything else, so long as you had a license. Didn't matter that it was only good for one thing, and that thing was cops. They couldn't outlaw fire and sunlight, and I suspected that the mummies and vampires weren't going to give up the one thing they had on the wolves. As squeamish as monsters were about using each other's weaknesses and phobias, they still hadn't outlawed the ability to use them.

Eight silver pellets, each one ready to end a wolf's life. I didn't think I was going to use them, but I had to know they were there, and when I put the magazine back, I went ahead and filled a spare, putting that in my jacket pocket. The Luger was hungry. Been starving since the end of the Night War, and now it wanted to gorge itself.

I wasn't even exactly sure what I was doing. Jaime was even more confused when I busted through the front door of the office and dumped a bag with a full rack of ribs on his lap.

"What's this?"

"Dinner for a family of five. You want it?" I went into the office, and heard Jaime respond from where he was.

"Yeah. Where'd you get it?"

"This wolf place in Gardena."

Jaime appeared in my doorway as I was shoving the second clip in my pocket. Serendipity appeared behind him. He flinched when he detected her there, but he didn't turn on her like he would have when he started here.

"We got another case? Need me to sit on someone?"

"No. Not exactly. I need to check on something."

Jaime and Ser exchanged a concerned look.

"You sure, Nick?" Ser asked. "You've been acting a little strange the last month or so."

"Don't worry," I lied to her. I needed to know what the wolves were doing at Español's place. That wall wasn't leaving my head, not after Moon's reaction to it. I didn't know what it meant, but it meant something. This decaying incestuous spiral was reaching the bottom, only because the bodies kept falling. I needed to know why. I gave the two of them a smile, but just by the expressions on their faces, I knew it looked ghastly.

The front door opened.

"What's with the kibbutz?" Mickey's voice was hale and loud from the front door.

Both Serendipity and Jaime turned around to face the newcomer. Ser's gills popped right out of their slits as she made her way behind her desk. "Mr. Cohen, Mr. Steele, so nice to see you."

"It's Mickey and Johnny, dollface. Where's the boss?"

I stepped up to the door, crowding the group. Sure enough, Mickey and Johnny were at the front door. Johnny's suit was dark gray, and he hadn't bothered with a tie. He was making promises to Ser with his eyes, and she was putting every one into her hope chest. As for Mickey, he leaned on a cane, and his right arm was gingerly cradling his belly, but other than that, he looked fine.

"Right here, Mickey."

"Stick. Oh, ain't youse a sight for sore eyes." He hobbled over and gave me an affectionate pat on the cheek before turning to address Jaime and Ser. "You shoulda seen this fella. Zombies roll up and give one of my guys the business. You know, street cannons. Your boss here starts shooting up the street like Wyatt Earp. Same old Nick."

"What about you, Mickey? I saw you get shot."

Mickey hobbled a few steps away to take the center of the room. "Barely winged me. Youse can teach a corpse to do a lot, but decent work with a shotgun ain't one of 'em."

It was impressive anyway. He wasn't shot but two days ago. Still, Mickey was a tough guy. I'd seen that firsthand in the Night War. He might look soft, but maybe all that belly fat was good for catching buckshot. First time an ice cream diet ever saved a fella.

"Well, it's great to see you up and around."

"Ain't it? And I'm happy to see your setup here. Who's the kid?"

"This is Jaime Alvarez. He's uh...a legman." Sure, that sounded good.

Mickey stuck a hand out. "Jaime. Pleased to meet you."

"Nice to meet you too, Mr. Cohen."

"Polite too!" Mickey said. He turned Jaime's hand over and had a look at the ink across the kid's knuckles, then peered up at the tats peeking from under the collar. Only then did he release Jaime's hand. "Normandie Knights, huh?"

"Yeah. What of it?"

"Good outfit," Mickey said, nodding. "Lotta humans don't know what time it is. Little direction, the Knights could really be something."

I kept myself from shaking my head. Mickey would get along famously with Liling.

"Johnny Stompanato," Johnny said, taking Jaime's hand. He was trying to loom over the kid. Johnny had some height on Jaime, but it wasn't working. Jaime's expression hardened and his chest stuck out.

"Settle down, Johnny," Mickey said. "Haze the kid later."

Johnny let Jaime's hand go with an easy grin. "Nice to see you again, Miss Sargasso. You're looking lovely as always."

That line was dripping with Velveeta, but Ser's gills frilled outward and she did the *Oh you* pose. Don't even think she noticed that Johnny had given her a different name. He sat down on her desk and started speaking to her in low tones.

"Smart, Nick. Good idea getting yourself some muscle. Nothing against you, but we're not as young as we used to be. Can I have a word with you?"

"Sure thing."

"Step into my office." Mickey hobbled out the front door and I followed. It was a perfect Los Angeles January: freezing in the shade, but like a nice bath in the sunlight. Mickey limped slowly down the concrete staircase leading down to Flower Street. My office was over a laundry, and Mickey paused in front of it, right next to a planter filled with ferns and a single tubby palm tree. Mickey settled down on the lip of the planter and let out a heavy breath. I wondered how much he was putting in to make the hit look like it had no effect.

"You know, Stick, you're a tough man to read."

"Really? Everybody just thinks I'm sort of nervous."

"The ones who never look any deeper. You're smart. You make sure no one thinks enough to look."

"What are you getting at?"

"You been reluctant. I'm trying to give you an opportunity, over and over. Join up with me. Get the kind of green and respect you're never going to get doing what you're doing. Get yourself a pretty spook to live with you, or one of them skin-dollies you like so much. But youse act like I'm trying to sell you a cobra to keep in your trousers. Not like a dear old friend finally getting his due from a man who maybe owes him his life."

I had already tensed, glancing up at the door to my office, half-expecting Johnny to burst out with another shotgun and put me on my back.

"And when I'm thinking youse might be a lost cause, you do something brilliant."

I blinked. "What?"

"Don't act like you don't know. It wasn't front page news, not like the other hits. But I seen the article. Bracken Mold, one of Sarah Bellum's enforcers, dead in his own kitchen. Top of his head shot clean off."

I swallowed. "How did you figure it was me?"

Mickey laughed. "Johnny saw you leave the club with the dead man. I expected maybe you would do collections, make book, that kind of thing. Leave the redder part of the business to the hard men. But then youse trick one of Bellum's top guys into taking you home and you bump him off? That's cold, Stick. Ice cold."

"Wasn't exactly like that."

Mickey laughed again. "I'm sure there were a lotta ins, lotta outs. Mold's croaked, and maybe the ledger's a little more even. Add a couple names to the list, and things are starting to look rosier than a virgin's blush."

"I still haven't found Jack."

"I know. I don't think we're going to find Jack. It's like you said, he's probably at the bottom of that bend in Mulholland. Bellum's people, probably Mold and those other corpses, took Jack for a ride, and that's the last we seen of him. Only you're the only one trying to balance the scales."

I shifted uncomfortably. Flower Street was pretty quiet, the city in a late afternoon malaise. Across the street, a meat golem walked a pair of stitched-together wolfhounds. I watched him going about his business, entirely unaware there was a gangster across the street.

Or maybe two gangsters.

"So it got me to thinking. If you're going to be bumping off Bellum's people, you might as well work for me."

"That was a one-time thing."

"It's always a one-time thing with you. You say, this time, no more. Then youse do it again. And again. And it gets easier, every time."

He wasn't wrong. When I'd shot Mold, I was putting a bullet through every last monster who had ever taken someone with the law on their side.

In that moment, I had been Liling Lam, and I still had the nerve to tell her she was the one who was mixed up.

"You gotta know, with the Gobfather shown the door, there's only two outfits worth mentioning in town. Mine and Bellum's. And we got her on the run, Stick. She hits hard and she's smart, but her guys go gaga if you give them a salted french fry."

"That's good for you."

"Good for us. We're the future, and youse can take that to the bank."

"Mickey, I got a job. I got a life."

"I'm offering youse a better one. Youse don't see all the cards on the table, but let me give you a tip. We got backers."

"Backers? What does that mean?"

Mickey pursed his lips, his dark eyes searching mine. "Some things I don't spill until you say yes. I will say that there's only one thing missing from it all. Nick Moss."

"What can I give you that you don't already have?"

"Johnny told me how youse talked to Mold. It was like youse knew him. That gets me thinking. You got some kind of in with Bellum's group. Youse can go where we can't. This is the opportunity, Nick. Youse do what you're going to do anyway, but youse do it on the winning side. Youse do it for me. And I'm not asking youse to be no bagman. I'm asking youse to be a captain. Youse follow orders from nobody but me, and youse keep your crew. That kid in there? Him and how ever many of his friends youse want to bring along."

A breeze rustled down Flower Street as Mickey watched me. Saying yes would have been easy. He wasn't selling me a bill of goods here. But I felt like I was back in the Gobfather's world, being bricked up into that well. I couldn't see the weasel, though. Or it wasn't coming to lead me out this time.

"I don't know, Mickey."

He grinned, but his eyes still looked like a pair of plastic beads. "Youse keep telling me you don't know. It was anybody else, I could tell 'em where to stick it, but it's you. Still, I ain't gonna take it forever. Youse gotta pick a side, Nick. Fellas who don't don't last too long."

I nodded, because I was certain my friend meant it. I was either joining up, or I was joining Big Jack in the ground. Or maybe both.

Forty-Five

I wasn't thinking about Mickey Cohen on the way into Beverly Hills. I was mostly thinking about my beat-up Ford Coupe and the chances of getting pulled over by wolves looking to prove a point. I got lucky, or maybe it was because they were all otherwise occupied. That's the conclusion I came to when I slapped eyes on Español's place.

Six prowlers were pulled up around it, and the other four buckets were probably unmarked cars. The front door hung off its hinges and loud bangs and crashes rolled from the house.

What the hell had Español done? It looked like this had been a standoff turned into a pitched battle. The cops had decided to charge headlong into the house. I didn't envy them, since I knew what was waiting inside. Between this and the mob the other day, if anything, Español's property was under-protected.

I didn't like phantoms, but I hoped this wasn't my fault. Moon had scurried out so quickly, I wasn't sure if he understood that I didn't think the pictures belonged to Español. In fact, I had an idea about whose they might be, although there I was on shakier ground.

I hadn't expected this. A rattle came from the interior; unmistakably a Thompson making life difficult for someone. If they were filling the air with lead, then I was already losing time.

I slipped through the front gate. Now I could hear other sounds in the relative quiet between the cracks of gunfire. Cursing from the wolves. Moon's familiar rasp barking orders at his men. The wolf lurked in their voices; all of them would be wearing their fur and muscles. I crept closer, ducking down behind cars as much as I could. I didn't think any bullets would come crashing through the windows, but better safe than sorry. Bullets, as long as they were lead, qualified as more or less non-lethal for wolfmen and phantoms. Oh, sure, give them enough and they'd give up the ghost, but that was a lot more than it would take for me.

As I ran up the aisle formed by a black and white and an Army-green Packard, I started wondering what I was going to do. Going in was suicide, but I needed to make it back to the hidey hole.

I paused by the front fender of the Packard, ready to sprint for the front door, mapping out the route in my head. I was going to get there, check the front foyer for monsters with guns, step over the tripwires, and make a beeline for the right bookcase in the hall. I broke cover and dug in, ready to run like I had a line of kraut bullets following me.

Ahead, a copse of banana trees fluttered, even though there was no breeze. No, fluttered was the wrong word. Two of the stalks went in opposite directions, then snapped back into place. That wasn't the strangest part. That would be the .45 automatic hovering about four feet off the ground, right next to a knapsack.

It was enough to bring me to a dead stop, gaping as both got closer. The gun rose, pointing right at my heart. "You have a car?" The voice was gravelly, but not especially deep; weary, but tight.

"Uh...yeah. It's parked on the street."

"Take me to it."

I took a leap. "Detective Bosch?" I asked.

The voice waited a few seconds to respond, and when it did, the suspicion cut through it like a blade. "Who wants to know?"

"Nick Moss. I was hired to find you."

Forty-Six

Wednesday, January 11, 1956
Moments later

The first thing Bosch did when he got into the passenger seat of my car was open up the knapsack, remove a fake mustache, and plant it right in the middle of where I assumed his face to be. After that, he looked like a caterpillar floating about half a head taller than me. The rod stayed pointed at me, the barrel a black hole looking to swallow me up if I so much as had a wrong thought.

"Drive," Bosch told me, and I did.

I left Español's place in the dust and went east, for lack of any other directions. If Bosch had other ideas, he could tell me. For the time being, he was content to let me choose.

"So who are you really?" Bosch demanded finally. His mustache twitched when he talked, like the caterpillar was dancing.

"Uh...what's with the mustache?"

"You don't like it?"

"No, it's fine. It's just...why are you wearing it?"

"So you have something to look at. Otherwise everybody stares over my shoulder. It's unnerving."

"Oh." It made sense. Never thought too much about what that did to invisible men. Sounded like they had a lot of difficulties. I hoped Bosch wasn't as crazy as they tended to be.

Bosch was quiet for the rest of the drive, the gun still pointed at my kidneys. I tried not to go over any bumps. That was the last way I wanted to go out. Okay, it was one of many last ways I didn't want to go out. Bosch didn't seem to have a destination in mind, and I let my old Ford pick. We wound up in a vacant lot on the southern border of Hollywood. A pair of gremlin flivvers were in the middle of an impromptu race, having attracted a crowd of like monsters cheering and taking bets. No two flivvers were ever the same, the weird genius of the gremlins taking whatever they could get their talons on and sculpting it into a vehicle that could more or less get from place to place and only exploded occasionally. One of them looked mostly like a disc, but it was lopsided, and seemed to get around via quick lurching spins. The other was halfway between a rocket and a bulldozer, and still had enough logos on it to say this gremlin had raided a garage or junkyard to build it.

The Hollywood Sheriff's Department wasn't around, so either they hadn't heard, or they had no desire to wander into the middle of this crowd. I didn't blame them. From the combination of gremlins, brainiacs, mad scientists, and martians who were watching, they were packing the kind of firepower that could make your hair turn green, turn you inside out, and give you a voice like Doris Day.

Me, I felt safe. Suppose that said it all. I turned the car off and settled down, watching the spinning disc lurch its way into a blistering climb, only scarcely avoiding pancaking into a brick apartment building on one edge of the vacant lot.

"So who are you, Moss?" Bosch asked. The gun was still on me.

I thought of Harry Braden, my old buddy who had gone invisible and, from there, mad. How many marbles were still rolling around in Bosch's transparent noggin? With no face, he was tough to read, and his voice was nearly a monotone.

"I'm a private detective."

"A dick, huh? Should have known it wouldn't take forever for a wolf to sniff me out."

"I'm, uh, I'm actually not a wolf. Still human."

"You said you're a detective."

"I get that a lot. I'm human and a detective."

"Can't be many of you."

"I'm the only one."

The rocketdozer flipped over on a blaze of white fire, slamming into the dirt. I figured it would stop, as the gremlin had crashed. It fired another set of jets and went skittering over the ground, igniting dry patches of cattails as it went. I realized then I had no idea which gremlin was ahead, or if this was even technically a race.

"You said you were hired to find me," Bosch said.

"Yeah. Back in October. I thought I'd found you, too. I watched you get set on fire by a goblin." I shuddered at the memory, the hungry beauty of the orange flames consuming something that wasn't even there, the burned pork-and-flour smell throttling the air.

"Wasn't me," Bosch said simply.

He didn't have to say anymore, because I saw it. I watched Moon sniff the body, then break the seal on the hanky and give that a whiff. Garou verified it right after.

"Someone switched the hankies," I said. "Do you know who the dead man was?"

"Probably grabbed an invisible man off the street. Told 'em what was what, and set them out of it."

The pieces fell into place one after the other. My mind was putting it together quicker than my mouth could keep up, so all I said was, "Let me guess. You found some kind of evidence that the Gobfather had one or more wolves in his pocket."

"Got it in one."

The pistol wavered, then lay flat on the car seat. I kept my hands on the wheel and watched the mustache bob up and down as Bosch spoke. Past his transparent head, the flivvers somersaulted through the air, always a blink away from a disastrous crash.

"Moore was the one who sent me under," Bosch said. "I know the press calls it the Wolf Pack because it's the wolves grabbing all the headlines. Easy to make print when it's a bunch of two-fisted wolfmen busting up some zombies. It's harder to make the spies into heroes, but without us, without invisible men and doppelgangers, the wolves wouldn't know where to hit. Wolfmen couldn't find a randy meatstick with both hands and a working sniffer. Uh...no offense."

"None taken," I lied.

"There was no threat like the Gobfather. Not even Bellum. We all knew it, but they needed someone with the guts to do something about it. I gave up my life and went under. Moore was the only one who was supposed to know how to get to me. My job was to find everything I could about Mab."

"By which you mean you started hanging around the Gobfather in the nude."

"Yeah. Why, what did you think I meant?"

"No, just...I wanted to hear it out loud."

Bosch paused, and the confusion twisted his voice. "Sure." He cleared his throat and got back to it. "I was supposed to get close to Mab. Once I got enough to throw Mab into the big house for a couple decades, we'd send in the wolves. Of course, this was before we knew what a nightmare he'd turned the Chateau Marmont into."

"Yeah. I wasn't prepared for that, either. Can't imagine the snow did you much good."

"It wasn't snowing when I got there. It matched up to the seasons pretty well, but not the seasons here."

"For what seasons we have."

Bosch snorted. "It got a little cold in the autumn, though. I don't know how invisible men live back east."

"Me neither," I said, realizing it was going to bother me all week.

"Wasn't just the weather, though. Mab's place is crawling with animals." He said "animals" with more venom than he'd used on the racist term. I must have shown my confusion on my face, because he said, "Animals can see me. Don't ask me how, but they do."

I started thinking about all the times my cat stared at nothing and shuddered.

"I couldn't sleep at Mab's—"

"So you bunked over at Español's place. They weren't too far apart, and their paths crossed enough that you could hitch rides back and forth."

"That's right. So I stayed as close to Mab as I could. Tough with all those owls around, but I did okay. I spent a lot of time with those three rhyming idiots."

"Flux, Murk, and Sawbones. Yeah, I've met 'em."

The mustache shook back and forth in disgust. "So they get to talking from time to time, and eventually I piece together that Mab has someone on the force. Maybe a lot of someones. I kept waiting for them to mention a name, but they never did. The one thing I knew for certain was that dirty cops like to be paid, so all I had to do was keep from getting found out until one of them paid up. It was only a matter of time."

Outside, the disk slammed into the earth, still trying to rotate but skipping like a scratched record.

"I had to stay in contact with Moore, and I had a meeting scheduled. The next thing I know, I'm reading my obit in the morning paper over the pig one's shoulder. I do a little poking around and get as much of the story as there is to get. Sounds to me like whoever was on the take got nervous. They couldn't get me, so they did the next best thing. Kill any old invisible man and make the world believe it's me. I show up, no one can identify me right away, and that gives the one who did it plenty of time to make sure I disappear permanently."

"That's what's on your wall. Your suspects."

"That's right. Only now I can't find out who. Mab was the only one who knew who the dirty one was, and Mab's dead and the gang is scattered. Whoever Mab bought is going to get away with it. All of it."

"No. There's still us. We can smoke him out. We can finish it."

"How? You got a way to talk to the dead?"

"You know, it's funny there isn't a monster who does that."

"Moss!"

"What were the Xs? Some of your suspects were Xed out."

"I know it's not them. One way or the other, they're in the clear."

I pictured the Xed out wolves. That included the chief and my old pal. "You sure about Garou?"

"Yeah, why?"

"He's the one who wanted me on the job. My very first night on it, I watch you go up in flames. Which, in retrospect, really starts to look like a setup."

"You really ready to make that bold a call?" Bosch's deadpan tone was admirable.

"I was a little distracted at the time."

"That's because you're not focused on the facts. The case is always in the facts. Not in gut feelings, not in hunches, not in intuition. If something is true, there will be facts."

"Well, the fact is, Garou hates me. If someone wanted to set me up, it'd be him."

"Wasn't you who was set up," Bosch said. "You were a witness. A mea...a human, sure. Maybe no human's word is getting used in a court of law, but you're also an outsider. You're not in the Gobfather's pocket."

He had a point. The Gobfather was the one mobster in town who hadn't tried to lease my soul.

"There are some people who would know," I pointed out. "The goblins. Don't suppose you know where we can find them."

The mustache shuddered. "They live in a bungalow court over in Silver Lake. But, uh...they have traps. Lots of traps."

The fear in Bosch's voice put a grin on my face. A simple flour bomb or even a cross on a wall would utterly paralyze a monster. And people wondered why I never wanted to be turned.

"It's okay, Bosch. I'll go in first."

All of my fears were entirely rational and I could ignore them. Most of the time.

FORTY-SEVEN

Wednesday, January 11, 1956
Later

If I hadn't known goblins lived in this particular bungalow court before I showed up, I'd have known within the first second of seeing it. It wasn't the two rows of eight identical white Spanish-style buildings arranged around a courtyard. It was pretty much everything else.

Big pine trees grew all around the houses. Hibiscus plants vast enough to get lost in, and ferns like something from a primeval forest grew around the bases. Birds of paradise sprouted around the fronts, and what in most similar courts would have been a neat lawn here was a miniature forest. As I pulled up in front, eyes shined from the shadows in the bushes, watching the both of us.

"We shouldn't talk to the little one," Bosch said, meaning Sawbones. "He's not going to know."

I was certain that's what was causing the reluctance and not the fact that Sawbones could kill Bosch with the snap of his fingers.

"If any of them know what we want to know, it's Flux. We'll talk to him."

Bosch let out a slow breath. "He's in number 3."

I got out of the car. Since the passenger door didn't open, I assumed Bosch stuck around inside. "All right. I'll go have a look and see what I can see."

"Watch out for the traps."

I just nodded. Mickey probably would have rubbed Bosch's nose in it. All that talk about meatsticks, and Mickey couldn't resist pointing out a meatstick rushing in where a monster feared to tread. I didn't feel like I needed it, though. Bosch knew what was happening. I knew it too. Let it stay unspoken.

Three concrete steps led into the court. Number 3 was the second one on the left-hand side. I didn't want any of the goblins to see me coming. It was a shame, since that made me a lot more suspicious to anyone who couldn't recognize me. I was wagering the other goblin residents weren't vicious little thugs like the one I was after.

If they were, well, I had enough mushrooms for everyone.

I broke off the concrete path immediately, and skirted the first bungalow. I kept low, moving as slowly as I could to keep from rustling. Every now and again, something hiding in the greenery bolted. I never got a good look at what it was, but I was going to pretend it was a cat. That was best for everyone concerned. Just a cat. Not a goblin monster pet from some other realm.

The backs of the bungalows were nearly flush up against a wooden fence separating the property line. I squeezed through there, once having to climb a pine tree halfway to get around it, and emerged on the other side. I dropped to a crouch, going still for a little while to catch my breath and to throw anyone watching off the scent. The floor here was mossy, a bright, heartbreaking green. I'd say this for the goblins, they knew home gardening.

About three feet ahead of me, I picked out a tripwire. I didn't know if I'd have seen if I'd kept moving. Best not to dwell. I approached it. It was stretched across a place where two narrow pathways met. Had anyone been creeping through the plants, they'd have naturally used one of the two avenues, and this was where they joined, pointed at a small window on the side of the bungalow. The wire was secured to the base of a fern on one end, and on the other, hidden in a fallen log, was a bomb.

I knew the type because I'd made enough of them during the Night War. Pretty simple. They functioned a lot like grenades, only instead of shrapnel, it was mostly just flour, or dust, or anything else you could coat someone with. They weren't easy to spot, and they played on the natural overconfidence invisible men often developed. Bosch had learned caution, and it was easy to see why.

I delicately gripped the wire, careful not to pull it, and with the dagger, sliced where it was tied around the fern. The trap effectively disarmed, I hid the rest of the tripwire in the same log along with the bomb. The glass by this window was frosted, so I was guessing it was the bathroom.

I paralleled the wall, and along the way disarmed two more of the flour bombs. The goblins were paranoid about invisible men, but then again, they had successfully been keeping them away. Might be a good lesson in there.

The next window had blinds in it, but putting my face right up to the glass let me see into an empty dining room. An open arch beyond showed off a front hall and a living room across the way. The lights were off. Looked like nobody was home. Only one way to be sure, though.

I wedged the blade of my dagger under the windowsill, and worried it until I could get my fingers under it. I wasn't going to dwell on the irony of using cold iron to get into a goblin's house. Or maybe that was something that just happened in my life now. I worked the window open and paused, peering underneath it.

The tripwire was nearly invisible in the gloom, but I caught it. It would be right where anyone coming in would step down. I got the window open enough for me to get my head and shoulders through. Now I was looking at the crossbow on the other end of that tripwire, waiting to stick a poisoned arrow into anyone who decided on an alternative entrance.

In the past couple months I had met a lot of people with truly excessive ideas of home security.

The way I was coming in, I was going to land right on that tripwire, so I needed to cut it before going any further. And I was going to have to do it with that arrow pointed at me. The flour bombs had been one thing; if I'd fouled up there, I'd just look like a ghost until my next shower. Screw up here, and Flux would get to clean my corpse out of the window.

I wiggled over, freeing up my left hand to draw the dagger. My weight was entirely on my chest now, my breath coming in aching huffs. Delicately, like I was performing surgery on a baby, I put my hand on the tripwire. The other end was secured to a radiator, so any thought of moving it was moot. I pulled as hard as I dared. The wire creaked. I froze, staring at the crossbow in mute suspicion. It hadn't moved.

I put the dagger up to the far side of the wire, and took as deep a breath as I could manage in my present position. Then, with as confident a cut as I could, pulled the blade through the wire. It gave with a twang, and I dropped it and exhaled at the same time. Then I wiggled into the room.

I slid onto the hardwood floor and rose, having a look around the room. Almost immediately, I thought I had the wrong house. I hadn't really noticed what was on the walls, or decorating the shelves and end tables in the form of knickknacks, or sitting on the dining room table as a centerpiece. Flux really liked fairies. You know, little mostly-naked people with bug wings. The one kind of monster I was comfortable saying not only didn't exist, but wouldn't.

Flux was obviously pretty depressed about that. I didn't think there was this much fairy stuff in the world, and he had it crammed into his bungalow, a structure barely bigger than the tiny box I owned in Watts. Between this small place and Mold's house in the hills, I was wondering if crime really did pay. For anyone other than the bosses, that is; Bellum and Mab had been doing quite well for themselves. The grunts got whatever crumbs were left over.

I went through the bungalow, a room at a time. The walls were purple or pink. The rugs looked like frosting and either sported flowers or butterflies on them. And on every shelf, in every bare patch of wall, another fairy bopping a frog on the nose with a wand, or bathing in a tulip.

Had the other goblins not seen this?

The rest of the house only had three more rooms, a bedroom, a bathroom, and a room whose only purpose looked to be holding the fairies that wouldn't fit into the rest of the bungalow. I supposed I could ask Flux whenever it was he got home. In the meantime, I would wait. I made sure the window was propped open and turned the crossbow to face the wall, then I went out the way I came and fetched Bosch.

"Bosch!" I hissed at the open window of my car. I was on the far side of the fence still.

"What?" said a voice beside me.

I nearly jumped right out of my skin. "Don't do that."

"Do what? I'm invisible." He had taken off the mustache, so that was literally true.

"I noticed that. Or didn't. It doesn't matter. Flux isn't home, so follow me."

"Are you sure?"

"I disarmed every trap between here and there. Just step where I step, okay?"

Bosch muttered something, but I ignored it. I retraced my steps through the bushes and shrubs, the whole way grappling with the uncanny sensation of having an invisible man at my heels. Bosch was nearly silent too, his steps and breath only just loud enough to raise my hackles. Had I not been certain he was there, those slight sounds would have given me the heebies something fierce.

"Are you sure?" he asked again when we got to the fork in the path.

"Positive. There was a bomb here attached to a tripwire, but it's safe as houses now."

"Depends on whose house," Bosch muttered.

I hoisted myself up through the open window. Once inside, I got to hear Bosch grunting, and the window wobbling whenever his back hit it. Soon, he and I were standing next to each other in Flux's house.

"You sure you got the right place, Moss?"

I picked a letter up off the end table by the door and held it up at approximately where his head may very well have been.

"This is not what I was expecting," Bosch said finally.

"Glad I'm not the only one."

I sat down in a chair in the living room facing the door. Periodically, the sound of one of Bosch's footsteps creaking on the floor would give me a fresh round of gooseflesh. I took out a smashed pack of cigarettes from my jacket and looked at them dubiously.

"You want a smoke?" I asked the air.

"So I can be seen? The hell is wrong with you?"

"Oh, sorry. I've been meaning to quit myself," I said. Truth was, I barely smoked. I never got the hang of it, and only did it for something to do with my hands. Only these days I hadn't needed to go for it. I shoved them back in a jacket pocket.

We waited for an hour in silence, before I had to break it with some conversation. "I read your file."

"Oh yeah? What'd it say about me?"

"Said you were a good detective."

Bosch *hmphed*. "Don't think I'd trust any of them to know good policework if it broke into their houses and turned them."

"You were also in the service."

"I was. Marine corps. Sounds like you were too."

"Army. Airborne."

"No kidding. They dumped you out of a plane?"

"Over France. Got a real good look at kraut flak."

Bosch chuckled. "They used boats with us. Threw us right into the teeth of Jap machine guns."

"Sounds familiar."

"You said it. One of these days, the brass needs to figure out a better thing to stop a bullet with than some poor kid." He grunted at some memory. "You from here?"

"Yeah. Santa Monica, born and raised."

"Don't live there now, huh?"

"No humans allowed."

"Yeah," he said. Sounded like maybe he had some thoughts on it, but wasn't going to voice them. "I'm from Hollywood originally," he said instead.

I was about to say something else when a key crunched into the front lock. We both went silent, and Bosch's light footsteps traced a path away from me. The front door opened, and there was Flux. He was wearing a pinstriped suit like some movie gangster, his greasy hair combed back over his distended skull. His face was fixed in a usual grimace, but his skin, usually a deep purple, was brighter around his eyes. Looked like a healing bruise to me. There was also the matter of the cast on his arm. When Jane saved my bacon, she must have really done a number on the three goblins.

Flux, without noticing me, stepped inside and shut the door behind him.

"Hey there, Flux," I said.

The goblin jumped like he'd been hooked to a car battery, his broken arm crossing his chest protectively. His black-on-black eyes took me in and his mouth twisted even further into something that was probably intended to be a sneer. His good arm snaked into his jacket. He hissed, "If suicide's your aim, I'd gladly stake my claim."

"I'd keep your hands where I can see them," I told him.

"Alone you arrive, alone you'll no longer be alive."

"Shaky meter, hob," Bosch growled, and for the second time Flux nearly had a heart attack.

Flux's jacket opened on its own and his gun floated out to be leveled at his head.

"It's a risk assuming I'm on my own here," I told him.

Flux scowled, putting his hands up. "Do what you came to this place for, filthy son of a scabrous whore."

"Mouth off that," Bosch said, and the gun came up and slammed down right behind Flux's right ear.

The goblin staggered forward, cradling his head as black blood welled up between his fingers. I didn't scold Bosch. Wouldn't do to present less than a united front, but I made a mental note about his hair-trigger temper.

I got up, gesturing to the seat I'd been using. "Siddown, Flux."

The goblin obediently went to the chair, continuing to cradle his wounded head. He couldn't glare at Bosch, so all his hatred bored into me.

"That's the hard way," I said, "and it gets a lot harder. We both know I have mushrooms and cold iron. Shows how nice I am that I'm keeping those in my jacket for now, but you keep up the tough guy act, they're coming out. The easy way is to answer a single question. You do that, we'll leave you alone."

Flux chewed on his lip. "If a question be my price, then I'll make that sacrifice."

"Good boy. We know Mab had a dirty cop on the payroll. Tell us the name."

"Policeman's name was always mystery, Gobfather knew, but Mab's history."

I pulled the vial of mushrooms from my jacket and shook three out into my palm. Flux cowered, trying to crawl up the chair and sink into the back of it at the same time.

"By claw and tooth, I speak the truth!"

"You're not telling us everything. My friend here has been listening to a lot of your conversations, Flux. You paid the cop somehow."

"A case of cash, a faceless drop, a furtive job to buy a cop."

"You took the cash to the drop?"

Flux nodded eagerly. "Where Western Ave. and Rosecrans meet, we hid the cash, oh so discreet."

I nodded to myself. That intersection sounded familiar, though I wasn't certain why. I put the mushrooms back in the vial.

"Good news, Flux. You're off the hook."

"Leave you now, but ere you go, hear that I will kill you slow. Meatstick, meatstick, you will know, the cost of bringing a goblin low."

"You're welcome to try. Just remember what happened the last three times we tangled. First time, I beat you in your own maze. Second time, a friend of mine put you in the hospital. Third time, I was in your house with cold iron. If I was you, I'd pray I never saw me again."

Those words came out of me before I knew what I was saying. Months with Mickey, diving into the Gobfather's dream realm, facing off with Mold, all of it. I told Flux exactly what had happened, and I believed it. He believed it, too.

Flux couldn't hide the terror on his face as I turned and left. Bosch, marked only as a pistol floating at hip height, followed me.

"Good god," Bosch said as we climbed back into my car. "Never seen a goblin piss himself before."

Bosch sounded like he approved.

FORTY-EIGHT

Wednesday, January 11, 1956
Late in the afternoon

The corner of Rosecrans and Western was nothing special, and Bosch wasted no time in telling me exactly that.

"That hob sent us on a wild goose chase. This is what we get for following some half-cocked leads. We should go for the files. I'm telling you Moss, the answer to the case is always in the files, just waiting for someone to make the right connection."

Bosch didn't notice what I was staring at. It wasn't the alley between a hardware store and a small market, which had ample hiding places for a case full of cash. It was across the street, where I was looking at a bar and grill I had been at only a few hours ago. It was the Moors, a favorite cop spot.

I swore under my breath.

"You said it. We can go back for him, but he'll be ready this time. Might have backup. Might even have those traps fixed."

"We don't have to," I said, staring the car. "I know who it is."

"Great. Where are we going?"

"I want to stop by my house. A little extra wolfsbane might not be a bad idea."

The clip of Flux's gun came out and levitated on its own. "The dumb hob is packing lead."

"Of course he is. A wolf's more likely to let him go if he's not carrying silver, and he's mostly using it on zombies."

"Don't suppose you have silver rounds for a .45."

"You're not coming."

"The hell I'm not!"

"Bosch, the wolves are on the lookout for you. I know they can't track you, but close enough, they'll sniff you. Chances are these are the only two who will recognize your scent. If you come, our goose is cooked."

"Doesn't feel right," Bosch muttered.

"What?"

"Me not getting to finish this."

"You were finished when Mab bought the farm. This is just cleanup."

I pulled up in front of my house. It was late afternoon, and the monsters had not yet started to gather on Juniper Street. I told Bosch I wanted to stock up on things, but that was only half true. I could have done that at the office, but I knew Ser would try to talk me out of this. It was stupid, maybe the stupidest thing I'd ever done. I had to do it, though. No one was paying me. Barely anyone knew there was anything wrong, and then only a fraction of them cared. But it came down to me. I was all that was left.

I went inside and held the door open for Bosch after breaking a line in the sand for him.

"This is your place? It's a dump."

"Thanks, Bosch."

I heard the shrug in his voice. "You have dents in the plaster."

"Yeah, someone tried to kill me by bouncing me off every wall in the place. Haven't gotten around to fixing it yet. Now keep your voice down. I have to place a call."

I called 77th Street Station and asked for Moon or Garou.

"Detective Garou," the wolfman snarled into the phone when they transferred the call.

"It's Moss."

"What do you want, Moss? You know I got a whole caseload that doesn't involve you."

"You hired me to find Anonymous Bosch. Well, guess what. I found him."

Garou laughed. "Pull the other one. Bosch is dead."

"He's not as dead as you thought."

"If this is some kinda meatstick prank—"

"It's on the level."

"Then bring him in."

"It's also not that easy. Meet me on Spruce Street, right up above Chinatown after sundown."

"After sundown? Taking your life in your hands there."

"Last I checked, it wasn't a full moon tonight. You going to be there?"

"We'll be there. If this is a trick, though, they ain't gonna find enough of you to bury."

Garou hung up without saying goodbye, because that's the kind of person he was. I hung up the phone, expecting my heart to be hammering against my ribcage like one of Capriccio Español's bongo players. It was giving me a steady *thump-thump*, like a sleepy metronome.

"Hope you know what you're doing," Bosch said, from way too close.

Now my heart was going. "You think you could put on your mustache? At least for a little while?"

"Oh, yeah. Sorry. It's in the car." I heard footsteps heading for the door, but they stopped.

A rapping came from my screen door. I turned, wondering why Bosch would be knocking. It wasn't Bosch.

It was Jane. She was dressed for work, but her posture was relaxed like it never was at the Nocturnist. She had one arm over her shoulder, and it looked like she had a half cape on.

I opened the door and she broke into a smile, giving me a small, staccato wave.

"Hi, Jane."

She gestured at the threshold and raised her eyebrows. I was pretty happy I hadn't lit the torches yet, or she'd never have gotten close.

"Yeah, come in. Can I get you something? Beer? Pen and paper?"

She nodded, and touched the end of her nose at the last one.

I pulled both off the fridge, tearing off the top leaf with my embarrassing bachelor grocery list and setting it aside. I returned to the living room and handed over the pad and pen. She set down what she was carrying, a handmade garment bag. At that moment, my cat wandered in as well. Its ears flattened against its skull as it hissed at Jane. Then it bolted from the room.

"That was my cat."

Cute, she wrote. *What's its name?*

"I never asked."

Her mismatched eyes crinkled. *You're so strange.*

"How did you know where I lived?"

Your secretary told me.

"Oh." That meant I'd be answering a few questions from Ser. This was much more welcome than the last girl she'd given my address to. That'd be Mira Mirra, her roommate.

I brought you something.

She shifted, her long legs looking more coltish than sexy. She was nervous. Hard to imagine that, but there it was. She picked up the bag and opened it, revealing a suit. The same one she had been measuring me on when I tried to get her to help me with Mold. She freed it from the bag and handed it over.

"This is for me?"

She nodded, color creeping into her cheeks.

"You made me a suit," I said, shaking my head. I couldn't quite believe it. "What do I owe you?"

Gift.

"That's a hell of a gift." I had a look at it. It was officially the nicest thing I owned. Just eyeballing it I could tell it would fit, and probably better than anything in my closet. She'd sewn extra pockets into the jacket too. "Thanks, Jane. That's—"

Words failed me. Hell, words fled right out the front door. Wasn't much I could say to her, not when I was holding the entirety of her attention. There was a time when all I'd have seen of Jane were the train tracks of stitches crawling over her body. I still saw them, but they were another one of her quirks, along with the mismatched eyes, the Roman nose, or the way she rocked back and forth slightly when she was nervous. She was pretty in a way I couldn't have seen as recently as six months ago, but I saw it now.

There was a time when I'd have been paralyzed, too. When I'd see a woman as remarkable as Jane and I'd let her pass me right by. Too scared about what I'd do. What she'd do. What the world had become. Not now. Not anymore.

I took a step to her, one hand going to her waist. She leaned in. Maybe I kissed her; maybe she kissed me. My brain shorted out for a second, and we were just together. Sure, she was the one bending down, and the force she was holding me with could probably have broken me in two. There might be those who'd think that was strange, but a fella likes feeling safe.

I probably could have stayed there all day. Jane seemed mighty content herself. It only occurred to me then to worry about how out of practice I was, but I threw that aside. I kissed Jane, and she kissed me.

"Good Christ, are you two going to breathe eventually?" Bosch complained.

Well, that broke the mood. We both jumped, and Jane hissed at the empty room, one strong arm corralling me behind her.

"It's okay. It's just an invisible man. I, uh, I forgot he was here, then there was the kissing."

Jane turned back to me, and her patchwork face was going greener and grayer at turns. She looked down, and picked up the pad, pen, and suit from where we dropped them.

"Sorry about that," I said. "It's really a great gift, but you know. You were there."

She nodded. I hung the suit in the hall closet and brushed a few stray cat hairs off it. When I turned, Jane had a message for me.

Why is there an invisible man?

"Part of this case," I said.

She nodded, still nonplussed. *You realize there is a naked man in your home.*

"I lead a complicated life."

She gave a wordless laugh, and I realized my life had just gotten a good deal more complicated. For Jane, though, I'd deal with complexity.

"I have to go do this now."

Be careful.

"I will."

Come back.

I had to smile. "I've got someone to come back to."

She nodded, her eyes clear.

"Bosch, you stay here," I said.

He grumbled but wasn't going to gainsay me. I checked over my jacket and I had everything I was going to need. My hand came down on the smashed pack of cigarettes. I pulled them from the jacket, turned them over. I didn't smoke. Never did. They went in the trash.

Jane and I walked outside. The cars were beginning to pull up as the monsters arrived to try to get past the wards of their favorite humans. Sam pulled up in his station wagon. Mira was walking from the nearest red car stop. Lurkimer's glowing eyes appeared under my porch. Purvissa parked her hearse on the sidewalk. I barely noticed them.

I paused at my car. Jane stopped as well, taking my hands in hers. Her skin was cool and dry. She'd left the pad inside, but the truth was, we didn't need it. I knew what she was telling me, and she could read the inside of my head as well. We wanted to be back with the other, safe and sound. She knew what I was doing was dangerous, but she also knew I had to do it. I don't think I'd have been a man she thought was worthwhile if I walked away.

She leaned in and gave me a peck on the cheek. It was hard not to chase.

I nodded to her, and we parted. She went to her car and left; the one monster leaving my neighborhood before sundown. If that didn't say everything that needed to be said about her, nothing would.

I glanced across the street. Will Hammond was in front of his house, in the midst of touching up his wards, but he'd stopped. He stared at me with more disgust and hatred than I imagined he was capable of. Yeah, my life was going to get a lot more complicated.

Assuming I survived the night.

Forty-Nine

Wednesday, January 11, 1956
Full dark

I stood at the crest of the street looking out over the blanket of lights. Somewhere in the dark above me, Liling Lam's house crowned the neighborhood. The one I was in front of looked like it had been half-melted by a death ray. There was another downside to living in this world: knowing intimately what death ray damage looked like. My car was parked a street away, accessible with a quick sprint over two abandoned properties and a half-collapsed fence.

I'd have been more nervous a few months ago, but being out after dark was getting normal. The strange truth was that a neighborhood like this was as close to safe as things got in the City of Devils. No reason for a monster to be out looking for anyone to eat or turn here. I was at ease.

Some of that might have been thinking about Jane. Or really the smile she'd given me after the goodbye kiss. Getting to see that particular quirk of her lips was a rare treat.

The sidewalk where I stood was broken from the weather and

pockmarked with small craters from explosions. Every house on the street was in sorry shape, with the best of the bunch looking like it was getting ready to fall inward at any second. Light came from a half moon hovering over the city. I didn't bother with my flashlight or lighter. Didn't need them.

At last, an unmarked police car turned onto the street, the headlamps splashing over me momentarily. It pulled up a few car lengths down the street, the brakes squealing softly. The doors opened with a sepulchral thump, and the two wolfmen stepped out. Both wore the beast on the outside that night. They were bulky, their newly inflated muscles straining against suits that were slightly elastic. Their irregular teeth poked upward from their underbites. Their eyes were red. Garou was covered in brown fur, Moon in gray. If they were wearing the wolf, it meant they were ready for trouble.

I looked from wolfman to wolfman. The calm never bled away from me. I had a full vial of wolfsbane, and a Luger that knew the taste of wolf blood better than anything in the city. They had claws, teeth, and guns packing enough death for me and then some.

"We're here," Garou growled.

"So cough it up, Moss, or my partner's liable to get bitey."

I glanced at the half-melted house. It was easy to picture the martian tripod coming over the rise, sweeping the area with its death ray, turning rocks into wax and people into shadows.

"I don't smell anything but a meatstick who sweats too goddamn much," Garou said.

Moon snorted. "Well?"

"Bosch is supposed to be dead," I said to the two of them.

Both wolfmen ambled closer. The headlights of their unmarked car haloed the three of us on that lost road.

"Bosch *is* dead," Moon said.

"We got a body. The scent matches."

It was a bit late to have second thoughts, but here they were, right on cue. Didn't mean I was going to stop. "Yeah, about that. Bosch found out the one thing you couldn't have him learning. He found out that you were on the take."

"You don't talk like that, meatstick," Garou growled, reaching into his jacket.

I stopped him with my next sentence, each word nailing him to the spot. "I'm not talking to you. I'm talking to your partner."

I turned on Moon. He stood straight as a ramrod. The truth was there in his eyes. He was surprised, yeah, but only that I'd sniffed him out. Any doubts I had were gone now.

"Yeah, you, Moon. You found out what Bosch knew. Maybe one of his reports, maybe he told you himself. He knew there was a dirty cop in the Wolf Pack, and as soon as he figured out which one, you were going down. So you worked out a great way to buy some time. You swapped his scent with some rookie on the force, and then you sent that rookie in. Only you made sure to tip your goblin pals off about it, and said rookie went up in smoke. You show up and dump the cold iron dagger near the body. You were the one who 'discovered' it, after all."

Moon was sputtering. Garou stared at me like I had sprouted horns and tried to sell him a condo.

"Now you had a body and you had a scent. Bosch was dead. If he came up for air, nobody would listen and you could croak him for real."

I went quiet. The only sounds rolling up over the hills were the yips of coyotes and the brassy hum of traffic.

Finally, Garou turned to Moon, already unsure. "Phil, tell this meatstick he's batty."

Moon didn't say it. I could see the story trying to claw its way out of him. Whatever it had been, it was too good, and he'd had his reasons. Reasons we could understand, that he desperately needed us to understand. Because if we did, then the guilt would go away, and he could start recognizing the face he saw in the mirror.

"Bellum was unstoppable," Moon rasped, his voice dying. His fur began to disappear in favor of his ruddy flesh.

"What? Phil?"

If Moon heard his partner, he gave no sign. "Wasn't a thing we could do against the gray matter. She's taking over the city one racket at a time, and there's not a goddamn thing we can do. Put one of her zombies down, she's got two more waiting in the wings. She's got more money than we do. I bet if you looked in Mayor Semerkhet's ledgers, you'd find some payments marked with an X that go right into Sarah Bellum's wallet." He snorted. "Or whatever the brains use."

He turned to Garou. I was just a meatstick, after all. I couldn't offer real absolution.

"Mab was actually making a dent. The elf was rolling her back. We were seeing zombies dropped in the street. She was taking hits. Real hits."

"C'mon, Phil," Garou said, practically begging his partner. The wolf was gone from both of them now.

"So I took Mab's money. Fed him what I could. He was practically doing the LAPD's job for us. *He* was paying *me* to help us take on our biggest enemy. Don't you see? It wasn't a devil's deal. I was getting a little money, sure, but the city was finally getting out from under the brainiac."

I barely heard what Garou whispered. Moon heard it, because he took a step back, wounded. Garou said it again, louder. "Wendell Paine. We thought the Monster Slayer had taken that poor kid. Hard to find the grave of an invisible man. Turns out, no, you set that kid up to die. You fed him to the hobs!"

"Lou, it was one guy."

Moon's voice didn't echo. It was like the night held its breath. There was only the three of us on that street. Only the three of us in the world.

Garou snapped that feeling when he went for his gun. So did Moon. The gunshots were so quick, it was impossible to know who fired first. Garou fell backward. Moon staggered, catching the fender of the car. I sprinted for the house. Two gunshots trailed me, but getting shot played hell on Moon's aim.

I threw myself through the half-melted doorway and rolled into cover. My Luger was in hand. Now on my belly, I poked the gun and one eye from the portal. Moon and Garou's car was on the street, headlights shining up the hill, and I could just barely see Garou's shadow, slumped on the ground. Sad to say, I wouldn't miss him.

A shadow moved beyond the car, and I heard two cracks, followed by the zipping sounds of pieces of the house being shot off. I sent a couple bullets his way. They didn't hit a single thing.

"Moss! Hold your damn fire! Let's talk. It's just you and me here now and we can come up with any story we want. Mab's dead, but that doesn't mean we lost the fight against Bellum yet. I could use a man like you. Resourceful. Smart. You and me, we could work together! We just have to stop shooting!"

"You're asking me to trust a fella just shot his partner," I hollered back.

"Lou was a hothead! You know that better than anybody! He was making a move, and you can't begrudge a man for self-defense!"

It would have been easy. Moon and Moss, against the Bellum mob. Finishing what Mickey had started. I might have done it had I thought Moon wouldn't air out my guts as soon as I came out of cover. And as it turned out, I had something to live for. A beautiful patchwork of dead girls who wanted to design clothes.

"I hate to turn you down, Moon, but no thanks."

"This is your last chance, Moss! I don't want to have to kill you!"

"I think we both know you have no intention of letting me walk out of here!"

"Suit yourself." He almost sounded sad. The bullets whining off my cover said he'd get over it, though.

I shot back, but I might as well have been shooting at a ghost. The lights from the car formed a nearly solid barrier, and beyond it, Moon was just a fat shadow. I slid up the wall, getting to my feet, pulling the vial of wolfsbane from my jacket. I threw a little across the threshold. There were plenty of entrances into this dump, but at least he couldn't use that one.

I backed along a wall to a doorway, peeked in, and found what had once been a bedroom. The wall had been turned into drippy taffy. The only recognizable bit of the bed was a corner; the rest had been turned to sludge, then hardened. The wall looking to the front had a nice mix of cover and view, owing to the slagged state. I took up position and waited until I saw the shadow again, then fired a few more times. My Luger clicked empty.

I released the magazine and pulled another from my jacket pocket.

"Hold it right there," Moon rasped.

He stood in the doorway. His suit was rumpled and he was covered in dirt. His right hand held a .38 snubnose revolver. His left cradled his side, now soaking and crimson. He lurched into the room, dripping as he went. I stayed still, holding the now useless kraut pistol in my hand.

"Really thought you were smarter than this, Moss," Moon said.

"You and me both."

"I'll tell your secretary you went out like a hero."

"She'll never believe you."

Moon coughed with some laughter. "Goodbye, Moss."

I heard the gunshot. You never heard the shot that punched your ticket, supposedly. That's why my eyes flipped open like blinds. Moon was staring at a fresh hole through his chest, the stain blooming around it like a rose. He fell that way, too. Never believed for a moment that he'd finally been done in.

My legs were rubber, but they were going to support me one way or the other. I stepped gingerly around Moon's body and went to the bedroom door.

"Hold it right there," Garou growled.

His gun was up, and he was on the other side of the threshold of the front door. His other arm cradled a wound on his chest. Guess neither one of them was so keen on offing his partner. There was a lesson in there somewhere, but I was too tired to learn it.

"Moss." Garou almost sounded relieved, and the gun went down. "You want to get this goddamn wolfsbane out of my way?"

"Sure." I took my time, picking up each piece, shaking the dirt off it, and returning it to the vial. Hey, that stuff's expensive.

Garou shoved past me as soon as it was gone, and even shot, he was plenty strong. I caught myself against the wall and tried not to take it personal. Garou made it to the bedroom door and looked down at Moon's body.

"You killed him?" Garou asked.

"Yeah," I said. I'd been pretty sure the shooter wasn't Garou, but now I knew for sure.

"He was my partner, meatstick."

"He was dirty."

Garou turned on me. His face was pale and ghastly, and the wolf was there, right underneath. Ready to tear its way out. "He was a hero and we were never here, you got me? Bellum's corpses cut him down in a shootout."

"Sure, Garou. Whatever you say."

"Now get the hell out of here before I change my mind."

I left the house and crossed the street, going up the narrow pathway to where my car was parked. I wasn't surprised at all when I saw the slender silhouette standing by my car, holding a scoped Springfield, barrel pointing at the lonely sky.

"Hey there, Liling," I said.

"Mr. Moss. Looks like you took quite a gamble."

"Not really. Assuming you were home, and I imagine you are at the early parts of the evening, it was a done deal. I knew you couldn't resist getting a wolfman served up on a platter like that."

In the wan moonlight, I caught her smirking.

"Thanks for not killing the other one," I said, the one and only time I'd thank someone for not killing Lou Garou.

"That's one you owe me, Mr. Moss."

"I get that a lot."

Liling melted into the gloom, and it was like she had never been there at all. I got into my car, and once my hands stopped shaking, I drove it to the nearest human flophouse in Chinatown. Not that I slept a wink that night.

FIFTY

Thursday, January 12, 1956
Morning

Carousel Ice Cream was too bright for that morning. I'd gone home as soon as the sun rose to get a few things, and found Bosch on my couch in an extremely embarrassing way. The less said about that the better. I'd gotten myself cleaned up and dressed in the suit Jane made me. There was still one more thing to do. One last thing. Then I got to see what all the days ahead tasted like.

The bell jingled as I pushed through the front door and leaned on it, breathing in the air from the ice cream and the clean scent of winter.

Mickey peered over the counter. He was in shirtsleeves, an apron over his girth. I didn't see any of his guys, but he was running low on those lately.

"Stick! How are youse this fine morning?"

"I'm doing good. You look like you're fully recovered."

Mickey laughed. "I put on a good front. Lots back here to hang onto, but if I'm coming out there, I'm gonna need my cane. You want a sundae?"

"Sure, Mickey."

"That's what I like to hear. That look on your face says you want to have a conversation."

"We have a lot to talk about."

"That we do, that we do. Hope you're taking my offer seriously."

"As a vampire in a blood bank."

"Nice to hear." Mickey pulled a glass sundae cup from a freezer and set it on his marble counter. He gave me a couple scoops of vanilla and began to dress them. "So, talk. Youse got reservations. That's normal."

"I actually wanted to talk to you about a conversation I had last night."

"Oh?"

"Yeah. Wolf named Phil Moon. He was telling me about how the Gobfather was the one doing all the damage to the Bellum mob."

"The elf did a lot of damage."

"Not really. The fella putting the hurt was you. You had Bellum so scared she was willing to try to pop you on a crowded street."

Mickey's grin was feral. "Fat lotta good it did, too."

"But I don't see how it all fits together. I don't see where the loyalty's coming from. Nothing quite adds up the way it's supposed to."

"Sometimes that's life," Mickey said, handing over the sundae.

I accepted it, walking back to the table and setting the ice cream down. "Oh yeah. I should probably pay you for this." I fished a coin from my pocket and flipped it to him.

Reflexes made Mickey snatch it from the air. A sound like the sizzle of ham in a hot frying pan hit the air. Mickey opened his hand with a squeal, releasing a puff of foul-smelling smoke. The coin fell to the tiled floor, jingling to a stop. It was a shiny new silver dollar. I'd picked it up from the bank a half hour ago.

"That's when it all came together. You taking a shotgun blast and shrugging it off. The gold flatware in your house. The fact that you recognized me that first night when I was dressed like a clown. Even *I* didn't recognize me, but with your sniffer you knew immediately."

Mickey's lips were pursed, his head forward, staring up at me through hate-filled eyes.

I kept talking. "Moon turned you, didn't he? Gave you the one advantage no one could fight, because they didn't know. Everyone thought you were human. Bullets were just an inconvenience, but silver would kill you dead. Moon kept the cops off of you, and you were free to cut into Bellum's business."

Mickey was breathing hard like a stray dog. He closed his eyes and nodded. "You got me. I'm a wolf. Nothing's changing, Nick. You and Moon are the only ones who know what I am. I turn you, and youse join the gang for good. Bellum's never gonna know what hit her. Hell, I'm already putting her corpses back in the ground quicker than she can dig 'em up. What am I gonna do when I got Nick the Stick with me? It's gonna be like the old days. You and me, croaking monsters, and the whole time we got an edge they never know."

Mickey puffed up his chest. No way I could say no to that pitch. I didn't want to believe it. Not from my friend.

"One thing, though, Mick. You told me who you made your money off of, remember? You gave me Big Jack's list of collections. Some monsters, sure, but mostly humans. You're living off of humans, Mickey."

"Human. Monster. Doesn't matter to me."

"It matters to me."

"What are you saying here, Stick?"

"You got everything you need?"

Mickey frowned. "What?"

"Yeah," said Bosch. "I got it."

Mickey's eyes widened, then turned crimson. "An invisible man? You bring an invisible man in here?" Fur burst from his skin, his finger curling into claws. He was ready to pounce.

My gun was on him, filled with silver. Mickey was fast, but I was always faster.

With my other hand, I pulled Bosch's cuffs from my jacket and tossed them. They halted midair as Bosch caught them. "Turn around."

Mickey did it, and Bosch slapped the steel on Mickey's wrists.

"This is what you do to your friend?" Mickey shrieked. "This is how you repay me? By god, Nick, when I'm out, you're a dead man. You weasel! You fuckin' son of a bitch! *You meatstick!*"

I left the store, Mickey's enraged screams trailing me.

That's me, I thought. *Nick the Stick.*

FIFTY-ONE

Thursday, February 2, 1956
Dusk

I arrived at Jane's place about an hour before she had to work. I mostly read while she got ready. It was nice just being near her, and it wasn't like I was very welcome at home. The only ones who were happy to see me were the monsters who wanted to turn me. The humans stopped speaking to me once it got around I was making time with a meat golem. Will Hammond had called her a skin-dolly, and I'd nearly hit him. I didn't like that the term stuck to Jane.

Got the pad?

I nodded, showing Jane. I carried a pad and pen around now, in case she wanted to talk while she was at work. I drove her to the Nocturnist, and settled into my usual booth. Sure, it was way in the back of the room, in the most shadowed corner, but it was mine. The monsters in the place knew who I was. Knew I was human. They stayed away.

The stage show started, and I drifted away to the close harmonies of the Salem Sisters. Capriccio Español had been killed in a shootout by the police. The Nocturnist was looking for a new act, and I got my friends a tryout. It was good to see them, and seeing them do well for themselves.

Sometimes I saw Johnny Stompanato on the arm of some monster or another. He was the only one of Mickey's gang I ever saw. Big Jack Whalen was never found. I kept my eye on Johnny, knowing that any bullet with my name on it was in his gun. Johnny pretended he couldn't see me. Good enough, especially with Mickey in the pen awaiting trial. I couldn't prove it, but I bet Bellum was making certain Mickey was being held without bail.

On that subject, Bellum had sent me a thank you in the form of a really nice bottle of whiskey and a thousand dollars. She didn't know I'd plugged Bracken Mold, and I was betting she would barely care if she did find out. All she knew was that I was instrumental in removing her two biggest rivals. It looked like the debt was paid, but I knew she could call in a marker whether or not it existed.

And she did owe me. All I'd succeeded in doing was handing a divided underworld over to her on a silver platter, no pun intended. Not much I could do about that, either. Monsters were going to do what they were going to do.

Jane brought me a cocktail and a plate of deviled eggs, but don't ask me what kind of eggs they were originally. The best thing she brought me was her secret smile.

It was far away from where I imagined I'd be. But I'd take it.

Happily.

THE END

Jane Stitch will return in...

A Stitch in Crime

Fine Dining in the City of Angels
by
Gaston St. Bolus, the Ghoul Ghourmet

The Nocturnist

If you want to keep a secret, don't put it on the Sunset Strip. For residents, the Nocturnist isn't much of a secret, but you'll never find a tourist behind its ornate double doors. This tinseltown salon is a locals-only watering hole, and for good reason. It's the only place where the glitz and glamor of Hollywood rubs elbows with the seamier side of the city, where the angels of the silver screen meet the devils of the vice sheets.

This Sunset stalwart's art deco façade implies a more modern interior, like one of those phantom clubs where the cuisine takes a backseat to the auditory charms. Like so much about this happening establishment, never let first impressions lull you!

I had the opportunity to visit the Nocturnist on a Friday night, when the doppelgangers emerge from their studios, the mummies shamble over from city hall, and the goblins and zombies head over from the mean streets. The Nocturnist's ambience is spoken of in reverent whispers, and dear reader, I would not be the respected gastronomical guide I am had I chosen a quieter night.

Once you pass the doorman, an impressive and impressively mannered ogre, you enter the interior of the club. The first thing you will notice are the cages of bats and wolves. Vampires love to make an impression, don't they? The decor is equally evocative, making the entire interior of the club appear as the exterior of a lovely old world castle. You're not dining in the Carpathians, but I've been assured it's the closest thing!

When the band took the stage, I was initially dubious. A club this swanky should really have an all-phantom orchestra. Though once the trio of gorgeous ladies started their close harmonies, I was sold. I'm no music critic, but the Salem Sisters have in me a devoted fan.

The Nocturnist is far more famous for its atmosphere than its fare, but that is an injustice to the talented staff in the kitchen. The head chef, Wyeth Wyrd, lends the flare witches normally reserve for potions to a varied and fascinating menu. As usual, I brought several of my inner circle, including your favorite maven of manners, the Countess d'Rigueur, director of stage and screen Blork, and clothier of the afterlife Medium Rare. The Countess pledged to try a selection of hemoglobin cocktails, Blork would sample the electrical offerings, and Ms. Rare would sup on the ectoplasmic taste thrills.

We started with cocktails. A Bloodier Mary (complete with a novelty stake!) for the Countess, something called an On the Fritz for Blork, an Elysian Fields for Ms. Rare, and for my traditional palate, an Old Fashioned. My drink was delightful, the selection of bitters giving this version of the venerable cocktail a pleasing autumnal bite. The On the Fritz proved to be a small, sparking device looking somewhat like a small television. Blork inserted his probes into either side, and after a puff of smoke and the not unpleasant aroma of burnt plastic, he judged it to be delicious. Ms. Rare approved of her vapors as well, but the most effusive praise came from the Countess herself. She declared her libation to be the best she had ever sampled.

No small surprise, since the Nocturnist is the creation of epicure of the evening Nyx Nocturne. She is always present, fluttering about like a perfectly coiffed raven. Her beauty might eclipse many of the starlets at her tables, but her attitude is always one of welcome. She stopped by our table to offer a brilliant smile, and was kind enough to say she read both mine and the Countess's columns! While this won't influence my review, I will say it's the skilled hostess who has such information at her beck and call.

Our meat golem waitress took our order and promptly returned. I would be remiss if I didn't order the signature dish of the Nocturnist, a refreshing bowl of their ant bisque. While some monsters might be squeamish about dining on these giant insects, I want to allay any such fears. The soup is delightful, warm and savory, with a hint of chili for a southwestern zing.

While Blork moved onto heartier fare of an open circuit board, the ladies stayed with their liquid or ectoplasmic diets. Blork was far less enthusiastic about the second course, though he allowed he'd had much worse. As for me, I continued my assault on the hors d'oeuvres offered by the kitchen. First a plate of deviled eggs, and specifically for their ghoul patrons, a delicious plate of ladyfingers. So many establishments refuse to age their ladyfingers, but the Nocturnist does admirably well. One would almost think they have a ghoul in the kitchen!

The Nocturnist's reputation for fine entertainment, swanky surroundings, and upscale ambience with the hint of danger is well-deserved! The price tag is high, but nowhere else can one find the delicious combination that makes the Nocturnist such a vital part of the famous Sunset Strip!

The Moors

There's something intoxicating about the Moors, a hearty grill in the Gardena area of Los Angeles. Maybe it's the long wooden tables, worn from the scrape of dishes and notched by the hungry knives of the diners. Maybe it's the officious attitude of the waitresses, wolves lurking under starched uniforms. Or maybe it's because at every table is a brave officer of the Los Angeles Police Department, working off a powerful hunger gained from cleaning the streets of evildoers.

The Moors is a cop hangout, and a more authentic picture of the City of Angels you could never find. The air is thick with cigarette smoke and the growling conversation of police. The tables are chest-level, with high stools, giving one the feeling of always sidling up to a favorite watering hole. Even the booths are lofted, so only an ogre could sit and keep their feet on the floor. Don't fret, though. The accommodations aren't big enough for ogres. This is a spot for wolfmen and their many admirers.

If the atmosphere didn't make the point, the menu certainly does. Meat, and plenty of it. This isn't an establishment to go on a date. This is a place for men to get to the serious business of eating. From the beginning of my meal to the end, I had to loosen my belt three notches, and still went home with leftovers (do not utter the phrase "doggie bag" inside the Moors!) that fed me for a week.

The rack of lamb is the dish the Moors is perhaps best known for. While I have had better lamb, I have never had more of it, and that means something. The rack looked to come from at least two animals, and the lump of mint jelly served alongside it was the size of a baby's head. While I found the lamb perversely underdone, the more carnivorous palates would be pleased. I was able to sample a few other entrees, including a porterhouse steak and the famous pork tartare, and can verify that the meat is so fresh, it's still mooing (and oinking and baaing) on your plate. I will confess, when I took my leftovers home, I aged them and added a little of my special touch, and I humbly submit this as an improvement.

If you find yourself with a powerful hunger, the Moors will satisfy you. Beyond that, I think it's best to leave it as it was intended to be: a well-needed haunt for the wolves in blue.

Café Calavera

Is there a sight more indelibly associated with our fair city than a shimmering giantess emerging from the surf in her barely-there leopard-print bikini? My heart sank the day Miss O'Heaven announced her departure from the Isla Calavera Resort and Casino. Oh, she can still be seen, by the luckiest among us, but her appearances are no longer as constant as the tides.

The resort itself is a must-see destination in the Los Angeles landscape. From the fun of the gaming to the swinging sounds of Jungle Jim and the Hepcats, Isla Calavera is always a diverting time. Some come to the world-famous Café Calavera to sate the hunger that comes from a night at the tables.

Located in the crown of the skull, the décor continues the delightful island theme that makes the entire establishment feel like a vacation even when you're still within sight of the city. Vines crawl along the walls, and even the soft sounds of the jungle are piped in through hidden speakers. Every table is topped with a basket of fresh fruit, prominently featuring, of course, bananas.

With its commanding view of the Catalina Channel, it is easy for diners to feel like kings of all they survey. And, dear reader, for this alone, the Café Calavera would be a worthy place to spend an enchanted evening.

Because you won't come for the food.

There is nothing especially bad about the fare at this most lovely of establishments, but what money was spent on the ambience was saved in the kitchen. There is a halfhearted attempt to keep up with the island theme, but it never amounts to the gastronomical adventure such a distinctive environment would demand.

I tried their island steak, a limp New York strip with a sad pineapple garnish and some kind of middling sauce, and, well, there's a better way to spend ten dollars. And the less said about the ham and banana salad the better.

The drinks menu is where the Café Calavera truly shines. Their piña coladas alone are worth the ferry ride, and the more adventurous can try their unique spin on the zombie. That libation is not capriciously-named. It will reduce you to a shambling wreck with a single sip!

A visit to Isla Calavera will never disappoint. But do it for the gaming, for the shows, and for the drinks. If you're there for a truly gourmet experience, stick to the mainland.

The Pixie Ring

It's a common misconception that a ghoul can't appreciate vegetable fare. While it's true that I might like my greens a little more wilted than perhaps others might, I have developed an appreciation for the new kinds of produce created by our more green-thumbed brethren. The kind of produce served up at the Pixie Ring, an elegant fey establishment on the border of West Hollywood.

This enchanted garden on the edges of the wilderness transports the diner back to a time of knights and princesses, of magic and wonder. It is easy to forget you are but a short distance from the hustle and bustle of the Sunset Strip. Look instead to the living furniture sculpted as if by sorcery, the quiet pools ready to dispense swords, or the soft chimes kissed by the night air.

The food is in every way the equal of its magical surroundings. Or perhaps I was so bewitched, I didn't notice. It doesn't matter. The ingredients fairly (or fairy!) sparkle with life. The vegetables are so vibrant, they feel as though they must have been plucked directly from the plant, passed under a spray of sweet water, and deposited on your plate. The pleasing crunch even evoked the first bite into a well-aged longbone.

The Pixie Ring does serve meat, and it's prepared in the traditional goblin style, pioneered in their kitchens in the Black Forest! Served on bone bread, the brain jam is such a delicious appetizer, it is almost unfortunate that no zombie will find themselves at the Pixie Ring. I myself shied from their hummingbird hearts served on a bed of rose petals, but my guests found them far more toothsome.

As is my custom, I attended with several companions to obtain a wider sampling, including the goblin publisher Ink, and of course my dear friend Lysander Oberon (and yes, ladies and gents, he's still single!). They found everything as delectable as I, if not even more so.

And you will be dining in the firmament. This starry soiree is a favorite of many of the silver screen's most ethereal presences. See them in their elegant element. Just don't gawk! They merely want a quiet meal with their stags. Whoops! Gave it away! Now she'll never forgive me.

The Pixie Ring is the jewel in the crown of the Los Angeles gourmet scene. If you've the means, you simply must go and join the stars in the tinseltown night sky.

ACKNOWLEDGMENTS

Thank you to my family, who continues to believe in me despite all compelling evidence to the contrary. Thank you to Candlemark & Gleam, who has shown me nothing but support in my continued exploration of this weird little world. And perhaps most importantly, thank you to my fans who are willing to take this journey with me.

Photo by Leora Saul

About the Author

Much like film noir, Justin Robinson was born and raised in Los Angeles. He splits his time between editing comic books, writing prose, and wondering what that disgusting smell is. Degrees in Anthropology and History prepared him for unemployment, but an obsession with horror fiction and a laundry list of phobias provided a more attractive option. He is the author of nine novels in a variety of genres including detective, humor, urban fantasy, and horror. Most of them are pretty good.

Follow the Author Online

www.captainsupermarket.com
Twitter: @weirdnoirmaster
Facebook: facebook.com/weirdnoirmaster